RUIN

Necrotic Apocalypse Book Four

D. PETRIE

MOUNTAINDALE
PRESS

ACKNOWLEDGMENTS

Thank you to all of my supporters on Patreon, Discord, and every other corner of the internet that has convinced a friend or family member to take a chance on a foolish zombie and his coven of misfits. Without you, the story couldn't continue.

CHAPTER ONE

"Gaaaahhhh…"

Digby's voice trailed off as a wave crashed over his head to pour seawater down his throat. He clung to a plank that stretched across the tiny boat of the Seed's imaginary space. The piece of wood usually served as a seat, but considering that the craft was at the mercy of an enormous wave, there wasn't a chance of sitting comfortably.

Wind spun the craft as it evened out in a valley between mountainous swells of water. Rain pelted every inch of Digby's body.

"Where the hell is that insufferable copy?" He snapped his head from side to side, searching for the Heretic Seed's representation that usually wore his face. Whatever that crimson-eyed irritation was, it was nowhere to be seen. Digby pushed past his doppelgänger's absence and focused on the storm that had replaced the calm waters that he was used to.

Another wave crashed over him, nearly capsizing the small craft he clung to. Clouds rolled through the darkened sky in a swirl of black and gray. Lightning flashed from within to illuminate a serpentine shape coiling across the heavens. The rumble of thunder grew as the shadow slithered across the sky. Digby's mind struggled to keep his imagination in check. It felt like the darkness might reach down from the canopy and devour him whole. Every instinct he had screamed at him to hide, yet there was no place to go.

He was alone.

The Heretic Seed's representation had vanished without so much as a snarky comment. Now he was adrift within its depths without a clue as to why. He had to get out.

He had to find a way to return to the others.

No.

Running away never solved anything. Not when he had worked so hard to find answers. Not when everyone was still counting on him.

"Damn it!" He shook his fist at the sky, the word 'luck' spelled out across his knuckles. "Show yourself! I'm right here."

The Heretic Seed didn't answer.

Digby cursed the sea around him.

Why has it changed?

Why now?

Before he could work through the meaning of what was happening, the sea swelled higher. The crest of its apex curled overhead like a million hands of white foam clawing at the air. The wave was so large it seemed to move at half speed.

Backing into the bow of the boat, he braced for impact as the water blotted out the sky. A singular shadow swept across his existence to plunge him into a roaring darkness. Digby shot a frantic glance to one side in a desperate search for escape. With a flash of lightning, he caught a glimpse of a familiar, yet horrifying sight. It was only for an instant, but that was enough.

A lone structure marred the horizon in the distance.

"How?" His mind screeched to a halt as he stared at the castle where he had died eight hundred years ago. He turned and raised his eyes to meet the mountain of water as the wave crashed down.

"No, wait!" He raised a hand to shield his head an instant before the boat splintered to pieces. Digby clawed at the wooden plank as it was torn from his hands. Over and over, he tumbled deeper into turbulence, his only saving grace the fact that he didn't need to breathe.

None of it was real.

It was all just a realm within the Seed.

Yet there was no way to know what might happen if he was destroyed within that imaginary space.

The windswept sea rose and fell overhead as Digby drifted below the surface. Lightning flashed and the serpentine darkness in the sky coiled, ready to strike.

He reached up as the muffled sound of thunder faded.

What do you want from me?

All he had were questions.

After gathering all of the Heretic Seed's fragments, he thought getting answers would be easy.

I should have known better.

CHAPTER TWO

"Shit, Dig! Are you okay?" Becca dropped to her knees beside the dead man's body and grabbed him by the collar. A glance to her HUD showed only hers and Alex's name listed as members of their coven.

"What the hell happened?" Mason crouched down behind her.

"Halp! Halp!" Asher cawed in a frantic cry that mostly resembled words, her wings flapping in panic.

"I don't know what happened. He just fell." Becca shook the necromancer, having no idea what sort of medical treatment a zombie could possibly need. His head lolled to one side at an odd angle.

"Is his neck supposed to do that?" Alex peeked over Mason's shoulder.

"He hit his head on the table when he fell." Deuce stood on his toes further back so he could see what was happening.

"Well, shaking him is obviously not helping. He's already dead; he's not about to get any deader." Bancroft stepped past the scene on the floor, clearly more interested in the obsidian obelisk at the center of the room.

The Heretic Seed.

"Stay back." Becca dropped Digby's lifeless corpse to the

carpet of the casino's high roller suite and stood. "We don't know if it's safe to touch that thing."

Charles Bancroft, Skyline's former commander, glanced at Digby before stopping. "You may have a point."

"Just let me think before doing anything." Becca inhaled in an attempt to calm herself.

She was exhausted and jittery all at once. It was only last night that they had carried out a near-suicidal attack on Skyline's base. During which, they had broken into Autem's secure facility and stolen the fragments of the Heretic Seed that Henwick had recovered over the last eight hundred years. The only reason she and the rest of their team made it home to Las Vegas was due to Digby and his insane idea of improvisation.

The necromancer had snuck into Bancroft's quarters while he slept and convinced him to switch teams. Skyline's fate had been on shaky ground with Autem, so it was only a matter of time before Henwick decided he didn't need Bancroft or his mercenary force anymore. Granted, flipping their enemy's commander had still required leverage. That leverage came thanks to a loophole that Digby had noticed, one that rendered a person's resistance to direct spells meaningless while unconscious. The realization had allowed him to animate Bancroft's skeleton, sending Tavern, his dude-bro infernal spirit, to take up residence within the man's bones. With that, all it would take was a word from Digby, and his minion would simply kill Bancroft anyway they could.

Sure, their former enemy could try to fight back or cast a healing spell, but eventually, he would run out of mana and Tavern didn't get tired. It might take some time, but Bancroft would fall in the end. It was crazy and a little evil, but Digby had forced an alliance that brought them a win in the end.

As soon as they returned to Vegas, they retrieved the Heretic Seed's fragments from Digby's void where he'd stowed them. After that, coffee was poured, and everyone got to work. There must have been thousands of fragments, and considering that each shard had been placed within its own glass vial to keep them from coming into contact with the rest, the process required everyone to lend a hand.

Deuce and Elenore were glad to help. As the settlement's primary organizers, they had been preparing to evacuate the casino to search for a new home. They both were pleasantly surprised when they found out that their location was still unknown to Autem thanks to Bancroft's paranoid need to compartmentalize information. Ultimately, Deuce and Elenore were just glad to stay inside where it was safe. After all, the streets of Las Vegas were now crawling with revenants. At least inside the casino, they could remain within the effective radius of the sun goddess statue that kept the vampiric monsters at bay.

Sax, Parker, and Mason had been ready to help the moment everyone returned from the heist. Even the six guardians that Bancroft had brought over to their side on his way out lent a hand. Becca had made a point to keep an eye on them, afraid they might get it in their heads to pocket one of the Seed's fragments while no one was paying attention.

The only regulars that were absent were Lana and Hawk. Hawk was still a kid and staying up all night had clearly taken a toll, leaving him nodding off no matter how much he wanted to help. Digby had made it clear that he was grateful for everything he'd done during the night before sending him up to his room to sleep.

As for Lana, her brother Alvin took precedence. The teen had been integrated into Autem's training process and indoctrinated into their belief system. Becca had never been the religious type, but she knew how strong of a hold it could get on people, especially when they were as young as Alvin. The result had left the kid's loyalty in question. As it was, he hadn't come with them willingly, even though it meant he would be reunited with his sister. Deprogramming him would be tough, but that was a job for another time.

They had bigger problems at the moment.

Becca turned away from Digby's corpse and stepped toward the obsidian obelisk at the center of the room. It was hard to believe it had been in a few thousand pieces just minutes ago. Once they had laid out the shards on a poker table, Alex had used a spell called Mend that he'd learned the night before when he had restored the goddess statue. According to its description, the ability could repair any single object. It couldn't fix things that were made up of multiple parts but a solid block of stone or, in this case, a monolith of an unknown substance, was no problem. The mana cost of the spell was high, but it worked.

Maybe a little too well.

Becca went over the events that followed in her mind.

Everyone had stood back to give Alex room to work as he cast the spell. The artificer started by picking one of the Seed's fragments at random and placing it in the center of the room. He moved to make sure that he wasn't standing between it and the rest of the pieces. After that, he'd held his hands out and rubbed his fingers together. Becca had smirked on account of him looking a little dumb, like a magician at a kid's birthday party. For an instant, the tips of his fingers glowed before a wisp of light floated from him to the floor where he'd placed the Heretic Seed's shard. The light faded a second later, leaving the fragments unchanged.

Of course, that had been when Digby started complaining that the spell had failed.

Parker wasted no time in telling him to shush.

The zombie did not, in fact, shush.

At least, he didn't until one of the shards shot through the air like a powerful magnet had ripped it from the pile on the poker table. The fragment slammed into the one on the floor with an audible snap. The force of the impact sent the two pieces, joined as one, tumbling a foot across the carpet.

That had been when everyone froze.

Then, a second fragment burst from the pile on the table to join the black clump on the floor. Another followed. Then more. One by one, the shards shot across the space to snap into the growing formation. Becca couldn't quite describe the sound. It was like glass shattering in reverse.

She had watched the entire process, entranced by Alex's spell as it weaved through the space. It was like nothing she'd ever seen. Even more, the Seed itself was a thing to behold. What started as a jagged clump of obsidian fragments grew, its shape smoothing out into an imposing obelisk. The larger it got, the more Becca could feel the power it offered. It was like a dam standing between her and an ocean of magic.

As the shining, black monolith regained its original shape, the last few fragments trickled from the table. Leaving only one empty indentation to mar its otherwise flawless surface.

That was where things went wrong.

As expected, Digby had begun to gloat in victory, but before he could finish a sentence, he let out a gasp and lurched forward. An image of the zombie clutching his chest flashed through Becca's mind. He'd dropped to the floor like the corpse he was only a moment later. The sound of his head hitting the table was still fresh in her memory.

What had happened was obvious.

At least, a part of it was.

The shard within Digby's heart had been caught in Alex's spell and it tried to rip itself out of the zombie's body. Checking his corpse, Becca couldn't find an exit point, so she was pretty sure the fragment was still in his heart where it belonged. If it wasn't for the bone plates that protected the necromancer's chest, it might have succeeded.

As for why he had passed out or why his name had disappeared from her HUD, though, she had no idea. Becca brought up his status by glancing at the tiny circle that floated at the edge of her vision and willed the Seed to show her the information she wanted.

At least that was still possible.

STATUS
Name: Digby Graves
Race: Zombie
Heretic Class: Necromancer
Mana: 341 / 341
Mana Composition: Pure
Current Level: 34 (4,710 Experience to next level.)

ATTRIBUTES
Constitution: 32

Defense: 38
Strength: 36
Dexterity: 36
Agility: 38
Intelligence: 60
Perception: 45
Will: 46

AILMENTS
Deceased

After the assault the night before, Digby had climbed a few levels. Actually, they all had. Alex had reached twenty-eight and she was just one behind him. She was still starving from the demand that the sudden progression had put on her body.

Looking over Digby's stats, there was nothing out of the ordinary. His mana was normal and there were no ailments listed other than the deceased status that was always there. It begged the question, what just happened to him? Starting down at his body, she couldn't tell him apart from an average corpse. She squinted.

Dormant Zombie Emissary, Level 34 Necromancer.

Becca breathed a sigh of relief. "Okay, everyone calm down. The Seed labels Dig as dormant. Thinking logically, he should be able return to being active. Plus, his race and class are still listed. If he was in danger or dead for good, I think that would have changed."

"Shame. I thought we might be rid of him." A woman's voice came from the edge of the room sounding board.

Becca glanced to the side, finding Clint, the zombie master that they had rescued from Henwick's holding facility. He stood there as if attempting to blend into the wallpaper. He had been so quiet all night that she had nearly forgotten about him. The poor guy had once been one of Skyline's Guardians until Henwick decided to use him to hijack Digby's curse. Apparently, all Autem needed was a pure source of death essence to graft on the modifications that created the revenants.

Unfortunately for Clint, this required him to become a zombie to conform his mana balance to Henwick's needs. A steady diet of hearts and brains had done the rest. The result was a necromancer similar to Digby, albeit with fewer spells, since the Guardian Core limited what he could access. The voice Becca had heard, however, had not come from him. No, it had come from the bloody, severed head in his hands.

She narrowed her eyes as she stared at it.

The macabre thing was the final remains of a Guardian seer named Kristen that had stood in their way during the heist. Her head was more of a skull now that Clint had eaten most of the tissue from its surface. Digby had cast a Talking Corpse spell on the woman to get information. When he was finished with her, he had tossed her head to Clint as a snack to keep him from biting anyone that was still breathing.

The spell should have worn off by now.

"Well, that necromancer seems pretty dead to me," the skull added in a ghostly tone that didn't quite sound human. "You might as well push his corpse into a shallow grave and move along. No sense wasting time there."

"How are you still speaking?" Becca tilted her head to one side.

"I…" Clint spoke up to answer instead, looking around the room like a frightened animal before continuing. "I refreshed the spell."

"You can cast Talking Corpse?" Alex chimed in.

"I… um, yes." Clint nodded. "Henwick thought it would help if he was able to execute one of you, so he added it to my approved spells."

"Wait." Becca snapped her eyes to Bancroft. "Is Autem able to get a location if someone accesses the Guardian Core to cast something?"

"No." He shook his head. "But the spell does get logged, along with the caster. They will know that Clint is still walking around. Plus, they will cut his access when they notice. If it wasn't for the damage you all caused last night, I'm sure they would have already." He turned back to the Seed's obelisk. "At the very least, it will piss Henwick off when they report it. Though, I feel Graves would only see that as a bonus."

Becca relaxed, relieved that their location was still secure. She probably should have confiscated Clint's ring on the way back to Vegas. After all, the zombie master was nothing if not unpredictable. She pushed the worry aside and focused on the more important detail. "Why did you recast Talking Corpse?"

"Am I in trouble?" The unfortunate necromancer froze. "I'm sorry. I didn't mean to. It was just that, it was running out of mana. The spell, I mean." He raised his voice as if he'd remembered something urgent. "If the spell wears off, we won't be able to recast it."

"So you thought you would keep it charged so it wouldn't run out of juice?" Sax stepped over Digby's corpse to look at the woman's head. He gagged as soon as he got close.

"I wasn't sure if…" Clint trailed off before looking to the floor. "I thought she might still be needed."

"That's actually good thinking." Becca stepped closer, trying to reassure the zombie that he hadn't made a mistake. He wasn't wrong. The spell could be refreshed as many times as they needed, but if they let it lapse, they would lose access to whatever information the seer knew. "Try to check with someone first before doing something like that again, okay?"

Clint gave a sheepish nod as Becca returned her attention to the skull in his hands.

"You were one of the only people Henwick trusted with access to the Seed's fragments. How much do you know about it?"

"Plenty." Kristen, the deceased seer, scoffed. "Though, I'd say I know more than you about most things."

Becca ignored the jab. "Do you know why Dig passed out?"

"Oh, I'm terribly sorry, but I have no obligation to answer you. I mean, I imagine that you think you have the upper hand. Ridiculous." The seer rolled the one remaining eye that Clint hadn't eaten.

Becca did the same with her two.

According to the spell's description, Talking Corpse was unpredictable. It could force the deceased to answer anything honestly. Though, it would only work if the question was asked by the original caster. Beyond that, Kristen could say whatever she pleased. Understandably, she was hostile to Digby. He had killed her and dragged her back into what must have been a hellish existence. She didn't seem to be in pain, but Becca wasn't sure how much of the situation the deceased seer was aware of. Besides, the bigger issue was that, with Digby incapacitated, the dead woman had no reason to tell the truth.

"Fine." Becca ignored the skull's rebellion and raised her gaze to Clint. "How long will your spell last?"

The zombie hesitated for a few seconds as if trying to do the math. "I used all of my mana, so a couple hours?"

"Good. She might not have a reason to help, but with a little more time she might have a change of heart." Becca tried her best to fill in for Digby. "If her position had her as close to Henwick as it seems, then I'm willing to bet there's a few important details about his operation still rattling around in that skull."

"I agree." Bancroft backed her up. "And if we cannot get anything from her, I will share whatever information and expertise I have on the subject. If I am going to be shackled to your cause, I would prefer that the outcome be less bleak than it seems."

"What is that supposed to mean?" Mason puffed out his chest as he addressed the man that had once left him to die along with the rest of the army back in Seattle a month ago.

"It means that this place is worse off than I imagined." Bancroft groaned. "I never thought Digby would be running an operation on par with Skyline or Autem, but I certainly expected more than this." He gestured to the high-roller suite around him.

"Hey!" Deuce stood up for the settlement that he'd had a hand in building. "We have had our own problems to deal with. Mostly because of your people's interference."

Elenore joined him. "If it wasn't for you asshats supplying this city's previous tyrant with weapons and ammo, we would never have been in such dire straits. Thanks to you, the best we were able to do was scrape by until Digby showed up. So don't go acting all high and mighty."

Alex cleared his throat. "Plus, your guys did attack us and release a hive full of revenants onto the streets last night. So, you know, thanks for that."

The squad of guardians that Bancroft had brought with him all looked to the knight standing in front as their leader.

"Hey, we were only following orders," he argued without so much as introducing himself to the room.

"Orders!" Elenore stomped a foot. "You nearly killed us all."

Bancroft held up both hands to calm the situation. "I realize that this arrangement will take some getting used to. And I did not mean any disrespect. The situation that you all faced over the last month was regrettable and not at all your fault."

For a moment, Becca was impressed at how understanding Bancroft was being. Then she realized that he hadn't actually apologized. "But everything you and your men did was just business, right?"

"Yes, that's exactly what it was." He nodded as if the answer had been obvious. "Putting that all behind us, the fact remains that we are currently exposed and under-prepared for the fight ahead of us." He glanced around the room. "You have plenty of food to feed your current numbers for some time, but none of it is sustainable. Not only that, but those supplies will only be stretched thinner as we recruit more to our cause. And let's not even talk about your reliance on generators for electricity. There will come a time where you will have no fuel left for them. Even worse, if you squander it all to keep the lights on, you will have nothing left for vehicles."

"Anything else you want to scold us for?" Mason leaned against one of the tables with his arms folded.

"As I said, none of this is your fault." Bancroft let out a frustrated sigh. "I may not be here entirely by choice, but I am here now, and I know what I am doing. All I mean to say is that we have our work cut out for us to bring this place up to speed."

"Okay, fine." Becca stepped between them before Mason got any more agitated. She understood how he felt but fighting amongst themselves wasn't helping. "We don't have to like each other, but we do have to work together."

"My sentiments exactly." Bancroft relaxed. "But before we can get to work, there is still the issue of the deal Digby struck with my men and I to secure our services. And I don't think he is in any position to hold up his end of the bargain laying on the floor."

"Are you serious?" Mason pushed away from the table he leaned against.

"I am." Bancroft nodded matter-of-factly. "My men and I gave up our status as Guardians when we betrayed Henwick and his empire." He held up his hand to display the gold band around his finger that granted him access to the world's magic. "This ring might as well be a crackerjack prize at this point. I know that this might sound selfish, but my men and I can build up this city into something great, but we will need strength to do that. So yes, we will need someone to make good on Digby's promises to share the Heretic Seed's power with us."

"Ah…" Becca glanced down at Digby's unmoving body, unsure what she was going to do about the problem.

"Well?" Bancroft eyed her expectedly.

She took a deep breath, grateful that the man didn't have access to his abilities as a level sixty Guardian tempastarii. "You will have to be patient. I'm sure Dig will wake up soon and you can talk to him about your deal then."

"How do we know he will wake up at all?" He seemed to be making an effort to keep the volume of his voice from climbing.

"He has always come back within a few minutes." She tried to sound knowledgeable.

"He's passed out like this before?" He arched an eyebrow.

"Kind of," Alex added. "Except usually it's because he's been shot in the head or something?"

"What?" Bancroft snapped his eyes to him. "Then he hasn't passed out like this before."

"Not exactly like this, no." Becca took over. "But the Seed has a kind of virtual environment that it uses to talk to him. I assume that's where his mind is now. The Heretic Seed probably just wants to have a chat."

"Really?" Bancroft's eyebrows climbed up his forehead as he

turned back to the obelisk. "The Seed speaks to him? It really is some sort of intelligence like what Henwick said?"

"Yes." Becca relaxed a little. "And I'm sure Digby will return to us once he learns whatever he needs to in there."

That was when a laugh came from the edge of the room. "Look at you, making assumptions about things you know nothing about."

"What was that?" Becca turned as Clint nearly dropped the talking skull in his hands.

Kristen, the deceased seer, chuckled in that unsettling ghostly tone of hers. "Do you honestly think that zombie will wake up? Honestly, my heart breaks for you. Well, it would, provided I still had one. But I don't. Remember? Because you all killed me."

Becca narrowed her eyes at the skull. "If you have something to say, then say it. Otherwise, shut up."

Kristen paused as if debating on adding something. There was no benefit to divulging more information, but on the other hand, she seemed to have gained a vested interest in irritating everyone. Clearly, she was going to make her undead condition everyone else's problem. "Fine, I will give you this little bit of information for free. But first I must ask a question of my own. Do you really not understand why Henwick had taken such measures to keep the Heretic Seed's fragments separated? Honestly, he even built a fortress on the moon to hide them."

"The moon?" Sax's mouth fell open.

"Yeah." Alex scratched at the back of his neck. "We kind of went to space."

"What?" Mason and Sax asked at once.

"How?" Deuce stepped forward to share in the confusion.

Becca waved away their questions. "The elevator we took to Henwick's private facility must have traveled through some sort of portal or something. I don't understand it either, but yeah, we saw Earth in the distance through a window. The moon is the only place that would present a view like that. But that doesn't matter now." She shook off the subject and returned her attention to Kristen's head. "What makes the Seed so dangerous that Henwick went through all that to keep it hidden?"

Kristen remained silent for a long moment before speaking. "The Heretic Seed doesn't give power for free. It is a devourer of souls. And if your necromancer is connected to it, well, he's no longer at the top of the food chain."

"What?" Becca stepped closer.

The deceased seer chuckled. "Graves will be lucky if he wakes up at all. And if he does, he may not be the same."

"All the more reason for us to move forward with exploring the Seed's power with or without him." Bancroft stepped closer to the obelisk. "Without more magic on our side, we might as well just surrender now."

Before Becca could say anything else, he placed his hand against the obelisk's glossy, black surface just below the empty indentation where Digby's shard belonged. He jerked his hand away a second later, shaking his fingers like he'd been burnt.

"What happened?" Becca jumped closer as he staggered and clutched his head.

"I'm alright." Bancroft held out a hand to keep her from coming closer. "The Seed, it…" He trailed off for a second. "I think it connected."

Becca shifted her vision to the obelisk as a dozen overlapping rings, made up of hundreds of tiny symbols, appeared on its surface like ripples on water. Each circle widened and vanished until the obelisk went blank once again.

"It seems Graves was able to make good on his end of our bargain after all." Bancroft let a self-satisfied smile show on his face.

Becca's mouth fell open as she focused on the man.

Heretic, Level 52, Tempestarii.

"You lost some levels." She eyed him, unsure why the Seed had penalized him.

"That's to be expected." Bancroft didn't seem surprised. "From what I know, the Guardian Core awards fewer attribute points than the Heretic Seed until level fifteen. So it makes sense that there would be an adjustment."

"Does this mean that the obelisk will give magic to anyone that touches it?" Mason stepped away from the Seed.

"I don't know." Becca shook her head.

"Only one way to find out." Sax stepped forward and poked the monolith with the tip of his finger. He remained there for a full ten seconds.

"Well?" Becca leaned closer.

"Nothing." Sax dropped his hand to his side before turning around. "Hey Parker, you try it."

Becca waited for the pink-haired soldier to respond, only to furrow her brow when she didn't. Usually, the woman was ready with a side comment here and there, but ever since the Seed had been assembled, she had been uncharacteristically quiet. "Parker?"

Leaning so she could see through everyone in the room, Becca found the soldier sitting in a chair with her head down on a table. She shook her head. It had been an understandably long night but now was not the time to nod off. "Okay, apparently Parker is too busy napping." She turned to Mason. "You're up."

"Shit!" Alex jumped past her before Mason had a chance to respond.

Becca got out of the way as the artificer rushed to the chair where Parker slept.

"What...?"

She trailed off as Alex shook the woman. "Hey, don't do this."

Parker's arm dropped limp to her side at an awkward angle the instant he moved her.

That was when Becca noticed the pool of blood on the floor. "What... happened?"

CHAPTER THREE

"Ack! Blarg… wart blah hurk."

Digby burst through the surface of the sea mid-curse word while simultaneously expelling a lungful of water.

"What the hell?"

His words came out with a wet rumble as he snapped his head from side to side to take in the realm that the Heretic Seed had created. Unlike when he had arrived, the sea was now calm. Its placid waters stretched out as far as the eye could see without so much as a wave to mar the horizon. The sky above was pitch black, save for a crimson moon hanging overhead like a drop of blood about to fall. Digby furrowed his brow.

"What the devil am I doing here?"

In the past, he'd only found himself in the Seed's imaginary space when his brain had been damaged. As far as he knew, that was not the case now. Not only that, but the Seed's representation that normally greeted him, wearing a copy of his own face, was still nowhere to be seen. A fragment of the boat he had been sitting in floated by. The craft had been smashed to bits shortly after he'd arrived.

Something was definitely different, but what? The only thing that had changed was that the Heretic Seed was no longer laying in a thousand pieces. He considered the implications.

Maybe mending the obelisk has triggered a change in the Seed's imaginary space?

He placed a hand over this chest, remembering how it had felt when Alex had cast his mending spell. Digby had thought the shard in his heart might rip itself straight out of his chest. He probably should have stood further back while the artificer's magic worked. Fortunately, the bone plate covering his chest seemed to have stopped the fragment from breaking free.

He treaded water for a long moment.

None of that fully explains why the Seed has brought me here now. Or what the purpose of this new realm is, for that matter.

Normally, he was able to leave the Seed's imaginary space by casting Necrotic Regeneration to repair his damaged brain, but with his body in perfect condition out in the real world, he wasn't sure how to escape. A sudden streak of panic shot through his mind, questioning if there even was a way out. For all he knew, he might end up treading water within this new realm until the sun burned itself out.

"That would be bad."

That was when he noticed something else. Both Rebecca and Alex were no longer listed on his HUD.

"What?" He panicked for a moment but reminded himself that they had been fine the last time he saw them. Clearly, whatever was wrong had more to do with him than it did them. They were probably standing over his body back in the high-roller suite in Vegas, just as worried about him. Once he pushed that out of his mind, he noticed another change to his HUD.

77/2

"What's this?"

It didn't make any sense.

Digby focused on the digits, hoping to get some information from the Seed about it. None came. He rolled his eyes at the new mystery and returned his attention to his surroundings as the fear bubbling inside him reminded him that he was floating in a sea of nothingness. The fear died down as he turned around and caught sight of land in the distance. He tensed back up when he saw what the cliffside in the distance held aloft.

"Well, that can't be good."

He'd thought he had imagined seeing the castle during the storm before, but now, he raised his eyes up to find the recreation of the structure sitting in the middle of the empty horizon.

The place where he had died eight hundred years ago.

He swam for it regardless. After all, where else was he going to go?

As he approached the rocky shore, he found that it only stretched a short distance. Instead of continuing, the stone simply cracked and split into increasingly smaller chunks until the landscape faded to nothing. Even stranger was the fact that each severed portion of land floated in place as if weightless and half-formed. It was like the laws of the natural world meant nothing within this realm.

He supposed asking the Seed to obey gravity would be asking a bit much.

The scene got stranger the closer he swam. At first glance, the castle had resembled the one from his memory, but up close it was so much more. The base was the same, sure, but the rest was something else altogether. Looking up, the structure lost cohesion as towers broke off to float in place, as if the castle was frozen mid-explosion. Ribbons of what looked like stone reached out at various points, before twisting up toward something dark floating in the sky above it all. The irregular formation above was hard to make out with only the light of the crimson moon, but from where he floated, it looked like some sort of land mass. Like an island in the sky.

If it wasn't for the fact that he was stranded on an endless sea with no other land in sight, he would have turned tail and swam away.

Seems going forward is my only option. He pushed on.

Before long, he swam his way into a recreation of the cave entrance from where he had floated out to sea all those centuries ago. The cavernous space inside was just like he remembered. The walls were covered with stairways and doors, like a colony of ants. At the center, the pillar that had held up the Heretic Seed's obelisk poked out of the ocean. He followed its length up to the jagged platform where it had broken. The other half of the pillar lay to the side where it had fallen. A partially destroyed dock lay underneath. Digby slapped a hand onto the wooden surface of what was left and pulled himself up. It was good to be out of the water.

"Now what have we here?"

He nodded at the scene around him. If the Seed was recreating the scene, then from the look of things, it was using his memories to do it. The thought made him feel a little more secure. At least his surroundings were somewhat familiar.

Sweeping his eyes across the cavernous space beneath the castle, he couldn't remember which doorway he had come in, back when he had been in the real castle so long ago. Familiar or not, his memory wasn't that good; it was over eight hundred years ago. He couldn't help but wonder how much the Seed might have altered things. If it had strayed from his memory to fill in the gaps, then there was no telling what awaited him further inside.

He checked his mana on reflex.

MP: 291/291

"Huh?" Digby looked down at his body. He was wearing the same clothes that he had been when he'd passed out. Just a pair of ordinary trousers, a button-down shirt, and a pinstriped vest. The only thing missing was his coat. "That explains that I guess."

His coat and the Goblin King's pauldron that was attached to the shoulder would have provided him with an extra fifty mana. Without it, he had been dropped back down to two hundred ninety-one. Digby thought back. He was pretty sure he had been wearing it back in the high-roller suite before he'd gotten himself abducted by the Seed.

Maybe this place is unable to recreate enchanted objects from out in the world. The thought begged the question, what else was different?

That was when he realized he was missing something else.

A shoe.

"That is less than helpful. I must have lost it in that storm." He stared down at his sock before pushing the loss from his mind and returning to the most important question. "Can I even cast spells here?"

Without a better way to check, he held up a hand, still dripping with seawater, and cast Frost Touch. The remaining water turned to ice in an instant, freezing all the way up to his elbow. He shook his hand to flake it off.

"I guess that's a yes."

Digby turned back to the doors set into the cavern wall. "But why would I need to cast spells? There aren't any enemies..." He trailed off, realizing that he didn't actually know that. He checked his void contents.

AVAILABLE RESOURCES
Sinew: 0
Flesh: 0
Bone: 0
Viscera: 0
Heart: 0
Mind: 0

"Gah!" He recoiled from the text. "Empty?"

The knowledge of what that meant was horrifying. If he cast so much as a Necrotic Regeneration to repair a paper cut, it would send him straight into his Ravenous state.

"I have to eat something fast."

Unfortunately, there wasn't anyone around within the strange place to add to the menu.

The last time he'd eaten had been the night before on the way back to the casino. With the Las Vegas streets full of revenants, he had been forced to drop several dozen of the creatures into his void just to get through the parking garage and into the casino. Lot of good that did him now. Sure, he had gained enough resources to unlock his Mend Undead mutation, but again, that didn't help him much, considering he was now trapped in a place with no minions.

In all honesty, it probably would have made sense to wait for what he needed to get his Body Craft mutation, but he had been feeling good after pulling off the heist, so he'd figured why not and taken Mend Undead anyway.

Bringing up the description of both, he growled at the choice he had made the night before.

MEND UNDEAD
Description: You may mend damage incurred by a member of your horde as well as yourself, including limbs that have been lost or severely damaged.
Resource Requirements: 50 mind, 100 heart.
Limitations: Once claimed, each use requires a variable consumption of void resources and mana appropriate to repair the amount of damage to the target.

BODY CRAFT
Description: By consuming the corpses of life forms other than human, you may gain a better understanding of biology and body structures. Once understood, you may use your gained knowledge to alter your physical body to adapt to any given situation. All alterations require the consumption of void resources.
Resource Requirements: 200 mind.
Limitations: Once claimed, each use requires the consumption of void resources appropriate to the size and complexity of the alteration.

"No sense crying over spilled milk." After having his void emptied in the Seed's realm, it wasn't like he would be reaching the requirements for Body Craft anyway. At least he had claimed something, even if it had been the less useful of the two abilities.

He checked his HUD again to distract himself.

MP: 281/291

He noted the loss of ten points from his total from when he'd cast Frost Touch. "I suppose that means I don't receive the benefit of my staff's enchantment either. Too bad Alex isn't here with me to craft me one within this place."

The realization wasn't ideal.

Next, Digby stared at his mana value to confirm a bit of good news for once. The number ticked up a point rather quickly. He blew out a relieved sigh. It seemed that whatever rules the Seed's realm operated off had created a mana balance in line with a proper night, meaning that the fact that his real body was within the area of effect of the sun goddess statue was not slowing his absorption rate like usual. Apparently, the real world's influence had no effect on this place.

That being said, he was still alone.

Digby stared at his name as it hung by itself at the edge of his vision where he was used to seeing Rebecca and Alex. He may have gained several levels in the attack the night before, but his accomplices had certainly pulled him out of the fire enough times to make him understand that he was still at a disadvantage.

He forced out a damp sigh.

"I suppose I'm just going to have to be careful regardless."

That was when the sound of water splashing came behind him. A hand clamped around his ankle in the same instant.

"Gah! Die!" Digby yanked his foot free and thrust a hand down at the unseen threat with the intent to open his Maw and cast Blood Forge. His mind slammed into a couple of obstacles. First was the fact that the spell was immediately canceled due to a lack of blood within his void. The other was a woman with pink hair slipping back off the broken dock and falling into the water.

"Parker?" Digby flailed in place for a moment before dropping down to grab the young soldier when he realized she wasn't pulling herself back up. He snagged her wrist just as she began to sink. She was mostly limp, like a dead fish, but his above-average strength was able to drag her from the sea regardless.

"What the devil are you doing here?" He dropped her to what was left of the dock.

Parker didn't answer, opting to cough out a lungful of water and collapse to the wooden planks where she gasped for air.

"Good lord, you look like a drowned rat." Digby stared at her in astonishment.

The woman panted and wheezed before rolling onto her back and looking back up at him. With a grunt of effort, she raised a hand toward him. Then she extended her middle finger.

"Yes, yes, good to know you're alive enough to perform obscene gestures." Digby folded his arms, unamused to be on the receiving end of the action.

He waited for her to catch her breath, realizing that she must have swam in from the same direction he had. It was actually quite impressive that she'd made it at all without the endurance that being undead granted him. From the look of her, she must have discarded her leather jacket on the way, leaving her in just a pair of denim trousers and a light tank top. The words 'I'd hit that' were spelled out across her chest over a picture of a pair of cards. Her daggers were nowhere to be seen. The weapons must not have been brought into the Seed's realm with her, the same as Digby's staff.

Parker coughed a few more times, then began to sit up. "Where are we?"

"You're within a realm created by the Heretic Seed. It is where I go when my brain is damaged too badly to continue functioning. Except it seems to have changed now that the obelisk has been restored." He let his attention drift away from her as she pushed herself up. "Now, how did you gain access to this space? And is anyone else coming? Where are Rebecca and Alex?"

"Wait." Her face fell. "You come here when you die?"

"Indeed."

"Oh fuck! Am I dead?" She immediately spun to Digby and grabbed the front of his vest. "Did you just necromance me? Am I a minion? What the hell, man?" She let out a whimper. "I don't want to be a minion."

He brushed her hands from his chest. "I have done no such thing. I have no idea what your being here means. And you would not be my first choice for a minion regardless."

"Oh man, oh man, oh man." She rubbed at her forehead. "I haven't been this freaked out since that time I got food poisoning and had to go to the hospital for nearly crapping myself to death."

"Yes, well," Digby shook his head, "that is more information than I require."

"Too bad, I talk when I'm scared. Deal with it." She dropped down and sat on the dock as if unable to move from the spot until she had worked through her situation.

"Good, then tell me what you remember." Digby stared down at her. "Reassembling the Heretic Seed seems to have triggered something that has brought me to this place. But that doesn't explain why someone who is not even a magic user would be drawn in as well. Did something happen that I missed?"

"No, I don't think—" She stopped speaking and slapped a hand onto her side mid-sentence. "Wait a sec."

"Remember something?"

"Shit yes, I remembered something." Parker sprang back up and pulled her shirt up to inspect her abdomen. She spun around a second later to show him her back. "Do you see a wound?"

Digby glanced at her. "No. Should I?"

Parker dropped her shirt back down and let out a breath. "I don't know. But when Alex cast that Mend spell on the Heretic Seed, something hit me in the back." Parker rubbed at her side. "It felt I'd been stabbed. Like a knife had gone straight through me."

"And this happened when Alex cast Mend, you say?" Digby scratched at his chin. "Was there anyone standing behind you? One of Bancroft's men, perhaps?" Digby struggled to keep his suspicions in check for fear that his worries might run away with him.

"I have no idea, I wasn't looking." Parker sat back down on the dock and buried her face in the crook of her elbow. "What the hell? I'm freaking dead and I don't even know how I died?"

"Oh, get up." Digby jabbed her with his knee. "If you really were wounded, I highly doubt that you perished from it."

She looked back up at him. "Really?"

He rolled his eyes. "We both were in a room with several capable people. People that have magic and the ability to heal you.

No matter what happened, there isn't a chance in hell that they would have allowed you to expire. I'm sure they all sprang into action the moment you keeled over. So no, you're not dead."

She remained still for a long moment before nodding to herself and hopping back up as if everything had been solved. "I can buy that."

"Oh good, glad to take a load off your mind." Digby rolled his eyes at how easily she had been convinced.

"Yeah, glad that's dealt with. I was starting to freak out." She blew her pink bangs from her face. "What does synchronizing mean by the way?"

"What?" Digby snapped his focus to her.

"I have this little circle here." Parker shifted her eyes to one side as if trying to catch something at the edge of her vision. "Every time I look at it, the thing snaps out with the word synchronizing in the middle. It's been like that since I got here."

"Well, that's unexpected." Digby furrowed his brow. "I suppose it's possible that you being here means you have stumbled upon a way to access the Heretic Seed's power."

"Umm, cool?" A vacant expression fell across her face as if she was staring at the Seed's information ring. "How long does the Seed take to synchronize?"

"I'm not sure." He considered the question. "For Alex, he passed out for a half-hour while the process completed. Though, he had a ring, and we have no idea what triggered your connection to the Seed's system."

"I don't like that." She cocked her head to one side.

"I don't blame you." He reached out and jabbed a finger into her collar bone. "But the fact is, you're here now."

"Goody." She groaned.

"Indeed." Digby nodded.

Her eyes widened a second later. "Shit, I might get magic."

"That was the whole point of stealing the Heretic Seed back, was it not?" Digby eyed her sideways.

"Umm, I guess I didn't think that far ahead."

"Yes, I get the feeling that thinking is not exactly your style." Digby frowned, realizing that he might have been better off if the

Seed had dragged someone else into its realm with him. Parker had been helpful in the past, but she had never seemed all that reliable, what with all the napping and unhelpful comments.

Digby glanced at the pink-haired soldier as she tried to wring out the bottom of her shirt and complained about the cold. Honestly, it was hard for him to see why someone like her would have had an interest in joining the military in the first place. Surely Mason, Deuce, or Elenore would have been a better choice to synchronize with the Heretic Seed. Being stuck here with Parker would be just as bad as when he'd given Alex magic. Back then, his apprentice had been of little use. Then again, Alex had proved himself time and time again since then. Maybe Parker would do the same if given time.

The soldier frowned. "My underwear is wet."

Digby rolled his eyes. *Or maybe not.*

Thinking of the others, he couldn't help but wonder how Rebecca and Alex were handling things out there. With him unconscious and Parker mysteriously wounded, they were sure to be worried. Especially Hawk, considering everything the boy had been through. Hell, the child deserved a pat on the back for all he'd done.

Digby tried to piece together a timeline for how long he had been away already. Ultimately, there was no way to be sure. There was also no way to know how long he was going to be stuck within the Seed's realm. He forced out a damp sigh along with a spattering of seawater. The implication was clear. Judging from the fact that he was no longer floating in that tiny boat as he had been before, it was safe to assume that his stay in the Seed's world might be longer than he was used to.

Then again, as inconvenient as the situation was, there was a chance that the castle above might hold more than what little existed in his memory. Considering whatever land mass was floating in the sky above it, there could be more answers there of what the Seed was and where its power came from. Digby grinned. That bit of information would be a treasure all on its own. Besides, it wasn't like the others couldn't take care of themselves without his corpse there to tell them what to do.

Rebecca was entirely capable of keeping everyone in line, and Alex had really begun to grow into his position as the apprentice to a powerful necromancer. Even Hawk had grown into someone he trusted. With a little luck, the boy might talk some sense into Alvin by the time he finished whatever it was he was supposed to do within the Seed's realm. Not to mention Asher would be with them to help keep any zombie-related problems in check.

Digby relaxed at the knowledge that Vegas would be in good hands until he could figure out a way back to them. Then, a surge of dread swelled back up.

"Bancroft!" Digby's eyes bulged as he choked on the man's name.

"Yeep!" Parker jumped to one side. "What are you suddenly yelling about?"

Digby slapped a hand to his face and dragged it down to his chin. "I was just trying to convince myself that everyone in Vegas would be alright without me, but I just remembered that Bancroft is there too."

"Well yeah, you did sorta force him to join us." Parker straightened her shirt after ringing it out.

"Exactly." Digby groaned. "The man is nothing more than an unwilling accomplice. Without me there to tell Tavern what to do, Bancroft has no reason to play nice." He shuddered to think what might happen in his absence.

"I guess." Parker stared up at the ceiling for a second. "But he did burn his bridge with Autem, so it's not like he can do much. And for all he knows, you could wake up at any moment and tell Tavern to kill 'im."

"I suppose that's true." Digby chewed on the thought. "I still don't trust him. Though, if one thing is certain, it's that Bancroft has a strong sense of self-preservation. Meaning he might at least wait before doing anything rash."

"Not like we can do something about it from here." She stretched. "Besides, you said it yourself when I was worried, Becca and Alex probably have things under control."

"Yes, yes." He let the worry fade. "We should get moving then. We won't get any closer to figuring things out by standing—"

His words were cut off by a panicked cry from beside him.

"Snake!" Parker plowed into his shoulder with a surprising amount of force for a relatively small woman. He fell in a heap with her on top of him.

"What do you think you're—gah, snake!" Digby repeated her cry as he jerked his arm to the side to avoid a massive black form as it streaked toward him. He rolled to the side to get away, tossing Parker off of him in the process. A set of jaws, large enough to take his head clean off, tore a mouthful of splinters from the broken dock where he'd been.

"Whoa!" Parker tumbled off the side of the dock and splashed into the water.

Digby kicked himself away from the scaled form that slithered past him toward the center of the cavern.

"What the hell is...?" He trailed off as he followed the length of the form with his eyes, watching it twist around the remains of the pillar that stuck up out of the water. The creature had to have been twenty feet long and as thick as a tree trunk. It coiled up the base of the pillar, culminating in a head of black scales and crimson eyes. A forked tongue flicked at the air as it focused between him and the woman splashing in the water to the side.

"Kill it with fire!" Parker crawled onto the rocks near the end of the dock.

"I would if I could!" Digby stared up at the menacing creature, unsure where it had come from. He analyzed it.

Caretaker, hostile.

Digby had no idea what a caretaker was, but he didn't need the Seed to know that the serpent was hostile. As much as he would have liked to oblige Parker's request to kill it with fire, that was out of the question. Without a source of dead tissue, his Cremation spell was useless. Casting it now would only kill himself with fire. Again, his first instinct was to cast Blood Forge, only to remember that he had nothing in his void to fuel it.

"Fine then. No time to be stingy." Digby retreated back along the dock toward where Parker coughed her way from the sea and cast Decay twice as he passed her.

Decay has increased from rank B to rank A. Area of effect increased to 8 feet, +50% due to mana purity, total 12 feet. Range increased to 40 feet, +50% due to mana purity, total 60 feet.

"Perfect timing." The spell was becoming more and more powerful. It still wasn't a useful attack against anything with a will value, but it did well to weaken what was left of the pillar.

Chips of stone fell as the serpent stretched its body across the space between them, its head swaying back and forth to lock onto Digby. A horrible screech echoed through the cavern as it opened its jaws to strike.

"Come on then!" Digby cast Emerald Flare at the exact spot where he himself stood. He turned and ran as ribbons of sickly energy streaked through the air to converge where he'd been. The serpent slammed into the broken dock, unable to change directions mid-strike. It claimed another mouthful of splinters right before the Flare spell detonated.

"Get down!" Digby leapt from the dock, splashing into the shallow water at the base of the cavern. Parker ducked under as well as an emerald flash lit up the space like a miniature star. An earsplitting crack struck the air the instant he surfaced, followed by frantic screeching. The serpent reeled from the blast, its body marred by burns. Scales curled and flaked off the damaged portions. He would have to get Parker out of the radioactive area of effect before it poisoned her, but the spell had certainly given the serpent something to think about.

"That wasn't enough." Parker peeked out of the water beside him.

"Wait for it." He thrust out a finger as the base of the broken pillar snapped under the strain of his two Decay spells and the force of the blast. The caretaker flicked its head back at the falling column of rock. It tried to slither away, only to let out an enraged screech when the pillar landed on its tail.

"Try biting someone now!" Digby laughed in victory.

"What is it?" Parker backed out of the water and got to her feet.

The snake let out a final screech as the weight of the stone pinned it down and crushed a portion of its body.

Caretaker defeated. 430 experience points awarded.

"Apparently that was called a caretaker." Digby stared at the deceased creature. His jaw dropped when it began moving again.

"I thought you killed it." Parker stepped back.

"So did I!" Digby did the same, unsure how the thing could still be alive even after it had been listed as defeated. He glanced up in hope of finding a stalactite at the ceiling of the cavern that he could break free to drop on the serpent's head. They were in luck, there were plenty. Though none of them were in range. At least not yet.

"Come on." He beckoned to Parker as he made for the rickety stairway near the edge of the cavern that led up to the walkways that lined the walls. "We have to get higher."

She looked up at the rock formations above, then followed without argument. It wasn't until they made it halfway up the stairs that she spoke up. "Shit, what's it doing now?"

Digby spun around as the soldier thrust out a finger behind them. The serpent ceased its screeching and stretched its body as far as it could with its tail still pinned, nearly reaching the remains of the dock.

Then, it opened its mouth.

"What the…?" Parker trailed off as a series of pops came from the creature's jaws.

Digby winced as its mouth opened wider than what seemed possible, even for a snake. It was almost like the serpent's head was folding back on itself. From deep within its throat, something swelled.

At first, Digby thought that the creature might vomit, but in reality, it was so much worse. All at once, the serpent's insides surged from its mouth. Recoiling in horror, he watched as the monstrous thing turned itself inside out. At the start, it was just flesh, but then, bone.

Then more.

From the beast's throat, a pair of large, human-looking hands reached out to grip the top and bottom of its jaws. They twisted and pushed until they tore the serpent's head in two.

"Holy hell!" Digby scampered back.

"I do not like that." Parker joined him.

The new, impossible creature continued to pour from the serpent, leaving an empty, scaled husk behind. A malformed skull burst from the center as rotted flesh formed around its base. Just before Digby thought the unnatural beast couldn't get any stranger, the hands that had torn the serpent's head apart split down the middle. Bones pushed forth to form a claw that elongated and curved until they each became a large scythe-like limb. They shifted along the creature's body until they were positioned near the front like a praying mantis. Six arms burst from its sides next, each a different size. The new limbs slammed down onto what was left of the dock to drag the disjointed mass of horror forward. A pair of undersized, almost child-like legs pushed from the back as the monstrosity heaved its weight toward him.

Evolved Caretaker, hostile.

"I am never sleeping again." Parker covered her mouth as if she might expel a meal.

Digby fought the impulse to flee, reminding himself that nothing had changed. He could still drop a stalactite down on the beast. The fact that it had transformed into the stuff of nightmares was inconsequential. It wasn't fast enough to get out of the way.

He kept moving.

All he had to do was make it a little further and he would be in range. He skidded to a stop as something white flew past his head. Flicking his head to the side, he found one of the creature's bone scythes lodged in the wall of the cavern.

"Crap, Dig!" Parker scrambled up the stairs behind him.

"Crap, indeed! If it wasn't for my heightened agility, that could have taken my head off." He reached out to grip the railing again, only to stumble forward in spite of his aforementioned heightened agility.

"I don't think it was aiming for your head." She ducked down to snatch something from the walkway.

"What the…?" Regaining his balance, Digby raised his hand only to find three of his fingers gone. The blade of bone had cut them clean off.

"I got them." Parker blew past him, shoving three severed fingers into his remaining hand as she passed him by. "Stick those back on. That thing is still coming."

He closed his hand around his missing digits and glanced back. The beast below had already reached the stairway. Its mutated form slammed into the rickety structure, smashing the steps to splinters. He relaxed for a moment, only to panic when the creature pushed past the broken stairway and stretched its amorphous body up the wall. A grotesque hand slapped down on the walkway to hoist itself up.

Digby cast another Emerald Flare to try to keep the thing back. The spell converged in the beast's path and a blast of radioactive power exploded into existence. A rush of displaced air swept past him as the spell lit up the cavern. Digby wasn't sure what effect the lingering poison aura might have within the Seed's realm, but it was safe to say that it wouldn't have much effect on the caretaker.

"Did you get it this time?" Parker slowed to a jog.

"I'm not sure." Digby hesitated as the creature's malformed hand slipped off of the walkway.

He watched his HUD for another experience message.

None came.

Digby would have made use of the moment to reattach his fingers, but with nothing in his void, he had no resources to work with. Hell, he couldn't even use his Limitless mutation for fear that he might damage himself and be forced to heal. He leapt back a second later when a sinewy, black tendril shot upward from the mass of flesh below.

"Good god!" Digby shoved his missing fingers into his pocket and ran.

A second tendril shot upward, cracking like a whip as it snapped around one of the railings. The creature's remaining bone scythe hooked itself over the walkway at the same time.

"I don't like the looks of those tentacles. I've spent enough time on the internet to know how this ends up." Parker sprinted along the walkway toward the nearest door.

Digby could have cast another Flare, but the first two hadn't done any good. Whatever lay deeper into the castle's catacombs was a mystery, but it couldn't be worse than staying to fight.

He ran for the nearest exit.

Relief swept over him when he saw that there was at least a solid door attached to the opening in the wall. He slipped through just as Parker shoved the heavy wooden barrier closed. Wasting no time, he slid a metal bolt into place on one side to secure the door. Then he backed up into the corridor to stare at the barrier from a safe distance. A lone torch flickered on the wall, bathing the stone hallway in pale orange light.

"Do you think that door will hold?" Parker asked from her place a few feet behind him, her hair still dripping with seawater.

A loud bang came from the other side before Digby had a chance to answer. The tip of a bone white blade poked through on their side.

"No. No, I don't think it will." Digby stepped away.

"What do we do?" Parker backed away as well.

Digby turned and started.

"We run for our lives!"

CHAPTER FOUR

Digby sprinted down the narrow stone corridor of the castle at an uneven gait. "I really wish I hadn't lost a shoe right about now."

"What happened to it?" Parker ran just behind him.

"I don't have any bloody idea." Digby finished his answer with a sudden shriek as the door holding back the caretaker burst into splinters behind them.

"That's not good." The pink-haired soldier behind him picked up her pace to run past him.

"Thank you for stating the obvious, Parker," he snapped back. His three severed fingers still rattled around in his pocket. Again, he cursed his lack of resources. With his void empty, he couldn't even reattach his fingers without sending himself into a ravenous downward spiral.

He checked his mana regardless.

MP: 208/291

He'd gained a few points after casting a few spells back in the cavern he'd started in. His thoughts were interrupted by a string of obscenities pouring from the woman beside him.

"It's gaining on us!" Parker panted as she looked behind her.

Digby glanced back in horror as the caretaker filled the narrow corridor behind them, its enormous, malformed skull leading the charge as its mantis-like arms hit the floor to pull itself forward into the space with a horrible click-clack. Its back shuddered and rippled as dozens more limbs burst from its body. Faster and faster, it moved as it shifted into a nightmarish centipede with all of its appendages pushing along the floor, walls, and ceiling.

"Now would be the time to do some kind of cool necromancer shit." Parker looked at him expectantly.

"Well, excuse me, but 'cool necromancer shit' requires minions or resources which I currently do not have." Digby groaned.

"That is not reassuring." She groaned back.

"I don't see you coming up with anything." He rolled his eyes and cursed the Seed again for choosing her to saddle him with. Would it have been too much to ask for him to be trapped within this strange realm with someone more capable? At this rate, the only help she might be would be as bait to slow the caretaker down.

He immediately felt bad for having the thought when a blade of bone shot past her. Parker leapt out of the way but stumbled into the wall. Bouncing off, she fell to one knee.

Damn. Digby skidded to a stop to buy her a few precious seconds. "Get up and run!" He cast Emerald Flare as soon as she was out of the way. He tried his best to estimate the speed at which that horrible creature moved so that the spell converged in the tunnel right as it passed through its epicenter. A blast of displaced air surged through the enclosed place to launch Digby off his feet as dust and debris rained down from the ceiling. Tumbling to the floor, he rolled onto his shoulder. He glanced up as dust settled to watch the beast shake off a few blocks of stone that had fallen as if nothing had happened.

"Damn!" Digby snapped his eyes to Parker. "Keep moving!"

They both pushed off the floor just as the creature slammed a bone scythe into the floor hard enough to crack the stone.

"Sorry I'm slowing you down." Parker heaved for air as she ran. "Thanks for saving my ass, though."

"Your thanks are premature," Digby grumbled. She was right,

she was slowing him down. He might have saved her, but there wasn't any guarantee he would succeed the next time she was in danger.

That was when something reached out from a branching passage. He looked down just as a gnarled hand tightened around the lapel of his vest only to yank him to the side. He tumbled into a branching passage as a hooded figure slipped past him.

"Keep running!" A raspy voice shouted from beneath a hooded cloak.

Parker skidded to a stop and shoved off the opposite wall to fling herself into the tunnel behind him. Digby froze for a moment, staring at the hooded figure. They were short, a bit hunched, and draped in black, moth-ridden cloth.

"I said run!" The hooded figure stomped a foot and turned away to face the caretaker as it barreled toward them.

"Sure!" Parker blew past him, not questioning the rescue.

Digby did so as well, despite his mind scrambling to place his savior's voice. It was ragged and hard, like a crust of stale bread. Even more, it was familiar. He ran regardless. If whoever it was wanted to take his place as that monster's prey, then, by all means, they were welcome to do as they pleased.

That was when he sensed mana flowing from behind him. He glanced back just as the figure threw out both hands toward the caretaker. His eyes widened as a dozen ghostly hands reached from the walls to grab hold of the creature.

What the—

He flicked his eye to the figure and focused.

Remnant Spark, level 35 Necromancer.

His mind raced as he read the line of text. Before he could get another word out, the hooded necromancer spun away and rushed toward him as if they had accomplished what they had set out to do.

"Move." They shoved past him, keeping their head down and hiding beneath their cloak.

"Now wait just a minute, who the hell are you?" He followed despite his protest.

"Yeah, who—" Parker tried to back him up before being cut off.

"I shall not repeat myself," the figure snapped back without slowing. "My phantoms will not hold that beast long. Unless you wish to be devoured, I suggest we slip away to a path unknown to it. We shall have a respite for questions in good time."

"Fine." Digby shut his mouth and ran, finding a lack of options to do otherwise. Parker did the same.

From there, they sprinted down one twisting passage after another. The cloaked figure remained silent as they raced along, only speaking to bark orders. Eventually, after passing through a heavy door, the hooded necromancer simply slapped him on the shoulder to signal for him to get out of the way so they could close and bolt a door behind them.

Parker jumped out of the way as well.

Digby started to ask for their name again but was cut off.

"Keep moving. This mere door will not be enough to stop that beast." The cloaked figure's voice echoed through his memory, sending a chill down his deceased spine. He had definitely heard it before.

"Then what is the damn point of closing a door?" Digby snapped back.

"Stopping that creature is impossible." Their hooded savior let out a sly cackle as they continued down the hall. "But hiding works like a dream."

Digby followed until his guide eventually stopped before a tapestry. He watched as they slipped behind it and opened a hidden door. Parker shrugged and followed as they found a hallway even smaller than the ones they had traversed prior. Digby felt mana flow through the necromancer's body as they snatched a long-dead torch from the wall. The torch sprung to life a second later without the necromancer doing anything to light it.

Their savior slowed but continued on.

"Can't that beast still reach us here?" He kept pace behind them.

"Reach us, yes. Find us, not so much." They chuckled. "The Heretic Seed is in a state of disarray. It was in a thousand fragments up until now, after all. One can expect its representative to miss a few things here and there, even if the Seed created it in the first place."

"The caretaker thing is the Seed's representative?" Parker's voice sounded lost.

"I assume so." Their guide led them to a spiral stairway traveling up.

"Why would—" Digby stopped abruptly as soon as he entered the stairway, finding the space at its center empty. He stared down into the seemingly endless dark below.

Parker swallowed audibly.

"Mind your step, dear." The figure spoke in a tone that made it clear they were smirking beneath their hood.

Digby shook off the initial shock and climbed the stairs. "Why would the Seed's representative be trying to kill me?"

Their guide let out a laugh. "I can think of more than a few motives as to why someone would want you dead."

"What the devil is that supposed to mean?" Digby growled at their words.

"Sorry, I jest." Their laugh faded to a quiet chuckle. "In truth, I do not have all the answers as of yet."

"There must be some mistake." Digby swiped a hand through the air. "I have spoken to the Seed's representative and that thing is not it. The Heretic Seed that I know wears my face and acts like an arrogant ass."

"Curious to see where it got that trait." Their savior scoffed.

"Yes, yes, I'm abrasive. I know and I don't rightly care." Digby stomped up the stairs behind them, wishing he still had all his fingers to point aggressively in their direction. "Why would the Seed suddenly change like that?"

"Obviously, the entity that you knew was merely a part of a larger whole. It was a representation built from whatever could be pieced together from very limited resources." Their ragged savior laughed, letting a strangely musical tone into their voice. For a second, it sounded feminine. Well, feminine for a woman who had died centuries ago.

Digby's eyes widened as the ancient, cloaked woman pushed through a door at the top of the stairs. A deluge of memory flooded back to him as their guide's identity became clear.

The witch!

Digby stopped short and held up a hand, to stop Parker from getting closer.

It was actually her.

The witch that had started it all.

The witch that had cursed him.

The witch that had doomed the world by loosing the dead upon it all those centuries ago.

"How?" Digby curled his remaining fingers into a fist. "How are you here?"

The woman stopped at the center of the room where she'd led him. It looked like some sort of workshop. A shelf of jars and tinctures lined the wall. Paper scrolls littered a table, held down by a mug placed on top to keep anything from being blown away by the draft of a nearby window. The dark sea stretched out into the infinite horizon outside.

Turning slowly, the woman pulled the hood of her cloak down to reveal a rat's nest of gray hair and an ashen face. Her eyes, shining like emeralds, locked with his. They were eyes he could never forget. He didn't wait for her to answer him, instead, he thrust out his hand, missing digits and all, to extend an accusatory finger in her direction.

"Witch!"

CHAPTER FIVE

"Witch!"

Digby continued to stand with his few remaining fingers pointed in the old crone's direction.

"Who the what now?" Parker's attention flipped back and forth between the two.

"What?" The haggard woman squawked in indignation. "You dare intrude on this castle again and call me witch?"

"Uh oh." Parker backed away toward the wall, clearly sensing the tension in the room.

"Indeed, if the description fits." Digby swiped his damaged hand to the side. "You are the cause of…" He shook his head. "The cause of everything. If it hadn't been for your curse, I never would have died. If it wasn't for your curse, the dead would have remained in the ground." His voice climbed higher with each accusation. "If it wasn't for you, everything wouldn't have gone so wrong."

The witch shook her head furiously and stomped forward. "And if it hadn't been for you and your friend, Henwick, showing up at my door, I would not have been forced to defend myself."

"Henwick was never my friend!" Digby stomped his foot right back.

"Hey, guys." Parker half raised a hand. "Maybe don't yell at each other. 'Cause that caretaker thing is still out there."

"Yes, thank you, dear. A wise suggestion. We shan't want to bring that entity right to my door." The witch gestured to the entrance that she had locked behind them before returning her glare to Digby. "And might I remind you that I have very recently saved your existence?"

"Fine." Digby quieted down. "But how are you even here?"

"I should ask you the same." She scoffed. "The last time I beheld you within these castle walls, you were falling to your doom after the Heretic Seed's obelisk exploded in your face."

"I'm harder to kill than most." Digby smirked and wiggled the finger and thumb that were still attached to his hand. "Apparently having a shard of the Heretic Seed lodged in your heart comes with advantages."

"Lodged in your heart, you say?" The witch arched an eyebrow.

"Indeed." Digby tapped his chest. "Right here."

She stared at him, clearly gauging if his story was true. "You really are dead then?"

"Indeed. I'm a zombie." Digby raised his head, unconsciously proud of his existence. "Go ahead and analyze me and see for yourself."

"A zombie?" Her eyes widened as she traversed the room to look at him. "How is it possible that you are speaking?"

"The same way you are, I should guess," he answered matter-of-factly. "I'm not sure what a Remnant Spark, or whatever the Seed has called you is, but you didn't look very alive the last time I saw you out there in the world."

"I was not a zombie." She frowned and stepped away.

"You weren't?" Digby didn't hide the surprise in his voice. "I had assumed from…" He trailed off and waved his hand in a circle around her haggard visage. "…this, that you belonged in the ground long ago."

Parker snorted a laugh at his comment before promptly covering her mouth.

The witch's face soured as she stepped forward and slapped

him on the side of the neck with a boney hand. "I am not dead. Least, I wasn't when I last beheld you. I didn't expire until later when that horrid man, Henwick, hunted me down."

"I'm no admirer of his either." Digby growled at the mention of his enemy's name. "But none of what you have told me explains how you are here now."

"A bit of a long story to that. " The ragged witch sighed and walked back to her workbench to drop into a chair. "After the obelisk exploded, Henwick fled from my zombies. I was left without a connection to magic, and I knew it was only a matter of time before he returned, with more men and better prepared. With that knowledge, I gathered a small chest worth of the Heretic Seed's fragments and fled. The castle burnt to the ground. I didn't understand enough then. I might have held my ground had I known what the fragments I carried could do, but I had yet to discover that. I didn't learn that they could be used to reestablish my connection to the world's magic until later."

"And you entangled your spark with the Seed's fragment once you figured it out," Digby assumed.

"Yes, I realized that when I saw that Henwick had become a Heretic as well." She gestured to the Seed's realm around her. "Apparently letting my mana system merge with one of the obelisk's fragments preserved my existence within it. I don't know what has happened in the world since, but I assume that the Seed has been restored. That is the only explanation for why I have become aware and how I am able to interact with you." She eyed him and Parker for a moment. "I assume from the fact that neither of you are labeled remnants like myself, that you at least exist out there in the world."

Digby nodded.

She groaned. "Then it seems I am in your debt for facilitating my return."

"Yes, it was I that reclaimed the Heretic Seed's fragments and restored the obelisk." Digby pushed aside his ill-will for the woman and focused on getting answers. "But let us start at the beginning. Just what were you doing in that castle, and how did you become a Necromancer if you aren't dead?"

She stared at him in silence, clearly debating telling him more.

"Do you have a name?" Parker added.

With that, her expression softened. "My name is Sybil, and you don't have to be dead to become a necromancer. You just have to cultivate your mana and spells until you discover the class. You can't force it, the Seed doesn't work like that, but if you're willing to make sacrifices and take risks, then you can gain access to a wealth of abilities that one might consider questionable in nature."

"Why meddle with something so dangerous?" Digby gestured to her corpse-like hands. "Clearly it has taken a toll."

She chuckled. "True enough. The body is not meant to contain high levels of death essence. I never came close to the pure mana balance that you must have as a full-fledged member of the dead. Yet, even partially shifting the balance of essence within myself was enough to leave me a shell of the woman I once was. You might not believe it, but there was a time when I was considered quite beautiful."

"You're right, I don't believe it." Digby dropped his tone into a solid deadpan.

Sybil ignored the comment. "As for why I meddled in the taboo. The answer to that is simple. The only way to truly under-stand life is to understand death. You might be right that it was dangerous, but what I learned from my sacrifice had the potential to help the world."

Digby narrowed his eyes, thinking back to what had started it all. The castle had belonged to a lord of the name of Axton, and the only reason Henwick had gotten involved was that villagers had been disappearing. "What about the people that had gone missing from areas near the castle? That was what brought Henwick to your door. What was it that you and Lord Axton were doing?"

Parker glanced back and forth between them. "Who is Lord Axton?"

"Axton was a scoundrel." Sybil placed a hand to her head. "And the disappearances were his doing. He was the one who obtained the Seed's obelisk originally. I don't know where it was found, but he had it brought to his castle and requested assistance in researching it. That was how I became involved. It wasn't until just before Henwick and you arrived that I discovered what Axton's true goal was."

"And what was it he was trying to do?" Digby continued to stare at the woman.

"I'm not entirely aware of the full scope of his plans." A chill entered her voice. "I was forced to kill him before I was able to discover that. All I understand was that he was trying to produce a way to give magic to others while maintaining a level of control over them. A way to ensure that he governed the power of the Seed, no matter how many new Heretics were created from it. That was why he had been taking people from the villages. To experiment on. With the Seed intact, all a person had to do was touch its obelisk and accept the power it offered. There was no need to entangle your spark with it the way you and I did with our fragments. From what I discovered, Axton was simply working from trial and error with no clear direction or understanding. Taking people from the villages was just a learning experience, during which, he gave them magic before promptly murdering them to dissect their bodies. It was crude method of gaining information."

"Shit." Parker breathed the word in a whisper. "That's some all-out horror movie stuff."

Digby suppressed a reaction to that bit of information, setting aside the similarity between Axton's goal and what Henwick had created with the Guardian Core. If what she said was true, then all that was needed to create a new Heretic was to have them touch the Seed. The other interesting detail was that Sybil didn't seem to know about the rings he'd found in the castle. He glanced at the crone's hands, finding no trace of the Heretic Seed's markings.

Interesting. There might be more to the rings that granted me my power originally than I had previously understood.

"How would Axton have gained control over another Heretic?" He dropped his hand to his side.

Sybil's eyes shifted up and to the left as she considered the question. "If he could craft some sort of item with similar properties to the obelisk and forge a link between them, then he could possibly use that as a barrier between the magic and a Heretic created after himself."

"But he hadn't succeeded?" Digby tried his best to make the question appear innocent.

She shook her head. "I think not, or else I shan't have been able to defeat him."

I wonder if that is true? It was possible that he had made more progress than she assumed but had not had time to implement it. There was no way to be sure. Either way, it was probably a good thing that Axton had perished all those centuries ago. Otherwise, he might have dominated the world then. Not that it mattered. Henwick had succeeded where Axton had failed.

That was when he remembered a second detail. When Henwick had asked him how he got his power, he had told him about his ring, thinking it better to keep the shard in his heart a secret. Perhaps that was the wrong choice. With this new information, the rings might have been the more important discovery. Then again, Henwick hadn't reacted, so it was safe to assume no one at Autem understood the ring's significance either. Digby shook off the thought and asked another question.

"Why didn't you investigate Axton's experiments further? Surely you must have been able to find out more."

"I would have liked to." She nodded. "After dispatching him, my intent had been to sift through his materials and secure transport for the obelisk to move it to a safer location. However, before I could achieve that—"

"Henwick and his mob showed up." Digby filled in the rest. At least that explained why she didn't know about the box of rings that he'd found. He shot Parker a look to make sure she didn't blurt anything out. The soldier kept her mouth shut, giving him a nod in return that drew Sybil's attention.

Before the witch could inquire further, a loud screech echoed up to the window from outside. Without a word, Sybil rushed to the sill and leaned out.

"What was that?" Parker stepped away from the window.

Sybil said nothing, her body rigid as she stood with her head cocked to one side, clearly listening for something.

"Don't just go silent here." Digby stepped toward her. "Was that the caretaker? Has it found us?" Before he could say another word she snapped her hand toward him and started pushing mana through her body. He jumped back on instinct, expecting an attack. Instead, a spectral hand reached out from behind him to grab hold of his hair. It yanked him back against the wall where a dozen more coiled around his arms and legs. One of the phantom limbs clamped down across his mouth.

Sybil raised a finger to her ancient lips to make her point clear.

Digby held still, unsure how to escape from her clutches.

The witch glanced at Parker, who immediately held up her hands and kept her mouth shut so that she didn't suffer the same treatment.

A long moment went by before another screech echoed up to the window again. With that, the old witch finally blew out a breath and relaxed. Though, even then she continued to restrain Digby as if making a point of the fact that she could. "That noise was most likely the caretaker. At least it sounded like it. The cliff-side is down below us. It must have circled back to the entrance where it found you to search." She pushed away from the window and strolled across the room to him. "I apologize for the rough handling, but it seemed prudent to lower our voices as the young lady here suggested." Sybil waved a hand in his direction as the spectral hands holding him to the wall vanished.

"Somehow I don't think you're as sorry as you say." Digby rubbed at his jaw where he'd been grabbed.

"Maybe so." Sybil let out a quiet chuckle before snapping her attention to Parker. "Speaking of the young lady, who are you?"

"Umm, nobody." Parker shrank back.

"Indeed." Digby nodded.

"Yeah." She agreed. "I just got sucked into this place along with him. I think it was some kind of mistake or something."

"Maybe, maybe not." Sybil grew quiet as if having a good think on the matter. "If you are here, then it means you have entangled your spark with the Seed, just as we have. You don't appear as a Heretic but that may be due to circumstance. Either way, you must have had a fragment pierce your body at some point."

"Shit." Parker slapped a hand to her side where she had said she'd been wounded. "That's what must have stabbed me."

"But how would…?" Digby tried to work out how that might happen. Then it dawned on him. "It was the Mend spell."

"What?" Parker cocked her head to the side.

Digby shook his head. "We must have missed one of the fragments and left it somewhere on the floor or something. You just happened to get between it and the obelisk."

"Seriously?" She screwed up her eyes.

"The shard in my heart nearly ripped itself from my chest. Had it not been for my bone armor, it would have." He pointed to her stomach. "I'm pretty sure that Mend spell got those fragments moving fast enough to shoot right through you."

"Fuck my life." Her mouth fell open. "I'm only here because I stood in the wrong spot?"

"I wouldn't be that sure," Sybil interjected.

"Why?" Digby flicked his eyes to her.

"Just a theory." Sybil waved a hand back and forth. "In my experience with the Heretic Seed, I find it hard to believe that such a strange turn of events could truly be by chance. The Seed has a way of getting what it wants, like it has some sort of survival instinct."

Parker frowned. "I don't like the sound of that."

"Yes, well, I'm sure you will be fine once the Seed works out what class you are." Digby tried to push past the subject.

"Agreed. Try not to worry, my dear." Sybil gave Parker a sympathetic smile that made her seem much less evil than Digby had originally assumed. He eyed her suspiciously, unsure if she was merely trying to lull them into a false sense of security. For that matter, he wasn't even sure if he should believe the details of her story so far.

If what Sybil said was true, then she may not have actually deserved the blame for everything that had happened to the world. It was just a series of accidents and coincidences. If Axton hadn't abducted anyone from his village, Henwick wouldn't have gathered a mob or gained magic, and Digby would have lived out his days as a normal peasant centuries ago. The modern world would have kept on going, had the pieces not fallen into place the way they had. His mind struggled to accept the fact that he didn't have anyone to fully blame for his fate.

"Alright." Digby tapped at his chin. "Suppose I believe your story. What did you do with the fragments of the Seed that you made off with?"

"I placed all but one in the care of someone worthy of my trust and continued to study the shard I retained whilst I led Henwick away. It was then that I discovered how to restore my magic by intertwining my spark with the Seed's fragment."

"But why?" Parker furrowed her brow. "Why tie yourself to the Seed again when you were free of it? Would Henwick have let you go if you showed that you were no longer a threat?"

Digby answered for her. "Obviously, there is no reasoning with a zealot like Henwick."

"Unfortunately, that is something we can agree on." Sybil nodded. "Besides, if I had not intertwined my soul with the Seed, I shan't think I would be talking to you now."

"It seems so." Digby allowed an air of superiority into his voice. "Though, unlike me, you do not have a body available in the outside world."

She scoffed. "I might be a prisoner here in this realm, but at least I can continue my work. If only for a little longer." She snapped her eyes to Digby. "And I suggest you stop feeling superior. I can't guess what might happen when that number at the corner of our vision drops to two, but I have my theories."

"What number?" Parker furrowed her brow.

"You see them too." Digby glanced at the mysterious digits that had appeared when he'd arrived in the Seed's realm.

77/2

"What do those numbers mean?" He stepped closer to Sybil.

"Like I said, I have my theories, but my guess is that there is a correlation between the number two, and the two of you."

"I do not like that." Parker shook her head.

"And what of the other number?" Digby tried to connect it to something.

"Well, that part is simple." She grinned. "Though I might be the only one that can shed some light on the answer."

"Spit it out, witch," Digby growled through his teeth.

She bared her teeth right back. "Seventy-seven is the number of fragments I took from the castle with me. Including yours and my own, of course."

Digby's mouth fell open at the implication of the information.

"What does that mean?" Parker looked back and forth.

"It means, the three of us are not alone here. There are seventy-seven heretics in this realm with us." Digby slowly closed his mouth. "And only two bodies connected to the Seed."

"Wait, what?" A panicked tone entered into Parker's voice as she connected the dots. "Does that mean only we can escape?"

"No, that means that anyone can." Sybil held up the fingers on both hands before closing all but two. "Provided they survive this place to be one of the final two."

As if to demonstrate her theory, it was that moment that the number in his vision ticked down.

76/2

"Looks like the rest of the Seed's population has gotten started without you." Sybil lowered her hand to her side.

Digby froze, his eyes locked on the woman. The witch stared back, with a wicked grin on her face as he realized there was nothing stopping her from killing him and fighting her way to be one of the last two standing. A tense moment passed where nobody moved.

Then she laughed.

"Oh, calm yourself, I am relatively sure I would not survive the gauntlet if I tried. And I have no interest in stealing your bodies. If I did, I shan't have saved you from the caretaker." She settled down. "No, I shall be satisfied by merely learning what I can about the Seed before I am done here. That would be enough for me.

I'm sure it will take some time for the other souls trapped in here to make their way to you, but within a few hours, that may change."

Digby struggled to wrap his mind around the situation, his dread dancing up and down his spine. Despite her words, he couldn't allow himself to trust her. After all, if he was in her position, he would have said anything he had to in order to fool her into a false sense of security.

"We have to go." Digby backed toward the door.

Sybil's face fell. "I said that I have no interest in—"

"You expect me to believe that?" Digby swept his damaged hand through the space between them.

"You still suspect me." The old witch followed for a few steps.

"Stay back." Digby held his good hand out toward her, ready to cast a spell. "I will refrain from fighting you for now in thanks for saving us earlier. But I am not about to sit here and wait for you to decide my usefulness has run its course." He pulled the door open. "Come on, Parker. I'm sure everyone is waiting with bated breath for me to return and we shan't find a way out of this realm hiding here."

Parker opened her mouth as if she had something to add but Sybil spoke up first. "Good luck to you then."

"What was that?" Digby hesitated.

"By all means, I invite you to try to find a way out of here." She turned back to her work table as if fixing to get back to her tasks. "But I sincerely doubt there is a way back to the world outside beyond surviving until the end."

"What do you know?" He glanced back with a sneer.

"I know that the path from here leads up, and I find it hard to believe that the Seed would create such a thing if you were not meant to make the climb." She sat down in her chair. "And you will need a lot more than luck if you think you're going to make it to the end."

"I'll survive. I always do." He shot Parker a look that said it was time to go before walking out of the room.

The pink-haired soldier gave the old witch a slight bow before hopping toward the door behind him. Digby didn't look back, not wanting to see that witch again. She had doomed him to walk the earth as a member of the undead simply because she had meddled in something she shouldn't have. It was thanks to fools like her that the world had been plunged into destruction.

He stormed off down the corridor.

One way or another, I will find a way back home.

CHAPTER SIX

Digby grumbled to himself as he climbed up the spiral stairway outside of Sybil's workshop. The steps finally let out into a much larger hallway than the one where he had last seen the caretaker. The walls were decorated with tapestries and sconces. It was nothing as grand as the casinos in Vegas, but it was as opulent as things got back in his day. They must have reached the castle's main floors. He relaxed a little, glad to be out of the bowels of the structure. Despite that, he kept his head hunched in frustration and marched onward with an unnatural gait, thanks to his missing shoe.

"Just who does that witch think she is?"

"Dig?" Parker followed behind, struggling to keep up.

He kept walking while balling his one good hand into a fist. "Who does she think has the upper hand here? She doesn't even know what century it is."

"Dig, wait up." Parker walked faster to catch up.

"Hell, I'm sure Becky is doing everything she can to get me out even as we—"

Parker called out again, but this time, her voice trailed off as Digby heard a thud behind him. Finally turning around, he found her resting on her hands and knees as if she'd lost her balance.

"What is it?" Digby walked back and dropped down to her level.

Parker failed to answer, her eyes practically going crossed as she looked up from the floor.

"Is something wrong?" Digby reached out with his undamaged hand, only to hold it just over her shoulder.

"I'm okay." Parker finally spoke up. "I just— Holy shit."

"What is it?" Digby lowered his hand as it became clear she wasn't hurt.

"The synchronizing message on my HUD just changed." Her eyes drifted from side to side as if reading something.

Digby stood back up. "What does it say now?"

She shook her head as if unable to make sense of it. "All it says is synchronizing failed."

"Well, that can't be good." Digby furrowed his brow.

"Wait, no." She sucked in a breath. "Now it says connection established. Shit, now it says translating."

"Translating?" Digby's mind crashed to a halt. "Translating what?"

"I don't know." She stood back up, supporting herself on the wall. Her eyes widened a second later. "Oh damn."

Digby arched an eyebrow. "What? Is the Seed still translating?"

Her eyes darted from side to side as if reading. "I think the Seed is finished. It says class recognized. Okay, now, new Heretic class discovered."

"New class?" Digby stared at her.

Heretic: Level 1 Messenger

"What?" Digby squinted at the information and willed the Seed to show him her attributes the way he had been able to with Alex and Rebecca's. The information ring at the corner of his vision remained where it was, apparently refusing to show him what he wanted. He tried to add her to his coven next, but that failed as well. He frowned. "What the devil is a messenger?"

"Is that not a normal class?" Parker cocked her head to one side.

"It's not any of the starting classes I've heard of so far." Digby shook his head. "Can you see your attributes?"

"Umm, all I see is mana." She looked like she might go cross-eyed.

"How much do you have?" Digby arched an eyebrow.

"Six-hundred and seven," she answered matter-of-factly.

"What?" Digby nearly fell over.

"Is that a lot?"

"Yes! It's a lot." He folded his arms. "That's far more than what even I have."

"Oh." Her eyes bulged before adding, "A circle that says attributes opened when I thought about it."

"Yes, and what are they?" Digby pouted a little.

Her eyes moved from left to right. "Umm, I've got, nineteen constitution, twenty-four defense, seventeen strength, fifteen dexterity, nineteen intelligence, thirteen perception, and five-hundred and five will."

Digby's mouth fell open, unable to reconcile her words. First of all, her intelligence was higher than he'd expected, but that was completely overshadowed by her will value, which was beyond impossible. "Five-hundred and five? There has to be some mistake. No one has a will that high."

"Maybe I'm special?" She shrugged.

"Oh, I doubt that," he snapped back on instinct.

"Maybe it has something to do with how I was pulled in here with you?" She grasped at whatever answer seemed to make sense. "Like, maybe something glitched out to give me a weird class and jacked up my will value."

Digby relaxed a little. "You actually might be onto something there. The Seed once told me that it would try to assist me when it had the ability to do so. The rules of its system don't allow for much, but on occasion, it comes through with a decent spell if there's a loophole to squeeze it through. Perhaps gaining magic through an unorthodox method left it some wiggle room for it to give you a leg up."

She relaxed visibly as if any explanation would have set her mind at ease. "Okay, that makes sense."

"More importantly." Digby pointed in her direction. "What spells do you have? Surely, a class known as a messenger must have a useful spell."

"Let me check." Parker's eyes focus on the space in front of her. "And don't call me Shirley."

Digby groaned. "Now is not the time, Parker."

"Sorry." She laughed. "But yeah, I have two spells. Mirror Link—"

"Yes, I know what that does. What about the other?" Digby circled a hand in the air to tell her to move things along despite having just interrupted her.

"The next one is Mirror Passage." Her eyes moved from side to side. "It says it creates a conduit between two reflective surfaces, capable of allowing passage. Looks like I just have to have a clear image in my head of the destination."

"Does that mean what I think it does? With that, we might actually escape this place." Digby grinned at the prospect of proving that witch wrong.

Parker shrugged. "Let's find ourselves a mirror and find out."

They both headed in opposite directions, looking for anything with a reflective surface.

Finding a mirror in the world outside was easy. In Vegas, the things were practically everywhere. Within the castle, however, it was a different story. Mirrors just didn't exist back in the time that their surroundings were based on in the way that they did in the present. No, in Digby's time, the best they could find was a polished piece of glass. If they got lucky, they might find one backed with lead.

Digby thought back to when he had been in the castle before. He was pretty sure he remembered there being a decorative mirror on the wall of the main hall. Before he was able to locate it, Parker rushed into the hallway behind him.

"Hey Dig." She stopped beside him looking a little pale.

"Did you find a mirror?" He spun toward her.

"No." She hooked a thumb over her shoulder. "But I found something else."

"What?" He deflated a bit.

"I kind of need to show you." She stared back in the direction that she'd come from.

"Alright, fine." Digby reluctantly abandoned his search for a mirror and followed.

Parker led him down a large hallway until she reached a corridor that didn't seem to match the rest. She pointed a finger awkwardly toward the other end. "Does that look important to you?"

Digby groaned. "How should I know? I am not an expert on whatever the Seed has decided to…" He trailed off as soon as he looked in the direction she was pointing. "Oh."

Not far down the passage, a large door sat on the wall. A flickering glass lantern hung on either side while the door itself was covered with a complex pattern of filigree.

"Yes, I suppose that is something that I would consider important." Digby glanced at the pink-haired soldier beside him.

"We should check it out, then?" Parker started walking without waiting for a response.

"Indeed," Digby grumbled as he joined her and pulled on the door's handle.

"Yes, indeed." She nodded enthusiastically just as a gust of wind blew the door the rest of the way open to knock her off balance. "Whoa, shit, hey…"

Digby stepped aside as the soldier fell at his feet and let out a judgmental sigh. "Let's hope Sybil was right that it will take a few hours for the rest of this realm's inhabitants to make their way to us and that the caretaker is back down below. Because I can't imagine all the noise you're making is helpful."

"Shut up. It caught me off guard." She pushed herself back up to stare through the door alongside him. "So is this something you remember being a part of the castle back in your day?"

Digby dropped his eyes down to the floor where a narrow set of stairs started. The walls and ceiling surrounded the steps, but only for a dozen feet or so. Beyond that, the surrounding stone began to become less stable, like it was falling apart. From there the stairway continued up at an odd angle with nothing to stop someone from falling off the side but their own sense of balance.

He thought back to when he had seen the place from the outside, remembering several ribbons of stone that reached up to a land-mass that floated in the sky. This stairway must have been one of those. He didn't like the look of it.

"No, I can't say that this was here the last time I visited this castle." Digby set a careful foot onto the steps and crept his way closer to where the wall ceased to shelter them.

"Yeah, probably not medieval architecture, huh?" Parker followed.

"None that I remember." Digby raised his gaze up the stairway, his eyes bulging as it twisted higher and higher. At one point, it actually folded over on itself, so the top of one step became the bottom of another.

It was madness.

"How do we even climb up there?" Parker gestured to the section of steps that twisted over itself. The wind blew through her hair, threatening to toss an unsteady traveler right off the steps into the sea below.

"I think the more important question is, should we?" Digby stepped back. "We have yet to investigate the rest of this castle, and there might be more to discover. Not to mention we still need to find a mirror. Hopefully, we will find a safer way up in the process. And let's not forget that we will find more opposition further up. I say it's best to get our bearings first."

Another gust of wind blasted Parker in the face. "Okay, yup, I vote we go back. Lots of castle to explore and whatnot."

"Indeed." Digby turned and headed back in the direction they had come from. "We'll take a pass of the upper floors and if we find nothing, at least we know where this door is."

Filing away the knowledge of what they had found, Digby returned to his search for the main hall. Fortunately, it wasn't long before he found a corridor that seemed familiar. They pushed into the main hall soon after. The room was smaller than the spaces Digby had become accustomed to in Vegas, but still it was large enough to drive a cargo truck through. On the walls hung several tapestries while a few wood and iron structures hung from the ceiling covered in candle wax.

"Ah, there we are." Digby gestured to a reflective surface of polished glass backed by lead that hung on the center of the rear wall.

"Nice." Parker slipped into the main hall behind him.

"Alright." Digby gestured to the mirror. "Just do whatever it is you do."

"Got it. Some cool messenger shit, coming right up." The pink-haired woman marched forward, looking a little proud as she approached the mirror.

Then she deflated.

"Do I just, you know, think the spell?" She gave an exaggerated shrug.

"Yes, yes." Digby pushed her along.

"Okay." She nodded, raising a hand toward the glass. "One Mirror Passage to Vegas on the way." She held the pose for several seconds while nothing happened.

"Well, get on with it, then," Digby grumbled from behind her.

"Sorry. I'm trying to focus on an exit point." She scrunched up her nose. "I don't want to send us somewhere entirely different."

Digby shuddered at the thought of coming out somewhere back in California or something. Hell, they could drop out in front of a horde of revenants if they weren't careful. "Good point."

"Okay, I'm going to try to connect us to the mirror behind the bar in the dining area back at the casino." She nodded to herself and reached out toward the glass.

For a second time, she remained like that for several seconds.

"What is it now?" Digby groaned.

Parker responded by sticking her tongue out and making a sound that was not dissimilar to flatulence. "It didn't work."

Digby forced out an exasperated sigh, again regretting that the Seed had sent her and not someone more dependable. "What do you mean it didn't work?"

"It says the spell was canceled because it is unable to create a passage between a material and an immaterial space." She furrowed her brow.

"So it's like my void." Digby rubbed at the bridge of his nose. "I can't access the resources I have in the outside world because they exist in a physical space and everything in here is just a representation of a physical space."

"That would make sense." She dropped her hand to her side. "So I can go from one mirror to another here, but not to a mirror back in the outside world."

"That is frustrating." Digby growled at the result.

"I don't make the rules." She shrugged.

"I suppose that's reasonable." Digby tapped a foot on the floor. "Actually, I don't know why I thought it would work in the first place. How could it? Would we just step out of the mirror and end up with two bodies out there in the world? Of course not."

"Oh, but I still have Mirror Link, though." Parker brightened up. "If we can't travel back and forth, maybe we can at least communicate. Right?"

"Indeed." Digby gestured to the glass. "We might as well try."

Parker reached out again, this time causing the reflective surface to ripple. A scene of the dining area in the casino filled the panel. Digby took a step forward as soon as it came into focus. Through the glass, he could see a number of people sitting at the tables and Campbell standing behind one of the food stations.

"Does something seem a little weird to you?" Parker ran her finger around the image. The view was crystal clear, but she was right, there was something off about it.

"Why isn't anyone moving?" Digby leaned closer to watch Campbell as he held a spoonful of food over someone's plate. The man stood stock-still, like a statue.

"Hey?" Parker waved both hands back and forth to try and get someone's attention.

"It's like they are all frozen in time." Digby placed his fingertips upon the glass, yanking them away again when the image changed. It was still the same room, but the people had suddenly moved. Not much, but a little. Campbell had emptied his spoon and was putting it away. It was almost as if several seconds had passed in an instant.

The image jumped again.

Then, it began to move normally.

Then, it sped up.

"Is there something wrong with the spell's link?" Digby stared at Campbell as he served food three times as fast as any normal person would think reasonable. The people at the tables ate just as fast.

"Your guess is as good as mine." Parker held both hands up empty. "I'm still new at this."

"It's almost like time is flowing at a different rate here within the Seed's realm." Digby ran his fingers down the glass.

"That's bad. It's like we're out of sync." Parker winced. "I hope my body is okay out there. I mean, sure, you're a corpse, so they can just throw you in a closet and you'll be fine, but me? Well, Lana is going to have to find a way to feed me and make sure I don't poop on myself."

Digby shot her a look that said, 'Shut up, Parker.' Just in case that wasn't enough, he added an extra, "Shut up, Parker."

"Sorry." She lowered her head. "But if time isn't moving at the same speed here then we could end up missing days, or even weeks out there. I'm just not sure what that would mean."

That was when Campbell looked in their direction. The image froze, then it picked up again with the large man running toward them. The picture skipped again to him standing right in front of them with his mouth hanging open.

"Can he see us?" Digby's eyes widened.

Campbell waved his hands furiously as the image sped up to several times past normal.

"I think so." Parker stared at the man as he seemed to shout something back at someone. The image jumped forward again showing Rebecca sprinting across the dining area to reach the mirror. Alex was right behind her. A moment went by where they all stared awkwardly at each other.

"Can they hear us?" Digby arched an eyebrow.

"I don't know." Parker took a breath.

They both immediately started speaking, each attempting to give their account of what was happening.

"Alright, listen up. We're trapped within the Seed with every Heretic that ever existed." Digby leaned close enough to leave spittle on the glass.

Parker, in turn, flailed about to give her story. "There's this monster called the caretaker that wants to eat us or something, and now we have to Hunger Games our way through a crap ton of other magic users. This place is huge, and I don't know if what's going on with my real body, or if I've pooped my pants out there in the real—"

Her explanation was cut off when Digby shushed her.

Everyone on the other side stared back at them with confusion, like nothing they were saying was getting through.

"Damn." He slapped a hand against his thigh. "The time instability must be too disruptive for communication."

"At least everyone out there looks okay." Parker gave them a wave. "Bancroft hasn't somehow taken over and imprisoned them all or anything."

"Indeed." Digby scratched his chin. "We have that, at least."

"I guess we still need to find a way out of here then." Parker blew out a sigh.

"Maybe not." Digby stared at the image for a long pause. "I would say Rebecca and Alex look to have everything under control back home."

"Okay?" Parker's voice climbed a bit as if she was asking a question rather than agreeing. "And you, what? Want to stay?"

"I don't want to, but I'm wondering if escaping this place should be our goal." He stepped back from the mirror. "If we know that everything hasn't gone to hell without us, then we can afford to follow things here a little further. If the Seed has some sort of process in place, then we might do well to see it through."

"Do you really think we can?" She frowned. "I mean, Sybil said we're basically in a battle royal with every Heretic in history. And who knows how strong they are."

"My guess is not very." Digby let out a mirthless laugh. "Other-wise, they wouldn't have lost their Seed fragments to Henwick. Besides, the only reason Sybil was able to theorize about our dilemma is because she knows how many shards there are and that it matched the number on our HUDs."

"Yeah." Parker sounded confused despite her acknowledgment.

"And if we happen to meet someone else in here, then we

might be able to convince them to throw in with us so that we stand a better chance." He let a crooked smile crawl across his face.

"And then what? We betray them when we get to the end?" She eyed him sideways.

"Well, betray is a strong word." He folded his arms.

"I didn't hear you deny it." She narrowed her eyes.

"No." He winked. "You didn't."

"Yeah, that's the Digby I know, right there." She deflated.

"Oh, don't judge me." He scoffed. "Besides, you are a Heretic now. Once we get a win under our belts, you should be able to gain enough levels to, well, be useful."

"Thanks." She groaned.

"You're welcome." Digby nodded as if her gratitude had been genuine and turned back to the mirror to give the gathering crowd on the other side a confident nod. "Alright, you can end the spell now."

"Okay." Parker clapped her hands together causing the image to vanish and return the mirror to their reflection.

Digby winced at the sudden loud noise. "There is still a care-taker somewhere out there."

Parker froze. "Oh yeah, the caretaker."

"Oh yeah," Digby repeated her words with as much sarcasm as he could muster. "The unstoppable monster currently hunting us. That caretaker."

Parker wrinkled her nose. "Don't give me that attitude. I had to remind you to shush, like, not even an hour ago when—" She snapped her head to the side just as something slammed into a side door that connected to the castle's main hall. "That can't be good."

"No, it's not." Digby scampered back to slip behind a tapestry.

"Shit, where did you…?" Parker glanced back, clearly unaware where he'd gone.

He poked his head out. "Get over here."

She darted toward him and pressed herself against the wall to hide beside him. "Do you think it's the caretaker?"

"No idea." Digby peeked out from the side. "It's either that or a Heretic like us."

"Still planning on tricking someone into joining us, if it's a person?" She peeked out from the other side.

"Oh, don't say it like I'm some sort of villain," he snapped back just as another loud bang came from the door, along with the sound of splintering wood.

Thunk.

The sound came again in a steady rhythm.

Thunk.

Thunk.

Thunk.

Digby squinted at the door. "It sounds like someone chopping wood."

"Okay, good." Parker nodded. "It's not the caretaker then."

Thunk.

Crack!

The wood began to splinter. Whoever was on the other side was coming through.

"Do we run?" Parker held her ground as if waiting for a command.

"No." He remained still. "We learn what level this Heretic is first. If they are higher than me, we try to stay hidden. If not, we try to recruit them."

"Gotcha." Parker gave him a thumbs up.

Digby tensed as the head of an ax pierced their side of the door. It squeaked against the wood as the person on the other side wrenched it free again, leaving a hole a few inches wide. He gasped as a familiar face pressed itself against the opening to look inside.

His blood would have run cold if it hadn't already held the chill of death.

"Who is that?" Parker kept her voice low as she squinted from the other side of their hiding place.

Digby's voice trembled as he answered.

"Henwick."

CHAPTER SEVEN

Becca stood in the casino's dining area and stared at an image of Digby and Parker in the mirror behind the bar. They seemed to be standing in the hall of some old castle. For a moment, it looked like they were trying to speak but the connection kept jumping around. One moment, they seemed to be moving in slow motion, the next they were moving at triple speed. In the end, Digby gave them a confident nod and left. From that, all she could glean was that he and Parker were alright.

"What in the world did we just see?" Campbell scratched his head.

"I think that was a Mirror Link spell." Alex tapped a finger against the glass.

"So the big guy is fine then?" Campbell glanced back to the stairs that led to the upper floors. "He's not just a corpse laying on a table upstairs?"

"It looks like we were right. His mind really is someplace else." Becca leaned against the bar in the dining area, feeling the tension melt away from her shoulders.

"But how is Parker with him?" Alex blew out a relieved sigh.

"I'm not sure, but at least we know she's okay." An image of the pink-haired soldier bleeding in a chair in the high-roller suite flashed through her mind.

Parker had appeared to be in some sort of coma after being wounded by something when the Seed was restored. Becca had been able to stabilize her easily, but that was three days ago, and she hadn't shown any sign of waking up. Physically, Parker was fine, but there was no one home.

Now, at least they knew why.

After investigating, the only thing Becca could think of was that a fragment of the Seed had been left on the floor and passed straight through Parker's body on its way to join the rest when the obelisk was restored. That was the only explanation despite how improbable it seemed. Then again, Dig did say once that the Seed sometimes took advantage of any loophole it could to lend him a hand. Maybe it somehow altered the course of the fragment to make sure Parker was in its path.

Granted, she wasn't sure why the Seed would want to pull the irresponsible woman into its virtual environment. Maybe to help Dig through whatever he had to do in there? Though, not to speak ill of Parker, there were a number of better choices. Becca assumed the Seed's loophole just hadn't allowed for much wiggle room. Then again, it could have just been bad luck.

After Bancroft regained his connection to magic by touching the Seed, they had brought Lana in immediately to do the same. With that, they had another magic user on their side. Sure, all Lana could do was heal, but at least that gave them someone to care for Parker in her comatose state.

The Heretic Seed didn't seem to have any effect on regular people, but it worked fine to restore magic to anyone that had previously been a Guardian. The downside was that the rest of Bancroft's men had also gained their power back. There was something unsettling about being outnumbered by their former enemies, even if they were playing nice so far.

To make matters worse, the Seed seemed to be having trouble dealing with experience. For some reason, it considered herself and Alex as being somehow different than the new Heretics. Sure, they could group together in their own party just fine, but they couldn't be added to the original coven with Becca and Alex. This wouldn't have been an issue, but the Seed didn't seem to want to award experience to everyone if more than one group of combatants were involved. Instead, the points went to whichever group dealt the finishing blow. The result made it hard to work together with Bancroft's men without stealing each other's kills. Becca hoped that whatever Dig was doing in the Seed might help to clear that up and give them more control of how experience was split or how parties could be formed.

On top of the inconveniences, with Digby lying unconscious upstairs, she had been hesitant to take on any significant operations. Though, after three days, she was reaching the limit of how long she could wait for Digby to wake up. Bancroft had sent his men out to recon the situation at Skyline's base, but they would be back soon and, depending on what they reported, she would have to start making decisions on her own.

"So what do we do?" Alex looked to her as Campbell went back to filling people's trays.

Becca turned and sat down at the bar. "I'm not sure. It looks like Dig was trying to convey that he had things under control."

"So we should stop waiting for him then?" Alex leaned on the counter.

"Well, we can't just sit here and wait for something to happen." Becca sighed. "Eventually we are going to have to take charge and start making moves to strengthen our resources."

"I can do that." He nodded with a smile.

"What has you so confident?" She eyed him sideways.

"I didn't want to just sit around while we waited for Dig to wake up. So I've been busy." He shoved his hand into his pocket. "I think I'm on to something big."

"Oh?" Becca winced, realizing she hadn't accomplished much in the last three days other than avoiding Mason. Sure, they weren't fighting or anything, but she still needed to have a long talk with him about her past and she wasn't looking forward to opening up that part of herself. Even now, just thinking about her parents and what they went through caused her to tear up. Not to mention she'd never even known any of it until it was too late. She shoved the thought into the back of her mind and kept her attention on the artificer in front of her. "So what did you find?"

"I have been experimenting with the warding rods that we stole from Autem's research and development lab." He pulled out a bundle of four engraved metal sticks and tossed them into the air beside the bar. A couple people watched from the other tables as the rods snapped into a position in the air as if guided by a wire. Most of the people ignored them, clearly getting used to seeing magic on a daily basis.

"Okay." Becca got up and walked over to stand in the square that the items formed. "So revenants can't pass this boundary, right? Like the ones we saw set up back on Autem's base?"

"Yeah. I haven't gotten far yet, but the runes engraved on these things are somehow capable of creating an enchantment that can be triggered by anyone, even without access to magic. If I can figure out how they work, I might be able to create more." He gestured toward the entrance of the casino. "That would do a hell of a lot now that Vegas is loaded with revenants."

"That would help us expand our territory beyond this one casino." Becca tapped one of the rods to watch it wiggle in place.

"I know. We could take over the whole strip." He nodded. "People could actually go outside freely again. Not only that, but if I can figure things out, I might be able to use the runes to produce a different effect. Honestly, just the fact that these rods levitate has given me plenty of ideas for interesting uses."

Becca gave him her most skeptical expression. "You want to make a hoverboard, don't you?"

"Umm, maybe?" He grinned. "But seriously, we could create an entirely new mode of transportation based entirely off magic. Hoverboards are just the first logical step, I swear."

"Yeah, that's classic Alex right there." Becca reached down and snatched one of the rods out of the air, causing the other three to drop to the floor. "How do they work for people that don't have access to magic?"

"Oh, that's the cool part." He gathered the other three rods. "They absorb mana just like we do. They can't seem to store anything, but what they pull in is just enough to power their enchantment."

"Sounds like you're off to a good start." She handed him back the rod in her hand, impressed at how much he seemed to be looking toward the future of the city. "Do you need anything to take this further?"

"You think I should focus on it?" He furrowed his brow as if not expecting her to be supportive.

"Yeah, you have some good ideas." She leaned to one side. "Minus the hoverboard."

He pouted with his arms folded. "Hoverboard is non-negotiable. I got to have something to show Parker when she gets back."

"That's fair." Becca shrugged. "I'll be counting on you to keep things running, then."

"Sure." He arched an eyebrow. "Why, you going somewhere?"

"Someone has to." She sighed. "As much as I hate to admit it, Bancroft was right when he said we weren't as prepared as we should be. I'm going to have to take a team to get things done. Bancroft has been keeping his men out of our hair, but I don't trust them enough to keep sending them out on their own. At some point, we are going to have to start working with them. And since Dig is out, that's probably going to have to be my job."

"Damn, that sounds stressful." He frowned.

She did the same. "No shit."

"Well, don't look now, but the source of your stress just entered the dining area." He gestured behind her with his eyes.

"God." She debated on ducking behind the bar. "Is he coming this way?"

"Oh yeah, straight toward you." He sucked air in through his teeth for a moment before trying to make his escape. "Welp, good luck."

"No you don't." Becca leveraged every bit of her enhanced physical attributes to snag his sleeve before he could make his getaway. Then she pulled him back into a barstool. "Sit down and back me up."

"Ms. Alvarez." Bancroft marched right up to them.

"Becca." She suppressed a smirk as her correction seemed to

throw the man off balance. It was a cute little power play on her part. Bancroft wasn't part of Skyline anymore, and the people of Vegas were not mercenaries. The formalities that he had gotten used to were a thing of the past.

"Yes, um, fine. Rebecca." He hesitated. The man probably didn't know most of the first names of the people he interacted with in Vegas. He actually looked a little disheveled, dressed in a pair of pants and a shirt that must have been found in the shopping center connected to the casino. Obviously, he hadn't been given time to pack before fleeing his own base a few nights ago. All he'd taken was the clothes on his back.

Becca made an obvious point of not offering him a seat and waiting until he spoke first.

"I have—" Bancroft started to speak before Alex, of all people, cut him off.

"Where are your guys?" The artificer shot Becca a look like he thought he was helping.

"Yes, Charles, where are your men?" Becca repeated Alex's question in a show of solidarity while using Bancroft's first name for an added effect.

"They have just returned, actually." He glanced back and forth between her and Alex.

"And?" Becca pushed again.

For a moment, a flash of anger swept across Bancroft's face. He closed his eyes a second later and took a breath as he opened them again. "I will get to that. But obviously I am picking up on your hostility, Ms. Alvarez, and—"

"Rebecca," she corrected him again.

"Oh stop." He frowned. "You are not my mother." He shook his head in frustration. "As I said before, I am on your side. So you can stop trying to intimidate me and work together like professionals?"

Becca smirked. "Are we professionals, Tavern?"

Bancroft's face fell as his mouth opened on its own to utter a simple, "Nah, bruh."

The man regained control a second later, raising his voice.

"Would you—" He stopped abruptly and lowered his tone. "Would you not do that?"

"Sorry." Becca tilted her head to one side. "I was just making something clear. And I understand how you feel, but what I need you to realize is that you were our enemy. Hell, you tried to kill everyone here just a few nights ago. I do agree that we need to work together, but you and your men have a lot of trust to earn."

"Consider your point made." He frowned before continuing. "What I came here to say was that my men have returned with intel on Skyline."

Becca leaned on her elbow. "Okay. What is Skyline up to?"

"Nothing." He nodded decisively.

"What do you mean nothing?" Alex asked.

"I mean, Skyline is through. Graves struck a more decisive blow than I would have expected with that insane assault a few days ago." Bancroft seemed to relax now that he was saying what he came to. "At least, you sent a clear message to Autem that Skyline had outlived its use. With me defecting, there wasn't much point in keeping the operation running."

"How do you know this?" Becca let go of her posturing and leaned forward like she was legitimately interested in what he had to say.

"Simple." A smug smile that Becca didn't like spread across Bancroft's face. "While we have been waiting for Graves to wake up, my men picked up a squad of low-level Guardians fleeing from Skyline's service. They had no qualms about spilling everything they knew."

"They were fleeing?" Alex leaned forward as well.

"Yes." Bancroft nodded. "It seems that after the attack, Autem decided to drive a final nail into Skyline's coffin. First, they gathered the remaining high-level Guardians and brought them into the Empire's forces. Then they simply stripped the base of its resources, boarded their remaining kestrels, and left."

"What about the mercenaries they didn't accept into Autem?" Becca flinched prematurely, sensing the answer to the question before it was given.

Bancroft shot Becca a knowing look before confirming. "They knew too much."

"Shit." Her stomach turned at how easily Autem had written people off.

"Yes, shit is right." Bancroft sounded disappointed. "After spending years building Skyline's forces, I can't say that having them wiped out doesn't sting. Although, I can't say it wasn't expected. Even I was able to see that Autem's need for Skyline had an expiration date and most of the recent recruits had only joined to survive this apocalypse." He shook his head. "Fortunately, a few squads of Guardians had the forethought to run before things got too far, which allowed my men to apprehend and interrogate them."

"What about their magic?" Alex tensed.

"Gone." Bancroft swept a hand through the air. "Without a need for them, Autem cut their access to the Guardian Core remotely. After that, the only advantage an ex-Guardian has is the increased attributes that they had achieved before losing their power. They can't gain any more experience, but they would be a little stronger than the average person."

Becca tapped a finger on the table. "Where are these ex-Guardians now? If they seem cooperative, we might be able to bring them onto our side and convert them into Heretics. Considering how things went for them, they should be motivated to fight back against Autem."

Bancroft's face went cold as he pulled a small pouch from his pocket. "I don't think that will work out. Like I said, most of the personnel we took into Skyline in recent weeks lacked discipline and were only there to keep themselves alive. They would sell us out in a heartbeat if they thought it would secure a place for them with Autem. I'm afraid bringing them back to Vegas would be too much of a liability. But if you can figure out a way to convert a Guardian ring into one that will work with the Heretic Seed, we might still be able to bolster our ranks."

Becca followed the pouch with her eyes as the man dropped it on the bar next to Alex. It jingled as it landed. "Is that—"

"Yes," Bancroft didn't let her finish her question. "Those are the rings my men recovered from Skyline's deserters. They didn't exactly give up the rings easily, but my men gave them some modest supplies in exchange."

Becca relaxed, fearing that his squad had simply executed the deserters and stolen their rings.

"And that actually brings me to my request." Bancroft gestured to her. "I would like you and that Mason fellow to organize and lead a mission with some of my men now that they have returned."

"Ah, okay." She furrowed her brow. "I was actually going to suggest that as well."

"It would provide an opportunity to help build an environment of cooperation for my men and your people here." He blew out a sigh. "I've been trying to give you time to handle the situation with Graves, but let's be honest, this is not Skyline. My men, while capable, will need to adjust to the change in leadership if they are to become productive members of this settlement. I'm not fool enough to expect that will happen without growing pains, but I'd like things to progress as smoothly as possible."

"I can agree with that." Becca felt a little bad for giving him a hard time before, now that he was being so reasonable. "I think it would be best to take half your men with me and leave the rest here to help clear the city of revenants."

Bancroft chuckled. "I suppose that is fair, considering they helped make the mess in the streets out there."

"What sort of mission did you have in mind?" Becca stood up to stand level with him.

"A simple but potentially advantageous one." He smiled, seeming more at ease. "As I mentioned the other day, our reliance on generators here is not going to last forever. Fortunately, there is a large enough power station in the area that can handle this city's needs."

"You mean the dam?" Alex dropped a hand to the bar.

"Yes, the Hoover Dam is plenty capable of supplying Las Vegas with the electricity it needs." Bancroft tapped a finger on the counter. "I sent a team to survey the area back before I left Skyline, and they found that the power station was manned by a group of survivors. What I want you to do is go there and negotiate an alliance. My men will back you up."

"That actually sounds like a good mission to test the waters with your guys." She checked the time. "Have your men get everything ready tonight and get me all the information you have. We can leave tomorrow."

"Thank you, Ms. Alvarez." Bancroft inclined his head in a way that could only be described as professional. "I will leave you to it then."

She nodded and he headed back in the direction from which he came.

"That was surprisingly easy." Alex reached for the pouch of Guardian rings.

"Yeah." Becca narrowed her eyes as she watched Bancroft walk away. "Maybe a little too easy."

CHAPTER EIGHT

"Can someone tell me what we did to piss these people off?" Becca winced as gunfire thumped through the air past the kestrel she rode in. The craft weaved to the side, giving her a look at the Hoover Dam as the sun shined bright in the sky.

Apparently, Bancroft had left out some details about the survivors that were inhabiting the power station.

Taking a step to one side, she compensated for the sudden movement of the aircraft. Having the agility of an Olympic gymnast had its benefits. She slapped a hand to her face a second later as Mason tumbled by her feet.

"Damn, crap! Ow." He came to a rest on the floor against Easton's legs, lacking the balance to stay standing throughout the turbulence.

"I hate air travel." Skyline's ex-comms specialist clung to the cushion of one of the seats that lined the wall. At least Easton had fastened his seatbelt.

Mason pulled himself up into a seat and strapped in. Becca couldn't help but smirk. Sure, there was still some awkwardness between them on account of her keeping her emotions and past hidden, but he was cute when he got flustered. She might be an emotionally closed-off ball of anxiety and stress, but she did like having him around. Hopefully she could work up the resolve to open up before pushing him away any further.

Becca's mind was pulled away from that thought as the craft veered to the other side. She took another small step to maintain her balance. Under normal circumstances, it was easy to forget that her stats had progressed so far above that of a normal human. Sure, her intelligence attribute had hit a wall, but her physical capabilities had continued to grow. After the levels she'd gained from the assault on the base a few days ago, she was pretty sure could put most athletes to shame.

Glancing to the Heretic Seed's information ring at the edge of her vision, she willed it to show her stats.

STATUS
Name: Rebecca Alvarez
Race: Human
Heretic Class: Illusionist
Mana: 366 / 366
Mana Composition: Balanced
Current Level: 28 (2,494 Experience to next level.)

ATTRIBUTES
Constitution: 46
Defense: 41
Strength: 40
Dexterity: 44
Agility: 41
Intelligence: 46
Perception: 70
Will: 42

Becca tried not to let the strength go to her head, but as far as she understood it, a value of twenty was normal for a person in peak physical condition. The fact that she had double that in all of her stats was mind-boggling. Especially after the rapid levels she'd gained recently from the attack on Skyline. She still couldn't believe how powerful she felt. It sure as hell was a long way off from the fear that had kept her hiding in the van only a few weeks ago.

"See something good in there?" a voice asked from the other side of the cabin. "Bet you have some decent stats for a girl."

Becca suppressed a grimace as she shifted her focus away from her HUD and to the man standing in front of her.

Malcolm Winthrop.

Of the three members of Bancroft's squad, Malcolm was the man in charge. He was a bit of an ass. Just one of those guys that turned everything into a competition.

He'd cast off his class as a holy knight when he defected along with his boss. Apparently, the Seed didn't like the word holy, since it redesignated him a Heretic paladin. He also dropped from level thirty to twenty-three on account of the difference in attribute points that the Guardian Core gave out at lower levels. Unfortunately, he'd regained enough levels while out doing reconnaissance for Bancroft to get back most of what he'd lost, leaving him even with Becca at twenty-eight.

According to Malcom, they had killed a swarm of revenants, which at least sounded plausible. Unfortunately, she hadn't cast her Veritas spell to check if he was lying or not.

Vegas's new knight stared at her knowingly as he adjusted his footing in pace with her. A smug smile let her know that he had caught her admiring her stats. His attributes were probably just as high as hers. Becca broke eye contact.

"They're firing again." Another of Bancroft's men called from the cockpit. Malcom had introduced him as Ducky. Becca wasn't sure if that was a nickname or not. She liked him even less, despite having barely spoken to him. No, the reason she wasn't a fan was because she had fought him way back in Seattle when everything started. Back then, Ducky had projected himself out to aid in the pursuit of Digby. Of course, that was well before she understood anything about magic.

The kestrel lurched to the side as another torrent of lead streaked through the sky.

"Why did we not approach cloaked?" Becca held onto a rail mounted to the ceiling.

"They didn't have the guns last time we were here." Malcom shrugged. "I figured showing up in a kestrel would be a solid show of force."

"That isn't how we do things." Becca rolled her eyes.

"You guys alive back there? That one was wicked fuckin' close," the last of three ex-Skyline mercenaries that had accompanied her called from the passenger seat in the cockpit. Malcom had introduced him as Sullivan, or Sully as the others called him. His class was pyromancer, and he was the most Bostonian man to ever walk the earth. During the flight from Vegas alone, he had asked her if they could raise the Sox from the dead and told both Mason and Easton to fuck themselves.

"Cloak the damn craft and slow the approach." Becca tried her hardest to sound authoritative. "And again, could someone tell me why the Hoover Dam is shooting at us?"

"That's on Skyline." Malcolm shrugged as if the situation was unavoidable. "They weren't hostile before. One of our squads scouted the dam a week ago before your necro ripped Skyline a new asshole. The squad was a bunch of newbies, so things got complicated. They came out on top in the end, but it looks like the survivors at the dam haven't forgotten it."

"Why am I not surprised?" Becca rolled her eyes.

"It was on the docket to send an assault team back to take the dam by force." Malcolm chuckled. "But as I mentioned, you and your necro saw fit to tear Skyline an additional number of assholes before we had the chance."

Becca groaned at the mercenary's continued use of the word asshole. "Since when does a power station even have machine-gun towers?"

"Since decades ago," Mason answered from his place strapped into a seat along the wall. "The towers were put in back in World War II when they were worried about being attacked. They never used them, but they didn't take them down either."

Becca arched an eyebrow at him.

"I took a tour of the place when I was sixteen. That part stuck out." He held up his hands empty.

"Good to know." She gave him an approving nod. "But we are

going to need to do something about the guns if we're going to land and try to negotiate a truce."

"I say we cloak the kestrel and get in close to take 'em out." Malcolm dragged a finger across his throat in the universal sign for unrestrained murder.

"How about we not execute a bunch of innocent people that are just trying to survive? Not to mention those defenses will be valuable later to protect the place if negotiations go well." Becca headed for the cockpit to take in the landscape.

Beyond the window stood one of the most impressive structures the country had ever built. The mass of concrete stretched across a ravine to hold back billions of gallons of water while feeding it into a hydroelectric system that could support all of Vegas.

Surrounding the dam was an expanse of stone and sand with a lone road reaching into the distance. The machine gun stations were set up sporadically around the area.

Becca furrowed her brow as another barrage of bullets erupted from one of the defense towers, unsure what they were shooting at. Now that the kestrel's camouflage was active, there was no visual to target.

"What the hell are they shooting at?"

Leaning forward, she focused on the area around the dam as a torrent of bullets cut a swath through the dry ground. They weren't even firing at the sky. Clouds of dust swept over the land, reducing visibility. Then again, with her senses heightened to where they were, she could sense movement.

"There!" She thrust a finger against the cockpit window at a pale streak. The Seed filled in the rest.

Revenant, Lightwalker, uncommon.

"I don't see anything." Malcolm shoved his head into the cockpit beside her, getting uncomfortably close.

"I do." Ducky nodded from the pilot's seat. Being an illusionist, his senses must have been on par with her own. "Shit, there's more of them."

Becca squinted at the scene, catching numerous threats darting through the blanket of dust. The Heretic Seed labeled them the same.

Revenant, Lightwalker, uncommon.
Revenant, Lightwalker, uncommon.
Revenant, Lightwalker, uncommon.

She stopped counting at three, having trouble telling if she was counting any of the creatures twice with the clouds of dust billowing across the ground. Suffice it to say, whoever was manning the defense structures surrounding the dam had more to worry about than a kestrel in the sky.

"Why are there so many Lightwalkers all working together?" Becca pulled away from the window.

"They do that," Malcolm commented. "I'm surprised you haven't run into it before. The stronger ones like to travel in packs once enough of them find each other. Some kind of instinct, like how the zeds herd together. Now that a few weeks have passed and the revs have had some time to feed, we're going to start seeing a lot more uncommons in general, as well as groups working together like this."

"Great." Becca sucked in a breath before pushing away from the cockpit. "Take us in low."

"What do you plan on doing?" Mason carefully unbuckled his seatbelt and stood up.

"I'm going to drop down there and earn ourselves some good-will. If we help, they might be a little more willing to listen." She struggled to sound confident, trying not to think about the fact that she had almost been turned by a revenant just a few days ago when Vegas had been under attack. Especially since Alex wasn't there to cleanse a bite.

They really should have taken an enchanter with them. Becca cursed Bancroft for failing to mention that the mission was more complicated than a simple negotiation.

"Are you sure you want to jump into this?" The concern in Mason's voice was palpable.

"Yeah, I can do this." She glanced to Malcolm, then back to him. "Plus, I need the levels to stay ahead of these guys, since the Seed won't let us share experience. Besides, I have an idea of how to stay safe down there." She slapped the open button on the kestrel's ramp.

"Are you sure?" Mason pushed himself out of his seat.

"Yeah." Becca gestured to a bundle on the cushion beside him. "Toss me my stuff."

"Fine, but be careful." He grabbed her things and tossed her a dark green poncho made of a heavy canvas as the rear of the craft opened. Obviously, she could have worn full body armor like Malcolm and his guys, but it was easier to move like this and her agility had been turning out to be one of her top strengths. Ultimately, she just needed to hide the fact that all she was wearing underneath was a pair of leggings, a Las Vegas t-shirt, and a basic bullet proof vest.

She pulled the poncho over her head and held out her hand for the other item that Mason was holding for her.

"Don't forget your crown." Mason held out the tiara that Digby had looted for her back in California. Alex had enchanted it to decrease the amount of mana she used to cast illusions, but she hadn't worn it since, on account of it looking ridiculous.

"Hang onto it for me." She didn't take it. "I have to negotiate with a dam full of people that don't seem to like us."

"Good point. A tiara isn't a good look for that." He set it down on the seat next to him.

Becca gave him a nod as she stepped to the ramp and checked her mana.

MP: 366/366

"Not so fast." Malcolm stepped to her side along with his pyromancer, Sullivan. "Not letting you steal all the XP."

"Of course." Becca let a note of sarcasm into her voice. "The thought never crossed my mind."

"I bet." Malcolm eyed her sideways.

Becca sighed. It was safe to say that Bancroft's men would

never be trusted friends, but with Malcom's competitive nature, they could at least be rivals working toward a common goal. Provided she could keep things healthy and didn't let herself fall behind.

She looked down as the craft lowered to the ground.

With the kestrel hovering only thirty feet above in the air, it wasn't so far that a level twenty-eight heretic such as herself had to worry about injury.

Jumping would certainly give her a head start.

With that in mind, Becca gave them a friendly salute and stepped off the ramp. "See you down there."

As a precaution, she cast Barrier on the way down, sending a shimmer of energy across her body. The wind blew through her hair as she rotated her body to land on her feet. She hit the ground hard and dropped to one knee as her barrier absorbed the impact.

Barrier has increased from rank D to rank C. Potential damage absorption has increased by 50%.

"Can't argue with that." Becca stood up as the kestrel's rotors stirred even more dust into the air.

The surface of the craft shifted color above her, its camouflage struggling to adjust to remain hidden with all the debris in the air. A sudden screech came from her side to announce a Lightwalker's approach.

"Not a chance I'm getting bit."

With her Barrier still active, there was little chance of a revenant's teeth getting through. Then again, the spell could fail at an inopportune moment. To be safe, she cast Conceal on herself, followed by Waking Dream to produce a copy of her image three feet to her left. The tactic was something she had been experimenting with, the result being a decoy that not only drew the attention of threats but one that also seemed to reinforce the believability of her Conceal spell so she could move freely without unraveling the illusion. The combination took a hefty seventy mana, but it was better than getting bitten and gaining a taste for blood.

A revenant Lightwalker put her spells to the test within seconds, rushing from the surrounding dust clouds and lunging for her decoy. She pivoted on one foot and slammed an icicle through its heart before it could get close enough to unravel the illusion.

Revenant Lightwalker defeated. 694 experience awarded.

"Not bad." She nodded at the notification. A few more like that and she might make it to level twenty-nine.

"Save some for us." Malcolm landed a few feet away, followed by Sullivan.

Initially, she was concerned that the mercs might scrutinize her decoy long enough for the Waking Dream spell to fail, but they had either been fooled by the effect, or they were used to working with an illusionist and had made a point not to doubt what they saw. Either way, her magic held out.

Malcolm snapped a sword from the sheath on his back before darting into the clouds.

Sullivan followed.

A burst of flame erupted from one side while the sound of a blade sinking into flesh came from the other.

Becca glanced to her HUD.

Still nothing.

"Shit!" Becca spun, reconfirming the race that she had just entered.

The Seed still wasn't willing to count members of her coven together with the new Heretics when rewarding experience. Hopefully whatever Dig was doing on his end of things would solve that problem. Until then, it wouldn't be enough just to kill the revenants. No, she had to kill them faster than her competition.

Another Lightwalker came for her decoy. She put an icicle straight through its eye.

Revenant Lightwalker defeated. 694 experience awarded.

"Come on!" she taunted the surrounding dust cloud, having no idea how many more might be out there. To her surprise, she wasn't even scared. For the first time since leaving her luxury prison back in Seattle, she didn't feel like prey.

"This must be how Digby feels."

Becca started to understand why the necromancer rushed into everything, cackling like a madman. Gaining a higher level had certainly made a difference in how she saw the world. If she was honest, it could easily go to her head.

The sound of the kestrel's rotors faded to silence as the craft fell back to find somewhere safe to land. A revenant's cry drifted across the dusty expanse. Malcom and Sullivan were off to a strong start, sending a bead of sweat running down her forehead. Becca focused her perception. Bancroft's men might have been experienced fighters, but she had the senses of a predator. She had to stay ahead of them.

Fortunately, the dam's gunners had stopped shooting, probably not wanting to fire on them blindly now that they were helping.

Listening close, revenants screeched in several directions. Each sound echoed through her mind to point her in the right direction.

"There!"

Becca launched an icicle out into the dust, hearing a solid thunk in return. A flash of pale skin streaked past, and she let another frozen spike fly in the direction of her target's path.

2 Revenant Lightwalkers defeated. 1,388 experience awarded.
You have reached level 29. 7,368 to next level.
All attributes increased by 1.
You have 1 attribute point to allocate.

"Yeah!" Becca's heart raced as the rush of a level up swept through her and she dropped her point into perception. Another revenant emerged from the debris only to meet an icicle, point-blank. The creature's head snapped back as its feet flew forward, its body slamming into the ground where it skidded to a stop.

Her effort was rewarded with a new rank of the spell, bringing it up to B as the revenant flailed at her feet. The increase gave her the option of forming either a larger icicle or three smaller projectiles. She used the spell's upgraded option immediately, firing a trio of frozen shards behind her like a shotgun. She hadn't fully pinpointed the location of her next target, but a pained screech told her she was close enough.

2 Revenant Lightwalkers defeated. 1,388 experience awarded.

Her ears twitched and her eyes darted across the terrain, but the only thing she picked up were the heavy footfalls of Malcolm and Sullivan nearby.

"Is that all of them?" Becca glanced at her illusionary decoy.

It shrugged back, following with her thoughts.

"Well, that's helpful." Becca groaned at her decoy as the dust clouds began to dissipate.

The entrance of the dam started to come into view.

"Let's hope the people inside are more willing to negotiate than those revenants."

CHAPTER NINE

The screeches of revenants faded as the dust began to clear from the stretch of desert on one side of the Hoover Dam. Becca swept her eyes across the scene, making sure that the last of the creatures were dead.

Satisfied, she released her Waking Dream spell, feeling confident that she no longer needed the decoy. Despite that, she kept her Conceal active. With the fading dust clouds, she still had the chance for misdirection, and considering the survivors holed up in the dam had shot at them earlier, it made sense to take steps to keep herself safe.

With that, she simply sat down and cast a Spirit Projection.

A moment of disorientation passed, leaving her standing next to her unconscious, concealed body. At least that would keep her out of the line of fire if someone decided to point a gun at her. The projection spell was more stable than Waking Dream anyway. It also allowed her to speak without having to cast Ventriloquism.

"How many you get?" Malcolm and Sullivan wandered back toward her as the dust settled.

"Eight," Becca answered, not mentioning the fact that she was a projection. They didn't need to know.

Malcolm let out a low whistle, as if impressed.

"Damn," Sullivan added with an approving nod.

"Dam is right." Becca pointed to the structure ahead of them.

She considered rubbing her kill count in their faces but suppressed the urge. Instead, she flicked her vision to the sky in search of the kestrel. Unfortunately, her perception had not quite reached the point where she could easily see through the aircraft's camouflage. She could hear its rotors but not enough to pinpoint a location. It must have been landing a little further away.

Becca dropped her eyes back down to the dam, finding the guns of the nearest tower pointed in her direction. Malcolm placed his sword back in its sheath before pulling a pistol. Sullivan drew his gun as well and took up a position a few feet away. Apparently, they still resorted to firearms when facing ordinary humans.

"Put those away," Becca hissed at them. "You're more dangerous with magic anyway."

"Not a chance," Malcolm grunted back. "These assholes didn't see our capabilities on account of the dust clouds. We need them to understand who's in charge."

Becca rolled her eyes, as the knight made it clear he had no intent of disarming. She would have argued but fighting with him would only make her side look fractured, and that was sure to hurt her ability to negotiate with the people inside the dam.

"Oh well, all I can do is try." She stepped toward the dam's nearest entrance, at the top of the structure to the side of the road that traveled across it. It was less than a hundred feet away.

A short burst of gunfire ripped through the ground in front of her before she could make it halfway.

"Not another step," a gruff voice shouted from the entrance she was heading toward.

"Okay." Becca halted her progress and raised both hands to show that she was unarmed. Her attempt at goodwill was immediately ruined when Malcolm stepped past her with his pistol ready.

"I don't think you're in any position to be telling us what we can and can't do." The paladin didn't even look in her direction before assuming command of the situation.

The gruff voice of the dam's representative remained quiet, as if still trying to figure out what he wanted to say. "This is your last warning. Your people killed three of ours the last time you were here. If you take one more step, we will open fire. And you can bet your ass that we'll hit more than the desert."

"Damn it." Becca shot Malcolm an irritated look. "You didn't say that Skyline killed three of their people."

"That wasn't our squad." Malcolm didn't back down, shouting his response so everyone could hear. "As far as I can see, we just saved your asses from a bunch of bloodsuckers. So you owe us a conversation. And let me remind you that we still have an aircraft out there capable of taking out your defense towers. So don't go thinking you have the upper hand."

"That right?" The voice in the entrance grew louder as an old man dressed in army fatigues stepped out with a rifle trained on Malcolm's position. His white hair hung down to his shoulder, while a beard framed his face. His chest was covered by a Kevlar vest. "You gonna tell that oversized drone to take out our towers? I'm willing to bet I can put a round between your eyes before that thing can even open fire. So I'll say again, this is as close as you get to this," he chuckled, "dam place."

"The hell it is." Malcolm took a step forward.

The old man with the rifle made good on his promise. His weapon barked before Becca had a chance to say anything. A splash of blue sparks erupted from Malcolm's right shoulder as a Barrier spell took the round.

"Wait!" Becca shouted as Malcolm recovered and took aim at the man.

"How?" The gruff man with the rifle let his gun waver, clearly stunned by the fact that his target was unharmed.

"We do this the hard way then." Malcolm grabbed for his radio and thumbed the button. "Take the towers."

"Don't you—" Becca shouted over him so at least Mason could hear her over the radio since hers was still on her body.

"We don't have time to play nice." Malcolm took aim at the old man just as his target did the same.

Not knowing what she could say to stop the conflict, Becca jumped forward to get between the two men with her hands up. "I said wait a damn second."

"Get out of the way." Malcolm didn't show any sign of letting up.

That was when one of the gun towers opened fire. Dry clay exploded from the ground just behind Malcolm as another three rounds slammed into his barrier. The spell held, but the impact knocked him on his ass.

Being a projection, Becca felt nothing.

A glance down showed a strange empty space where her chest should have been. A swirl of multicolored particles flowed around her for a moment before drifting back to reform her projected body. She was just glad she hadn't used Waking Dream to represent herself. If she had, the attack probably would have unraveled the spell.

"I said hold your fire until I gave an order," the gruff man with the rifle shouted into a radio of his own as he crouched against the entryway of the dam. Clearly, the shots from the tower had not been on his orders. He snapped his vision back to Becca as her form solidified once more. "What the hell was that?"

Becca stared down at Malcolm as he sat on the ground. "You tried your way, now let me do mine."

"Fine, go right ahead." He rolled his eyes and raised a hand as if to say, 'have at it.'

"Thank you." She breathed her words at the mercenary through her teeth before spinning around to give her attention to the old man and his rifle. Her mouth fell open a second later when she realized she didn't know what to say.

"What are you people?" The man in the doorway shouted again, making a point of keeping his weapon aimed at her. "I've seen a lot of weird shit this last month, but I haven't seen whatever you just did."

"Think, Becca think, what would Dig do?" she whispered to herself.

"What was that?" the old man called out, obviously noticing her talking to herself.

"Shit, I really need an inner monologue," she scolded herself before throwing up both hands again to show she wasn't a threat. "Hi, there!"

The man stared at her with his rifle raised for a long moment before responding with an awkward, "Hi."

"Okay, so, I know how things look." Becca cringed as the kestrel revealed itself and landed a few hundred feet behind her. "But we are not here in the same capacity as the men that hurt your people were."

"Killed our people," the elderly man corrected her. "They killed three of our people."

"I understand that." She took a step closer. "But I assure you, we mean you no harm now."

"You expect me to believe that when you come here in one of those sci-fi helicopters and have some of your guys threaten us?" He wasn't buying it.

Becca hesitated as the kestrel opened its ramp to let Mason and Easton out. The pair kept their distance and made sure not to make any movements that could be interpreted as hostile.

"You're right, these two men with me did threaten you." She gestured to Malcolm and Sullivan before adding, "And they were wrong to do so. But I will add that they are not the ones in charge here." She puffed out her chest. "They are also no longer affiliated with the organization that attacked you before. None of us are."

"Alright, so you're in charge, then." The man seemed to accept that.

"Yes." The word felt like a lie even as she said it. She continued regardless. "And if you would allow me to approach, I can explain things."

"Nah, I don't think I can take that chance." The man didn't budge. "Those men from—what's it called? Oh yeah—Skyline, killed some good friends of mine. They had families."

Becca let out a sigh. "Unfortunately, I understand all too well what Skyline does to families."

"What is that supposed to mean?" He let his aim falter.

Becca glanced back at Mason. It wasn't exactly the time or place for her to share the details of her past, but she shook off the concern and took a step forward hoping her experiences might help to convince the stranger. "Skyline tore apart my family as well."

"What's that?" The man sounded surprised.

"I was taken from my parents under false pretense when I was still young and trained as a surveillance operative. I grew up thinking that my family had abandoned me. It wasn't until last week that I found out that it was all a lie." She took another step. "Skyline, and the organization behind them, spent years blocking my parents from seeing me while telling me their letters had stopped coming. I never knew how hard they tried to get me back. I didn't even know I had a brother. I didn't learn any of this until they were all dead."

"How did they die?" The man lowered his rifle to his side.

"How do you think?" Becca gestured to the world around her. "It was Skyline and their parent organization, Autem, that spread this curse through the world, and it was them that created these bloodthirsty creatures that hunt those of us that have survived. This is all part of their plan."

"And you're what, defectors?" The elderly man leaned to one side.

"Yes, but also, we're so much more." Becca released her projection as well as her concealment spell, causing her form to disperse into a cloud of glowing particles.

The old man did a double-take between the spot that she had been standing and her real body as she stood up further away.

"I know that things are strange, and I will be glad to explain everything." She lowered her hands and began walking toward him. "But we're never going to understand each other if we don't stop aiming guns at each other."

"Now, hold on now, just tell me how you did that, ah, teleport thing." The old man jabbed a finger at the air before sweeping it back and forth between where she was and where she'd been. "That can't be possible."

"It wasn't teleportation." She shook her head. "Hell, I wish I could do that. No, that was just an illusion to protect myself. I've been hiding over here the whole time we've been talking."

"How is that—"

"It's magic." She cut him off, remembering how Digby had revealed the existence of the absurd to her a month ago. "I know that sounds crazy, but this is the power that Autem used to plunge the world into the apocalyptic hellscape that it has become. My people intend to use the same power to fight back. In fact, we have already delivered a solid blow to their mercenary force. Because of that, they shouldn't be coming back here anytime soon. That's also why we are making use of the aircraft we stole in the process."

"I saw some pretty strange things back when those men came here the first time." The man scratched at his scruffy gray beard. "And with that display you just put on, I'm not sure what I can believe. Honestly, I'm an old man here. I can't even put a photo in Microsoft Word without it screwing the formatting up."

"No one has figured out how to do that." Becca smirked.

He laughed and shook his head. "Well, you can call what you do magic or even science…" He laughed again. "Hell, you can call it pixie dust, if you want. Either way, it's over my head. All I know is hydroelectrics and that there are people here that depend on me to keep them safe. Now you say you don't mean us any harm, but your reason for being here is obvious. You want the same thing that those men who came before wanted. The dam."

"That's fair." She stepped closer until she was only a few feet away.

"So why should we help you and not them?" He slumped against the entryway as if it had taken significant effort to hold his rifle up for as long as he had. The barrel of the weapon shook back and forth.

"Because Autem plans to conquer the world and indoctrinate everyone they can to their side, until they have erased everyone that could stand up against them." Becca reached out to catch his rifle when it slipped from his grip. She leaned it against the wall beside him, making sure to place it close enough for him to reach it. "I won't lie, there is a chance that standing in Autem's way may end up getting all of us killed. But really, that would happen eventually anyway even if we don't fight. Unless you want to join them and help steal people's children."

"Those are not great options." He eyed her sideways. "You get that, right? You aren't giving us much of a choice here."

"I understand that," she answered him matter-of-factly. "I wish the future was bright, but—"

"I know, it's too much to expect sunshine and rainbows at this point." He fell silent for a moment before finally blowing out a heavy sigh. "The name's Jameson."

"Were you military?" She leaned closer.

"Used to be." He shrugged. "Long time ago. Seems I've been drafted back to duty though, whether I wanted it or not."

"I get that." She nodded. "We have a few former soldiers that have done a lot for us so far." She glanced back at Mason, who was still standing further away to make sure he didn't disrupt the negotiations. "I'm not sure what I would have done if I hadn't met them."

"That's good to know." Jameson gave an approving nod.

"Well, one of them is pretty cute, so, you know." Becca tried to lighten the mood, getting a laugh from the old man.

"That so?" He leaned forward to glance at Mason for a second before returning to the entryway. "Not bad. If I were younger, I might give you some competition." He finished his comment with a wink.

"I'm sure." She chuckled.

"Okay, fine." Jameson held out a hand. "You have yourself a power plant."

CHAPTER TEN

Digby fought the urge to turn tail and run as the face of his sworn enemy stared through the cracked door of the castle's main hall.

Henwick!

How?

How in the hell is he here?

He ducked back behind the tapestry that he and Parker hid behind to eliminate any chance of being seen.

"Wait, that's Henwick?" Parker did the same, running into his side as they both tried to stay hidden. "How is he here?"

"I don't know, I don't know, I don't know. Unless…" His face fell. Unless the man had been brought into the Heretic Seed the same way as Sybil.

Digby's mind raced, trying to figure out how that could be possible. Could the man's spark have become trapped within the shard that had once been lodged in his arm? Not only that, but was it possible his spark had somehow been separated from him when the fragment had been removed? Henwick was clearly still alive and well out there in the world beyond, so what else could it be? Digby suppressed a gasp. Could it really be possible that the man out there was somehow walking around without a spark? Without his soul?

There was only one way to be sure.

Digby leaned back to the edge of the tapestry, being careful not to be seen. Then he focused on the growing hole in the door. If he was able to see Sybil's level, then there was a chance that he could catch a glimpse of Henwick's as well. His enemy had been a level one hundred high priest when he had last set eyes on him, but if this version of Henwick had been severed from that man long ago, then it should be lower. Digby watched him give the door another few chops to widen the hole before he tried to reach in for the lock.

Remnant Spark, level 31 Cleric.

"Huh?" For a second, he was surprised that the Seed even had a cleric class, considering its connection to things that might not be considered holy. He shook off the question and focused on the more important part. That being the fact that the version of Henwick trapped within the Seed's realm was only level thirty-one. "We're in luck. I think I could beat him if I had to?"

Henwick returned to chopping after being unable to reach the lock on the door.

"Got it, let's go pick a fight?" Parker started to step forward.

"No." He grabbed Parker's shoulder and dragged her back. "Are you mad?"

"But you just said we could take him," she hissed back.

"I know what I said." He held up a hand. "But I didn't mean fighting was our first option, just that it wasn't out of the question."

"Sorry, just trying to help." She backed down.

"Well don't." He kept his voice low. "Henwick might actually be the perfect rube for us to recruit."

"How so?" She cocked her head to one side. "Isn't he hell bent on destroying the world?"

"Yes, but he wasn't back when he had his fragment removed. My guess is this version of him will be a little more cooperative." Digby glanced at the numbers that showed the population of Heretics still active within the Seed's realm.

Parker must have looked as well because the next word from her mouth was, "Noice."

Digby arched an eyebrow. "What is?"

"Just, um, you know, sixty-nine." She shrugged.

Digby held back a groan. "I'm going to assume that was a reference that I don't understand, and I'm not asking questions on account that it will probably annoy me."

"That's probably wise." She nodded.

"Yes, but the situation is nice, indeed. Henwick doesn't have all the information that Sybil had, plus the naiveté of his previous self should make him pliable enough to recruit to our side."

"Until we betray him, right?" Parker added.

"Yes." Digby nodded briefly before shakings head a second later. "No. I mean, maybe. We'll see how things develop."

"Ah, gotcha." She gave him a thumbs up and went silent.

"Yes, just follow my lead." Digby started to slip out from behind the tapestry only to glance back at her. "Oh, and probably let me do the talking."

"I'm not an idiot, you know?" She narrowed her eyes at him.

"Yes, yes, I'm sure." He broke eye contact.

She let out a huff and blew her bangs out of her face but refrained from adding any further argument. He just hoped she wouldn't blurt out anything incriminating that might cause a problem. With that, he stepped into the open and headed for the door.

"Henwick?" He shielded his face as he approached, as if he was worried he might get hit with debris from the man's continued chopping. "Henwick? Is that you?"

The ax pulled away from the door as the level thirty-one Heretic on the other side peered through the hole. "Who's there?"

"It's me, Digby." He rushed forward to the door. "Thank god I've found someone."

"Graves?" Henwick stepped away from the door. "How are you here? I saw you fall to your death."

"Yes, and I thought the same had happened to you." Digby made a point of keeping himself hidden by the door so that the cleric couldn't get a good enough look to analyze him. "Here, let me get this door open for you. No sense chopping it down if I can simply unlock it."

"Please do." Henwick stepped away to give him space. "How did you survive the fall? I thought for sure you were…"

The cleric trailed off just as Digby pulled on the bolt that secured the door. Henwick went eerily silent the moment he made it into the main hall. A look at his face told Digby why. The man wore an expression of confusion mixed with horror.

"Well, damn. You analyzed me, didn't you?" Digby deflated.

Henwick glanced around the room for a brief moment before raising his ax, light glinting across the blade as he did. "You foul creature!"

"Wait, wait, wait!" Digby leaped back to avoid a swipe aimed at his neck. The air crackled in the weapon's wake as he felt mana move through the cleric's blood. "I can explain."

"You shall explain nothing." Henwick lowered his weapon only to thrust out a hand. "Whatever you are, you have been twisted by the vile power of the Heretic Seed."

Digby threw out a hand in kind to cast Absorb. "That's rich, coming from a level thirty-one Heretic."

The shimmering light of a healing spell met the purple vortex of Digby's counter to swirl into his palm. The power of the spell funneled its way harmlessly into his mana system for later.

"You think I wanted this power?" Henwick took another swing with his ax. "No, I have hunted your kind in penance for months."

Digby filed that little tidbit away as he jumped back to dodge. The man had only lived for a few months before removing the Seed's fragment from his arm. Understanding that, the version of Henwick that was standing before him now couldn't possibly know anything of the last eight centuries. Digby grinned, remembering how little he understood when he'd thawed out a month ago. If Henwick still had the mindset of someone from the past, that would certainly make him easier to manipulate.

"Hey!" A blur of pink hair slid out from behind the tapestry as Parker lobbed an object in the man's direction. "Back off!"

Henwick snapped his vision to her and jerked his head to one side just as one of her boots flew past his head. He furrowed his brow at the new opponent and thrust the head of his ax to point in her direction.

"Oh shit." Parker started taking off her other boot, probably to use as a weapon despite the fact that it hadn't worked out well with the first one.

Henwick shifted his attention back to Digby while keeping his ax held toward her to keep her at bay. "Graves, what have you done to this young lady?"

"What the hell sort of question is that?" Digby scrambled to the side of the room and dragged a chair between him and the hostile cleric. "I've not done a bloody thing to her."

"Clearly you've used whatever power you have to enthrall this poor creature." He winced. "I shudder to think of how you have mistreated her. Her hair is unnatural, and her clothing is indecent."

Parker's face fell as she looked down at the tank top she wore. "And what is wrong with what I'm wearing, you ass?"

"Well said." Digby peeked out from the side of the chair he hid behind to address Henwick. "As I said, you ass, I have done nothing to this young lady. She is a soldier, far more capable than any you might have known. And it would do you well to allow me a moment of conversation before resorting to violence."

"Yeah, so drop the ax." Parker stood a little taller from the compliment.

"I think not." Henwick didn't budge. "You are one of those creatures, one of the dead. Even worse, you have followed in that witch's footsteps and given in to the temptations of necromancy."

"Temptations, my deceased ass," Digby spat from behind his chair. "Had it not been for my poor judgment in following you, I shan't have ever perished in the first place. My class is as much a choice as yours was."

Henwick furrowed his brow as if considering Digby's situation as similar to his own, then he shook his head and returned his gaze to Parker. "I can't imagine what you must have been through, young miss, but if you could step aside whilst I handle this vile miscreant, then I shall tend to your safety afterward. You have my word."

"Oh, for crying out loud." Digby gave up on trying to reason with the hypocrite and simply willed his mana into action. He had a good mind to open his void and swallow him whole, but he resisted the urge and opted for an Emerald Flare instead. The blast probably wouldn't kill the man if he positioned the spell's epicenter about ten feet away from his target. Hopefully, the shockwave would cause enough damage to subdue the pompous ass.

Parker got her other boot off and prepared to launch the improvised projectile, keeping Henwick distracted as streaks of sickly energy swam through the room behind him to coalesce into a bright point of unstable power. The light of the spell grew until it bathed the large room in an eerie glow.

That was when Henwick finally turned around to search for the source. "What the—"

The spell detonated in a blast of emerald power that tore the man off his feet. An instant later, he hit the wall, nearly twenty feet away, like a rag doll. His ax slammed into the wall next to him, nearly shattering the mirror they had used to check on Vegas. The ax clattered to the floor as Henwick's body crumpled against the wall.

Digby immediately cringed.

"Damn." Parker dropped her boot, having no need to throw it anymore. "Overkill much?"

"Well, yes." Digby sucked in air through his teeth. "That spell might have been a little more impactful than I intended."

"Ya think?" The soldier went about collecting her other shoe. "Is he dead? Also, am I going to get sick from the area effect? Because I don't have a healing, or purification, or really any spells to deal with that."

"We'll just have to drag him to the other side of the room away from the spell's radius and remain there. As for if he's dead, I'm not sure?" Digby watched his HUD for an experience message.

None came.

"See right there." Digby pointed to a wound on Henwick's head that seemed to be closing. Probably due to the man's regeneration spell activating on its own. "He's fine, just a little unconscious is all."

"Oh, is that all?" Parker repeated with a heavy dose of sarcasm.

"Yes, now help me find something to tie him up with." Digby rushed over to the tapestry they had been hiding behind and began yanking on it.

"Okay." Parker pulled her boots back on and ran to help. "So what, we gonna roll him up in this, like a corpse in a carpet?"

"Corpse in a carpet?" Digby paused for a second. "Is that a thing?"

"Maybe?" Parker didn't seem sure. "I think it's a mafia stereotype."

"Oh." Digby continued tearing the tapestry from the wall. "Well, if it's good enough for the mafia, I say it's good enough for me."

Between the two of them, the fabric came free, and they spread it out on the floor. With it flattened out, they saw to moving the unconscious cleric. Digby grabbed Henwick's shoulders while Parker took his feet. After getting him into position, Digby dropped him. Parker winced when Henwick's head hit the floor with a solid thud.

"Oh, don't be squeamish, he's fine." Digby brushed off her concerns. "He's a Heretic, and one that clearly has the Regeneration spell. It will cast automatically while he's unconscious until he's in top shape. That's one advantage of being alive, it seems."

"You can't do that?" Parker began rolling their prisoner up.

"Sadly, no." Digby bent down to help. "Seems you can't have spells cast on their own while unconscious if, in most cases, the only way to be knocked out is to have your brain crushed beyond recognition."

"Good to know that someone can even be knocked out here." She stood up as soon as Henwick was secure. "Actually, it seems like this whole place functions a lot like the real world."

"It seems so." Digby nodded along.

"And thanks for the compliment earlier." She helped to drag Henwick away from the Flare spell's poisonous area of effect.

"What's that?"

"That I am a soldier more capable than any Henwick has met. Didn't think you liked me much, actually." Parker wrinkled her nose at him, clearly realizing that the compliment might have had more to do with intimidating Henwick than genuine respect. "And you didn't mean it, did you?"

"Well, I, ah… Of course I did." Digby tilted his head from side to side. "Though, in all honesty, fighters back then mostly ran at each other in an open field whilst swinging around pointy things. So the bar wasn't exactly high."

Parker looked annoyed for a second but quickly nodded. "That's fair, I guess."

"Indeed." Digby poked at their prisoner with his foot, the man's body rolled up in the tapestry like a sausage.

"What do we do with our friend here?" She held a hand out toward the man in the carpet.

"Well, first we need to find out what he knows." Digby tapped a dead finger on his chin. "Nearest I can tell is that good old Henwick was busy hunting down Sybil and anyone who might have come in contact with the Heretic Seed's shards. We'll have to see how much of that happened before he removed his fragment." Digby crouched down to examine the man. "The Seed had to consume his spark to grant him power, if I understand things right. So that's what we're seeing here."

"And a spark, is like, a soul right?"

"Indeed." Digby placed a hand on the cleric's chest, feeling it rise and fall as if truly alive despite being a disembodied spirit within an immaterial realm.

"So if his soul is here." Parker crouched down beside him. "What the hell is walking around out there in his body?"

"That, I have no idea." He shook off the question. "But what we do know is that this version of Henwick has no idea of what has become of the future or anything that I might have done. And I aim to keep it that way."

"So we lie to him?" Parker caught on.

"We lie to him." Digby nodded in confirmation. "With some convincing, we just might be able to trick him into taking our side in here. Having a level thirty-one cleric would certainly increase our chances."

"Do we have to worry about the Seed labeling us as hostile if we have an ulterior motive?"

He considered the question. "I don't think so. It should label us as friendly as long as we are working together. That will change if the situation does."

"How long do you think he'll be out cold for?" She reached out and pushed one of his eyes open. His iris stared back with no reaction. She wrinkled her nose. "Sorry, just checking to make sure he wasn't already awake and playing dead to eavesdrop on us. That's what I would do if I was in his position."

Digby glanced at the woman, surprised at her forethought. That sort of planning hadn't seemed like one of her strengths. Of course, that was when she pressed a thumb against Henwick's nose so that it resembled a pig's snout and giggled while making oink noises. Digby blew out a disappointed sigh.

"Parker, is that helping?"

She stopped and looked back at him mid-oink. "No, probably not."

Digby shook his head as she backed off, only to crouch down and take her place. Then he picked the ax up off the floor to make sure he had something to threaten Henwick with. Then he slapped him on the cheek. "Time to wake up."

"Is that helping?" Parker repeated his earlier question.

"Well, we can't just let him nap the hours away. He's not you." He gave her a judgmental look.

"Hey, I do plenty more than nap." She folded her arms. "Sometimes."

"Like what?" Digby eyed her sideways.

"I don't know, stuff." She looked away.

"Oh yes, stuff, very helpful." He antagonized her further, the way he usually did Rebecca when they had nothing else to do.

"Eat a bag of dicks, Dig," Parker grumbled.

His face fell, realizing that he wasn't going to get a witty response back. Then he blurted out the first comeback that came to mind. "I'll have you know I've swallowed many men whole, so I've eaten plenty of dicks."

Parker burst out laughing. "That's the best you could come up with?"

"Oh, shut up, Parker. I'm not used to such lowbrow insults." He rolled his eyes. "Rebecca is usually a little more eloquent with her jabs."

"Well, I'm sorry I'm not Becca." Parker threw out both hands. "Obviously, I'm going to try my best to help you here, but if you're gonna annoy me, I'm going to tell you to eat a bag of dicks."

"Joy." Digby rubbed at the bridge of his nose just as their prisoner stirred and opened his eyes.

Henwick winced as if his head hurt before frantically glancing around and struggling to get free. "Release me, you foul creature. I know not what this bag of dick is, but I wish for no part of it."

Parker snorted.

"Good lord, don't you start in with that again." Digby shoved the ax under his chin to keep him in line. "And don't even think about casting anything. We just want to talk. And I can easily take your head off before you have the chance to hit me with something."

Henwick stared daggers at him for a long moment before he finally acquiesced. "Very well, I shall talk, but I demand you release me once you are satisfied. If that really is all you want."

"Good, good." Digby nodded. "Now, how did you get here?"

"I... I'm not sure." Henwick shook his head.

Digby furrowed his brow. "I find that hard to believe."

"It is the unfortunate truth." He narrowed his eyes. "I removed that blasted fragment in my arm and..." He trailed off for a second. "I'm not entirely sure what happened next, but I woke up here?"

"Alright, that does make sense." Digby removed the ax from Henwick's neck, making sure to keep it within sight. "You're just like the rest of us then. A soul consumed by the Heretic Seed."

"Consumed?" Henwick's eyes widened again. "No, that can't be right, they told me that removing the shard would free me from the Seed's influence."

Digby arched an eyebrow at that last statement. "What do you mean, they?"

Henwick shut his mouth tight.

"Don't you close up on me now," Digby growled through his teeth. "We were just getting somewhere."

"No," the cleric snapped back. "I answered your question, I shan't say more unless you answer mine."

"That's actually reasonable." Digby relaxed. "You are not currently in a position to be making demands, but in an effort to keep you from attacking me the moment you are released, I believe it best that we come to some sort of understanding." He stood up and handed the ax to Parker. "Alright, Henwick, what would you like to know?"

"How did you come to be what you are now, and how many people did you kill to reach your level?" Henwick asked the question as if he already knew the answer.

"Oh please, you might as well start gathering firewood to burn me at the stake, considering you've obviously made up your mind of my guilt already." Digby rolled his eyes as hard as he could manage. "I have been bestowed the Heretic Seed's power the same as you and, in doing so, it allowed me to regain my conscious mind after I became a member of the dead. And yes, I have certainly been forced to defend myself against those that would seek to do me harm." He made a point to make eye contact with the man. "But I have also used my magic to protect hundreds of innocent people from those that would threaten their survival."

"You expect me to believe you a saint, then?" Henwick scoffed.

"Obviously not." For once, Digby made no effort to lie. "I'm just a scoundrel that happened to have fallen into a position where good people depend on him. I do what I can to protect them, and fight when I have to."

"He's not lying." Parker gave the cleric a sincere look.

"In short, the world has changed, and it's all out of heroes." Digby held out an empty hand. "For the people out there in the world, I am the best option available. At the very least, I'm a fair bit better than the people currently trying to grind the world under their boot."

"The world?" Henwick's eyes darted to Parker, then back to Digby. "What do you mean?"

"Not so fast." Digby waved a finger. "I answered your question. We're back to you now. What did you mean by they told you that removing the Seed's fragment would free you of its influence? Who are they?"

Nothing could have prepared him for Henwick's answer.

"Autem."

"What?" Digby nearly choked. "What did you say?"

"Autem," Henwick repeated as he looked up. "They hunted me down for the same reason I was hunting other Heretics, to rid the world of this power."

Parker let out a gasp.

"You've heard of them?" Henwick stared up at them.

Digby's mind hit a wall, struggling to process the information. Henwick hadn't created Autem. He brought a hand to his mouth. No, it had been the other way around.

"Indeed, one might say Autem and I have crossed paths." Digby kept his answer vague. "But to confirm, they approached you?"

Henwick nodded. "When I explained that our goals were the same, they gave me a choice. Well, more of an ultimatum."

"Let me guess." Digby crouched back down. "Join them or die."

"Yes. Though they did not use those words. They offered me a place as a member of their order so that I might continue my pursuit of the Heretics alongside them. They didn't have to mention what would happen if I declined. And why would I? They offered me salvation from the Seed's darkness."

"Yes. Salvation, indeed." Digby gestured to the realm around them that had become the man's prison.

"Clearly there has been some sort of mishap." Henwick locked his eyes to Digby's. "Wait, did they offer you the same thing?"

"A representative of their organization tried to enlist my help with a spell they were trying to cast. Apparently, they wanted a source of pure death essence," Digby answered honestly but left out the fact that it was Henwick himself that had made the offer.

"Although they were not quite so keen on allowing me my freedom. If I had agreed, they would have thrown me in the deepest hole they could find for safekeeping."

"I take it you refused?" Henwick tilted his head to one side.

"Considering they would have also murdered my companions, who had done nothing wrong but exist in the wrong place at the wrong time." Digby eyed the cleric. "Obviously, I refused. Not to mention I didn't like the idea of being used to fuel the spell they had planned."

"A spell?" Henwick cocked his head to one side. "That is not possible. They would not have tainted their ranks with the Heretic Seed's power."

"It seems things have changed since your interactions with them." Digby debated on how much to tell him. "They have created their own version of the Heretic Seed, most likely by using the fragment they got from you as a template."

Henwick dropped his head down as if trying to work something out. "But they said they were trying to rid the world of magic."

"I think that only applied to magic that they didn't control," Digby added. "The Heretic Seed was a variable they could not allow to exist. As far as magic itself, they have no qualms with wielding it as long as they can decide who has access."

The cleric began to tremble. "They lied?"

"Seems so." Digby slapped a hand to the man's shoulder. "I'm also sorry to say that Autem hasn't exactly used that power for altruistic purposes."

"What?" Henwick flinched.

Digby tried his best not to laugh. The man before him had been held in high regard by everyone back in their village, while he had always been looked down upon. Now, Henwick just seemed weak. Digby had assumed that he had created Autem and ran the organization for centuries, but no, he had merely been taken advantage of. His soul had been ripped from his body and imprisoned along with his fragment of the seed. Whoever or whatever Henwick had become after that must have climbed the ranks of Autem over the centuries until he was sitting at the top.

The misguided man had thought himself a hero, yet all he had done was plunge the world into ruin. In trying to rid the world of the Heretics, he had given the power to someone worse. Digby shook his head. The urge to talk down to Henwick was almost too much. He wanted nothing more than to rub it all in the man's face.

Despite that, he pushed the impulse aside.

Following Henwick back then had thoroughly destroyed his life, yet there was nothing to be gained by kicking him while he was down.

Instead, he blew out a long sigh and told the truth.

Well, a half-truth, at least.

"I'm sorry to be the one that has to tell you but, as I mentioned, there are people that depend on me. And, sadly, Autem is the reason why."

"What?" Henwick froze, clearly more interested in hearing what he had to say rather than getting free.

"Autem has unleashed a new curse upon the world." Digby squeezed his shoulder. "They found a way to cast their spell without my help, and created a new breed of creature far worse than my kind. The world perished in a matter of days, leaving few capable of standing up against the empire that Autem is now building from the ashes. As the only ones with magic, they alone are capable of rebuilding. Now, they steal children from survivors to train and indoctrinate them as soldiers that will secure their rule for eternity."

"My god." Henwick started to squirm. "I demand you release me. I must—"

"Easy now." Digby grabbed the man and rolled him over to loosen the tapestry, feeling confident that he had said enough to keep him from attacking. He'd certainly left a few things out. He wasn't sure if he had glossed over things to manipulate the poor man, or if he was simply trying to spare Henwick's wounded pride. Though, either way, it was best to keep him in the dark.

"Come on. Let's get you out of there." Parker helped to unroll the cleric.

Henwick staggered to his feet as soon as he was free. "If what you have said is true."

"It is." Digby placed a hand to his chest. "I swear on my unbeating heart."

"Then we must find a way out of this realm and confront Autem for what they have done. They claim that their intent was to save humanity." Henwick grabbed both of his shoulders tight just like he had all those centuries ago when he'd insisted that he follow him. "But if they have lost their way…"

"Alright, alright." Digby brushed the cleric's hands away. "I agree that we should work together to find a way out of here, but let me make one thing clear." He hooked a thumb back to himself. "I shall not follow you any longer. I am not the man you once looked down on. Far from it. I am Lord Graves, and I am merely accepting your assistance."

Henwick stepped back as if about to argue.

"It's best if you just agree." Parker stepped to his side. "I mean, he's gonna do what he wants anyway. And if you want to go after Autem, then sticking together is probably best."

"Very well, I agree to your terms." Henwick held out a hand.

"Excellent." Digby gave him a firm handshake with his undamaged hand, grinning as the man shivered from his cold grip. "I'd hoped you would see this my way."

"Ah, yes." Henwick pried his hand free as Digby spun away.

He gave Parker a wink. "Yes, I think this will all work out."

CHAPTER ELEVEN

With Henwick on board, the next step was to investigate the castle further. There was no telling who else they might find or where the safest way up to the next area of the Seed's realm might be.

Stone surrounded them on all sides and shadows hung like tapestries.

Digby walked in silence as Henwick led the way toward the castle's upper towers. They had formed a fragile truce for the time being, but it didn't seem like the cleric had much interest in getting close. Not that Digby minded. The less they spoke, the less likely it was that anyone would say something that would get them into trouble.

Unsure of where to start, they made their way up, hoping to find an easy path up to whatever hung in the sky above the castle. If not, they would have to take their chances on that treacherous stairway that he and Parker had found down below.

Strangely, as they got further from where they had started, the castle's layout made less and less sense. The hallway they walked seemed to stretch into infinity, as if the Seed had gotten lazy in its recreation of the structure. Looking from side to side, identical doors lined the walls. Inside of each was an equally similar bedchamber. After investigating the first few, they found that they were copies of the first. Without anything else to find, they marched forward to look for a part of the castle that made more sense.

Unfortunately, the walk gave ample opportunity for idle chatter.

"So that's the infamous Henwick, huh?" Parker tilted her head from side to side as she walked beside Digby far enough behind the cleric that he wouldn't be able to hear them.

"Indeed." Digby eyed the woman, unsure what the sudden interest in the man was.

"He's weirdly hot when he's not judging me on my outfit." She snorted. "The whole Gaston look is kind of working. Very rugged."

"I don't know who Gaston is." Digby forced out a sigh. "And need I remind you that he is still trying to kill us and take over the earth out there in the world?"

"True." She shrugged. "Plus, he looks thirty-something so the age difference is weird. I'm still a spring chicken, you know. Only twenty-one." She furrowed her brow. "I think."

"Good for you." Digby rolled his eyes at the conversation.

"I'm just saying." She squinted at Henwick walking further ahead. "He's got an appeal is all. Not like I would jump him or anything."

Digby let the comment lie, hoping for a moment of silence if he failed to respond.

"Sorry." Parker shattered his hopes. "The silence is freaking me out." She deflated a little. "I don't handle stress well."

"Really?" Digby wasn't exactly surprised, though he could see a bit of a contradiction. "I should say, then, why join the military?"

"Huh?" Her pace slowed.

He furrowed his brow as he thought further. "You don't exactly seem the type, if you get my meaning."

"Is that another dig at me being irresponsible?" She narrowed her eyes.

"Oh please, Parker. You aren't exactly the most diligent person in the world."

She scoffed at his accusation as if it wasn't spot on. "I'll have you know I was a highly dedicated soldier."

"Really?" he asked in his most incredulous tone.

She immediately let out a laugh. "No, not really. They probably hated me in boot camp. I barely paid attention, so it was all pretty much a blur. I think I joined up 'cause I didn't know what else to do. I didn't really have a purpose after high school and working a summer job wasn't going to cut it anymore. Besides, I was a burden to the people that were nice enough to take me in. I guess I just enlisted out of desperation."

Digby caught a detail in her wording. "You were taken in?"

"Yup, by my aunt and uncle." She nodded. "After my parents," she stuck her tongue out and made a choking sound, "died."

An ache echoed through Digby's deceased chest. "I'm sorry to hear that."

She shook her head. "Don't be. Obviously, it was a bad time for me, and I miss them and everything, but it was a car crash. Not like they were murdered or anything. No need for a quest for vengeance. Plus, I was still pretty young, so it's been a while." She paused and took a moment to stare into the distance.

"They were good to me though. You don't find supportive family like that every day."

"That's, umm, good to hear." The ache in his chest persisted, clawing at an old wound of his past. "I lost a parent as well. My mother."

"Shit." She slapped a hand to her forehead. "I'm sorry if this is digging up stuff for you."

"No, no. I'm fine." He held up a hand, not sure if he really was alright or why he had even brought up the detail with her. Talking about his past wasn't exactly something he enjoyed. Despite that, he continued. "I never knew her, to be honest. She passed in childbirth. Nothing anyone could have done."

"Oh…" Parker fell silent for a long moment. "Anyway, back to Henwick being hot. That's less depressing."

"Oh, good lord." Digby rubbed at the bridge of his nose. "Could we not?"

She smirked. "We could always talk about who is more your type, Dig."

"Parker, I'm dead. No one is my type." He folded his arms. "Besides, I was more interested in stealing things, even when I was alive."

"Ah, that makes sense." She nodded. "Sorry, I get bored easily, and a bit of hypothetical thought is fun."

"Well, excuse me for not providing entertaining commentary." Digby groaned. "Though honestly, I'm surprised you don't have this sort of talk with Alex. Lord knows the two of you spend enough time together. Hell, at this point, I always make sure to knock when entering his room just in case you both are in there. Don't want a repeat of that time I walked in on Rebecca in bed with Mason."

"Ha!" Parker squealed with laughter, before promptly slapping a hand over her mouth to quell the outburst.

"What's going on back there?" Henwick snapped his head back to them.

"Nothing, nothing." Digby waved a hand in his direction.

"It best be," the cleric grumbled, clearly still unhappy about the prospect of working together.

"Sorry." Parker wiped a tear from her eye.

Digby tried to put her reaction out of his mind but failed a moment later. "Wait, what's wrong with my apprentice? I should say he's a fair bit better than Henwick for a romantic partner, even with that ridiculous blue hair."

Her shoulders shook with silent laughter as she swept a hand back and forth. "There's nothing wrong with him. I sent a few signals up the flagpole here and there back when we first met, but he didn't seem to pick up on them. I don't think he thinks of me like that, or if he even has an interest in that sort of thing. Probably for the best too. My relationships don't exactly go well and now that I know him better, I think we're much better friends than we would have been if I had jumped on him."

"I suppose that's a reasonable response." Digby cringed at Alex's lack of awareness. It wasn't surprising that the artificer had missed whatever signals Parker was sending. Then again, she might not be that adept at doing so either.

Parker let out a sigh. "I'm actually really grateful that I met him. I'm not sure I would have handled this whole apocalypse thing without having him as a friend to lean on. I try not to think about my home town, but everyone back there is probably gone now. It's the same for him, so just having someone to hang out and play board games with is a huge deal. There's nothing wrong with hooking up like Becca and Mason, but everyone is different, and for me having a friend is helpful in hard times. Romance is nice and all, but I'll take a partner in crime any day."

Digby considered her point, understanding that he might actually agree with the pink-haired soldier more than he'd realized. He still had trouble thinking of the people in his orbit as friends, but that was probably more appropriate than accomplices at this point. He might bicker with Rebecca at every turn, but she was probably the person that understood him most. He knew what it was like to be alone, and at the very least, things were better with her around.

"I suppose you're right." He nodded.

"I usually am." She patted herself on the back. "My love life is a mess anyway. I assume Lana is in charge of my body out there in the world, since she is the closest thing to healthcare in Vegas. So at this point, I think the only one getting in my pants is her." Parker stopped short and tilted her head to one side. "Actually, now that I think about it, Lana is cute. Like, I would totally—"

"Thank you, Parker. That's quite enough." Digby kept walking.

She jogged a few steps to catch up. "I guess you're right. I mean I'm a couple years older and she just turned nineteen, so that's a weird age-gap. Plus, there is some serious family drama there with Alvin."

"That we can agree on." Digby nodded. "I hope Hawk is able to talk some sense into that boy."

Parker flashed him a warm smile. "You know, it's surprisingly sweet how much you trust Hawk."

"Bah." Digby didn't give her comment a second thought. "Hawk just happens to be a competent ally for his age. I would be a fool not to be impressed by him."

"It's still sweet. Granted, it would be nice if you trusted me half as much," she grumbled to herself.

"Well, maybe don't throw your shoe next time we face an enemy." Digby eyed her sideways.

"At least I still have both shoes." She stared down at his sock.

"Thank you for reminding…" Digby trailed off as a sound came from down the hall. "What was that?"

Parker stopped in her tracks. "I didn't hear anything."

Digby turned back to listen. He might not have had the super hearing that Rebecca did, but he was sure he'd heard something.

That was when the quiet jingle of a bell echoed down the hall. To his surprise, Henwick was the first person to act.

"Quick." The cleric spun around and darted toward them. "We must hide." Henwick pivoted back and forth on his foot, scanning the hallway before grabbing hold of Parker's wrist and making a break for one of the identical bedchambers that lined the walls. "Come, milady."

"What?" Parker nearly fell as he pulled her forward.

"Hey, where are you going?" Digby glanced back in the direction the jingling had come from, before reluctantly following Henwick. He found Parker attempting to get free of the man's grip.

"Let go, you weirdly attractive jerk."

"Hush." He held tight.

Digby slapped Henwick's hand away from her. "Let her go, she can manage on her own."

"Fine, but we must—" Henwick locked his eyes with the open door as the sound of a bell came again, this time sounding closer.

"What is that?" Digby's body tensed in response to how worried Henwick appeared to be.

The cleric fell silent for a moment, then lowered his voice to a whisper. "A foe far worse than that witch."

"What?" Parker let out an awkward laugh.

"Yes. What?" Digby gave the man an accusatory look. "What other enemies have you made?"

Henwick's gaze shifted back to Digby. "After I dispatched that necromancer, I discovered that she had passed a handful of the

Seed's fragments on to an accomplice. I tracked them to a nearby city. It was there that I ran into Autem's representatives. After revealing their organization to me, they assisted me in passing judgment on that witch's accomplice."

"They had already passed on the fragments to someone else, but kept one for themselves to…" He trailed off.

"To what?" Digby stepped closer.

"What was their class?" Parker lowered her voice.

That was when the sound of a bell came from even closer than before. Henwick's response was instant.

"It's them."

Digby grabbed the man by the shoulder. "It's who?"

Henwick turned back. His face was white as a ghost.

"The fool."

CHAPTER TWELVE

Digby held perfectly still as he locked his eyes on the open door of the castle's bedchamber. The hall outside was dark, save for the flickering light of a torch growing close. The sound of bells jingling continued in rhythm with the footfalls of whoever Henwick was so worried about.

They were coming and there was no time to hide.

Surely, they had seen them enter the bedchamber that they cowered in.

"Who is the fool?" Parker whispered from her place standing by a tapestry.

"A monster." Henwick uttered the words with a quiver of fear in his voice. Then he stepped toward the bed on the other side of the room as if preparing to take cover. "We must be ready. If it had not been for Autem's assistance, the fool would have killed me."

"There's no use in hiding." Digby rolled his eyes. "Clearly, they know we're here." He stomped forward to assert himself, not wanting to look frightened in front of Henwick. "I don't know who is out there, but hurry up and make your move."

Digby sensed a bit of mana flowing just as the jingling stopped.

Silence filled the hall next.

"Be on guard," Henwick whispered as he tightened his grip on his ax.

A playful voice echoed back from the hall. "Yes, please do be prepared."

Digby narrowed his eyes. Making irritating comments to his enemies was his favorite way to start a fight, though he didn't enjoy being on the receiving end. For a brief moment, he opened his mouth to try to taunt the threat back, but before he could get a word out, the flickering light in the hall grew.

From the glow reflecting off the wall, the foe must have been running at a full sprint, yet not a sound came. Digby opened his maw on the floor within the doorway to catch the foe off guard. His face fell when no one entered. Instead, an arm simply tossed a torch into the room without its owner not so much as looking in to acquire a target.

Digby watched as the flaming object twirled lazily through the air. It hit the floor square on the butt end of its handle. Embers burst from its head on impact. The torch bounced once before toppling over a foot away from Digby's leg.

"I'm not falling for that." He snapped his eyes back to the door, refusing to let the distraction work on him. That was when Parker thrust a finger in his direction.

"Dig! Your pants!"

"What?" He looked down to find his right leg aflame. "Holy hell!" He leaped back and slapped a hand to his pants in an attempt to put out the blaze.

How?

He had been sure the torch had landed a safe distance away.

"Oh no! He's in here with us!" Henwick held his ax up as he backed up to the wall.

"What?" Digby swatted out the fire on his pant leg.

Judging from Henwick's reaction, their enemy must have been capable of concealing their presence, including the sounds they made.

A rogue, then. Digby nodded to himself.

He'd never fought the class before but from what he knew, the capabilities lined up.

The foe must have slipped into the room while everyone was focused on the torch, then moved it closer to his foot when he looked back to the door. Digby swept his vision across the room in search of the concealed enemy. "Come out, then. Don't think being invisible will protect you for long."

That was when his assailant chose to strike.

"Of course, how rude of me." A slender man appeared directly between him and Parker. Digby sensed a surge of mana flowing through his blood, however, no spell followed.

"Gah!" Both he and Parker leapt away.

Digby hit the ground and rolled, snapping his vision to the man's feet. He did a double-take when he saw a pair of shoes, each with a bell on the heel. His mind raced for a way to attack. He couldn't cast Flare in such a small space, Decay wouldn't do much against an enemy with a will, and there were no corpses to work with. This only left his maw as a method of defense.

He focused on the floor beneath one of the man's ridiculous shoes. They moved in a blur of black and white. Every movement was accompanied by dead silence.

Digby snapped his maw shut a second too slowly as the strange man grabbed ahold of a tapestry that hung near the mirror. It was a struggle to follow his movements as he placed a foot against the wall and hung from the fabric as if he weighed practically nothing.

Heretic, level 37 Rogue.

A form-fitting jester's tunic clung to their frame, a pattern of two-toned sections dividing their body into quadrants. Getting a look at his face, a half mask covered his eyes, a black diamond overlaying one side. Locks of black hair framed his face like the curtains of a window. If Digby didn't know better, he would have thought the man a jester.

A fool.

The bells were starting to make sense.

"Get down from there." Digby opened his maw on the wall where the tapestry was supported, hoping to drop the rogue to the floor.

"I think not." The jester didn't even flinch as the fabric he clung to came loose. Instead, he kicked off the wall and yanked. The tapestry came free as he jumped, revealing a narrow mirror behind it. Digby made a note of the discovery but kept his focus on the rogue. He couldn't believe his eyes as the man twisted in the air to land behind Parker. She froze as he drew a small dagger with his free hand.

The blade moved in a blur before anyone could react. He pulled his fingers back, a lock of her pink bangs held gently between them. "I do like the hair."

"Leave the young lady alone." Henwick stepped forward, a beacon of chivalry in a dark world.

"Sorry, I mean her no harm." The jester launched his dagger with a snap of his wrist. "You, on the other hand."

Henwick jerked his ax up to block only for the blade to sink into his hand, pinning his flesh to the handle of his own weapon. He cried out in pain.

"Now where was I?" The jester turned back to Parker just as she lunged forward and thrust a knee up toward his chest.

"Back off!"

"Of course." The jester slipped to the side like water to dodge the attack. Parker's face went blank, clearly confused that she'd missed from so close. The rogue's hand snapped out to grab one of her wrists in response.

"Hey wait!" Parker lost control of her momentum as he swung her to the side. At the same time, he whipped the tapestry he held in his other hand into her path in a maneuver that Digby would not have believed had he not seen it. Parker hit the floor tangled in the fabric like a fish in a net.

Digby got himself up, his eyes darting around the room for a weapon. The jester did the same as their gaze fell to the torch that lay on the floor at the same time. Digby flinched as another surge of mana flowed through the jester's blood. He'd expected a spell, but like before, none came.

"Mine!" He pushed the question of what the spell was out of his mind and dove for the handle of the torch. The rogue did the same. Digby's hand closed around empty air as the jester tumbled past him to snatch it up first. He skidded across the floor before rolling himself back up into a crouch.

"Sorry, did you want this?" The jester tossed the torch in Digby's direction. He raised a hand to block, only to realize the flaming object had passed by overhead. For an instant, he thought that the rogue had missed. Then he heard something hit the wall behind him.

Oh no. Digby panicked as something hot landed underneath him.

"Gah!" He leapt up, realizing that the torch had bounced off the wall, and rolled into position to set his pants alight again. As far as how the jester had achieved such a throw, he had no idea. Either way, he needed to put it out before he could do anything else. This of course left him slapping his own ass. Everything was harder with the three missing fingers on his hand.

Parker was no help as she struggled on the floor, still wrapped in a tapestry. Henwick, meanwhile, unpinned his hand from his ax.

"I demand you cease this assault and surrender." Henwick tossed the rogue's dagger behind him and got back into a fighting stance. The wound on his hand healed as mana flowed through his blood.

At least one of them was ready to put up a fight.

Henwick rushed forward with his ax raised. The jester spun to one side as a downward chop missed him by mere inches. The weapon landed harmlessly on the nearby bed. He raised his ax again, this time swinging it horizontally. The energy of a spell trailed from its edge and the air crackled. For an instant, the jester seemed to trip backward in an uncoordinated dodge, only to fall back into a roll. As chaotic as the move was, somehow, he was able to flip right back up on his feet. It was like watching someone fall in reverse.

The flames licking at Digby's rear threatened to tear his attention away from the fight, forcing him to yank off his vest and swat himself.

Henwick kept up the fight in his place.

Mana swelled through the cleric's body before bursting from his fingers in the form of a dozen motes of shining light. The rogue darted to the side, taking a few particles of energy to his leg.

"Lucky shot, cleric." He hopped away, clearly injured.

On the sidelines, Digby extinguished his pants and got back into the fight. "Think you can keep me at bay with a little fire, do you?"

"I did." The jester thrust a hand down toward the ground just as a blast of smoke engulfed him. Digby sensed a momentary flow of mana just as it happened.

"Is there seriously a smoke bomb spell?" Parker coughed as she kicked the tapestry she'd been wrestling with off her legs.

"It seems so." Digby waved his hand through the cloud of smoke in search of the jester.

Gone.

He swept his vision to the side. Had the foe escaped, or were they still in the room?

The answer came a moment later when Parker pointed a hand in his direction. "Dig, behind you!"

"What?" He spun to find nothing just as he began to feel heat on his back. The flicker of a reflected flame danced across the wall. "I'm on fire again, aren't I?"

"I got you." Parker grabbed one of the lumpy pillows of the bed and slammed it into his back. "He must have lit you up again when we lost track of him."

"Yes, well, at least he didn't set my pants alight this time," Digby grumbled as he scanned the room for the threat.

Parker snorted. "I want to make a joke about your pants being on fire for lying but it's probably not the right time."

Before Digby could respond with an annoyed comment, a gleeful laugh came from behind Henwick. The jesters reappeared in the same second to add, "I don't get the joke, but I like her."

Another surge of mana punctuated his comment like a period at the end of a sentence. Again, no spell followed.

Henwick stepped away from the threat. "Damn it, Graves, stop letting yourself be set on fire and help me fight."

"Oh yes, do try to help." The jester didn't skip a beat before snatching his dagger from the floor and stabbing Henwick in the gut.

"You foul—" was all Henwick was able to get out before the rogue dropped backward to land on the bed and kicked him in the chest. The jester's movements were fluid, though he winced on impact. The spell that had hit him earlier must have landed some solid damage.

Henwick let out an embarrassing yelp as he stumbled back from the kick and dropped his ax.

Reaching out with his uninjured leg, the jester caught the head of the weapon with his toes. He held it there for a moment, balancing it on the tip of his foot before flicking it up into the air. The rogue sat up and snapped his fingers around the handle a second later.

"Chop, chop, cleric." He grinned down at Henwick, ready to strike.

Digby tried to rush in to help, but something grabbed his foot to send him tumbling to the floor. He glanced back at his feet to find the laces of his one remaining shoe untied. He must have stepped on them with his other foot. He suppressed a groan, realizing that the rogue must have pulled on the knot while he was invisible, on top of setting him on fire.

The rogue stopped mid-chop to lock eyes with Digby and winked. "Sorry, I couldn't resist such a comedic vulnerability."

Then with a chuckle, he brought the ax down on Henwick.

The cleric cried out as his own weapon cleaved a chunk of flesh, the size of a decent steak, from his bicep. The slab of meat hit the floor in the middle of the room with a wet slap.

Hello there.

Digby wasted no time, opening his maw to claim the scrap. A free meal had been hard to come by in the Seed's realm and he still had fingers to reattach. Obviously, Henwick would disapprove but he was too busy pushing himself away from the jester to notice.

The foe tossed the stolen ax from one hand to the other, occasionally twirling it in the air as he stalked toward the helpless cleric. "Sorry, but I don't need you."

"What do we do?" Parker looked to Digby for orders.

He tried to think. Clearly, he had misunderstood the capabilities of the rogue's class, having thought they were merely a fighter that had specialized in perception to get a concealment spells. Seeing a more powerful example, the class changed everything he thought he knew. It was as if the jester had somehow enhanced his attribute points into perception, agility, and dexterity.

But that doesn't make sense. Digby's eyes widened.

Unless the rogue had a way of boosting them. That must have been what that spell was doing. Whatever the jester had been casting must have been giving him a temporary boost to some of his numbers. It was the same as Digby's Limitless mutation.

If that was the case, none of them were fast enough to fight the foe. There was no way they could win.

As a level one Heretic, Parker might as well have been a small child for all the chance she had of landing a blow. Even with her ridiculous will value. Digby himself, was of little threat as well, considering he was unable to use most of his spells.

Still, they had to do something.

Digby narrowed his eyes.

There had to be a way to cheat.

"Get away from him." Digby slid his good hand across the floor to find the edge of the tapestry that Parker had been wrestling with earlier.

"Oh, do stay down. I will be with the both of you once I deal with this one." The rogue adjusted his grip on the ax and hefted it back up as Henwick raised his other arm to block his head.

"I will have to insist." Digby flicked his eyes to Parker's, then glanced to the other corner of the tapestry. She nodded and began inching her way toward it. He snapped his eyes to Henwick next, before flicking them to the Jester's leg. Hopefully the cleric would get the point.

Digby shoved his damaged hand into his pocket and curled his thumb and pinky around the three severed digits he carried. Then, he simply threw them at the rogue's face. He accompanied the act with a ridiculous battle cry with the hope of throwing him off balance.

"Go, Dead Fingers!"

The jester dodged to the side as Digby's severed middle finger sailed past him. The other two struck him right in the face. A look of confusion fell across the rogue's face for an instant.

It was enough.

"Now, Parker!" Digby sprang forward with one end of the tapestry clutched in his good hand.

"Got it." Parker did the same, taking his cue to snatch up a corner of the tapestry and rushed the foe.

The jester shook off the shock of being hit in the face with a pair of severed fingers and moved to dodge. That was when Henwick reached out with his uninjured arm to snag the jester's foot.

Digby and Parker plowed into him, using the cloth between them like a net to keep the foe from slipping away.

"What's wrong, can't handle us if we all work together?" Digby let a low cackle rumble through his chest as he and Parker shoved the jester down. The strange man shrieked as he fell. His cry was cut off the instant his head hit the stone wall. The bells on his feet jingled for a second as his body went limp. Then, everything went still.

Digby held the jester firm just in case. "You alive, Henwick?"

"I shall survive." The cleric rolled over, clutching his wounded arm as a swell of mana repaired the damage.

Parker pushed herself up from the floor and threw her weight onto the jester's unmoving body.

"Oh damn, did we kill him?"

CHAPTER THIRTEEN

"Is this a normal occurrence for you both?" Henwick loomed behind as Digby and Parker positioned the jester's unconscious body on the tapestry that they had tackled him with.

"Just be glad you aren't on the receiving end this time." Digby stood up and pushed the strange man's body with his foot to roll him up.

"It is handy that there's so many tapestries hanging about." Parker helped secure the prisoner. "They make great human burrito wrappers."

"Indeed." Digby stared down at the foe, having trouble believing that he'd had so much trouble with the rogue.

"That was weird, though, right?" Parker stood beside him. "The way that this guy moved was wild."

"It was a spell." Digby waved a hand through the air as if it should have been obvious. "I could feel him casting something, but I wasn't sure what at first. My guess is he has a way of enhancing some of his attributes."

"What do you mean you could feel him casting?" Henwick eyed him.

"Ah…" Digby's mouth fell open, realizing he had just let an important ability of his slip. "I can sense mana flowing when a spell is cast. It's a zombie thing." He opted for honesty, having already said too much.

Henwick gave him a suspicious look before wincing and clutching his arm.

"You going to survive, there?" Digby chuckled. "If not, be sure to expire someplace nearby. I could use the minion."

"I do not see the humor. Such acts would be an affront to God." Henwick narrowed his eyes. "And yes, I shall live. My Regeneration spell is merely taking its time replacing such a large portion of missing flesh."

"Ah, yes, that makes sense." Digby looked away and scratched at his cheek, remembering that consuming the scrap of meat had given him what he needed to reattach his fingers. He'd already gathered up his missing digits from where he'd thrown them during the fight with the rogue, but he wasn't sure he wanted to repair them in front of the cleric.

Henwick merely sighed and turned away as if he was ashamed to have thrown in with their lot in the first place. Then, a second later, he snapped his eyes to the bloody spot on the floor where a chunk of his arm had landed earlier. He immediately brought an accusatory look to Digby. "Did you—"

"Alright, yes, I ate a bit of your muscle tissue." He rolled his eyes, hoping that if he owned up to it, the cleric might let it pass. "It wasn't like you could put it back on, and I need the resources to repair the damage I've sustained. Like it or not," he pulled his missing fingers from his pocket and held them in place to cast Necrotic Regeneration, "we are going to need me in top condition if we are to navigate this realm without further incident."

"That's..." Henwick stared at him, his face growing paler by the second. "That's horrible."

"Yes, yes, I'm a monster." Digby waved away the complaint. "We have covered that."

Henwick let out a harumph but refrained from any further comment. Though Digby was pretty sure he heard the man mutter something along the lines of 'abomination' under his breath.

"Oh, pout if you like. We have other things to worry about." Digby turned his attention back to the jester. "Like what are we going to do with our new friend here? In all honesty, this would have been easier if he'd been killed in the fight. Then I could simply eat him and move on."

"You wouldn't." Henwick recoiled.

Digby cringed, remembering that he shouldn't talk so freely with such a judgmental ally around, less they become enemies sooner rather than later.

Parker jumped in to help before he had a chance to answer. "Of course not. He only eats monsters out there in the real world. Right, Dig?"

"Yes, that is true." Digby fell in line with her lie, surprised that she had come up with something so fast. Maybe she would prove useful after all.

Then she gave him the most obvious wink that had ever been given. Digby tensed, expecting a tongue lashing from Henwick. He relaxed when he realized the cleric hadn't been looking at her.

"Regardless." Digby scratched his chin. "That still leaves us with the problem of what to do with our prisoner."

Henwick hefted his ax back up. "We should find out what he knows about this place and why we are here. We can pass judgment based on what he says."

Digby tensed right back up, realizing that the jester could easily say something that might clue Henwick into the wrong details of their situation. He cursed himself for not using some form of lethal force during the fight. None of this would have been a problem if the jester had perished. Thinking back, there had been nothing stopping him from killing the rogue.

Perhaps his time amongst the humans over the last month had been rubbing off on him. Something inside him felt a little warmer. Maybe there was hope for him after all. Regaining his humanity had been his original goal anyway.

He shook off the thought, returning to the problem at hand. He couldn't let Henwick interrogate the rogue. Unfortunately, the cleric started moving before he had time to come up with a plausible reason to stop him.

"We should start by finding out what sort of man hides behind a mask." Henwick reached for the jester's face only to jerk his hand back when he spoke.

"Take it off if you can." The strange man snapped his eyes open.

"Hey, shit, what!" Parker jumped. "Probably should have checked to see if he was really unconscious or not."

Digby ignored the vague threat and crouched down. If he couldn't stop Henwick from interrogating the foe, then he could at least take the lead. "Very clever. I assume you have been faking being unconscious long enough to understand that your life may depend on what you say next. And don't even try to cast that enhancement spell of yours, or any other for that matter. I will know."

"Oh yes, of course." The jester nodded happily as if not in any danger. "I shall do no casting. Though, I can't say what might happen when you decide to release me."

"Sure, fine, whatever." Digby brushed off the threat. After all, this wasn't his first time questioning someone that he'd rolled up in a tapestry. As far as he saw it, he could skip over the introductions. "Start talking. Why did you attack us?"

"That's not much of a question." The jester gave him an irritating grin. "Obviously you have something I want."

"And what is that?" Henwick knelt as well.

"Nothing you can offer me, I'm afraid." The jester turned his nose up at the cleric. "I'm only interested in discussing things with your two accomplices here."

"Alright—" Digby started to speak but Henwick talked over him.

"They are not my accomplices, and what is it you want of them?"

The jester answered with an elegant glance to the corner of his vision, right where the numbers hung on the Seed's HUD. Digby looked as well.

66/2

A few more Heretics must have perished since last he checked.

The jester left a pregnant pause. The implication was clear. He understood the situation well. He must have. If this man really was the person that Sybil handed the Seed's fragments to, then it was likely he made the connection between the number of shards and the numbers on their HUDs. Not only that, but he must have caught enough of their conversation while faking unconsciousness to know that his alliance with Henwick was fragile at best. Digby arched an eyebrow to convey that he understood as well.

The jester confirmed it all with his next statement. "I apologize. I have no ill will toward the two of you. I only attacked because you were accompanied by a former enemy of mine. Eliminating him was my priority. I'm sure you cannot blame me for that."

Digby raised the other eyebrow level with its mate. It wasn't the apology that was important, but instead, it was what the rogue neglected to say that mattered. He was keeping the details of the Seed's realm between them. Digby took that as a cue that it was safe to ask questions without worry of the jester letting something slip.

"Alright then, I can understand that. Henwick has already admitted that he fought you in the past." Digby nodded.

"I assure you I was in the right." Henwick folded his arms. "I may have been allied with Autem, but they had not yet lost their way. I was merely passing judgment on a Heretic who used the power of the Seed for personal gain."

"That is where you are wrong." The rogue stared up at the cleric through the holes in his black and white mask.

"How so?" Digby gestured for him to continue.

The jester blew out a well-rehearsed sigh and lowered his head. "It was true that I bear no ill will toward those of you that I have just encountered. However." He looked back up. "I would have killed you all if it meant I could escape this place. My return to the world is just that important. Autem cannot be allowed to do as they please, and I am willing to sacrifice whatever is necessary."

"Can't argue with that." Parker sat down on the edge of the bed in the middle of the room.

"Indeed." Digby began to relax. "Autem has done much

harm."

The jester shifted his position as if trying to sit up. "Yes. Autem has sought to control the world by eliminating those that disagree with their perspective. Myself and my associates meant to stand in their way."

Digby grabbed the tapestry that held the man prisoner and hefted him up so that he could at least lean against the wall. "And what do you suggest we do now?"

"Thank you." The jester looked between the three of them. "For the moment, I insist we work together. I have already proven myself a valuable ally. Surely you can see the benefit of me joining your efforts. I can also share with you the location of an easy to traverse passage that leads up to whatever is floating above us."

Henwick scoffed before Digby could respond.

"And what shall we do when this man decides to stab us in the back? He may be right that Autem's true nature was not as pure as I was led to believe, but he is still a willing user of the Heretic Seed's power. He was not forced into it like you or I. Not only that, but he saw to it that the fragments of the Seed traveled far and wide to spread their corruption. How can we trust someone like that?"

"What do you suggest we do, Henwick?" Digby gestured to the rogue. "Hold a trial for witchcraft and burn him at the stake?"

"I regret that there isn't time for such things, though, an execution would not be an unreasonable end given our situation."

"What?" Digby snapped his attention to the cleric in shock. "You just literally called me an abomination because I wanted to eat him."

"You only joked about eating him." Parker jumped again to help.

"Yes, yes, of course, it was just a funny joke," Digby agreed to maintain innocence and continued to focus on Henwick. "But if that was so bad, what made you suddenly so murder happy?"

"Like I said, he is a willing user of the Heretic Seed's power. There is no defense of that." Henwick tightened his hands around the grip of his ax. "If you are unable to take the life of this man, then I shall handle the task."

"No, you absolutely will not." Digby waved a hand through the air. "I may have taken my fair share of lives, but only in the fight against Autem. I have never executed anyone for having a difference of opinion. Hell, we don't even know if using the Heretic Seed is wrong."

"Of course it is." Henwick nodded decisively. "It is an affront to God."

Digby groaned, having trouble getting through to the man. "No wonder Autem was able to take advantage of you."

"Might I interject?" The jester spoke up.

"No!" Both Digby and Henwick responded at once.

"Or maybe we could hold off the witch trial for now and work together." Parker stepped in to make a case for the rogue. "There will be time to debate things later."

Digby hesitated. Adding the jester to their group would certainly give them an edge in the fights to come. Then again, it was clear he understood that only two of them could survive the gauntlet ahead to its end. It was likely that he would turn on them eventually. Though, he would most likely side with them over Henwick if anything threatened their alliance. Digby wished he had another infernal spirit to animate his skeleton with. That would keep him in line.

"I agree." Digby nodded to Parker. "The advantages outweigh the risks."

"But—" Henwick started to argue.

"But nothing." Digby held up a hand. "I am taking no side in your little crusade. There is a chance you are right and that the magic is evil, but right now we need it to stand up against Autem. No matter what you believe, you cannot deny that much."

Henwick stood with his mouth hanging open, clearly having trouble coming up with a valid argument.

Digby forced a warm smile to try to reassure the cleric. "I understand how you feel. This power was thrust upon me as well, and we know so little about where it comes from, but why don't we hold our judgments for now. We have a long way to go here, and we may learn more as we progress."

Henwick closed his mouth and finally acquiesced.

"My gratitude." The rogue gestured to the tapestry that held him with his chin. "Now, may I be freed from my improvisational prison?"

Digby reached for the jester's feet to drag him into an open space on the floor. He stopped momentarily before unrolling him. "I meant what I said. No casting things unless we run into enemies. I will know if you do."

"Understood." The rogue nodded before looking to Henwick. "How about a push?"

The cleric grumbled but obliged, shoving the jester hard enough to get him rolling out of his prison. He let out an abrupt laugh that seemed entirely inappropriate for the situation, which of course caused Parker to chuckle as well.

"Good, good, you're free." Digby stared down at the strange person, making sure he didn't cast anything the moment he was loose. "Now, you said you knew something about the fragments of the Seed that Sybil gave you."

Digby hoped he wouldn't say too much, but also that he might know something about the type of people that had also used the shards to become heretics.

"Ah yes, of course." The jester stood up and brushed himself off, the bells on his shoes jingling as he did. "I'm afraid I have no idea what became of the Seed's fragments, or what sort of people might have come in contact with them. Obviously, I hope they fell into the hands of those that might stand up to Autem, but I fear they could have granted power to anybody by now."

"That is less than ideal." Digby grimaced, realizing that he might not find many cooperative Heretics from here on out.

The jester immediately held a handout toward Henwick. "Truce. At least until we learn more."

The cleric stared at his hand without shaking it. "Have we all forgotten that this man attacked us first?"

"And you also attacked me out there in the world with Autem by your side." The jester kept his hand extended.

"I cannot be blamed for that." Henwick grew agitated. "They claimed to march to the guidance of angels and that they served the will of god himself to protect mankind at all costs."

"You are right, I cannot blame you for your actions. Many before you have fallen prey to Autem's words." The jester lowered his hand only to raise his other and place it on the cleric's shoulder. "Under the guidance of god and the Nine or not, sweet words have often driven good men to do terrible things."

"Indeed." Digby grimaced, remembering the twisted ceremony that he'd witnessed back in the underground cathedral on Autem's base. "Now, how about you lead us to that passage you found?"

"Of course." The jester spun back toward the doorway before looking back to take a bow. "I am at your service." He raised back up. "Besides, we must make haste before that caretaker finds…"

The jester trailed off.

"Yes, spit it out." Digby beckoned with a finger to draw out more just as a mouthful of blood sprayed from the rogue's mouth.

"Shit!" Parker leapt back as Digby did the same.

"What in god's name is——" Henwick retreated as well, his words falling short when the boney fingers of an oversized hand reached in from the shadows of the hallway to grab hold of the jester's head. In the same instant, a blade of bleached bone ripped through the rogue's neck to tear his head clean off.

"Holy hell!" Digby recoiled in horror as the rogue's body fell to the floor, revealing the nightmarish form of the caretaker occupying the hallway behind them.

The mass of decaying flesh and disjointed limbs contorted and swayed as a dozen hands gripped the door frame to block any chance of escape. A chittering screech erupted from the enormous skull that sat at its center. Digby watched in horror as the beast pushed the jester's head into its body. It vanished into the creature's bulk, only to reemerge next to its oversized skull. The jester's eyes flicked around the room as the head twitched.

"That's just wrong." Parker spoke while gagging.

Henwick held his ax out in defense. "We have to get past it."

"There's no way. It's bigger than the door." Digby focused on the jester's headless body. "We have to fight."

With a thought, he cast Forge to send every ounce of blood from the rogue's corpse rushing up into the beast. The crimson spike slammed into the creature just below its skull. He would have pushed it further but there was a limit to how much he could do with the quantity of blood that the average corpse held.

The beast barely noticed the attack, wrapping several of its hands around the crimson spike to snap it in half.

"We don't stand a chance. Yet I shall fight till the end." Henwick raised his ax and prepared to rush forward.

"Wait!" Parker thrust a hand out toward the mirror that hung on the wall. "There's another mirror back in the main hall. I can open a passage."

"We run then." Digby snapped his eyes back to the glass as the caretaker began pushing its bulk into the room. "Quick, open a passage."

"Yes, do that with haste!" Henwick immediately abandoned his previous strategy of going down fighting and ran to join them by the mirror.

Parker slapped a hand against the reflective surface just as it began to ripple like water. Then she swallowed hard. "I hope this works!"

"Only one way to know for sure." Digby tested the passage by shoving Henwick forward with an inappropriate cackle. The cleric disappeared into the mirror's rippled surface like a stone that had been tossed into a puddle. Digby looked at Parker. "Well, he didn't explode or anything."

"Move!" She gestured to the glass. "I have to go last to close it."

"Hang on." Digby glanced back at the caretaker as the collection of legs beneath it began to trample the Jester's body. He didn't have the luxury to pass up a meal. Opening his maw, he claimed the jester's corpse before turning back to Parker's escape portal.

"You done?" She let out an annoyed huff as she grabbed his shoulder and pushed him toward the glass.

"I have to take what I can get." He dove into the mirror as a few dozen limbs clawed toward him from behind.

The sound of the creature dragging itself along the stone would stick with him for the rest of his days.

CHAPTER FOURTEEN

A bead of sweat rolled down Becca's forehead.

She glanced to one side, then to the other.

She was not in a place she wanted to be.

That place being an elevator traveling down into the Hoover Dam with an old army vet, her boyfriend, Easton, and three ex-Skyline mercenaries.

There was a lot to unpack.

Jameson, the army vet that had been leading the survivors held up in the dam, kept glancing at Malcolm, Ducky, and Sullivan. The three mercenaries had threatened him only minutes ago, leaving him understandably suspicious. Not to mention he was still in the process of wrapping his head around the existence of magic. Then, of course, she couldn't fully trust Malcom or his men not to do anything to make things worse.

To her other side was Mason, who kept fidgeting awkwardly with the strap on his bullet proof vest after she had blurted out her entire tragic backstory in front of everyone as a negotiation tactic. It was everything that she had been putting off telling him for fear of reopening an emotional wound. From the look on Mason's face, he didn't know what to say about it either. Nor would he get the chance anytime soon. Unless he wanted to bring it up in front of everyone like she had.

The last of the tension came from Easton. The unfortunate ex-comms specialist had clearly picked up on the tension coming from both sides and was now doing his best to diffuse it.

"So, this apocalypse thing is crazy, huh?" Easton looked up briefly only to drop his eyes back down to the floor.

Becca suppressed the urge to slap a hand to her forehead.

"Your guy's awkward," Jameson said with a chuckle.

"I know." She glanced back at him as he mouthed the word, sorry.

Jameson glanced around nervously. "I'll take awkward over violent any day."

"Well, we have plenty of that to go around." Becca added an awkward laugh of her own only to completely freeze when the doors opened.

A group of twenty men waited outside in a long but narrow hallway. Every single one of them held a rifle pointed in their direction. The only reason Becca held back was the fact that Jameson was standing between them.

"I'm sorry." He stepped out and turned around. "I want to trust you all, but we still have to take precautions. There is a lot we don't know. So please, think of this as just another safety procedure for our comfort."

Becca held her ground, hoping Malcom and the others would follow her lead for once. She cast Veritas a second later, just in case. "And where does this procedure take us?"

"Nowhere bad." Jameson gave her a friendly smile. "We just want to talk a little more about things, someplace where we are less exposed. Once you catch us up to speed, I will be happy to give you a tour of the dam and our capabilities."

TRUE

"Let me guess, you want us to give up our weapons before moving forward." Malcom stepped up to stand beside Becca.

"That would be part of the arrangement." Jameson nodded, clearly treading carefully.

"That's fine." Becca stepped out of the elevator as an example to the others and raised her hands. One of the men in the hallway lowered their rifle and gave her a pat down.

"Thank you." Jameson nodded to her, clearly appreciating her compliance.

It was mostly for show anyway. He could disarm them, sure, but there was nothing he could do about their magic. The men with the rifles looked like civilians, though their weapons seemed to be military. Even with that, she and Malcom would probably be able to kill them all if they worked together. When the math was done, her side still had the tactical advantage.

She was pretty sure Jameson was aware of it as well, so she couldn't blame him for doing what he could to minimize the threat they posed. If she had to guess, he would separate them next. That's what she would do.

Becca shook off the concerns and stepped further into the hallway so Jameson's men could pat down Mason and Easton. She relaxed when Malcolm went along. Ducky and Sullivan followed as well. At least the three mercs were starting to follow her.

The men in the hall followed her with their rifles on both sides as she walked. When she got to the middle of the group, half broke off and started moving. The other half moved to the rear to keep them surrounded. Jameson stayed near her as if trying to convey an element of trust despite the situation.

Becca cleared her throat. "I understand your concerns and precautions. Though I will assure you that there is no need."

"I know." The old vet took a deep breath. "But technically you only need the dam, not the people inside it. So we're going to have to do this my way, so everyone feels safe."

TRUE

Becca nodded and followed along. They hadn't gone far when Jameson directed Sullivan and Ducky into a room on the left. After a few feet more, he sent Malcolm and Easton off to the right. Then finally he asked her and Mason into a room further down.

Becca relaxed as soon as she was inside, finding it a simple break room. They must have been in the office section of the dam.

"So, what do you think about our chances here?" Mason stood next to a simple folding table. He tapped one finger on its surface.

"We should be fine." She made a point to look around the room as she spoke. "Jameson never lied, so I think he's on the up and up. If everyone plays nice, we should get through this."

"Oh, good." He didn't seem to relax. "Forgot you can tell if people are being truthful."

She hesitated. "Yeah, I cast Veritas just to make sure."

"Was all that stuff true?" He stepped closer to her. "You know, about what Skyline and Autem did to you?"

A sudden jolt of pain echoed through her chest when she realized the conversation she had been dreading was happening. Even worse, they were trapped in a room with no way out. She couldn't even make an excuse and run away.

All she could do was nod.

Mason blew out a sigh. "Okay, I get it."

She shifted her gaze to meet his. "Get what?"

"Why you didn't want to talk about it." He held up his hands as if admitting defeat. "It's no secret that you have some trouble communicating like a normal person—"

"What?" Becca narrowed her eyes.

"You know what I mean." He dropped his hands to his sides. "My point is, I get you better than I used to. There was a time where I thought you were being a little ridiculous, or that you didn't trust me, but even with what little I heard up there." He shook his head. "Well damn, that is a lot of weight for a person to bear. So what I'm trying to say is, you've said enough. If something is hard to talk about, then don't worry about it."

"Why the sudden change?" She let out a slow breath.

"I can tell you've been stressed out and avoiding me. I don't expect you to suddenly be an open book, and I'll be here when you want to talk. So you don't have to force yourself to need me. I care more that you're comfortable."

Becca stared at him for a long moment before finally relaxing. "Thank you." She let out a long breath. "You have no idea how much I was worrying about it. It was like, I knew that most people would want to open up, but just knowing that it was expected made everything worse. Finding out my parents went through so much without me and that I kinda had a brother I never knew. It all hit me real hard."

That was when she realized she was actually talking about it.

Becca closed her mouth as she felt her eyes begin to well up. "Oh shit, now is not the time."

"Hey, it's okay." Mason leaned forward and pulled her close. "It's all good."

"I know. Sorry." She wiped her eyes.

"Nothing to be sorry for." He gave her a squeeze.

"Thanks for being patient with things." She let go. "I know you're technically the only guy I've dated, but as far as boyfriends go, you're a good one."

"Can't argue there." He gave her a charming grin. "I am pretty great."

She rolled her eyes. "I guess I can't argue with that either. And I'm glad you're here."

"Of course." He laughed. "I love you, so there's no place I'd rather be."

Becca's entire body tensed as her eyes bulged. "What?"

"Oh, ah…" Mason's eyes darted around the room, clearly realizing that neither of them had said I love you before. "I, umm, just meant that…"

Every thought in her head failed to launch as her eyes locked on the lone word that floated at the center of her vision.

TRUE

Her breath froze in her throat, leaving her unable to speak. It was probably for the best, considering the only words running through her head were, what the fuck?

Her Veritas spell confirmed it.

He meant it.

No one had ever said that to her before. Hell, she'd never even dated before. She hadn't even intended to date him. They had only been a fling. Just an exercise in her newfound freedom after escaping captivity.

That was when she became painfully aware that several seconds of her standing, mouth agape, had gone by.

Mason's charming grin had fallen to an expression of social panic.

Then, right on cue with the worst timing in the world, the door opened.

"Okay, I'm sorry for all the theatrics, but I get the feeling you're under…" Jameson trailed off as he closed the door behind him. His attention fell on Becca first. Then he glanced at Mason. Then back again.

She shifted her attention to him, dragging her jaw off the floor in the process.

Mason did the same, his face turning red.

Jameson held his hand on the knob of the door that he had just closed, as if he might open it right back up again and leave. The tension was just that palpable. Finally he shook his head. "Anyway, I hope I'm not interrupting anything."

"No!" Becca heard herself say, before adding, "Nothing happened."

"I'm sure." Jameson eyed her sideways, clearly picking up on plenty. He sat down at the table anyway. "Okay then, why don't you both have a seat and tell me everything you know about, well, everything."

Becca glanced at Mason for a fraction of a second just as he did the same. They both looked away immediately.

The best she could do was slide into a chair across from Jameson and try to move past the moment. After a few minutes, the situation faded into a nagging echo in her mind rather than a blaring air horn of miscommunication.

Fortunately, Jameson's questions filled the time.

It wasn't long before both she and Mason were going over the events from their first night of the apocalypse. Once Becca was able to get her bearings, she recast her Veritas spells and slipped in a few questions of her own to make sure Jameson really was the man she thought he was.

Explaining Digby was probably the hardest part, but it wasn't something she wanted to hide. It was understandable that Jameson might have some reservations about working with a member of the dead. Then again, the fact that they could potentially gain the protection of a horde was a powerful bargaining chip.

After about twenty minutes and a few demonstrations of magic, he seemed ready to take them for a tour.

They stopped in to make sure Malcom and the others were behaving themselves. Jameson had one of his people join them to discuss the logistics of supplying Vegas with power from the dam. There would be several missions to various locations to handle the project. It would be a difficult undertaking but worth it in the end.

Fortunately, it was a perfect job for Malcolm and his guys. Easton proved a solid choice to handle the logistics of the project.

Once the agreement was ironed out, Jameson asked her and Mason to join him for a tour. They both nodded and followed along.

It became obvious that the situation was not quite as simple as it seemed when Jameson spoke next.

"Look, I, ah, do have one more question for you all." The elderly man rubbed at the back of his neck.

"Yes." Becca stated to follow him down the hall toward the turbine rooms.

He stopped. "I have no problem with supplying Vegas with electricity. That would at least give meaning to this place again. So, yeah, I think the people here will be happy to be keeping the lights on somewhere again. But…"

"That sounded like a one hell of a but, there." Mason stood between them.

"Maybe." Jameson took a deep breath. "I guess what I'm getting at is if my people there are able to throw our support behind your cause. Well, what are you able to do for us?"

"Oh, is that all?" Becca exhaled. "You were acting a little like you had an unreasonable request. Obviously, you would get our support in return. Ideally, your people would become our people, though you would still oversee every aspect of the dam's functions. Currently, Vegas has plenty of supplies and is working on more sustainable methods to support a large number of people. So you and everyone here won't have to worry about food and medicine. And, of course, there's magic. We can offer that as well once we have a way to do so."

"Yeah, that sounds relatively standard for a deal like this." He started walking again. "But would you also be willing to let some of our people live in your city?"

"Of course, that would be no problem." She added, feeling confident, "We have a little under three hundred people now and there is room for more."

"Good, that helps." He scratched at his neck again. "You see, when the shit hit the fan a month ago, I headed straight here. Having some experience with the military and how slow the government can act, I assumed the dam would be an important resource. Figured whoever was here would need all the help they could get, and I had nothing better to do."

"That was smart." Mason nodded, clearly relating to the old man.

"What I didn't expect was that the situation would get away from us so fast. I thought when I got here, there would be boots on the ground already trying to secure it." He sighed.

"Same." Mason deflated. "We thought we would be recalled from the quarantine line, but the order never came."

"Yeah, it seems like we just weren't prepared for a magic-fueled zombie-revenant apocalypse." Jameson shrugged. "But when I got here, I found no one but the dam's personnel and their families. Seemed they had the good sense to evacuate to here."

"That's how you ended up in charge?" Becca nodded along as they walked.

"Yep. Someone had to do something, and after a few days I just kind of fell into the role. It wasn't so bad, either. We converted some of the office space to family dwellings for the staff here. It worked well."

"I'm sensing another but coming." Becca eyed the man.

"That's just the thing." He glanced back at her. "This went smoothly, but that was before more people started showing up."

"More people?" Mason arched an eyebrow. "How many more?"

"That's just the thing." Jameson reached the end of the hall where a set of double doors waited. "Apparently, I wasn't the only one that thought of this place as a possible refuge. Seems others had the same thought. Who could blame them? This place is built like a fortress, and they thought the government would be along to secure the place just as I did."

Jameson paused as he pushed open the doors.

"Oh my god." Becca's eyes bulged as soon as she stepped inside.

"Yeah, it seems we took in our fair share of strays." Jameson stepped to the railing of a walkway that overlooked the turbine room.

"That is one hell of an understatement." Mason followed behind.

The floor below held a row of massive turbines, all shut down on account of having nowhere to send the power they generated. They were impressive, but even more so were the tents that littered the floor surrounding them.

There must have been hundreds.

Becca swept her eyes over the scene, taking a count of the people and noting the conditions they were living in. There were well over a thousand men, women, and children.

At first glance, they looked healthy and in good spirits, but looking closer, there were signs of overcrowding. They were doing the best they could, but they had reached the limit of what their facilities could hold.

Becca shuddered to think what would happen if Autem came back to find the place full of potential child Guardians.

"So..." Jameson turned to her and leaned an elbow on the railing. "You still on board with taking in our people?"

CHAPTER FIFTEEN

Becca rolled in frustration, unable to sleep on the cot that had been set up for her deep within the Hoover Dam.

The day had gone smoothly.

She and Mason had spent the time giving presentations to the survivors living in the dam's improvised tent city. Many were uneasy about the idea of leaving but the knowledge that they would be moving into one of the biggest casinos in Las Vegas helped. It was one hell of a step up from a camping tent next to a turbine.

As for magic, her illusions gave her the ability to demonstrate their capabilities safely while also putting on a decent show. Not to mention she was able to introduce them to Digby by creating a suitable stand in. Surprisingly, that part got a few solid laughs despite her creating the image of an undead monster. After an hour or so, pretty much everyone was on board.

From there, everyone started packing. There were too many people to take to Vegas in the kestrels, so Ducky was to fly back a small group first thing in the morning and return with a few buses to transport the survivors to their new home. It would take a couple days of going back and forth to get them all. As long as one kestrel traveled with the vehicles, they could shoot down anything that might pose a threat. Autem should still be too busy with their recovery to be patrolling anywhere, so now was the best time for everyone to make the trip.

The other kestrel would head out with a crew to work on setting up the delivery of the dam's electricity to Vegas. For that part, Becca was going to be needed to help plan and take care of the important decisions since there was no one else to do it. Her work was certainly cut out for her.

With all that ahead of her, getting a good night's sleep was key.

So why was she struggling?

Well, that probably had something to do with the most awkward pause that had ever transpired in the history of humanity. That being the one she let continue just after Mason told her he loved her.

Thankfully, the rest of the day had been so busy that there had been no time to follow up. Plus, her near superhuman senses had made it impossible to tune out the noise of the dam's turbine room and its massive tent city. After explaining things, Jameson put her in a small maintenance closet far away from the communal living space. Mason, conveniently, stayed behind. He said he didn't want to wake her with his snoring, which was a legitimate concern, but she was pretty sure he was just trying to avoid being alone with her after the aforementioned most awkward pause in history.

Becca groaned and pulled the poncho that she had been using as a sheet over her head. After the day she'd had, all she wanted to do was sleep.

After a few more minutes of staring at the concrete ceiling, she kicked her poncho off and sat up. "Argh, why am I like this?"

It was hopeless. She didn't even feel tired.

"Maybe if I get up and go for a walk." She glanced at her HUD. "Actually, I wonder if there are any more revenants lurking around up near the entrance?"

She considered the thought, having half a mind to go check.

If she could take out a few of the creatures at night while they were active, she could gain a level to keep ahead of Malcolm. Sure, he, Ducky, and Sullivan had been getting along with everyone better as the day progressed, but that didn't mean she was going to let them get ahead of her. As long as she kept her barrier and decoy active, she should be fine, considering how powerful she had been getting.

Rolling out of her cot, she pulled her poncho on and headed out into the narrow hallway outside. She stopped short as soon as she closed the door behind her. The sound of footsteps came from further down the hall. They were casual and slow.

"Who's there?" She spun toward the source, finding the silhouette of a man.

"You weren't lying about that hearing." Jameson clicked on the light at the end of the hall around fifty feet away. "Not sleeping?"

"Unfortunately, no." Becca relaxed.

Something about the old vet seemed to set her at ease. After working with him all day and seeing how he handled the survivors in the dam, it was clear he was the type that took to leadership naturally. It didn't hurt that everyone seemed to like him on top of it. Digby could really learn a thing or two from him.

For that matter, so could she, considering how terrible she was at dealing with others.

Watching Jameson work had the strange effect of making her feel secure and insecure at the same time. It was good to have someone reliable around, but he also reminded her of what she lacked.

"All that magic hoo-hah really has an impact on you, huh?" He walked toward her.

"Yeah, the perception makes it hard to sleep, but it definitely has its advantages." Becca shrugged, glad that he had stopped asking for demonstrations earlier that day. "I was going to head outside and do a sweep of the area. Figured if I can't sleep, I might as well get a little stronger."

"Trying to keep an edge on Malcolm and the rest of the Skyline guys, huh?" He arched an eyebrow.

"Umm." She hesitated, which pretty much answered the question in and of itself.

"Relax." He chuckled. "It isn't hard to see there's some tension there."

Becca sighed. "Yeah, they are new and still finding a way to fit in. They have a different way of doing things. All force and no flexibility. It doesn't always mix with the way the rest of the Heretics do things."

"Should I be worried?" Jameson eyed her sideways.

Becca shook her head. "They are beginning to fall in line. They just need to adjust."

"Good to know." He gave her a sympathetic smile. "Though, if things hit the fan, I'll back you. I've seen enough to know their type. Not hard to see which side would give my people the better deal if I'm not around. You and your Heretics don't exactly come across as professional, but I'll take that over subjugation any day."

"Um, thanks?" Becca furrowed her brow.

"Relax, I'm just a good judge of character and professionalism is overrated. Give me a resourceful band of misfits, and I'll put money on them surviving when the dust settles."

She laughed. "I'm glad you see things our way. Honestly, resourceful misfits is pretty much the closest description that you could have come up with."

"Told you I'm a good judge of character."

"Guess so." She nodded and started walking toward the exit where she had entered earlier.

"Hold up." Jameson caught up to walk beside her. "If you're going out there to hunt those, what do you call 'em, revenants? You're gonna want to head down to the river bed on the south side instead. There's always a few of those things out there being a pain in the ass." He pulled a radio from his belt and handed it to her. "I'll grab a rifle and watch your back from the top. There's a guard house up there that has a view that can see the whole area. As long as you don't go too far, I can keep you covered."

Becca hesitated before taking the radio, feeling a little uncomfortable putting herself in an open space where a man she just met was watching her with a rifle. Then again, it would certainly help build trust between her and Jameson. She took the radio and clipped it to her belt. "Thank you. Just don't shoot me by mistake."

Jameson chuckled. "Don't worry, I'm a good shot. Besides, I'm no stranger to insomnia. I could use the distraction as well right now."

Jameson gave her a brief explanation of how to get to the lower exit before heading up to the top of the dam. With that she headed down, sighing occasionally when she remembered her conversation with Mason earlier. She forgot all about it the instant she stepped outside as the screech of a revenant greeted her along with the night air.

"Bla!" She jumped backward as a set of jagged teeth lunged for her.

Active Revenant, common, hostile.

"Oh, shit no!"

Becca cast Barrier without a second thought and planted her foot flat against the concrete behind her. She kicked off, thrusting her opposite knee into the creature's chin. The crunch of shattering teeth told her she'd hit home. The revenant cried out and flailed as it fell down the metal stairway that the door had led her to.

"That's right." Becca gloated as she sailed over the creature, only to realize that she had, essentially, just launched herself into the air with nothing below her but a flight of metal stairs. She might have had the agility of a tight rope walker but there was a limit to what a circus performer could do in the dark without planning.

"Oh shit."

Flailing her arms, she plummeted back down. Her first instinct was to brace for impact, yet her body had other plans. In a maneuver that resembled something a squirrel might perform, her eye locked on to a surface that matched her trajectory as her body twisted to meet it. Her feet touched down a heartbeat later, in the middle of one of the narrow, metal railings that lined the stairs. Every stabilization muscle in her body flew into overdrive to keep her from toppling off.

"Oh shit!" Becca repeated as she wavered back and forth, her internal gyros waging war with gravity.

Nothing but the empty riverbed lay before her while the injured revenant flailed behind her on the steps. The sound of its fading shrieks told her that the damage she'd caused was healing.

It would be on her in seconds.

Her balance stabilized, leaving her standing on the railing as the slap of a cold hand hitting metal announced the attack she knew was coming. Without much in the way of options, she did the only thing she could. She crouched down and sprang back up. The act was insane, after the ridiculous amount of effort it had taken to keep from falling the first time. Jumping again was the last thing an intelligent person should have thought of.

The Heretic Seed's influence told her otherwise.

Twisting in the air, she cast a Fireball, making use of her momentum to launch it straight into the revenant's face as it reached for her leg. The creature fell back flailing as she came back down on the opposite railing from the one where she'd started. Her internal gyros screamed when her foot came to rest unevenly. She slipped forward, extending her other leg on instinct to keep herself upright. She came to a stop straddling the stairway over the flaming creature below her.

"Okay." She paused before realizing that she wasn't even winded. Then she checked her mana.

MP: 330/375

The revenant's body sizzled, filling her nose with the smoky scent of burning flesh. The creature was badly hurt, yet still, it was attempting to stand.

"Nope, not happening." Becca dropped an extra-large icicle down through its chest to finish it off.

Active Revenant defeated. 92 experience awarded.

"What are you doing down there?" Jameson's voice came from the radio clipped to her belt. "Haven't you heard of waiting for your support to get into position before rushing out there?"

Becca pulled the radio from her belt and tapped the button.

"Sorry, it rushed me the second I opened the door. I wasn't expecting it. I handled it, though."

"I guess so," Jameson added. "Well, needed or not, I am in position up here."

Becca took her thumb off the radio's call button and dropped from the railing to land onto the steps in a perfect crouch. Technically the crouch wasn't necessary, but it made her feel a little cool. She immediately rolled her eyes at the ridiculous landing. "Who am I, Alex?" Shaking her head, she deflated a little. "Grow up, Becca."

Raising the radio to her mouth, she added a request. "Could you turn around for a moment?"

"Umm, sure." Jameson sounded confused but didn't ask questions. "This some sort of illusion thing?"

"It is." Becca cast Conceal and Waking Dream to set up her decoy system, then checked her mana.

MP: 240/375

She thumbed the radio's button again. "Okay, you can look now."

"Got it." He paused. "What'd you do there?"

"It's best if I don't explain it, otherwise the spell could fall apart if you think about it too hard." She willed her illusionary copy to turn its head up to the top of the dam where he was positioned. "The main thing to know is that you don't have to worry too much about my safety. So don't feel the need to shoot if a revenant gets close. Also, if you do need to fire, try not to kill them, since it will waste experience."

"Understood." He paused again. "Well, not really, but whatever, just do your thing. I'll wound anything that looks like it's getting the drop on you. Also, heads up. It looks like that last monster's screams have drawn a couple more."

Becca glanced down the metal stairs finding another two revenants creeping up from the concrete landing at the bottom, their bat-like faces illuminated by the flickering light of the still-burning corpse of the last creature she'd killed. She took a deep breath and stepped behind her decoy to stay safe. "Okay, let's go."

The pair of revenants rushed her without hesitation, their jaws streaking up the stairs.

Becca threw a hand up in the air to cast Icicle, then dropped it back down to guide the three shards of the evolved spell straight into their skulls. "That's what you get for standing so close together."

2 Active Revenants defeated. 184 experience awarded.

She nodded at the message, surprised at how strong her Icicle spell had become. The fact that the frozen spikes were hard enough to penetrate a revenant's skull was impressive. She could only imagine what it would be capable of at its final rank. For that matter, there was a chance that getting it that high would discover a new spell. Considering that, it made sense to prioritize the spell over the others.

From there, Becca made her way down the steps to the concrete platform at the bottom. She tossed a Fireball into some nearby brush for light, making sure to stand close enough to her decoy so that it wasn't obvious that the spell had been cast from behind it. Becca snapped her eyes to the side as she caught movement in her peripheral. It vanished as soon as she noticed it.

"Okay, that was weird."

Her mind flashed back to when she and Digby had fought a revenant blood stalker a couple weeks ago. The one that had the ability to conceal itself. A chill traveled down her spine at the thought of one of those oversized monsters catching her off guard. It wasn't out of the realm of possibilities. She glanced back to the door, wondering how fast she could get back up there if her fears proved true.

It wasn't far, but it wasn't close either.

"Maybe this was a bad idea after all."

Focusing on the sounds that surrounded her, she pushed her perception to the limit. If she couldn't trust her eyes, then her ears would be her best bet. Unless the revenants had evolved a way to deal with that too. The answer came at her from behind a second later.

"Wait, shit!" She leaped forward as a normal-sized revenant blinked into existence directly behind her, despite having heard nothing. Not only that, but it was also ignoring her decoy and going straight for her. Becca stumbled forward and cast Icicle twice, sending six daggers of frost behind her without looking.

The revenant let out a shriek in her ear so close she could feel the breath of the creature on her neck. The sound of a gunshot rang out, and a bullet punched into the ground somewhere behind her, sending a burst of concrete fragments into the air. Becca fell forward into a roll but reached a hand down to pivot to the side. Snapping her vision back, she caught the revenant for an instant. It shrank away, with an icicle in its gut just as the air wavered around it.

"I don't think so." She locked her eyes on the creature to make sure she didn't lose track of it. If she took her eyes off it for even a second, it would be able to conceal itself again.

Revenant Sensebreaker, uncommon, hostile.

"Holy shit."

It was a new type. "It must mask the sound it creates as well."

That was probably how it saw through her decoy. Deafening the noises she made was something her conceal spell didn't do. The sensebreaker must have tracked where she really was by sound, while paying no attention to her decoy.

"You okay down there?" Jameson's voice came from the radio.

"Yeah, that was a good shot though. The thing almost got a bite in." Becca sucked in a breath. If it weren't for her barrier, she was a hair's breadth from being turned. She shook off the thought and refocused on the revenant as it stood there watching her. "You going to make a move or what?"

The creature responded with a short chitter before turning and making a run for it.

"Damn." Becca launched another burst of ice in its direction to keep it from fleeing. If she let it get away, it would probably come back and attack as soon as it could conceal again. "Get back here."

One of her icicles grazed its leg.

The revenant let out a shriek but didn't slow down.

Becca ran after it, her feet hitting the concrete in a steady staccato. The creature leaped down from the manmade slab of stone at the base of the dam to land on the edge of the river not far below.

"God damn it, stop making this harder." Becca followed and launched another cluster of ice spikes, this time piercing its shoulder. A screech from the side reminded her that the sensebreaker was not the only threat out there in the night. She blasted a common revenant in the chest with three more frozen shards and kept running.

She glanced back as the creature flailed on the ground to make sure it succumbed.

Active Revenant defeated. 92 experience awarded.

"No!" Becca snapped her vision back to the sensebreaker she was chasing as she realized that she'd taken her eyes off of it. She slowed to a stop as finding no trace of the creature. "Damn it."

She kicked at the dirt in frustration. To make matters worse, Jameson added more bad news.

"You might have run a little out of my range there, Becca. I'm a good marksman, but I'm not sure if I can make a shot that far."

Becca held her breath, not sure what to do. With the sensebreaker concealed again, there was no way to know where it had gone. It could be a foot in front of her face for all she knew. She started creeping back to the safety of the dam where she would still be in the range of Jameson's rifle.

That was when she slapped a hand to her face. "I'm an idiot."

If the revenant could conceal itself and mask the noise it made, then there was still an option. She held still and inhaled through her nose. If she could tell what was for dinner back at the casino from a couple floors up, she could probably find a revenant. They didn't smell as bad as the dead on account of them still being alive, but they didn't smell great either.

She breathed out when she picked up a slight presence of the creature's telltale scent.

"Okay, it's still out there, but not close." Becca turned and started walking back to the dam, making a point of checking the air the entire way.

After a few more steps, the scent got stronger. "Come on, just a little closer."

Becca reached the base of the dam just as the odor following her began to swell. The direction was a little vague, but it was good enough. She turned and focused on the ten-foot area behind her, causing the air to ripple about five feet away. She launched an icicle straight into its center as the revenant's conceal ability unraveled.

"Yes!" Becca jumped and thrust a hand in the air as the sense-breaker fell back and flailed on the ground as its healing ability slowed and failed.

Revenant Sensebreaker defeated. 692 experience awarded.

SKILL LINK
By demonstrating repeated and proficient use of the non-mage skill or talent, Sense Tracking, you have discovered an adjacent spell.

REVEAL
Description: By combining the power of the enhanced senses that you have cultivated, this spell will reveal the position of any threat that may be hidden to you and display as much information as available. This spell may also be used to see in low-light situations.
Rank: D
Cost: 30 MP
Duration: 10 mins
Range: 30 ft

> **Limitations: Some information may not be revealed, depending on your enemy's capabilities.**

Becca cast the spell without hesitation, causing her vision to fade to grayscale. A second later, a figure was highlighted near the edge of the spell's effective radius. The information ring that waited at the edge of her vision snapped out as if she'd just analyzed the threat.

> **Revenant Sensebreaker, uncommon, hostile.**

"Oh shit." She slapped a hand to her mouth. "There was another out there."

Apparently what Malcolm said about uncommon revenants working in packs was true.

"Well, this one should go a little different than the last." She turned and climbed her way back up onto the concrete portion of the dam.

"Everything alright down there?" Jameson asked.

"I'm good." She glanced back to find the sensebreaker creeping around about twenty feet away. "I have another one right where I want it."

Reaching the top of the concrete edge, she stood tall and surveyed the area. A second sensebreaker slipped into her field of view about twenty feet from the other. She arched an eyebrow as they both inched their way toward her. She couldn't help but feel a little like the predator as the Heretic Seed highlighted each of the threats.

"Hmm. I guess sensebreakers are more timid than the normal ones."

The behavior made sense for a pure ambush predator. As a bonus, the fact that her reveal spell didn't cause the creature's abilities to unravel left them unaware that their positions had been compromised. Becca made a point not to look at either of the revenants for long or let them linger on her thoughts to make sure she didn't break their concealment. It was better if they thought they had the drop on her rather than the other way around.

She checked her mana.

MP: 75/375

Watching the sensebreakers move, she made a note to project herself to Alex later to let him know there was a type of uncommon revenant that they hadn't run into before. Even if they weren't that strong, the ability to sneak up on anyone was dangerous all on its own. It would be easy for someone in Vegas to fall prey to an ambush attack.

For a moment, she wondered how the Reveal spell was able to identify her targets. Then she remembered what the description said. It used a combination of her senses to identify her prey. Becca waited for the pair of creatures to creep their way up to the concrete wall below her. Then she dropped a pair of extra-large icicles into their skulls at once. She brushed her hands together as they fell.

"I could get used to this."

2 Revenant Sensebreakers defeated. 1384 experience awarded.

"That will work." Becca stepped back toward the base of the dam and leaned against the wall to watch the surrounding area for more as she waited for her mana system to absorb more of the ambient essence around her. She raised her radio to her mouth while she waited.

"Are you intending on going someplace?"

"What?" Jameson responded.

Becca thought back to their conversation before she'd gone outside. "You said earlier that it was easy to see that joining us was the right choice for your people if you weren't around. So, were you planning on leaving?"

It was a valid question. With what he now knew of their operation, it would be a problem if he decided to head off on some personal mission.

"Oh, not really. But the way I see it, you'll need someone to stay here at the dam to run things, so I don't see myself moving to Sin City anytime soon. And most of my people will be joining yours in Vegas, so I won't be around for them. I'll have to leave the survivors that have been under my care to you and yours." He paused for a moment. "Plus, I've got a bad ticker. Had it diagnosed back before all this happened. You know, when hospitals still existed and all that. I was on the books for a bypass, but I guess that isn't gonna happen now. Too many cheeseburgers."

"How long do you have?" Becca regretted the question as soon as she'd asked it. Apparently, she hadn't grown as much as she'd thought if her first instinct was to probe for more information that might impact Vegas rather than opting for something more comforting.

"Right to the point, eh?" He laughed. "I have enough prescriptions for a while but that isn't gonna cut it long term. It'll last a few more months. It's more than most of the world's population got, so I'm not complaining."

"You know, there might be a way to change that." Becca considered the Heretic Seed.

"You gonna magic me up a new heart, there?" He chuckled.

"Not quite." She shook her head. "But we are working on a way to create more magic users. If one of our people back in Vegas can figure some things out, then it would be possible to give you access to the same power I have."

"You mean that Heretic thing?"

"Yes, the Seed." She nodded. "If you are going to stay here and run this power station, you would be a prime candidate to be given magic first. Not to mention you have valuable experience that would help our side. I can't guarantee how magic will interact with a bad heart, but in theory, it should repair the damage without the need for medical treatment."

"How?" His voice sounded skeptical.

"Well, my assumption is that your stats have fallen as you age. So your starting values will be low, but they should climb back up to match those of a healthy person. You probably won't become as powerful as someone who became a Heretic in their prime, but natural causes should stop being a threat. Plus the immortality that comes along with magic should help." She laughed. "I mean, I know you haven't met Digby yet, but if the Seed can keep him walking around, then I'm sure it can keep you ticking."

"I'm sorry, but did you say immortality?" Jameson's breathing came out strange, like he'd just nearly choked on something.

Becca chuckled. "Did I forget to mention that earlier?"

"You did." He let a long beat pass by. "And this Graves guy that saves everyone from Autem, he's really a corpse?"

"Yes, a zombie, actually," Becca added matter-of-factly.

"Jesus." Jameson's tone lowered to a whisper.

A long pause went by before he added, "Wait, are you telling me that he is a magic zombie, named Dig Graves?"

Becca blew out a sigh. "The irony has been pointed out."

"I'm sure." Jameson let an awkward laugh travel across the radio. "How did the world get this weird?"

Becca laughed. "Tell me about it. A friend of mine back in Vegas is trying to make a magic-powered hoverboard."

Jameson chuckled. "Sounds like a nerd."

She shrugged. "You hit the nail right on the head with that one."

Jameson blew out a sigh over the radio. "Zombies, revenants, Heretics, and Guardians. This world is pretty much FUBARed at this point, but honestly, I'll be damned if I'm checking out while there's more I can do."

"I take it you're interested in gaining magic then?" She glanced up at the guard house where he was positioned.

"Well, shit, lady. Of course I am." The sound of him slapping his thigh was audible over the radio. "I ain't ready to leave this world yet, and I'm not afraid of things getting weird. I mean, I lived through the eighties. Weird might as well be my middle name. So yeah, I'll stay aboard this runaway train all the way to the end."

"That's good to hear. I think." Becca recast Reveal as her MP ticked back up to around fifty percent.

That was when something blew against her foot.

Becca glanced down, her heart climbing to her throat at the

sudden contact that her spell hadn't sensed. She furrowed her brow when she saw what it was.

"The hell?"

A slightly worn cowboy hat sat, resting against her foot.

"You alright?" Jameson's tone grew worried. "I can't quite see you down there where you're standing."

"I'm fine." She bent down and picked up the hat. "A random hat just blew into me."

"Oh, that happens." He didn't sound surprised.

"Cowboy hats happen?" She arched an eyebrow.

"Yep. Tourists used to lean over the top and lose them in the wind." He laughed. "Go look in the ditch to the right."

Becca shrugged and walked to the side to peek down into a lower portion of the dam's base. Her mouth fell open at the sight of a few hundred cowboy hats all laying in the ditch.

"Ok, that is weird."

"Yep," he responded matter-of-factly.

"Why are they all cowboy hats?" She stared at the strange collection.

"Near as I can tell, the brim is wider, so they catch the wind real well." He snorted. "They all collect right there eventually when they blow against the dam."

"Well, that's a new and useless fact." She placed the hat she'd picked up on her head. The fit was a little loose.

"You should grab one for that rugged soldier boy of yours," Jameson added with a laugh. "He'd look pretty fetching in a Stetson. Might just smooth over whatever happened right before I walked in earlier today."

"Oh jeez." Becca groaned. "You know me one day and start giving me relationship advice."

"Sorry, I call 'em like I see 'em." He chuckled wholeheartedly. "What was that I walked in on, by the way?"

"Seriously, you're asking me this?" She walked out a few steps and stared up at his sniper perch.

"Yep, there's no TV anymore. Have to get drama somewhere."

"Good lord." She folded her arms before blurting out, "Fine. He told me he loved me."

"You say it back?"

Becca could hear him scratching his beard. "Nope."

"Met him recently?"

"Three weeks ago."

"I see." He inhaled audibly. "Not a lot of time."

"Nope." She leaned back against the dam.

"Do you?"

"Do I what?" She frowned.

"Do you love him?"

"I don't know. Maybe. Probably." Becca slapped a hand against her thigh. "I'm bad at this."

That was when Jameson started laughing. "No, you aren't. The world ended and someone loves you. You're doing fine."

"I'm glad the stranger I just met thinks so," she responded with as much sarcasm as possible.

"Eh, like I said, I'm a good judge of people." He chuckled. "I'm sure you and your guy will work things out just fine."

"Thanks." She rolled her eyes before adding, "Anyway, I'll get myself a level out here, then head back to bed. Sound good?"

"Sure, whatever that means," Jameson agreed.

Becca took her finger off the radio's button and pulled the hat off her head.

"Why am I like this?"

CHAPTER SIXTEEN

"Not good!" Digby spilled from the mirror in the castle's main hall as he fled from the caretaker. The floor came at him fast as his body twisted to meet the stone. His foot slapped down, leaving him standing in an awkward crouched position that made it clear that he had not expected to actually land upright.

Mere moments had passed since that malformed monstrosity had torn that jester's head off. He lamented the loss of a potential ally.

Henwick stood not far away, clearly annoyed that Digby had shoved him through the mirror to test the passage that Parker had created. The only person missing was the messenger herself.

He snapped his vision back to the mirror.

"Parker?" He stood up slowly just as a wild shout erupted from the reflective surface.

"Outta the way!" Parker tumbled into the room, bowling into Digby with all of her weight.

"Gah!" He flopped onto the floor, his head coming to rest staring up at Henwick from his feet.

"What is wrong with you?" The cleric stared down at him. "Get up, man."

"Hey, crap, watch it!" Parker flailed around on top of him with all the coordination of a level one Heretic.

"Get off of me." Digby shoved her off before she kicked him on accident.

Standing up again, he snapped his attention back to the mirror, wondering if the nightmarish monstrosity on the other side could follow them through the passage that Parker had created.

"Close the portal!" Digby jabbed a finger at the rippling mirror.

"I can't. It's supposed to close on its own when I go through. Oh damn…" Her voice trailed off a second later.

"What is—" Digby's eyes bulged as he spotted the problem.

A tendril of sinewy black tissue was reaching through the bottom of the mirror. He followed it with his eyes until he reached the other end that was currently wrapped around Parker's boot. The passage must not have been able to close while something was obstructing it. Everyone held perfectly still for a moment as if the slightest movement might remind the beast to pull the soldier back through the glass.

"Young lady." Henwick swallowed hard. "Try to remove your footwear."

"Ya think?" she hissed back as she slowly reached for her boot-lace. Of course, that was when the creature decided to yank back on its tendril.

Digby dove forward as Parker slid toward the passage. Henwick did the same, each of them grabbing hold of her hands. Despite the added weight, the three of them continued to slip toward the mirror, albeit at a slower pace. The glass rippled as the beast's oversized skull emerged from the passage. It was immediately followed by a scythe of bone that slammed down hard enough to crack the floor.

The creature let out a horrible screech as it squeezed what it could through the mirror's portal. The only saving grace was that its bulk was too large to fit.

"I didn't get to untie my shoe." Parker struggled to hold on as her boot remained firmly attached to her foot.

"Damn." Digby cursed the situation as well as the fact that he didn't have enough blood in his void to make use of his forge spell. It had been his best attack ever since he'd learned it, but now, it was all but useless. Emerald Flare was out as well, considering the beast was pulling them closer and closer to the epicenter of where he would have to target.

He checked his HUD.

MP: 291/291

Digby growled at the numbers. He had plenty of mana but so few usable spells within the Seed's realm. All he had left was Decay. It wasn't powerful, but it would have to do.

Scanning the room, Digby found a row of chandeliers, candle wax coating every inch of the heavy framework. The support ropes for each ran through a ring attached to the ceiling before traveling through a second ring on the wall before finally reaching a hook at eye level where it was tied off.

There wasn't time to guess at the math.

Digby focused on the support ring embedded in the ceiling and cast Decay. It snapped in an instant, releasing the heavy chandelier above.

"I suggest we all duck." Digby flattened himself to the floor as the mass of wood, metal, and wax fell straight for them. Parker and Henwick did the same just in time for the chandelier's free fall to end, the second ring catching its weight. A solid crack came from the wall as the tension threatened to tear the metal support from the stone.

It held.

The chandelier swooped over them with only inches to spare. Both Parker and Henwick sucked in a breath as Digby winced. He half expected the swinging object to shave off the nose that he had worked so hard to regain. Instead, all it did was leave a few crumbles of wax on his face.

Digby sat up to watch as the chandelier swung toward the mirror on the wall with the momentum of a charging bull. The caretaker cried out just before its voice was cut off by the sound of shattering glass. Black blood sprayed the wall as the creature's skull and top portion of its body splattered to the floor.

Caretaker defeated. 2,432 experience awarded.

"Woooo!" Parker threw her arms up as she lay on the floor. "I just leveled up, a lot. What do I put my points in? Maybe dex? You know, cause I do daggers?"

"Yes, yes, don't get over-excited." Digby resisted the urge to relax. "That thing regenerated before, so there is a solid possibility that it will again."

"Abomination." Henwick immediately scooted himself away from the severed portion of the beast.

"Indeed." Digby stepped away from the skull, its jaws still open wide having been cut off mid-screech. "If it does regenerate, let's just hope the thing decides to regrow itself back up in the room where the bulk of it remains."

"As long as it's not trying to rip my leg off, I'll count it as a win." Parker stood up and brushed bits of wax from her shirt.

That was when a horrid gurgle came from the creature's throat.

"Of course." Digby groaned before heading toward the door. "Come on, lest that thing grows into something even worse than its last form." He hesitated to think about what the creature might become. He may have gained experience with each victory, but the caretaker had simply come back stronger with each death. Judging by the number of points awarded, the first form had been an equivalent to common, the next uncommon. Whatever was coming next was sure to be considered rare.

They had to lose the beast before that happened.

"Where do you plan on going?" Henwick caught up to his side as he took a left down the hall.

"Yeah, we can't go back upstairs, that thing will just find us again, and we don't know if there's a way out up there." Parker flanked him on his other side.

"Indeed. That jester knew of a passage, but he isn't quite able to share that information anymore." He didn't slow down. "That's why we're going to climb that twisted stairway we found earlier."

"Can we even climb that?" Parker shrieked.

"I have no idea, but we don't have much of a say in the matter." Digby flinched as a strangely human shout came from the main hall behind them. "But every second we waste is one less we have before that monstrosity is upon us."

With that, they made their way as fast as they could back to the strange door that they had peeked through earlier. Henwick brought up the rear with his ax in hand. The beast behind them continued to scream the entire way, like it was gaining on them with each step. Even worse, each time it cried out, its voice seemed to grow more human.

Digby's skin crawled with every labored scream.

It wasn't until the creature began forming his name that he recognized the voice. He kept running, cursing the Heretic Seed for using his own memories against him.

It was a voice he never wanted to hear again.

"There it is." Parker thrust a hand out at the door that led to the treacherous stairway.

"I don't like the appearance of that." Henwick started to slow as he reached the door.

"I don't care." Digby ran faster, not wanting to catch a glimpse of the monster, his imagination already presenting an image that had plagued his dreams since childhood. His only saving grace was the fact that he didn't sleep anymore. "Keep going!"

Practically running straight into the door, he wrapped his cold fingers around the handle and pulled with all his strength. Parker jumped to his aid as Henwick's mouth fell at the sight that lay beyond.

The cleric froze in place as the impossible path of steps twisted up and folded over on itself. "What in all that is holy?"

"It's a way out." Digby stepped outside.

The Seed's realm stretched out below as a swell of vertigo coiled around his body. Gusts of wind battered the unprotected pathway, each threatening to throw him from the tower and down into the waves that crashed against the rocks below. If it hadn't been for his enhanced attributes, he would have lost his balance and plummeted into the sea after only a few steps.

"Grab on." He threw a hand back to Parker as she placed a foot on the first step. The soldier would never make it alone. She reached up without hesitation. He panicked as soon as she did, catching the sight of a hulking figure entering the hallway behind her. Digby's eyes bulged. It was almost human. Well, if a human was twice as tall and had a skull for a head, that was.

"Digby!" a gruff voice shouted at its highest volume, echoing down the hall from the caretaker's new form, its body made of glossy, black flesh that rippled with every movement.

No! His hand trembled at the sound of the familiar voice, but Parker tightened her fingers around his.

"Keep going." She nodded to him.

"Yes. Make haste." Henwick planted his foot at the base of the stairs with his ax at the ready. "I shall guard your flank."

"Don't be a fool, you halfwit," Digby growled back at the man's idiocy. "That thing will tear your head off, and I'm not letting your body fall into the sea where I can't even eat it."

"Must you continue your vile comments?" the cleric gasped before adding, "But you might be right." Henwick lowered his ax and followed them up the stairs, clearly having second thoughts about fighting.

Digby pushed on at a steady pace, making a point of keeping Parker close. She might have gained some levels, but she was nowhere near where she needed to be to make the climb. Especially since the steps grew steeper and more uneven the further they got. Eventually, they had no choice but to continue on all fours for stability.

"Digby!" the caretaker below howled as its over-muscled form stepped out onto the base of the stairway. The severed head of the jester was embedded in the rippling tissue that covered its neck. The eyes continued to twitch horribly beneath its mask. "Digby Graves!"

"Why does that abomination know your name?" Henwick crawled up behind Parker.

"I don't know," Digby lied on instinct before adding a plausible reason. "That thing is an unstable representation of the Heretic Seed. It probably knows the names of every soul trapped within this realm."

"Maybe we'll get lucky, and it will just fall off the stairs," Parker added with an awkward laugh that was entirely inappropriate for the situation.

Digby glanced down as the human-shaped monster slapped a meaty hand down on the steps only to have its finger snap and break to form tendrils that clung to the stone.

"No, I don't think we're lucky enough for that thing to fall on its own." He climbed higher with Parker close until they reached the section of stairs that folded over on itself. A vertical section of stone stood in their way before it bent over and returned to normal above.

"Shit! We're out of room." Parker clung to the edge of the steps, clearly struggling to hold on to the vertical surface of the notched stone. The wind matted her pink hair against her face.

"We're going to have to climb around to the opposite side of the stairs to keep going." Digby searched for something to get a solid grip on.

"That's much easier said than done." Henwick reached the step right behind them. "The young lady will never make it."

"Oh, will you shut it with the young lady crap?" Parker reached for the step above her. "I was in the damn army. If I can do that, I can climb a stupid cursed stairway."

Digby winced as she pushed off the steps and reached up with her other hand, half expecting her to slip right into the sea below. When she didn't, he started to climb as well, hoping to make use of his attributes to make it to the other side first where he might be able to help her. The look on her face was a mix of annoyance and absolute terror as she struggled to pull herself up. Digby wished the soldier had remained in Vegas where she was less likely to become a liability. The last thing he wanted was her death on his conscience.

With a final push of effort, he yanked his upper body up onto the topside of the steps, his legs dangling free over the sea below.

"Almost there." Parker slapped a hand onto the top as well and hoisted her chin up. For a second, she looked like she might make it. Then she slipped. Panic flooded her eyes just as Digby threw his hand out to reach hers. It was the same hand that had been supporting his weight.

"I have you!" His fingers curled around her wrist an instant before she disappeared over the edge. A grunt of effort erupted from his mouth as he caught her weight, leaving him with both legs hanging free on one side of the steps while she kicked at the air on the other side. From their awkward position, it was near impossible to make the climb. All they could do was hold on to each other's arms and use each other as a counterweight as they struggled.

The creature below shouted Digby's name again in the same voice that threatened to drag him back into the misery of his past. He couldn't tell how close the caretaker was. All he knew was he hadn't heard Henwick scream, so it stood to reason that the beast hadn't reached him.

That was when Parker let out a surprised yelp.

"Hold on, young miss!" Henwick's voice called out from below. "I shall aid you! Hold your place, Graves, whilst I assist the lady."

"What?" Digby immediately began to fall as Parker lurched upward, no longer able to act as his counterweight. He dropped down, letting go of her to keep from pulling her over. His hand caught the edge of the stone, leaving him hanging from the steps by his fingertips. From there, he watched Henwick shove Parker's feet up with one hand whilst clinging to the steps with the other.

It was all rather heroic.

Digby rolled his eyes.

Then he looked down.

The caretaker's fingers stretched into tendrils that slithered their way toward Henwick's foot. His mind raced to get a warning out but the only sound he could force his mouth to make was a meaningless gasp. Despite that, the cleric shoved Parker the rest of the way up with one final push and leaped up to follow just before the caretaker reached him. The beast's tendrils snaked through empty air.

Henwick locked eyes with Digby as they both hung from the

stairs together with that monstrosity and the sea beneath them, the wind slipping through their hair. The cleric proceeded to do a one-handed pull-up to reach the top of the steps. Digby didn't attempt anything as flashy, using both hands to hoist himself to safety. The caretaker let out another howl of his name as they both slipped away from its grasp.

"What do we do now?" Parker peeked over the edge at the creature as they both joined her in the relative safety at the top side of the twisted stairway. She immediately ducked back. "That thing is gonna get up here any second."

"I was forced to abandon my ax in the climb, but I will use magic if I must." Henwick got ready to fight.

"Don't bother." Digby swept his eyes up the stairway to find that it did indeed reach the land mass above further up. "Now move, I have a plan."

"Very well." Henwick nodded and stood up, grabbing Parker's hand without giving her a chance to refuse. They both made for their destination as fast as reasonably possible upon the uneven stairs.

"Keep going." Digby did the same, making a point to hang back a bit.

After a few dozen steps, the stairs began to even out, giving him a more stable place to work. He spun just in time to see the beast reach up from the underside of the stairway. Its macabre visage of bone came into view a moment later.

"Dig Gravessss!"

"Shut up!" Digby shouted back. "I won't be called that by you. Not anymore."

The creature didn't listen, crying out again as it pulled its body up to the topside of the steps, its oversized form looking strange standing on such a narrow path of stone.

Digby held his ground as he focused on the space directly in front of the monster. It was true that thing would never simply fall on its own, but nothing said that Digby couldn't give it a push.

He cast Emerald Flare.

Emerald streaks of angry energy streaked through the air,

converging into a point of unstable power as the beast took a step forward.

"Stop following me!" Digby snapped his fingers.

The spell detonated in a sudden blast that bathed the stairway in a sickly light. The image of the creature vanished as the brightness of the spell blotted its form out of sight. The steps beneath it cracked and shattered into fragments that flittered off into the night. A gust of displaced air blew Digby's hair back just before the wind reasserted its dominance. He took a step forward as the spell faded, searching for the monstrosity in hope that it was gone.

There was nothing left but a spatter of black fluid upon the broken stone. Below, the water rippled out from the epicenter of an impact. Digby relaxed. The horrid thing had fallen into the sea.

"Good riddance."

"It's not dead," Henwick shouted back from further up the stairs.

"Yeah, I didn't see a notification," Parker added as she pulled her hand free from the cleric's grip.

"It likely wouldn't matter anyway." Digby started toward them. "The creature would only regenerate into something worse. The experience would be a boon, but we might be worse off if it becomes too strong for us to handle."

"Agreed." Henwick nodded. "As it stands, we shan't win against that abomination under normal circumstances."

"Indeed." Digby caught up as they waited. "At least we should get a bit of peace while that thing climbs back up from the bottom."

With that, they climbed the rest of the way up.

It was hard to get an idea of what the next area of the Seed's realm looked like from the stairway. Below was the castle, but above was something else entirely. From the towers beneath them, stretched several forms of darkness that spread out like the branches of a tree. Several other stairways similar to the one they stood on twisted and reached for a new mass of land above.

Henwick gasped. Digby suppressed one of his own.

The section above was so much larger than the castle they had left behind.

Looking down at the steps as he walked, the stone shifted from solid slabs to a cobblestone path that grew wider and wider as it spiraled upward until it was the width of a street. Wrought iron fences topped with wicked-looking points began cropping up at the path's edges the closer they got to the top.

It wasn't long before they were looking up at the barred gates of a city.

Buildings, larger than any of the village where he'd been born, filled a street lit by lanterns mounted on posts. Though, none of the buildings held a candle to Vegas. Through the bars of the gates, he took in a long row of what looked like rundown shops with broken windows and darkened doors. It was like the place had been abandoned. The state of it must have been due to the Seed's instability.

It was just another memory, just like the castle. As to who it belonged to, he had no idea.

"Do you recognize this place?" Henwick approached the gates.

"I should say not." Digby shook his head.

"It looks like a scene from a period drama or something." Parker placed her hands on the bars.

"I don't know what that is." Digby joined her, testing the strength of the barrier with a good shake.

"It's a movie that…" She trailed off, glancing at Henwick as she did, clearly not wanting to say too much in front of him. "I mean, this place looks Victorian."

Digby rolled his eyes. "I don't know what that means either."

"Umm…" Parker's face went blank for a moment before she leaned close and lowered her voice so that it was barely audible. "I mean it's back in England, like almost two centuries ago."

"You don't have to whisper." Henwick eyed them, his voice growing cold.

"Nonsense." Digby brushed off the comment.

"Cease your lies, Graves." A severe frown settled across the man's face as his eyes narrowed. "I'm not a fool. I know when I am being lied to."

CHAPTER SEVENTEEN

"Now wait just a second. I have no idea what you're speaking of."
Digby threw up his hands, pretending that Henwick's accusation
that he had been lying was wrong. Sure, all the evidence pointed to
the contrary, but he wasn't about to admit it now after lying
continuously since they had run into him.

"I shall not, and will not, let you wriggle your way out of this."
Henwick slapped a hand down on his shoulder, grabbing a fistful
of his clothing, and shoving him against the barred gates behind
him that prevented their access to the strange city street that lay
beyond.

"Hey, so, like, maybe this isn't the place for this." Parker tried
to slip between them as if there was actually something she could
do to stop the conflict. "You know, 'cause we just escaped a
monster, and we probably want to keep moving."

"Indeed." Digby brushed off Henwick's hand. "That's the
most sensible thing you have uttered this whole time."

Parker gave him a dirty look, clearly to imply that she had
uttered plenty of sensible things. Digby couldn't think of any.
Though he also didn't try too hard. Not when Henwick was still on
him about lying.

"Very well." The cleric let out a breath. "But don't think that I am letting you off. We will discuss this further when we find some-where less exposed."

"Alright, alright. You can tell me whatever it is you think I've lied about as soon as we're safe." Digby forced his body to relax in an attempt to give the cleric the idea that he was being more honest than he was.

In actuality, a series of panic bells were echoing through his mind. The first was a reminder that he was indeed lying his deceased ass off and had almost certainly been caught in a decep-tion. The second was the fact that he had no idea what had given him away. That jester had seemed to understand enough not to let anything slip, and Digby was pretty sure he hadn't said anything either. Lastly, there was the loudest of his panic bells, the one that questioned what Henwick might do when the truth came out.

That was the real problem.

There was a limit to how long he could stall, but in the end, their temporary alliance might just end in violence. If Digby failed and played his cards wrong, Henwick could become just as much an enemy within the Seed's realm as he was out there in the world outside.

He checked the number of Heretics still in the running for the final two places.

54/2

Technically, the cleric could kill him and escape this place as one of the survivors.

Then where would the world be?

Sure, Henwick would have to take the body of a zombie, or a young woman, but still, one of him out there was bad enough. He could only imagine what would happen with two.

Digby pushed aside the thought and focused on buying himself time.

The gate barring entrance to the street beyond was tall and topped with a series of unfriendly-looking spikes.

"Looks like we're not climbing over easily." Digby followed the bars to the center of the gate, finding a large locking mechanism.

The thing looked to be in severe disrepair like the rest of the buildings on the street within. Ravaged by time and rusted beyond function. "No matter."

Digby placed his hand against the lock and cast Decay. The spell had nearly reached its maximum rank, making it far more useful a tool than it had been back when he'd learned it in Seattle. The thought crossed his mind to stall, but the caretaker was sure to come after them the moment it climbed out of the sea below.

He checked his mana.

MP: 271/291

He was still down a bit after casting flare back on the stairway to handle the caretaker. Best not to use so much that he would be at a disadvantage if Henwick decided that their partnership had run its course. Then again, the lock wasn't going to decay itself. He cast the spell anyway, hoping for the best. With a couple uses focused on the lock, the entire thing began to crumble in his hand, leaving him more than two-thirds of his mana remaining to deal with whatever Henwick might decide to throw at him. It was something, although he did wish that Parker had gotten a class that could at least assist in combat.

Some help she turned out to be.

"Alright." Digby snapped the gate open and pushed it in. A loud creak came from the hinges to announce to anyone within that they had arrived.

Parker cringed. "If anybody's home, they know we're here now."

"Yes, but more importantly." Henwick cleared his throat. "I have questions—"

"Yes, yes, I know." Digby waved a hand at him without even looking in his direction. "But let us get inside and find someplace more secluded. Ideally with a change of clothes, considering I was just set ablaze and would like to find some trousers without holes burnt in the rear."

Parker snorted. "Speaking of. Your ass is pale. And I mean really pale."

"You're not helping," he grumbled back.

"I know." She jogged up to walk beside him, leaving Henwick to walk behind. Digby just hoped the man would let things lie a little longer.

The street stretched out in front of them, lined with rundown buildings of brick and wood. Alleyways snaked off into the shadows on both sides. Following the rooftops to their apex, a latticework of what looked like dead tree branches climbed into the sky to hold up some sort of ceiling. It reminded him of some of the casinos in Vegas, the way that the space appeared to be a city street, but in actuality was just inside an enormous structure.

"This place looks like something out of Dracula." Parker stared at the buildings from beside him.

"What is a Dracula?" Henwick asked from behind them.

"What did I tell you about questions, Henwick?" Digby glanced back at him. Antagonizing the man might have seemed like the wrong move considering the situation, but since he was trying not to act suspicious, it made sense to behave consistently. Acting nice all of a sudden would have given Henwick far more reason for alarm. That was when he stopped short. "Actually, what is a Dracula?"

"A vampire," Parker added in a nonchalant tone.

"Hmm, you mentioned that word before when discussing the revenants back when we met." Digby scratched at his chin.

"Revenants?" Henwick caught up to walk beside him.

"Yes, horrible creatures." Digby decided to answer the question rather than antagonize him further. There was sure to be a limit to what the man would put up with. "Bloodsuckers, all of them. I suppose these vampires are similar, then?"

"Yeah." Parker nodded. "They're people that drink blood and live forever and such. Not a real thing, obviously. Though, who knows at this point what's real and what's not. I mean, I'm a Heretic messenger, so I'm not gonna go passing judgment on what people want to believe."

"Fair enough." Digby nodded.

"Besides, I'm no expert." She let out a laugh. "I didn't even watch, or I mean, read Twilight."

"Is that a book about these vampires you mentioned?" Henwick arched an eyebrow.

"Yeah."

"I'd like to read this book." He sounded genuinely interested.

"No, you don't." She kept walking.

"Whatever, no one cares about Twilight." Digby hastened his pace as he spotted a rundown garment emporium of some kind. "We have windows to break and merchandise to loot."

Without hesitation, he pressed his face against the dingy glass. The inside of the shop was dark and covered in a layer of dust. He quickly cast Decay to shatter the barrier and climbed through, finding what looked like a tailor's workshop.

"Ah, this should do." Digby clawed his way through a corner where garments were hung, finding a pair of old trousers, a shirt, and a rather nice vest. After a little more searching, he found a pair of shoes as well. Claiming them all, he shook off the dust and got changed.

"Should we get you a spray tan or something? You look like you haven't seen the sun in years." Parker snickered at his appearance.

"I'm dead. It would be far stranger if I had a healthy glow about me." Digby paid the comment no mind. "You might want to find something as well." He jabbed a finger in her direction, sweeping it up and down. "At least find something with sleeves to help protect yourself."

"Yes." Henwick cleared his throat. "Your current clothing does not leave much to the imagination."

Parker rolled her eyes at the comment and grabbed a short coat and vest, along with a hat. "There, you happy now? I look like Oliver Twist."

Digby arched an eyebrow at the name, remembering that someone had mentioned it before in regard to his accent.

"I wonder why this place is even here and why it's abandoned." Parker adjusted her hat in a dusty mirror. "I mean, why would the Seed create all this?"

"That part's obvious." Digby stepped into his looted pants. "Clearly, this is the unstable memory of a Heretic. Just as the castle was. This place must resemble the world known by another of the Seed's magic users. There is a good chance whoever this area belongs to is still lurking around, too."

"And that is why I need you to start explaining why you are here." Henwick stepped forward, standing tall as if to make himself appear intimidating. "We do not know when we will next find a moment of peace."

"You will have to be more specific." Digby fell back on his earlier deception that there was nothing afoot. "I still have no idea what you are talking—"

That was when Henwick slapped a hand down on a table. "Don't give me that. I am not the fool you take me for. I know that I am dead."

Digby's face fell, unsure what the man meant, considering the fact that his body was still very much alive. "What?"

"I am dead out there in the world beyond this one." Henwick deflated. "I saw what the Heretic Seed called that jester when I focused on him. A remnant Spark. Not a Heretic, such as what appears when I analyze both of you."

"Nonsense." Digby tried to wave the question away. "Why would that mean you are dead?"

"It lists the same categorization within my own information. A remnant Spark." Henwick made a fist with both hands, his knuckles turning white. "I watched that rogue die at the hands of Autem's witch hunters. Clearly, they must have killed me when they removed the Seed's Fragment from my arm. Thus, why my soul became trapped here. And I assume the two that is listed in the corner of my vision has something to do with the two of you."

Digby hesitated. The cleric had just confirmed what he'd feared. He had, in fact, worked out the situation at hand. He glanced at Parker, hoping for at least a distraction. Her confused expression told him he wasn't going to get any help there. Without a better option available, he did what any reasonable zombie would do.

He doubled down on his lie.

"I don't know what it is you're on about. We have no way of knowing what that number on our HUDs is—"

"Please stop." Henwick cut him off before lowering his head. "That jester attacked you and seemed to think there was still a way out of this place, even for him. Which means there is still a way out for me, if I survive to be the last Heretic within this realm." He looked back up. "Is that it? Is that what you have been keeping from me?"

"Oh damn, not good." Parker inched her way back against a rack of clothing and pulled down her new hat, as if trying to blend in before the fighting started. She grabbed a wooden coat hanger as well, as if planning to use it as a weapon.

"Alright, but just wait a moment." Digby took a step back and held up both hands, making a point to move closer to a pair of tailor's shears that lay on a counter. "I know this looks bad, but—"

"I don't—" Henwick raised a hand.

"Back off!" Digby threw off his attempt at civility and leapt backward to snatch the shears from the counter. He swiped them through the air. "No one is making use of my body but me. It may be dead, but it's mine and I'm not about to give it up without a fight."

Henwick blew out a long sigh and lowered his hand. "I have no interest in fighting."

"You don't?" Digby furrowed his brow.

"Wait, seriously?" Parker pushed her hat back up with the wooden coat hanger in her hand.

"No," Henwick growled back as if insulted that they thought he would. "I may not like you, Graves, but I can't blame you for protecting yourself. Especially when you have a war still to fight out there in the world. Nor could I stand in your way, knowing what Autem has done."

"Oh…" Digby hesitated a moment before realizing he was still holding the pair of shears in the cleric's direction. He shoved them behind his back. "Okay, well, I wouldn't blame me, either."

Henwick grimaced, clearly not appreciating the response. "I wouldn't want to possess the body of an undead monster, regardless. Nor should I desire to rob a young lady of her existence, either. I am a man of honor. Such acts would be unthinkable."

"Whew." Parker swept her hand across her forehead cartoonishly. "That's a relief."

Digby ignored her, opting to try to ascertain Henwick's plan. "What is it you intend to do then?"

Henwick closed his eyes for a moment before snapping them back open and locking them with his. "I wish to enter into a pact with you."

"A pact?" Digby tightened his grip on the shears he held behind his back, not liking the sound of the idea.

"Swear an oath to me, that when you return to the world, you will do as you have said you will. End Autem's reign and set things right." The cleric placed a hand to his chest. "In return, I will aid your survival long enough to escape this realm."

"But what about you?" Parker furrowed her brow, clearly doing the math.

"Once you have secured your escape." Henwick nodded decisively. "I will lay down my existence to ensure that you reach your home. You may be an unholy abomination and a scoundrel, but as you have said, there are people that need you. For now, I see no other way but to extend a chance for redemption."

Digby glanced around the abandoned shop for a second, having trouble processing what he'd heard. It had to be some sort of trick. If their situations were reversed, he would have clawed his way to the finish and absconded with Henwick's body without a second thought. Not to mention it was clear the cleric didn't like him. Obviously, he was trying to throw him off guard.

"Why should I believe you?" He held his ground.

Henwick screwed up his eyes as if Digby's continued suspicion was unthinkable. Then he blew out an exasperated gasp. "How truly twisted are you, Graves, to have so much trouble believing someone when they are trying to help you?"

Digby glanced at Parker, who only gave him a shrug, leaving him just as confused. Could Henwick really just want to help? Could he actually have no interest in double-crossing him? Would he really sacrifice his very existence to help him?

Could Henwick, really, just be a good person?

No. That would be ridiculous.

This was the man that ended the world. This was a man that would stop at nothing to destroy him and everyone that he'd ever come in contact with. Hell, this was the man that had ordered his men to steal children and indoctrinate them into his future army.

No. There was no possible way that the same man would have a truly altruistic side to him.

That was when Digby remembered what had transpired on the stairway earlier. Back there, in the face of danger, Henwick's first instinct was to stand his ground to buy time for him and Parker to escape. He had even risked his existence to help Parker reach the top when she nearly fell. He hadn't even thought twice about it.

Sure, Digby had never liked the man back when they had lived in the same village, but if he was honest, that might have had more to do with jealousy than anything else. Henwick had been well-liked by everyone back then. It wasn't hard to resent that fact when no one could stand being around him for more than an hour.

Digby furrowed his brow.

The Henwick he knew out in the world was a shrewd man with no qualms about leaving someone to die if it meant he could strengthen his grip on the world. Hell, from what Bancroft had told him, the man was a complete monster.

Then how could he be so noble here?

Unless the man out there had somehow changed? Eight hundred years was a long time and living without a soul for all of it could very well have taken a toll. Digby hesitated for a moment before reaching forward to place the shears back on the counter.

Then, he told the truth.

"You aren't dead, Henwick."

"What?" The cleric looked relieved.

"You aren't dead, but your body isn't exactly available either. So there is still no way for you to regain it. Though, you should know the truth, even if it hurts. If you plan on helping me, then I owe you that much." Digby forced out a sigh. "Autem didn't kill you after they removed your fragment of the Seed. You just sort of kept going without your spark."

"So I'm still alive?" Henwick's eyes darted around before adding, "How is that possible? I would have no soul!"

Digby shook his head. "I don't know how a man can live without a spark, but you did."

Henwick started to open his mouth, but Digby held up a hand to stop him.

"There's more, and I'm afraid it gets worse. I wasn't around for much of what happened. After I died, my zombified corpse drifted north in a small boat where it got trapped in ice. It wasn't until eight hundred years later that I got out."

Henwick's eyes bulged as his body began to tremble. "Good lord. How?"

"I don't know." Digby shrugged. "Something about melting ice. I was found and taken to—"

"Not your escape from the ice, Graves." Henwick shook his head frantically. "How is it possible that I have survived there for eight centuries? I removed my shard and cast aside the power of a Heretic. I should have grown old and perished without it."

"Yes, but as I said before, Autem discovered a new power," Digby added.

"You are one of their Guardians," Parker helped explain.

"Indeed." Digby leaned on a nearby counter. "Everything else I said was true. Autem manufactured a curse and spread it through the world to destroy everything that stood in their way."

"And you believe that I accepted their magic and joined them?" Henwick shook his head. "I never would have gone along with such a plan."

"As I said, it gets worse." Digby lowered his head. "You didn't just join them. You became their leader. You must have risen up the ranks while I was frozen. They don't share their immortality with many within their organization but, apparently, it is a perk of the few that sit at the top. That's why you haven't aged."

"At the top?" Henwick's face fell. "Impossible. How could I?"

"I don't blame you for having doubts, and I don't know how it all came to pass." Digby laid everything bare. "But I have seen you with my own eyes. You sit at the apex of the organization. The man you have become out there holds sway over all of Autem's actions. None dare oppose you."

Henwick slammed a first down on the table. "You mean to tell me that I destroyed the world. You expect me to believe that I murdered millions."

"Billions," Parker corrected in a tone far too serious for her. "The world's population had grown since your time."

"Billions…" Henwick staggered as he placed a hand to his head.

"I wish I was lying." Digby pushed off the counter and stepped closer. "Just imagine how it was for me. I woke up centuries after my death and had to make sense of all this while finding out that the most popular hunter from my village was still around and wanted me dead."

"But I wouldn't do any of that." Henwick heaved several deep breaths. "I wouldn't—"

"I know, I know." Digby stepped closer but refrained from touching him. "I am realizing that the person you are here within the Seed is not the same man that I have encountered out there. I don't know if it was the weight of the last eight hundred years, or the fact that you have existed without a soul the entire time, but the Henwick beyond this place has become someone else entirely."

"I… I need to sit down." Henwick struggled to stay standing.

"I got you." Parker grabbed a dusty chair and dragged it over just in time for him to drop into it.

"We'll give you a few minutes to process this." Digby stepped away, gesturing to Parker to follow as he slipped away from the distraught cleric. If there was one thing he understood, learning so much so fast was hard to handle. If there was a second thing he understood, it was that he was not good at helping someone cope.

"Is he going to be okay?" Parker followed him to the back of the dark shop where the cleric was less likely to hear them.

"I don't know, but he had to hear the truth." Digby glanced in Henwick's direction, as the man sat with his hands pressed to his face. "Now we just have to see if he finds some sort of resolve or if the knowledge of what he has become breaks him."

"It's weird." She looked away. "Other than being kind of grabby and a little sexist, he doesn't seem evil."

"I know." Digby deflated. "That was something I was not expecting. I certainly had no love for the man back in my day, but

I'm starting to think that my disdain for him had more to do with who I am than who he was."

"And are you okay?" She looked up at him.

"What? Yes, I'm fine." He brushed off her concern. "It will take more than my enemy revealing that they are not the monster that I thought to shake my deceased nerves at this point."

"No, I don't mean with Henwick." She placed a hand on his arm. "I mean about the caretaker."

Digby froze as soon as she mentioned the monster, its familiar voice still fresh in its mind.

"You looked really freaked out when that thing started shouting your name." She held onto his sleeve only for him to yank his arm away.

"I'm fine." He tried and failed to suppress a shudder.

"You don't seem fine." She didn't let up.

"Oh look, Henwick looks like he's doing better." Digby tried to change the subject.

Parker glanced at the cleric, who was still very much not alright. "He still looks pretty bad. But honestly, you don't look better. Sorry I hit a nerve, but you should probably talk about it with someone."

"Fine," Digby snapped at her. "That thing sounded exactly like my father, okay? Are you happy now that you dragged that outta me?"

"Umm, no." She looked embarrassed. "I didn't mean talk to me about it. I meant, like, talk to Becca later when we aren't hiding in a weird shop that's built from the memory of some Heretic of the past that may or may not be Dracula. I don't know how to deal with your past family of trauma. I can barely handle my own issues."

"Then why did you ask?" he growled back.

"I don't know." She shrugged. "I'm not good at this stuff and I'm trying my best."

"Good lord." He rubbed at the bridge of his nose. "I say, your best is not quite working."

"Clearly not." She pulled off her hat and slapped him with it. "We both know I'm a mess, so let's not hold that against me."

"Alright, alright." He raised a hand to defend himself until she ceased her attack. They both remained silent for a moment before she spoke again.

"But, now that I know, why would the caretaker make itself sound like your dad?" She stared at him again despite her previous statement of not wanting to. "You have father issues or something?"

"Of course I have issues, Parker." He dragged his hand down his face in frustration. "My mother died in childbirth and my father blamed me for it. Named me Digby and everything. Said I dig the graves of people better than me. The man hated me more than I have ever hated myself."

Parker's eyes widened. "That's fucked up."

"Indeed." He turned away from her only to feel her arms wrap around him. "What the devil are you doing?"

"Oh, you poor zombie, so much makes sense now." She held firm. "Anyone would be all kinds of screwed up with a childhood like that."

"Yes, yes, now get off of me." Digby pried her hands loose.

"Sorry." She gave him a dumb smile. "Just thought you needed a hug."

"Well, I don't." He folded his arms in defiance.

"Yeah, you do, but I won't force it." She leaned to one side. "Not like I want to hug a corpse anyway. I was just taking one for the team."

"Whatever." Digby stepped away from the maddening woman. "I'm checking on Henwick."

"That's fair." She pulled her hat back on and followed.

When they returned, the cleric did indeed seem to be doing better. The panic and uncertainty in his eyes were gone, though Digby wasn't sure how he felt about what had replaced it.

In short, the man looked angry.

"Graves." Henwick snapped his eyes up to him as he placed a hand firmly on the table before him. "I understand that there is no hope that I will ever leave this place, but I will say this. Everything Autem has done has been in the name of God and His nine angels. And I refuse to believe that the Almighty would desire such a thing. Which is why I say that, in the name of God Himself, Autem must pay for its crimes. The world must be set right."

"I can't say I believe in the Almighty, but I agree." Digby tried to stand tall. "What Autem has done is unforgivable."

Parker stepped closer. "And you are okay with helping us, even if that mean you will—"

"Yes." He didn't let her finish. "If I have done everything that Graves has said I have done out there, then so must I pay for my crimes as well." His face softened a bit. "All I ask is that you continue on in my stead."

Digby opened his mouth to accept the terms of the man's last request. He closed it again as a scream echoed from somewhere outside. It sounded feminine. All three of them snapped their eyes to the broken window that led to the street as the lingering reverberations of the sound trailed off.

"It seems our earlier assumption was correct." Henwick clenched his fist.

"Indeed," Digby added. "We are not alone here."

CHAPTER EIGHTEEN

"That was a scream, right?" Parker peeked out from the edge of the shop's window.

"I think that's safe to say." Digby crept forward as well.

"That must have been the voice of another Heretic that has been trapped here the same as I." Henwick set a foot on the broken opening of the window to climb out. "She may be in danger. We must make haste before a potential ally falls victim to whatever has caused her to cry out."

"I don't think so." Digby glanced to his HUD to check the Seed's current population.

48/2

The total had dropped by a few recently. Odds were, that scream had belonged to one of the Heretics that had perished. Though, he couldn't be sure.

"Could the caretaker have caught up to us already?" Parker followed him through the window.

"Not likely." Digby went through last. "Despite that monster's persistence, it was not what I would call fast."

"Which way did that scream come from?" Parker spun around, taking in their surroundings.

The street was dark, with only the dim light of lamp posts to illuminate the space. Digby's shadow stretched out across the stone. There was a layer of grime on practically every surface as if the city was actively rotting.

"I'm not sure where that scream came from." Digby stared down the stretch of cobblestones and darkened windows. "I certainly wish Rebecca was here right now."

Parker folded her arms. "Well sorry, you're still stuck with me."

"Oh, don't be childish." Digby groaned. "Rebecca has the perception attribute of a bloodhound. I would simply feel more comfortable with her senses to alert us of a threat."

"That's fair." Parker nodded. "I'm only good for dumb jokes and profanity."

"Indeed." Digby followed behind Henwick, who seemed to have a renewed interest in moving forward. Apparently, finding out that a soulless version of himself had ushered in the apocalypse would do that. "Over there."

The cleric took off running toward an alleyway further down the street, forcing Digby to break into a run to keep up. It wasn't easy to spot through the shadows of the street, but as he approached, he sensed the blood.

A human foot stuck out from behind one of the buildings.

A woman's shoe lay nearby.

"She might be alive." Henwick dropped to a knee to help.

"No, it's too late." Digby slowed to a walk. "I don't sense any blood flowing."

The reason why became obvious when he rounded the corner.

Blood pooled around the body, soaking through the woman's clothing. Digby didn't recognize the style of her garments. It didn't seem to fit the time that he came from, nor did it fit the designs of the present that he had come to know. All he could tell was that it looked uncomfortable.

"Damn, we're too late." Henwick sighed and rested an elbow on his knee.

"Check her throat." Parker peaked around the building. "You know, in case of Dracula bites."

"Oh yes. Of course." Henwick tilted the dead woman's head as if Parker's suggestion hadn't been a joke.

Digby rolled his eyes. "It wasn't Dracula. There's a wound on her abdomen."

Henwick gasped as he rolled the body over to find a six-inch gash across her stomach. "Who would do such a thing to a lady?"

"You would be surprised at what people will do." Digby tried to ignore the man's naïveté. "The world is an unfriendly place. But more importantly. Where did she come from? And does this place come from her memory?"

"Judging from her clothes, she was from Victorian England, like the rest of this place." Parker gestured to the street around them. "She must have been a Heretic from back then."

"And are you basing that assumption off this Dracula movie you keep mentioning?" Digby eyed her.

"Kind of." She frowned. "Okay, yeah, I'm not an expert on history. Sue me. I'm right, though. I mean, sure, there's no Keanu Reeves or anything, but everything else fits."

"I don't know who that is." Digby ignored her.

"That's a shame," she added.

"Yes, I'm sure this Keanu person is very important." Henwick stood up. "But the question still remains of how this woman met her fate. I don't see anyone else around."

"Maybe she wasn't the only Heretic that lived close to this time period." Parker hopped over the corpse to stand on the other side of the alleyway, being careful not to step in the blood. "The Seed might've created this place from the memories of more than one person and shoved them together. I mean, that jester got tossed into the castle down below with you guys, so the same is probably true up here."

"If that's the case, then there could even be several more Heretics skulking around." Digby checked the number at the corner of his vision.

46/2

A couple more Heretics must have killed each other in an attempt to be the last ones standing. The competition was beginning to heat up now that the souls trapped within the Seed seemed to have begun to run into each other. Digby fidgeted with the buttons of his new vest. "Considering our situation, we should be careful. I doubt we will find many friendly faces here."

"True, though we may also find a potential ally that can be swayed to our side," Henwick added.

"Yes, yes, of course." Digby humored the man despite being pretty sure they would find no more allies. Besides, things were complicated enough with just the three of them. He shifted his focus to the woman's body on the ground and opened his maw. "Either way, I have a corpse to eat."

"What in the devil are you doing, man?" Henwick grabbed his shoulder.

"Unhand me," Digby snapped back as he lost focus on his maw. It closed just as the woman's body was sinking into his void. The resulting division severed the woman's head with a pop before sending it rolling into the wall with a wet spatter.

"Ew! That sound is going to stick with me." Parker shuddered and closed her eyes as she flailed her hands a bit.

"You cannot just devour a woman's corpse. Show some respect, Graves." Henwick finally let go of his shoulder.

"It's a little late now." Digby gestured to the head. "And what does it matter? This place isn't even real. We're all just essence swirling around within the Heretic Seed."

"Well, yes, but—"

"But nothing. Waste not, want not." Digby snapped his fingers and opened his maw again. "Considering our situation, I shall be eating every corpse that I get the chance to. I'm still working off a fraction of my capabilities, and we need every bit of power we can get if we are to make it to the end of this ridiculous contest."

Henwick stood for a moment with his mouth open, as if he still wanted to argue but couldn't come up with a valid reason.

"That's what I thought." Digby glanced to Parker. "Do me a favor and kick that head into my void."

"Ew, no." She scrunched up her nose. "Do it yourself."

"Fine." Digby forced out a long sigh at her refusal before taking on the task. The head vanished into his maw a second later. "See? Nothing to be concerned about."

"Okay sure, but that definitely is." Parker thrust a hand out to point back into the street behind him.

"What?" Digby spun around, ready to cast Flare at whoever was sure to be sneaking up on him. His brow furrowed a second later as he caught a glimpse of two glowing red flickers in the shadows of the alleyway across the street. "The hell is that?"

A second set of glowing lights appeared as well, followed by a third. Then, slowly, a foot stepped into the light. Digby arched an eyebrow as a man wearing a long, ragged coat appeared. His body was thin and his eyes glowed crimson in a way that reminded Digby of the serpentine form of the caretaker. The same grime that clung to everything within the street coated his skin and clothes.

Two more men stepped out of the shadows behind him, a strange stiffness about their movements. Something supernatural, like their limbs didn't quite want to obey their minds.

"Who goes there?" Henwick stepped forward with a hand raised.

"Holy shit, it is Dracula!" Parker threw a hand out in the figure's direction.

"Don't be foolish." Digby focused on the man, getting a message from the Seed in response.

Fractured Spark, Hostile.

"That's enough confirmation for me." He immediately cast Flare, sending the trio darting out of the way as the spell gathered power. A detonation of energy lit up the street for an instant, yet the blast caught nothing.

"Damn!" Digby struggled to keep the three figures in his view as they scattered. He checked his mana.

MP: 246/291

"What the hell is a fractured spark?" Parker retreated to his side and pulled out a wooden hangar that she'd apparently taken from the shop they'd looted.

"I don't know, but they are fast and don't seem to have an interest in talking." Digby ran through his spells in his mind, trying to think of something that he might actually be able to catch one of them with. A part of him regretted eating that woman's body a moment ago. At least if he had a corpse around, he could animate it or use it for parts to cast Cremation.

Before he could come up with a way to fight, the fractured spark wearing the tall hat dashed forward.

"Very well." Digby raised his fists. "We do this the non-magical way."

That was when the thin man stopped short and snapped his fingers.

"What?" Digby's jaw dropped as the temperature around him and Parker began to rise, embers flickering into life on all sides. Sparks grew into a circle of flames before constricting inward. "Get down." He grabbed the collar of Parker's new jacket and yanked her to the cobblestones.

"Oof." She dropped as Digby threw up an Absorb in panic.

The fractured spark spell swept inward and burst into a column of flame. It poured into his palm, leaving him a little singed. Digby's eyes widened. That must have been the next tier of fire-based spells after Fireball.

Parker shot back up.

"Shit! I almost had my hair burned off again." She pulled her hat off to check.

"Indeed." Digby flicked his attention back to the fractured spark in the tall hat. He could open his maw, but he was sure that the man would simply leap out of the way.

Not if I pin him in place.

Digby opened his maw, keeping it small, and cast Blood Forge, hoping he had enough resources in his void at least for what he needed. A small barb shot up through the shadowy hole in the street at an angle to pierce the foot of the man in the tall hat. The fractured spark tried to jump away.

"Too late!" Digby opened his maw and dragged the man down. He snapped it shut the moment he vanished, leaving only his ridiculous hat.

Fractured Spark defeated. 930 experience awarded.

Digby snapped his vision to Henwick, ready to shout at him to demand that he lend a hand. The complaint got lodged in his throat when he realized the cleric was already battling the other two threats. A blast of light came from Henwick's hand, knocking the legs out from under the larger of the two fractured sparks just as the other sent an icicle into his shoulder. Henwick let out a pained grunt but didn't flinch.

"We need to help him." Parker got moving.

"You think?" Digby kicked off as well, checking his mana as he ran.

MP: 186/291

Still plenty.

Digby raised a hand to focus on the ground near the spark that had been tossing icicles around. "Hold on, Henwick, we're—"

His words were cut off as the other threat threw a hand out toward the street, causing all the moisture in the air to condense and freeze in a layer covering the stone. Digby lost his focus as he struggled to stay upright. His arms flailed as his feet slid forward. Finding his center, he raised a leg to stop himself as he careened toward a wall. He planted his foot against the bricks, letting his deceased muscles absorb the impact.

"Nice try." Digby spun around just as Parker flew past him. Unable to stop, she hit the wall with a solid thump before bouncing off and landing on the ground next to him.

"What the shit, that hurt." She held her elbow and hissed air through her teeth.

Digby suppressed a groan and returned his attention to the fractured spark that had produced the sheet of ice. Without another thought, he dropped his eyes to the street and opened his maw to cast Forge. A barbed spike shot up, but this time the spark saw it coming and hopped back.

"Damn, guess that isn't going to work twice." Digby lamented the fact that he'd wasted valuable resources, even if it was just a little. The foe responded by casting another spell to cover the ground around it in ice. Clearly, the spark was trying to defend itself. Digby changed his strategy, looking down and casting forge on his own feet. The spell sent the blood in his body down to pierce his new shoes and form a layer of spikes for traction. Sure, he wouldn't be able to get them off easily, but at least he could move on ice without struggling. The Heretic Seed rewarded his improvisation with a new rank for the spell.

The spell, Blood Forge, has increased from rank C to B. You may now reform your forged objects one time after creation at the expense of 10 MP.

WARNING: A blood forged object will lose durability when reformed.

"That should help." Digby rushed forward, his spiked shoes chipping into the frozen ground with each step. The fractured spark raised a hand as moisture swirled in the air to form a spike of ice. Digby responded by throwing out a hand to open his maw on his palm. He cast forge to block, sending a spiral of crimson out from the center of his hand to make a one-foot-wide shield. The spark launched their attack, the icicle shattering against Digby's Blood defense. He kept running, his shield plowing into the threat.

With a thought, he tested out his spell's new upgrade.

All at once, the disc of blood folded in on itself, some of it partially becoming liquid again before reshaping into a thick spike that exploded out of the spark's back. The forged weapon snapped off a second later, demonstrating the loss of durability from being reforged.

Fractured Spark defeated. 930 experience awarded.

"I am going to get a lot of use out of that little enhancement." Digby tossed aside the remaining piece of what was once a shield. He glanced at his HUD as more messages came in.

You have reached level 35. 10,244 experience to next level.
All attributes have increased by 1.
You have 1 additional attribute point to allocate.

For an instant, he nearly willed his extra point into intelligence like he usually did, but thought better of it before the choice locked in. It was true that he would always need the mana. That fact was especially true now, where he lacked the minions to Leach MP from.

Is that really the best choice?

Technically, he could drain mana from Parker if she was willing. It wasn't like she had any spells to make use of the power anyway. Besides, after witnessing how strong that jester was earlier, Digby was starting to see the benefits of investing in agility. He had already seen some benefit to it as it was.

He glanced at his mana.

MP: 123/298

Digby nodded to himself and tossed the point into his agility. He'd always been a hands-on kind of necromancer, so the choice made sense.

With that, he turned his attention back to his most recent kill and spent another few points to open his maw wide enough to get the body in. He snapped it shut as soon as the spark vanished. It wasn't much, but he was at least able to use a few of his abilities again.

That was when a loud boom drew his attention behind him. Spinning to find the source, he found Henwick on the ground near a building, clutching at his chest as if injured. The remaining spark stood several feet away, larger than any of the others.

"What are you doing down there, Henwick? You can't handle one of these things?" Digby stepped toward the cleric.

The cleric answered him by coughing out a mouthful of blood and casting a Regeneration spell.

"Fine, I'll do it myself." Digby marched up to the last and largest of the sparks and opened his maw in his hand.

"Wait!" Henwick choked out. "Don't get so close—"

His words were cut off as the fragment turned to Digby and clapped his hands together. There wasn't even time to cast Blood Forge before a shockwave of energy slammed into him. Flipping through the air, end over end, he flew until he hit something solid. The sound of a dozen bones snapping struck his ears as he landed on the ground. A moment of confusion passed before he was able to clear the fog from his senses. Sitting up, he realized he had been thrown clear across the street. He raised a hand, only for his wrist to flop to the side like a sack of rocks.

"That's not good." Digby cast Necrotic Regeneration and watched as everything began to pop back into place. Then he snapped his eyes back to the spark, standing in the middle of the street. His vision drifted over to Henwick who was still regenerating his own body. The cleric must have been hit with the same shockwave like-spell.

Come to think of it, what even was that spell?

Probably something from the knight class.

One spark had used fire magic that Digby hadn't seen before as well. Whoever these foes had been in life must have been fairly high-level Heretics. The only question was how the hell they got there. He had no idea what made someone a fractured spark instead of a remnant spark.

He checked the numbers at the corner of his vision. They still read forty-six out of two, even after Digby had killed two of them. Apparently, whatever a fractured spark was, it wasn't considered part of the Seed's little death match. Either way, they were still hostile and considering they showed little interest in speaking or even a reaction to pain, he assumed they were no longer sentient. Just some kind of lingering ghost of someone that had once come in contact with the Seed's power.

Considering the strength of the spark's magic, the only reason he and his accomplices had not been killed outright was that these entities didn't seem capable of strategy or conscious thought. Then again, with that weird shockwave spell in play, there was no way to get close.

That was when the fractured spark suddenly lurched forward.

The familiar sound of a blade sliding into flesh met Digby's ears. He squinted at the threat, finding nothing around it. Then, the air began to ripple behind the spark, revealing a slender man wearing another one of those ridiculous tall hats. A billowing, black coat hung from his shoulders.

"Dracula!" Parker thrusted out a finger as she struggled to stand up on the sheet of ice where she'd slipped earlier.

"For the last time. It is not." Digby tried to analyze the man, hoping his view wasn't obstructed too much by the dying spark in front of him to block the Seed's analyze ability. For a moment there was nothing, except the vague sense of mana flowing through blood, as if the spark was trying to cast one last spell. Its hand began to rise, only for the man behind to drive a blade deeper into the spark's back.

Heretic, level 58 Rogue, Friendly.

Digby let out a relieved sigh, thanking the Seed that the man wasn't, in fact, a Dracula. Well, that and the fact that he was labeled as friendly. "See, he's just a rogue."

"Oh." Parker looked a little disappointed.

"Who are you?" Henwick demanded as he spat out a mouthful of blood and started to get to his feet.

The rogue answered by stabbing the fractured spark another ten or so times before dropping the body. The corpse crumpled to the stone at his feet, leaving him standing there with a bloody knife gleaming in the dim lamplight.

"You heard my accomplice over there." Digby stepped forward with caution at the man's level. "Who are you?"

The slender man merely pulled a handkerchief from his pocket and wiped the blood from his knife. The blade was narrow, like something a medical professional might use. He slipped it back into a hidden sheath in his jacket, then took off his hat and bowed.

"It is a pleasure to meet you, my fellow Heretics." He kept his body bent but looked up to make eye contact as a warm smile grew across his face. "I believe the newspapers have been calling me Jack."

CHAPTER NINETEEN

Hawk crept through the hall of the casino toward the stairwell that led to the high-roller suite where the Heretic Seed's obelisk was kept. It had been days since Rebecca and Mason had gone off on that mission to the dam. From what he'd heard, it had gone well. The only reason they hadn't come back yet was that they were working out how to get the dam's electricity to the strip. It would definitely be cool to be able to run more lights than just the bare minimum.

Then again, the darkened hallways were perfect for sneaking.

After eavesdropping on every conversation for the last few days, Hawk had figured out how Bancroft and his guys had gotten their magic back. Apparently, all he had to do was touch the Seed's obelisk and all the power he had as a Guardian would be given back. Except he would be a Heretic instead. He may have only been level one, but still, he had two spells and the ability to get stronger. He wasn't about to sit in his room and do nothing when he had a shot at getting his magic back.

At least that way, he could actually do something to help while Dig was out of commission. A little fantasy of surprising the zombie with a new class or a useful spell when he woke up passed through Hawk's mind.

Yeah, that would be badass.

With Becca, Mason, Parker, and Dig all away, that only left Alex to ask if he could have his magic back. Unfortunately, the nerd had been locked away in the forge to work for days.

Hawk assumed Alex's busy schedule had something to do with the fact that Parker and Dig were out cold. He'd played enough board games with them to know that Alex would be worried. Hell, so was he. They were the closest things to a family that he had. Sure, one of them was a sarcastic walking corpse and the other was a lazy pink-haired soldier, but it was the apocalypse, and he wasn't going to be picky.

That was why he hadn't been nagging Alex for magic every five minutes.

If he was working on a way to get Parker and Dig back, then he wasn't about to disturb him while he was working. Well, that wasn't the only reason. There was also the fact that he wasn't entirely confident that Alex would let him have his magic even if he asked.

There was no way he was going to ask Bancroft either. He wasn't even sure what that guy was in charge of in Vegas.

Hence the need for sneaking.

Hawk slinked up against a wall to make sure the coast was clear. There wasn't anybody in sight. He wished he still had his magic. At least then he could use it to cancel out the sound of his footsteps. After all, he was pretty sure that getting caught would mean no magic.

Ever so gently, he opened the door of the stairwell before slipping inside. Heading down from the guest floors, he made his way toward the high-roller suite. The sound of voices trailed up from the bottom as he peeked over the edge.

"You hear we're getting electricity?" A man with a rifle stood near the door that led to the high-roller suite. "No shortages or rationing either."

"Yeah, that's gonna be sweet." A second man bracketed the other side.

Hawk released a quiet sigh. Of course they'd have guards keeping people out.

He'd seen the two men before. They weren't Heretics or anything, but they did work for Deuce. According to Hawk's investigation, the Seed's fragments had been put back together to make some kind of big ass block of obsidian. He'd assumed it was still in the high-roller suite, but the fact that Deuce had guys guarding the floor confirmed it.

As annoying as it was that they stood in his way, he couldn't really fault Deuce for wanting to keep the obelisk under watch. Especially with Bancroft hanging around. Supposedly there was no way for the guy to steal the Seed and betray them without Tavern killing him in the process, but it was still better to be safe than sorry.

He shook his head. It didn't matter why the guards were there.

No, what mattered was finding a way to get past them without getting sent straight back upstairs with nothing to show for his effort.

Again, Hawk grumbled to himself at the loss of his magic. He searched his pockets for something to distract the men with. All he found was a pack of gum and a poker chip. His first thought was to throw the chip down the stairs and hope that the guards went to investigate. He actually got into position, holding the item over the railing, before thinking about it further.

Wait... He pulled his hand back. *This isn't a video game. It's not like they will just go looking and assume it was the wind.* Hawk shoved the chip back in his pocket.

Then he got a better idea.

Why the hell am I even hiding?

If there was one thing that Dig had taught him, it was that stealth wasn't the only option. Not when you could just walk right in. Hell, after everything that he'd done back on Autem's base with Alvin and whatnot, the guard should give him a fist bump and let him right on through.

Hawk stood tall and waltzed down the stairs like he hadn't been sneaking around a moment before and tried his best to act like he was not up to no good.

"Whoa, kid." One of Deuce's guys held up a hand the moment he saw him. "Whatcha doing here this late?"

"Oh hey, what's up?" He kept up the act. "Alex asked me to meet him in the high-roller suite to help with something."

"He asked a kid for help?" The other guard arched an eyebrow. "'Cause Deuce said not to let anyone in."

"Oh yeah, you definitely shouldn't let anyone in." Hawk stepped forward and reached for the door as if he was somehow exempt from his own statement.

"Umm. Yeah." One of the men stared at him awkwardly as he moved to block the door. "So that means you don't get to go in."

"Oh, that's funny." Hawk let out a chuckle. "I just snuck into Autem's base to help Dig take them down. Trust me, if anyone has a pass to go through, it's me."

"Wait just a sec—" one of the guards started to push back, but the other stepped in to cut him off.

"Okay, yeah, that's true. I was there when you warned us all about Skyline's plans." The guard placed a hand on his shoulder. "That was hella brave for a kid. Letting yourself get taken and all just to give us an edge."

"Umm, okay." The first guard backed down.

"Thanks." Hawk nodded. "I know it's hard for everyone to stay organized with Dig out. I just hope Alex can figure out a way to wake him up soon."

With that, he pushed through the door and into the hallway.

For a moment, he half expected one of the guards to grab his shoulder or call out, but in the end, neither did.

Like clockwork.

Unable to resist the urge, Hawk circled back to the door as soon as it closed behind him and placed his ear to its surface. The muffled voices of the two guards were still audible.

"That kid really did all that?" one of them asked.

"Yeah," the other answered. "Probably saved all our asses in the process."

Damn right. Hawk let a giddy smile take over his face as he continued along, creeping his way toward the high-roller suite and the Seed's obelisk.

Reaching the door, he slipped inside. He nearly froze as soon as he did.

There it was.

The Heretic Seed.

It was so much smaller than he'd thought it would be. For some reason, he was expecting it to be massive, but in reality, it was no taller than the average adult. Despite that, he could practically feel the power within calling to him. It was like it wanted him to have it. For a moment, he questioned if he should touch it, like that might be something that he couldn't take back.

He shook off the thought.

Now wasn't the time to hesitate. The Heretic Seed's power was needed. Even if it came with a side effect, after seeing everything that Digby had sacrificed to fight Autem, he was willing to take his chances. Hell, all those kids he'd met back on the base needed to be saved. He may not have gotten along with any of them, but that didn't mean they deserved to be twisted by the Guardian rings the way Alvin had been.

Hawk took a deep breath. He would have his magic back. That much he was sure of.

That was when someone turned on the light.

"Eep!" He jumped several feet in the air as he spun to find Alex sitting in a chair by the door.

"Hi Hawk." He waved at him with a notebook that he had in his other hand as if he'd been sitting there the whole time working on something.

"Shit hell bitch!" Hawk hissed and let out a growl as he simultaneously caught his breath.

"That was an awful lot of swear words for a twelve-year-old." Alex laughed.

"The world ended; I'll swear if I want. What the hell were you doing sitting in the dark?" Hawk tried to draw the focus away from why he had been sneaking around at night.

"I wasn't sitting in the dark." Alex shrugged. "I turned the light off when you started down the hallway. I thought you might be one of Bancroft's guys."

"Okay, well, I'm not. And how did you know I was in the hall?" He kept the questions coming to steer him away from why he was there.

"Oh, that part's cool." He pulled an object from his pocket and tossed it into the room as if he couldn't wait to show it to someone. Hawk watched as it fell toward the floor only to split apart right before landing, leaving two metal rods floating near the floor a few feet apart. In the center between them, sat a third, resting on the carpet.

"Umm, okay?" Hawk stared at the things.

"It's a security sensor." Alex stood up and grabbed the piece that had fallen to the floor before handing it to Hawk. A second later, he turned and walked between the two rods that were floating. The instant he did, the piece of metal in Hawk's hand vibrated, like a phone on silent.

"Oh weird." He flinched, not expecting the sudden sensation.

"Cool, right?" Alex reclaimed the item. "This piece notifies me when someone passes between the other two. I have a pair set out there in the hall at both ends. That way I'll know if anyone goes near the Seed no matter where I am in the city." He slapped his notebook down on a table and waved Hawk over, clearly excited to talk about his work. "Check this out."

Stepping to his side, Hawk looked over a page filled with some kind of runes. Alex had scribbled hundreds of combinations, circling some and crossing out others. A few runes were drawn larger with a word underneath. One was labeled float, while another read ward. "What are they?"

"It's like a programming language, but for magic." He sighed. "I haven't cracked it yet, but I'm getting there. I wish I had taken some classes in Java or something back in college, instead of majoring in English. I don't really have the knowledge I need, but I have talked to a few people that do to point me in the right direction."

"So you just have to carve these symbols into things?" Hawk furrowed his brow, having trouble believing that things could be that easy.

"No. I had hoped that was the case, but when I tried, I didn't get any results." He held a hand out over the edge of the poker table as a rune etched itself into the side. "I gained an engraving spell after trying it several times. That was the key. It takes a ton of mana, though."

"Why?"

"The runes seem to need a flow of mana to jumpstart their enchantments." Alex pumped his eyebrows. "I'm just glad I'm a class that can learn it. Actually, I'm starting to think that this is an artificer's real purpose."

"That's neat." Hawk did his best to humor the big nerd while he geeked out.

"Honestly, I can't stop imagining the things that I can create. I mean, hoverboards are first on the list, 'cause you know, cool. But after that, the sky's the limit. Actually, we know magic can get us to the moon, so maybe setting the limit at the sky is thinking too small." Alex glanced upward before adding, "Maybe space?"

"I don't know if I want to go to space in something you made." Hawk snorted while glancing at the Heretic Seed's obelisk, wondering if Alex would say anything if he approached it. That was when the artificer turned his head halfway to look at him sideways.

"What are you doing here so late?"

"Umm." Hawk stalled and glanced around the room. "I'm here to check on Dig, you know, just kinda missed him is all."

"Really?" Alex arched an eyebrow. "'Cause we moved him upstairs with Parker where Lana could keep an eye on them."

"Oh, I didn't know that." Hawk played dumb.

"Really?" the artificer repeated in an increasingly skeptical tone. "'Cause we weren't quiet about that, and right now, it looks like you were trying to sneak in to touch the obelisk to get your magic back."

Hawk's face fell. "I don't know what you're talking about."

Alex didn't say anything in return. Instead, he let his eyes do the accusing for him.

"Okay, fine." Hawk pouted as he blew out a frustrated sigh. "I want to help and I can't do that without magic."

"Ah." Alex stood there for a long moment without responding. Then, to Hawk's surprise, he simply gestured to the Seed with a nonchalant, "Go for it."

"Wait, what?" Hawk's jaw dropped.

"I mean, have at it, I guess." Alex walked up to the obelisk and sighed. "I've only known Dig for a month, but I think I know what he'd want. And I think he'd want you to be a Heretic."

"But he didn't want me to be a Guardian." Hawk cocked his head to the side.

"Yeah, but that was only because of the risks it posed to you and Vegas. I don't think he cares if you have magic. Actually, I think he'd rather you get a few levels to make you a little more resilient if things ever go bad." He scratched at his head for a second before abruptly hopping between Hawk and the obelisk to stop him from touching it. "But you do have to agree to some rules first."

"Like what?" Hawk stared at him, not sure if he was going to like what he was about to hear.

"Okay, well, it's like…" He seemed to be having trouble putting the thought together before finally coming up with something. "No taking risks. Like, at all. Magic or not, I know Dig wouldn't want you putting yourself in danger."

"But how am I supposed to get stronger?" Hawk raised his voice on instinct, sensing the usual unfairness that adults usually forced on him.

"I know." The artificer held up his hands. "I get what it feels like for people to exclude you from the important stuff. It wasn't that long ago that I felt kinda left out of things too. But if I let you touch that obelisk, you have to trust that I have more experience out there. Things can go wrong fast and if you get yourself killed, it's only going to hurt Dig."

Hawk opened his mouth to argue but something about Alex's last statement stuck with him. Digby wasn't exactly affectionate, but he was the only adult that had treated him like he mattered. No one had done that since his adoptive parents.

"Alright, fine. I won't do anything risky."

"Good." Alex nodded. "Once we have a few things figured out, we can put together a group to take you, and probably Lana, out to get some experience. We should be able to get you through the low levels pretty fast, and that should be enough to give you what you need to be safe. Beyond that, you are not to go out on your own. You have to respect that, okay? No cheating. Do you get it? And I say that as someone who has played a lot of board games with you."

"Yeah." He groaned a little but didn't argue.

"Okay, then." Alex stepped aside to let him pass.

"What will happen?" Hawk stepped toward the Seed.

"When I got my magic, I passed out for a half-hour in the middle of Seattle while Dig and his horde surrounded me." Alex gave him a wicked smile before adding, "But none of Bancroft's guys lost consciousness, so I'm pretty sure you'll just regain whatever you had before without a problem."

"Okay?" Hawk didn't like the uncertainty in Alex's voice. Though, it wasn't going to stop him either. He reached out and touched the obelisk without hesitation. It seemed best to do it quickly, like ripping off a Band-Aid.

A few seconds passed where nothing happened.

"What the hell, where's my—" He abruptly closed his mouth when he noticed a tiny circle floating at the corner of his vision. His mana readout appeared next.

MP: 122/122

"Oh." The numbers faded away as soon as he stopped looking at them. It was so much better than the Guardian Core's HUD. That thing had been a pain in the ass and gave him a headache if he kept it active. Fortunately, the Seed seemed to be less intrusive.

He took a moment to look over his stats.

CONSTITUTION: 15
DEFENSE: 9
STRENGTH: 10
DEXTERITY: 17
AGILITY: 15
INTELLIGENCE: 18
PERCEPTION: 17
WILL: 16

It was good to see the numbers again.

"You good?" Alex leaned down a little to look him in the eyes.

"Yeah." He nodded, unable to suppress a childish grin. He was back on track to becoming a rogue.

"Cool." Alex grabbed his notebook off the table. "Now why don't we head down to the dining area? It's late, but I bet we can find something to celebrate with, right?"

"Fuck yeah!" Hawk hopped toward the door, getting a judgmental look from Alex in the process. "What? I said it's the apocalypse, who cares if I swear?"

Alex just sighed. "Yeah, I guess."

After that, they closed the door to the high-roller suite, checked on the magical alert system the artificer had rigged up, and headed downstairs to the dining area.

They both hesitated as soon as they reached it.

The tables were mostly empty with it being so late, but a few people were still there. Most had probably missed dinner due to whatever task they had been working on to support the casino. With Becca sending so many people from the Hoover Dam, the place needed a lot of work in order to get everyone settled.

Hawk assumed Alex was hesitating for the same reason as him. The reason being that one person, in particular, was sitting at one of the tables near the edge of the room.

Alvin.

The slightly older boy sat with his sister, Lana, looking just as down in the dumps as usual.

"We should probably go check in with them, right?" Alex looked down at Hawk as if he already knew the answer was yes but was still hoping he might say no to give them an out.

Hawk didn't give him the exit. "Yeah. That's what Dig would want us to do."

"Probably right." Alex started walking again.

Campbell waved as soon as he saw them. Hawk was surprised that the big guy was still there. They had enough people working the kitchen at that point, so it wasn't like he needed to be there all the time. Then again, he might have just been a dedicated person.

Hawk followed Alex's lead as they approached the table where Lana and Alvin sat.

"Hey." Lana gave them both a polite wave when it became obvious that they were heading for her. Then she elbowed her brother in the ribs.

"Hi," Alvin added, avoiding eye contact.

Hawk remained silent, having no idea what to say to the kid. He had only really interacted with him before under the cover of lies.

"What're you two doing here so late?" Alex sat down.

"I just went to check on Parker." She hooked a thumb at her brother. "Had to take this one with me on account of his tendency to defect to the enemy whenever you turn your back."

"You…" Alvin started to speak but closed his mouth a second later, prompting her to elbow him again.

"Spit it out, you don't get to play the quiet role anymore." Her voice was harsh but with an element of warmth lurking underneath.

"You don't have to treat me like a prisoner." Alvin finished his comment.

"Umm, yeah, I do. 'Cause, you know, you are a prisoner," Lana responded in the way a sister might when trying to remind a brother that they were in trouble. "You know, for the treason and stuff."

An awkward silence fell over the table, tempting Hawk to make up an excuse to abandon Alex and head back to his room. He suppressed the urge, telling himself that Dig would want him to try harder. Alvin was obviously going to take a lot of effort to bring back after everything Autem had done to manipulate him.

That was when Hawk had a thought.

I'm dumb.

The realization came with a shock of understanding. The reason that he wanted his magic back so badly was that he wanted to help, but there was actually something important that he could do without power. As hard as it was, maybe helping Alvin break free from the chokehold that Autem had on him was what he should have been focusing on from the start.

If anything, it was the job he was best suited for.

"I'll be right back." Hawk spun on his heel and ran off across the casino floor toward one of the function rooms.

Rushing through the doors, he snapped his vision to a row of shelving units that they had brought in. On each shelf sat the boxes of several board games. Without internet or tv, board games had become the most popular thing to do in the city, so it hadn't taken long for them to set up a modest library where people could check things out to play with a group.

Weirdly, the practice seemed to have an impact on the people there, helping them to get to know each other and build bonds. His adoptive parents had done the same thing. He may not have spent that much time with them, but he had felt like he'd belonged with them, so maybe there was something more to family game night than he realized. Alvin might not have been his brother, but with what the world had become, family was what you made of it.

At the very least, a game couldn't hurt, and it would help them push past the awkwardness and hostility that was hanging over them.

Hawk grabbed a box labeled Grim Forest, and tucked it under his arm before heading back out onto the casino floor. Everyone but Alvin looked up when he returned to the table.

"So, I know it's late and there's a lot going on." He avoided making eye contact with anyone. "But maybe you guys would like to play something."

Alex gave him a slight smile, clearly getting the point of what he was trying to do. "I could definitely go for a distraction to reset my brain a little."

"Same." Lana blew out a sigh, before nudging her brother again. "Right?"

Hawk dropped the box to the table without giving the older boy time to answer. "Of course you want to. It's gotta be boring being a prisoner of war and all."

Alvin looked up, briefly meeting Hawk's eyes before glancing away. "I guess so."

"Fuck yeah, you do." Hawk started handing out game pieces, getting a sigh from Alex at his continued swearing.

Before the artificer had time to complain, Campbell dropped a bowl of chicken nuggets on the table along with a tray filled with packets of dipping sauces. "Looks like you all could use something to munch on. I'm getting ready to clean things up for the night, so do me a favor and take care of my leftovers."

"Thanks." Hawk didn't hesitate before grabbing one along with a packet of buffalo sauce.

"No prob." The big guy gave him a wink as if understanding what he was trying to do.

It took a minute or so but eventually, Alvin reached for a piece of breaded chicken too. After that, the game got underway. Hawk made a point of treating their prisoner like any other survivor from then on. There were enough people keeping an eye on him, the kid didn't need another. Not like it was his fault that he'd fallen down the rabbit hole that Autem led him to.

After witnessing how their people operated, he was just lucky the same hadn't happened to him. Alvin may not have been innocent, but he wasn't bad either.

Just lost.

Hawk claimed a few game pieces off a board at the center of the table, catching a smile on Alvin's face as he dipped a piece of chicken into some ketchup. He smiled back.

It was a start.

Sometimes when someone gets lost, they need help finding their way home.

CHAPTER TWENTY

A gentle wind blew over the Las Vegas strip as the sun shone down at the rivers of black rock below. Asher adjusted her angle to glide into one of the many structures that filled the city. Dark stone engulfed her as she slipped into one of those layered buildings. She liked those ones. They had no windows to run into.

Windows were always hard to see.

She was pretty sure that was how she'd died.

There wasn't much she was sure of, but that seemed to stick out to her. At least, it explained why her neck had been broken when Lord Graves had brought her back to the world.

Landing on the back of a car, she took a moment to rest. She didn't actually need to, considering she was dead, but it seemed to make the living feel more comfortable with her if she made some effort to mimic them.

The vehicle she stood on was nice, or at least, she thought it was. There was a lot she didn't understand, but the car was shiny and that was enough. She hopped toward the nearest window and pecked at her reflection. Her white feathers stood out in the shadows of the structure. She still had trouble understanding why she had been incorporated into her lord's… family?

Was that the right word?

Sure, they were both dead, but beyond that, it was obvious that they weren't the same. She had feathers, her lord didn't. Then again, her lord had also been joined by several of the living as well, which was strange enough considering they were usually food. Taking that into account, it didn't seem that weird that her lord had accepted her. Maybe the differences between them didn't really matter.

Things had changed so much in the time since she'd died. Asher could barely remember things from the beginning of her new existence, but they had become clearer and clearer as time went on. She seemed to be growing along with her lord. Some of the changes were good, though plenty only served to confuse her. As it was, she had trouble organizing her thoughts, which were a mix of concepts, images, feelings, and words.

The words were the hardest part.

Just finding the right one for what she meant was confusing. She often knew what she wanted to convey and understood what her lord and the rest of her family meant, but she had trouble fitting the meaning into language. Even harder was putting the words in the right order. To avoid miscommunications, Asher tried to keep her speech simple and only called out when needed.

In truth, she didn't enjoy it.

Judging from the expressions of those she spoke to, her simplistic words didn't make her sound smart.

At least when she spoke to her lord across their bond, he was the only one that could hear her. When it was just him, he never gave her judgmental looks. Maybe it was because he understood what it was like to be a mindless corpse and how hard it was to exist. After all, even he had started that way. The thought of Digby reminded her of the unnerving silence she sensed across their bond.

He had been quiet for days.

Usually, she sensed his stray thoughts drifting across their connection. A vague sense of superiority or spite every now and again. There was always something. Now it was quiet. Like he wasn't even there.

Asher missed him.

She had begun to panic when Digby first went silent, but Alex had told her everything was alright. That it was a normal thing. Despite that, she couldn't shake the uneasy feeling in her mind.

Her attention was pulled away from her anxiety by the low chitter of a dormant revenant. The creature huddled alongside another dozen of its kind. She hopped away from her reflection in the vehicle's window and stared at the pale form. The city was crawling with the things. They had been trapped in one of the buildings on the far side of the area but had since been released to run free. The nights were theirs, but in the light of the day, the humans sought to bring the city under their control.

Asher flapped down to the floor and hopped closer to the revenants. Other than a few wary glances, the creatures paid her no mind. There wasn't much she could do to them alone, and she hadn't done anything that might provoke them.

She took a mental picture of their location.

The dead still roamed the city here and there, and if she was to find and bring them together, they would need food. At the very least, that new zombie that her lord had returned with, the one with magic, would be hungry.

What was his name?

Click? Clark? Clint?

That was it.

Clint.

The zombie had seemed even more confused with his situation than she was. Though, it was obvious to her that he had lacked the support that she had been given through her time as a member of the dead. Despite that, she was still glad to have another zombie master to aid in the management of a horde. As powerful as she knew her lord to be, not even he could compel anything more than a handful of uncommon dead.

Asher shoved the thought away and continued her search for more of their kind.

From there, she took flight down the incline that led to the level below. The cool air of the shadowed structure was comforting under her wings. Passing by another cluster of revenants, she memorized their location as well and kept moving. Another group of creatures huddled near the entrance. She slowed as she flew by, if only to catch a glimpse of herself in the reflective circle mounted to one wall nearby.

She regretted indulging in the distraction as a bullet shattered the silence, the head of one of the revenants exploding into a spray of crimson.

Asher dropped to the floor, her talons scraping the stone as she skidded to a stop. She came to rest against one of the abandoned cars near the structure's entrance. A panicked squawk fell from her beak as she checked her wings to make sure that they weren't injured. Another gunshot went off, along with a second burst of blood from one of the revenants.

"STAPP!" Asher flapped and cawed trying to let someone know she was there. "STAPP!"

More guns went off. She hated the weapons more than her lord did. The revenants screeched and tried to escape, but with their limited ability during daylight hours, they were just as slow as the common dead.

"STAPP!" Asher cawed again and again, too scared that she might be hit if she took flight. Even worse was the way she pronounced the word. She knew it wasn't right, but couldn't manage better with so little preparation.

Then finally, someone came to her rescue.

"Hold your fire!" The voice was familiar but held a strange air of authority.

The assault ceased as a man vaulted over the half-wall that marked the parameter of the structure's ground level.

Alex.

Her lord's apprentice.

Asher had spent a fair amount of time with him. Despite the fact that he was alive, she had grown to trust him. In fact, he was one of the few people that stuck out in her memories from a month ago. He'd seemed so weak back then, yet now, well, he was different.

"Oh shit, Asher." The young man gently brushed a hand along her wing to make sure she was unharmed. She moved it to show that she was alright. "Oh thank god, Dig would totally eat someone if something happened to you."

Asher appreciated the sentiment, feeling a little more important that her lord might devourer one who had the gall to harm a feather on her body.

The remaining revenants near the entrance cried out, each reaching toward Alex while his attention was on her. He paid them no mind, as if they posed no threat. A gunshot came from outside, tearing one of the creature's jaws off.

"I said hold your fire, you jerks," Alex shouted at whoever was outside before pushing Asher behind him and snapping a sword from a sheath on his back. "I have this."

She watched as he launched a ball of flame to put down the first of the revenants as they approached. The rest moved closer, each stepping over the first as it flailed on the stone floor in front of them. Alex held his ground and remained focused, throwing a shard of ice through the head of one only to toss a ball of fire directly in another's face. The sphere of flame burst on contact to engulf the creature just as Alex planted a boot on its chest. With a kick, he launched the revenant at least fifteen wingspans away.

Alex's sword began to glow like molten metal a second later just before he cut down the final two. The corpses fell, one of their heads landing a single wingspan from Alex's foot. Asher remained behind him, feeling safe again.

After glancing down to make sure that she was alright. Alex turned to whoever was outside. "What the hell is wrong with you?"

Asher's first instinct was to flap up to the partial wall so that she could see who he was shouting at, but the scent of the revenants cooling on the stone drew her attention. She hopped over to the corpses and snatched up a bit of gray matter before flapping up to the wall where she could peck at her meal and watched the scene outside.

"Relax, kid." A man dressed in black armor held a rifle low while a sword was strapped to his back. Another two men dressed the same stood behind him. Asher tensed when she saw them, letting a scrap of brain fall from her beak.

Ever since her lord had brought that man, Bancroft, and his

group back with him, she had been listening to everything in case they turned out to be a threat.

If there was one thing she knew, it was that she didn't like a single one of them. All she had to do was watch Alex's body language to know that he agreed. No one seemed to feel comfortable with the newcomers.

Bancroft himself seemed to be the most agreeable. Though, there was still something predatory about him. As for the rest, well, it was a mixture of problems.

Three of the men had gone off somewhere with Rebecca. Asher had struggled to remember their names, feeling terrible when she couldn't come up with anything. It had been a few days since she'd seen them last. She hoped she might remember when they returned. Fortunately, the three that remained in the city were a different story.

Asher was actually a little proud that she had been able to remember who they were.

The first was Roland. She remembered that one easily. He was a rogue and the fact that his class and name started with the same letter helped a lot.

The second was a little harder. His name was Louse. Wait, no. That wasn't right. It was Louis. She had just been calling him Louse to help remember his actual name. The reason for that was because he was nearly a full wingspan shorter than the others. He was small like a mouse, which led her to Louse, and that kind of sounded like Louis. It wasn't the best method of remembering a name but at least she knew his class, which was enchanter or possibly artificer. She could tell that much from the flasks of water that he carried.

The last of them had been near impossible to recall. The only detail she had to remind herself with was his way of speaking, which sounded a little like her lord's. She didn't know why their pronunciation matched, though. Maybe he and Digby came from the same place? From that, she had been calling him Not Graves. Fortunately, that became a good way to remember in and of itself. His actual name was Nat. He was a cleric, according to what she had overheard.

All three of the men made her uneasy, like they were only loyal to themselves.

Asher kept her head down as Louis shrugged off Alex's complaint. "Hey, everything's fine, so relax."

"I will not relax." Alex didn't let up. "You nearly hit Asher. Do you have any idea how important she is?"

"It's a bird." Louis groaned back.

"That bird is a zombie master, and capable of commanding a horde of thousands. She's one of the most powerful creatures in this entire city." Alex's words struck her with more impact than she was prepared for.

I'm powerful?

Asher raised her head, proud of the complement. Sure, she was aware of her capabilities, but had assumed she was weaker than the rest of her family. Thinking about it, other than the fragile nature of her body, she could actually be quite dangerous if she chose to be, or if her lord had asked her to. Asher cawed in Alex's direction to help back him up.

"Holy shit, kid. She's fine." Louis threw out a hand toward her. "See, she's squawking over there, just like always." He swept his hand back toward the casino. "Just go back to the forge and leave sweeping the city up to us."

"I will when I am sure this city can rely on you three." Alex stepped forward and jabbed a finger into Louis's chest. "I know you have gotten used to doing things the way they were in Skyline, but here in Vegas, we don't take risks like that. The people here are too important."

That was when someone else stepped onto the scene.

"Um, excuse me?" The new zombie master, Clint, stepped out from behind the others with one hand raised and a small bag slung over his shoulder. He looked better than the last time Asher had seen him. He must have grown a little stronger. Clint still seemed frail but at least the new necromancer didn't look like he might fall over at any second. Still, the zombie struggled to be heard over the shouting. "Hello?"

"What?" Louis shouted at him.

The zombie shrank back. "Is anyone going to eat those revenants?"

"No, Clint, they are all yours." Alex waved him on with an exasperated sigh.

"Thank you, I'm very hungry." Clint walked past the two men, ducking as if fearful that someone might harm him. Thinking about it, it was equally possible that he was afraid he might bite one of them. The zombie didn't seem to have much in the way of self-control. Clint gave Asher a bow as he entered the garage, pausing as if asking for permission to eat.

Asher flicked her beak in the direction of the corpses to wave him on.

"Thank you." Clint kept going.

"Don't thank that creature." A woman's voice came from the bag he wore slung over his shoulder.

Asher eyed the satchel. It must have held that talking skull that Digby had brought back from their enemy's nest. She had trouble understanding why the necromancer was keeping the thing active, but she assumed it was similar to her appreciation for shiny things. With all of the changes that being dead brought, it was probably comforting to have something that reminded Clint of the life he'd lived before. In his case, the unpleasant skull was someone that he'd spoken to at some point, even if all that was left was a magical recreation.

Clint set his bag down next to the corpses and went about digging for a heart. Asher looked away. It wasn't that watching was unpleasant, but there was a strange uncertainty that accompanied everything the zombie did, like there was a part of him that hadn't accepted what he'd become. The idea of it was absurd. She had never minded being dead, and her lord carried himself with a confidence that she found infectious. Hopefully, some of that might rub off on the new addition to their family.

With Clint out of the way, Asher hopped off the barrier wall and down to the ground outside the building. She held a piece of brain that she'd claimed in her beak. It had started to cool in the shadows of the stone structure, so she dropped it on the sidewalk in the sun. A minute there would be sure to bring it back up to a more appetizing temperature. That seemed to be one of the perks of living in the sun-drenched city.

Her meal was interrupted yet again.

"We've got a zed here." Roland, gripped a zombie by the back of its clothing and yanked it out from behind a dumpster. Most people probably wouldn't risk grabbing a member of the dead, but he had the might and magic to back up the act. A lone zombie just wasn't a match for someone like him.

The walking corpse let out a moan that, to anyone else would have sounded like just another sound, but to Asher, it told a story of hunger overshadowed by fear. The zombie wanted food and was clearly tempted to bite Roland as he dragged it along, but the fear of retaliation was stronger. Instead, all it wanted to do was get away.

Asher let out a caw carrying a compel to help calm the walking corpse so that it would at least stop struggling. From where the zombie was found, it must have been a part of their previous horde but wandered off from the rest. If there was one thing Asher had learned as a master, the dead weren't exactly easy to keep focused. It took near-constant compels to keep them in line. The fortunate thing about their behavior was that there was a good chance she could find enough stragglers around the city to start a decent horde.

Letting out another compel, Asher tried again to calm the zombie. It wasn't helping that Roland was shoving it along and being so rough. As it was, the poor monster had worked itself into a panic, making it hard to reason with.

Clawing at the air, the zombie caught Nat's arm as Roland shoved it past him. The blow landed a solid scratch.

"Fuck!" Nat shoved the zombie into the street and planted a boot on its side to kick it to the ground. "God damn thing clawed me."

"Yeah, and I would too if you kept shoving me around like that." Alex moved to put himself between Nat and the zombie.

The monster remained on the ground, clearly unable to find a safe route for escape. Asher spread her wings to fly to it but to her surprise, she was beaten to the scene by Clint.

"Stop!" The necromancer choked the word out as he rushed to the entrance of the structure he was in. "You're scaring us."

"Everything's fine, Clint, just go back to eating some brains or something." Louis ignored him.

"Nothing is fine!" Clint stepped out into the sun and scurried toward the conflict. He snapped his jaws as he delivered another complaint. "You're upsetting us."

"Okay. Christ." Nat backed off along with the rest.

"Sorry. I didn't mean to..." Clint trailed off, clearly self-conscious that he'd snapped at them while speaking. Despite that, he shifted his attention to the cowering zombie to hand it a scrap of the revenant that he had been eating.

"Don't be sorry, Clint." Alex eyed the men. "You didn't do anything wrong."

"The hell he did." Nat pointed to his arm. "What if he had actually bitten me?"

"Then either I or Louis would cleanse you. There would be plenty of time. That's why we do this in the daylight when the curse moves slowly." Alex let out a long sigh and shook his head.

All three of them started to speak at once, but Alex held up a hand.

"I get it, okay." He lowered his voice, sounding strongly friendly for the situation. "Life in Skyline was different. You guys were the alphas there and the dead were just experience points to you. But you need to get over that and learn a few things now that you've joined up with us." Alex's voice shook a little, but he held his ground and stood firm. "First, this city is a group effort. And second, the dead are a part of that effort. I know that's weird but at this point, I'll take a zombie on my side more than most people."

"Yeah, sure, but you'll throw the dead to the wolves when it's convenient. So don't go acting like you're better than us." Louis swept a hand through the air. "Isn't that what you did to take down Skyline? You sacrificed a whole horde back there on the base."

"That's true." Alex nodded. "But that is what makes treating the dead with respect more important."

"LISTEN!" Asher flapped up to his shoulder to help him stand against them, pushing aside her discomfort with speaking. The fact was that most of the dead lacked any real awareness beyond instinct and that left them with nothing more than a list of priorities. At the top of that list was always the safety of their horde.

"Thank you, Asher." Alex nodded to her before continuing. "The dead are a part of this city and they have saved us time and time again. Most of them may not be much more than animals at this point, but that doesn't mean it's okay for us to mistreat them. We are just as much a part of their horde as they are, and that is why they sacrifice themselves for us. So try to give them a little more respect. Because if you remain a part of this city, a time will come when you will owe the dead your life."

The three men stood silently for a moment as if processing his words.

"Got that?" Alex raised his voice only to have it crack a little.

"Yeah," they responded.

Asher nodded to Alex, appreciating his effort. She would not have been able to explain things nearly as well.

Once the frightened zombie on the ground had finished the scrap of meat that Clint had given it, the necromancer cast a control spell to return it to the horde.

"Come on, follow Clint." The awkward zombie master hesitated. "I mean me, follow me. We eat."

Together, the walking corpses returned to the structure where the revenant's bodies were. Asher decided to let them have the rest. There were plenty more of the creatures out there to eat and it was best to strengthen the horde no matter how small it was.

With that, she flapped off of Alex's shoulder and left the scene behind. She still wasn't sure if her family would be able to work with these new Heretics, but Alex had become far more capable in the last month. The only question was if the men from Skyline would try as hard as he would to get along.

Climbing high into the sky, Asher soared over the city. She had to do her part. The city was counting on her to rebuild its defenses.

There had to be more of the dead out there.

All she had to do was find them.

CHAPTER TWENTY-ONE

"This should do." Alex looked over a maintenance room down in the basement of the casino.

After dealing with Louis and the rest of Bancroft's guys all day, he was ready for something a little less stressful. Setting up a new space to experiment with the Guardian rings that Bancroft had brought him was as good a way to unwind as any. Not to mention his exploration of the runes that Autem's R&D had been working on still held plenty of secrets. Secrets that he was going to need some space to explore if he was going to use them to reproduce every amazing thing from his childhood fantasies. For the good of the city, of course.

The forge just didn't have the room.

The maintenance room, on the other hand, was large, with tools of every kind lining a pegboard that hung above a work-bench. The lighting wasn't great, but that could be changed. With a little luck, he could get some work done without Bancroft or one of his guys looking too closely.

The sounds of the forge could be heard through the door behind him as the crew out there closed up shop for the day. They weren't so loud that the noise was distracting, but just enough to know what was going on. In truth, he liked the noise, making the location of his new workshop perfect.

Plus, he needed to stay close during working hours, considering it was his magic that kept the forge's equipment running. They had enough workers now, so he didn't need to be as hands-on as he had been. Mostly, he just helped with some of the weapon designs and recast his Heat Object spell every half hour to keep the temperatures up.

Alex made a mental note to find a way to use the runes to maintain the forge's temperature to further remove him from the process so he could focus on his other work. Not to mention he needed to keep an eye on Bancroft's guys for a while before he felt comfortable letting them do as they pleased. Granted, setting up a rune-powered forge was still a ways off. There was just so much to figure out first and he was still trying to figure out how to convert a stolen Guardian ring into one that could create new Heretics. That was the real task that lay before him.

Dumping the sack of gold bands on the workbench, he opened up his notebook and started working. It wasn't long before he shoved his scribblings aside and brought down a whiteboard from one of the function rooms upstairs. He needed more room to write down his thoughts.

The warding rods he'd worked with previously were child's play compared to the rings, leaving him lost every time he tried to understand them.

None of it made sense.

It was like he was missing part of the equation. Like the runes on the rings were somehow incomplete. After banging his head against the wall, well into the evening, he pushed away from the workbench and paced around the room. A minute later, he slowed to a stop.

"I need a break."

That was when he remembered the two display cases that they had stolen from Henwick's little museum up on the moon along with the Heretic Seed's fragments.

A chill slithered down his spine at the thought.

He'd forgotten about the moon. That part was still something he was trying to get over. It wasn't every day he found out he'd taken a giant step for mankind. He couldn't help but wonder if he would need to go back there.

Alex shook his head and kept walking; it was too much to think about right now. Not with the pressure of everything else.

Considering the fact that neither Bancroft nor his men knew about the items that they had obtained, it had seemed like a good idea to keep them hidden. At least that was what Digby had said back when they had returned from the attack on Autem's base. That was why they never actually brought them inside the high-roller suite where everyone had helped to reassemble the Seed. Instead, they had simply stashed them in a closet near the parking garage.

With Digby unconscious, there hadn't been time to investigate the cases, especially with Bancroft and his guys roaming the casino. Keeping it on the down low, the only person Alex had told about the cases was Deuce, who he'd asked to move the items to the high-roller suite when no one was looking. It had been difficult to find a good moment, but fortunately, the time that Louis, Roland, and Nat spent causing trouble out on the streets earlier provided Deuce the perfect opportunity to get it done.

Heading back upstairs, Alex went straight for the high-roller suite. The guards that Deuce had placed on the stairs waved him through without a second look. He passed by his detection rods as soon as he entered the hall, feeling the receivers vibrate in his pocket.

Cool.

At least he had made some progress with the runes even if he hadn't figured out the rings yet.

The Heretic Seed's obelisk stood right where it had been when he got inside. He walked past it and looked behind the bar to find both display cases covered in a table cloth right where he expected them. Of course, he had been concerned that Tavern might force Bancroft up there to get themselves a drink and stumble upon the hidden items, but the detection rods he'd placed outside had done their job. The only unauthorized person that had gained access to the suite was Hawk.

Dragging both of the cases out from behind the bar, he was grateful that Deuce had been able to hose the things off so that they weren't covered in the liquefied remains of the dead that filled Digby's void where they had been stored. As it was, they still smelled a little weird.

"Okay." He clapped his hands together. "Let's see what we have here."

Staring down at the pair of glass cases, each was a simple two-foot by two-foot box. Well, maybe not that simple. They were at least an inch thick and bulletproof. A pedestal of polished wood was adhered to the inside of both, though the contents were no longer resting on them. Against the wall of one lay a pair of sequined shoes, while the other held a sheet of some sort of red fabric balled up in a corner.

"Well, I have a guess of what the slippers are."

Alex crouched down next to the shoes, assuming they had gained a mass enchantment from the fact that so many people had seen them during childhood. There was a whole lot of belief in that. Although, he wasn't sure how the feelings of that many children could bestow an enchantment that was powerful enough to merit storing the shoes up on the moon.

"I guess there's no place like home."

He turned his attention to the red fabric, the origin of which was much less obvious.

"Okay, only one way to find out what you are."

Alex pulled a folding knife from his pocket, cast enchant weapon, and carved an X into one side of each case. Once he was satisfied the lines were deep enough, he started chipping away at the center until it finally shattered. The process was slow, but it worked. His brow furrowed as soon as he reached for the shoes.

Slippers of Possibility, unique, legendary.
MASS ENCHANTMENT: Due to the belief and admiration
shared by a large number of people, this item has gained a
power of its own.
PASSIVE TRAITS:
WISH

The wearer of this item will be granted the ability to cast one spell regardless of if they have access to it or not. This trait may be used multiple times but can only be used once by any given caster, and each spell may only be cast once. The user of this trait must have the mana and mana balance required to cast the resulting spell.

"Okay." Alex pulled both shoes out and dropped them on the floor next to his boots. Aside from the fact that they were too small for him, he wasn't sure why they were powerful. If all they did was cast one spell, then they certainly weren't good for much. Plus, the limit of one per person coupled with the inability to cast the same spell twice even with a second user restricted their usefulness further.

Unless… He considered the possibilities.

"Unless there are a lot more powerful spells that we don't know of." From what he'd seen, magic could do a lot and he wasn't exactly sure where the limit was. He thought back to a video game that he'd played where an endgame boss was able to summon a meteor that destroyed the entire solar system. He immediately stepped away from the shoes. If there were spells that dangerous, then those slippers could technically destroy the planet. All it would take was a stray thought.

"Okay, mental note. Do not put on the shiny slippers. No matter how pretty you want to feel. Also, find someplace safe to hide them." Alex dropped the shoes back into their display case, feeling better once they were out of his hands.

Finding a silver lining, there was a good chance the slippers could be used to strike a blow to Autem. Provided they knew exactly what they wanted to cast and were able to do it without screwing it up. Otherwise, it might be too dangerous to even try.

Pushing the first case aside, he turned to the pile of red fabric that was resting in the corner of the second one.

"Let's hope this one is a little less scary." He reached in to pull the item out, his heart soaring the moment the Seed filled his HUD with text.

Cape of Steel, unique, legendary.
**MASS ENCHANTMENT: Due to the belief and admiration
shared by a large number of people, this item has gained a
power of its own.**
PASSIVE TRAITS:
DRINK THE SUN
**This item contains a self-sustaining mana system that is
capable of continuously absorbing and storing life essence.**
MAN OF STEEL
**When worn, this item produces a continuous barrier around
its wearer that cannot be penetrated until its mana supply
has been exhausted.**

"Oh, my freaking god. I cannot believe what I'm holding."
Alex jumped up and unfurled the red cape so that it hung from his
hands. He stared at it a moment before sweeping it around himself
and holding it to his back. There were no strings to tie the cape on,
just two buttonholes. He would have to make some adjustments to
his leather jacket to add matching fasteners. A ridiculous image of
himself standing proudly with his hands on his hip flashed through
his mind.

Then he deflated.

As much as he wanted to stand tall as the man of steel, his role in
the fight had been becoming more support-based. In contrast, Digby
was always in the thick of things. For that matter, even Becca had
started entering the fray more and more. The zombie didn't need
much in the way of armor since he could pretty much repair any
damage that might happen to him. Becca, on the other hand, needed it
more, especially considering her refusal to at least wear regular pants.

Alex laughed to himself, imagining her running around in
leggings and a cape like some kind of spandex-clad comic book
hero. With that, Becca could become nearly invincible. Well, as
long as the sun was up to feed the cape's mana system.

"Probably not her style though." He pulled the fabric off his
shoulders and slung it over his arm. "And I guess the rule of no
capes makes sense. It wouldn't really be practical and could get in

the way. Although, I have seen her wear a poncho before to cover up."

Alex thought for a moment, picturing something that would work with her style. He wasn't sure how she would feel about his idea of fashion design, but if he could alter the cape, he might be able to make something that looked cool.

"I guess I should take this down to the workshop and find someplace to hide these shoes." Alex glanced down at the slippers before looking around the room for something to stuff them in. He found a cardboard box laying off to the side near the bar. It would do. At least with the enchanted items out of sight, none of Bancroft's guys would be able to analyze them.

Tossing the shoes and cape in the box, he folded the flaps down and picked it up. For a moment, he couldn't help but feel good about his discovery. Then he deflated, remembering the Guardian rings he was supposed to be figuring out.

"Welp, break over." He dragged his feet toward the door before stopping short. "Actually, these aren't the only things that we stole from Autem."

He grabbed his radio and called the one person that might be able to help with his ring problem. "Hey Clint, you there?"

A long pause of silence went by before the radio clicked and a raspy voice answered.

"Hello?" The zombie master sounded as unsure as ever. A loud clatter followed as if he'd dropped the radio.

Alex cringed.

The zombie must have picked it back up before repeating, "Hello?"

"Hi, Clint." Alex tried to sound friendly to avoid making the zombie nervous. "Do you still have that skull on you? The one that belonged to the seer?"

"Yeah. Do you need to talk to her?" Clint responded.

"I take it from your response that the Talking Corpse spell is still active?" He started for the door.

"It is." Clint's tone grew concerned. "Should I not have kept her functioning?"

"Don't worry, you did good. Bring the skull and I'll meet you in the forge."

"The forge? In the casino? Where the, the humans are?" Clint sounded even more worried than before.

"You'll be fine. Most of the people are starting to turn in for the night. Just try not to bite anyone you run into. And if you do, I'll be there to cleanse them." Alex shoved out the door and took off for the forge. "We have work to do, and that seer might have the answers I need."

CHAPTER TWENTY-TWO

"Okay, how's that?" Alex placed the skull of Kristen the seer down on a plate of iron.

Silence answered.

He continued to stare while sitting in his workshop. The only light came from a hanging fixture and the narrow window that ran along the upper wall and the sound of metal being hammered into shape came from outside his door.

He let out a sigh.

It was nice to have so many crafters working the forge, but he missed his partner. Not having Parker around to bounce ideas off of had slowed him down. Not to mention she kept the mood light and would have geeked out about things with him. Instead, he was stuck with a deceased seer.

Alex tapped on the skull sitting on the table before him.

"This will go a lot faster if you cooperate. I can always just let that Talking Corpse spell lapse and put you on a shelf to use as a bookend. You know, if I had books to hold up, that is." He cringed, realizing he wasn't nearly as good at vague threats as Digby.

"This will do." The skull grumbled in a tone that made it clear that an eye roll would have accompanied the statement had the skull had eyes to do so.

"That's better." He folded his arms and let out a sigh.

Until now, the seer had been kept active by Clint who had been refreshing the Talking Corpse spell. However, now that Alex had made some progress with the runes that Autem had been using to power their warding rods, he had found a better way. There was still a lot to figure out, but so far, he had been able to write out a mana absorption system of sorts.

The result was an uneven plate of iron covered with engravings. A few lines of runes had been scratched out where he had made mistakes. Overall, his creation wasn't pretty, but it worked. Sure, the thing wasn't able to store mana like he had originally wanted it to do, but it could absorb and feed it into the waning Talking Corpse spell before Kristen returned to being an ordinary skull.

He just wished she was a little more grateful about it.

Then again, being a skull probably wasn't the best existence, so maybe he wasn't actually helping as much as he thought.

"What's it like?" Alex knelt down to look into the hollows of Kristen's empty eye sockets. There was nothing left of the skin or tissue that had once encased the bone.

"Being dead?" The skull huffed. "Peachy."

"I was being serious." Alex tapped his fingers on the table.

"It's like falling from a cliff but never hitting the ground," she responded.

Alex pulled back, surprised by the sudden willingness to speak with him despite the seer's obvious disdain. "What do you mean?"

"I mean, I'm dead." She paused. "Or at least Kristen is. The person I was is gone. Whatever soul I had, has passed on."

"Then how are you still talking?" He arched an eyebrow. "How does this work?"

"The spell that your necromancer cast is like a net meant to catch an imprint of the person that I was. And that net continues to hold me, forcing me to answer whenever Graves asks me another asinine question." She fell silent.

"Does it hurt?" He probed deeper trying to understand.

"Not really." Kristen let out a ghostly sigh that sounded like a quiet breeze. "I know there is something wrong with me, but I am not inclined to fix it. I have little desire or direction. I don't appreciate the state of my existence, but at the same time, I do not wish for it to end. Even if I know that this existence is false. I am simply adrift."

"I can get that, I guess." He leaned back. "For a long time, I felt like nothing mattered. It really wasn't until the world ended and I met Digby and Becca that I started to feel like I had a purpose."

"And what, you think I will find some sense of purpose now, as a damn skull on an iron plate?" Her voice climbed a little higher. "You think I should just betray everything that I worked my entire life for, and join up with that undead monster like the rest of you?"

"I suppose that's true." Alex leaned to one side. "But as you said, you are not the person that once lived, you're an imprint created by a spell. So technically you have no loyalty to Henwick or Autem."

The skull gave a simple harumph. "No thank you."

"Okay, that's fair." He reached into his pocket for one of the Guardian rings that had been giving him so much trouble. "As much as I would like to work on other things, I could certainly use some help figuring out how to get the Heretic Seed to recognize these."

"Sorry to disappoint," Kristen added in a tone that made it hard to judge if she was being sincere or antagonistic.

Alex scratched at the back of his head. Other than the security sensors that he'd rigged up and the absorption plate, he hadn't been able to craft anything else that worked. Granted, so far, all he'd been doing was making alterations to the runes that were present on the warding rods through trial and error.

Sweeping his vision across a workbench of materials, he reminded himself of a few failed experiments. A collection of metal objects littered the table's surface.

There was a plate that he'd been trying to make levitate. He'd thought he'd cracked it at one point but ultimately only succeeded in making a metal disc that floated for a few seconds before firing off in a random direction. It had actually fractured his shinbone during his last test. After healing the damage, he decided that working out levitation could wait until he understood it more.

As far as why the plate didn't work, that was a mystery. He had thought he'd had the right runes engraved. From the warding rods, he'd been able to separate out a few enchantments that he made small changes to and copied them to the plate. Though, he still couldn't figure out why the engravings worked fine on the metal rods and not on this new item. It was like the different enchantments were interfering with each other and causing them to glitch out.

Next on his list of failures was his mana battery. That one was even worse. The goal was to absorb the ambient essence in the area and store it within a metal ring that could be worn. It worked, kind of. It wasn't that it couldn't store the mana if absorbed, but more that it couldn't do so without exploding. Any more than a few points of MP and the ring would just detonate, similar to a bullet that had been enchanted to deliver more damage. The blast wasn't anything significant, but it made the prospect of wearing the ring a little less appealing as the resulting explosion was enough to blow off a finger or two.

Ultimately, it was clear that the material wasn't suited to conduct mana. His conclusion was that a mana system, like what a person carried within them, was needed to actually absorb and store mana with any kind of real stability. He'd given up shortly after that.

Then, there was the mana grenade.

He groaned at the stupidest thing he had created so far. Since he'd already succeeded in replicating the destruction of an enchanted bullet through the use of runes, albeit by accident, the obvious next step was to scale up the item and make a bomb. With that in mind, he had crafted a large metal rod and covered it with the correct runes to produce a mana powered grenade that could even be used by a non-magic user.

It didn't quite work as intended.

Instead of absorbing enough mana to become unstable and detonate, it simply drew in a few points worth of MP before dumping them back out and repeating the process. Near as he could tell, the use of a larger object seemed to stabilize the process enough to prevent an explosion, but the poor mana conduction caused the material to reject the energy. The result was a metal rod that vibrated in a steady rhythm of low to high intensity.

Alex slapped a hand to his face. He could practically hear Parker laughing at the fact that he'd created a magic sex toy. Even worse, it kind of looked like a dick. He hadn't noticed it when he was making it, but now he couldn't unsee the similarity. He dropped a cloth over the offending phallus and groaned.

Despite his original excitement at the prospect of what the runes could do, he was beginning to think he was in over his head. No matter how much he learned, there was always something missing. It was like trying to translate a language without a dictionary. Like he'd just been dropped in a foreign country and told to figure it out.

Slipping the Guardian ring he held onto his finger, he slid it down to rest just above the string of tiny black runes that his Heretic ring had etched into the skin. He'd done this several times to compare the pattern. Of course, he had tried copying everything onto a new ring already to no avail. Clearly, whatever process that had been used to create his original Heretic ring was more complicated than anything he could do. The fact that it had been absorbed by his body was proof enough of that.

In frustration, he pulled the Guardian ring off and slapped it down on the work table to cast Heat Object. It was time to get aggressive. With so few rings to experiment with, he'd been hesitant to destroy any of them, but after hitting a dead end, it was the only thing he could think of that he hadn't already tried.

Holding his hand over the gold band, he felt the heat radiating from it as he pushed the temperature higher. It wasn't long before its shape began to deform. His eyes widened the moment it started to melt.

"Holy shit!" Alex yanked his hand away to put a stop to the spell as a dark ring of metal emerged from the center of the gold band.

"Congratulations," Kristen said from her place on the workbench. "You figured it out."

"Hell yeah, I did." He didn't let the skull's snarky tone bother him. He was going to take the win for what it was.

As soon as the gold had cooled, he grabbed a jeweler's loupe that he'd taken from a store in the casino's shopping center and examined the inner layer of the guardian ring. At first glance, it appeared to be iron.

"Well, that makes sense." He nodded, remembering how the first spell he had discovered, Detect Enemy, had required an iron object. That had been the reason he'd been using the metal to experiment with. He'd assumed that it would make for a good conductor for mana.

Maybe this layer was centered around stabilizing the enchantments?

On closer inspection, there were more runes that he didn't recognize visible on the iron portion of the ring.

"That must be why I've been missing something in the translation. I was literally only working with half of the runes."

"If I had hands, I'd clap." Kristen continued her snarky commentary. "But I don't, because I'm dead."

Alex spent the next few minutes removing the rest of the gold from the ring while being careful not to damage the second layer's engravings. Once he had a clear picture, he copied down the symbols and started to heat up the second layer the same as he had the first. Considering he had been working with only part of the puzzle and nearly blown off a finger, it seemed best to make sure there weren't any more surprises hidden within the second layer.

"Yes!" He drummed his hands on the table as a third layer began to show through the iron ring. "Who's the best artificer?"

Kristen's skull simply let out an annoyed sigh at the discovery.

"That's right, I am." He hopped up from his seat and picked up the Seer's head.

"Hey, stop that!"

Making use of his increased dexterity, Alex tossed the skull in the air, spun, and caught it in his other hand. Ignoring Kristen's complaints, he finished by letting her roll down one arm, across his shoulders, and into his other hand before placing her back on the absorption plate. After so much frustration, he needed a moment to celebrate.

The Heretic Seed seemed to agree because it chose that moment to give him a new spell.

SKILL LINK
By demonstrating repeated and proficient use of the non-mage skill or talent, Examination, you have discovered an adjacent spell.
INSPECTION
Description: Similar to a Heretic's Analyze ability, this spell examines an inanimate item with more depth, allowing the caster to see what materials an object is made of as well as enchantments that might be present.
Rank: D
Cost: 50 MP
Range: Touch
Limitations: Some details may remain hidden depending on spell rank.

Alex turned his attention back to his work, placing a new Guardian ring on the table and casting his new spell. The result was impressive.

The spell started the same as his analysis ability usually did, with the tiny circle at the edge of his vision snapping out to surround the item. The words 'Guardian Ring' ran along the circle's edge. Then, the details came in. The ring itself began to glow just before the image split into three spectral bands of energy each floating in a column directly above the real one. Letters appeared to the side of each to label the materials.

Shell: Gold
Mid-layer: Iron
Heart: Steel

He focused on the runes that showed on each piece, getting an explanation of each enchantment. The shell was for identification and security. That was the part that locked the ring to a user and logged each spell usage with the Guardian Core.

The mid-layer was exactly what he assumed, insulation. The runes acted as a buffer to keep the enchantments on the shell and heart from disrupting each other and the use of iron maintained the stability of the ring.

The heart was the most complicated, with its runes serving to connect a person to the mana that surrounded them. It still needed a system to link to like the Seed or the Guardian Core, but it wasn't specifically locked to either. At first, he was shocked that the ring's secrets were so easy to access.

Then, he found out why.

A jolt of pain lit up Alex's head, like a migraine but ten times worse as soon as he attempted to copy down the runes that encircled the heart of the ring.

"Unhggg…"

An unintelligible sound dripped from his mouth as confusion blew every thought from his mind like a shotgun blast to the temple. He hit the floor an instant later, unaware that he'd even fallen. It was like he had suddenly lost the ability to perceive time. Another slurred sentence spilled from him as Kristen's skull let out a mirthless laugh at his pain.

"Do you really think Autem would make things that easy? No, of course, you didn't. You're just a moron that walked right into the trap that lay waiting for anyone stupid enough to poke around those enchantments." Her voice drifted through the air, making it hard for his senses to figure out which way he was facing. She added a final, "Good riddance, you moron. Oh, I said that one already. Well, no matter, it fits."

The world began to fade.

One obvious thought clawed its way to the surface. *I'm dying!*

"No… funding… may!" Alex fought the darkness as it closed in. He shoved a hand into his pocket to wrap his fingers around one of the small flasks he always carried. He cast Purify Water without hesitation and yanked the cap off. He coughed and choked as he emptied the container into his mouth, then he went limp. The sound of his heart beating echoed through his throbbing head, the pulsating ache slowing to a crawl. It was like the signals coming from his brain were failing to reach the rest of his body.

Don't give out on me now! He willed his spell to keep his heart beating, wondering if this was what it felt like for Digby back when he'd died eight-hundred-years-ago in that tiny boat as he drifted out to sea.

"I am not... dying like that!"

His heartbeat grew stronger as he realized he had just spoken a coherent sentence out loud. Then, slowly the world came back into focus with him staring up at the ceiling. His face and shirt were wet. His eyes bulged. It was a miracle that he'd swallowed enough water to heal himself.

"Oh good, you're alive." Kristen's voice commented from the table in an unimpressed monotone. "Quick, how many fingers am I holding up? Oh wait, I don't have hands. Never mind."

"You suck, you know that?" Alex blew out a long sigh.

"As do you," she added in an antagonistically polite tone.

"So that was a boobie trap, huh?" Alex asked, hoping that there was no point in hiding things now that he had stumbled into it.

"Yes. Anyone that tries to tamper with the ring's heart layer gets hit with a preloaded spell that causes severe brain damage, usually stopping the victim's vital functions."

"Why was it able to bypass the resistance of my will?" Alex closed his eyes. "Nope, never mind, don't answer that. It was because I examined it, wasn't it?"

"Yes, Autem is aware of the Inspection spell and how it works, as it is common to the artificer class. The connection you established to see the enchantments served as a conduit into your brain."

"So it's a loophole like the one Digby used to animate Bancroft's skeleton?" He groaned.

"Yes. Technically, the trap can only attack gray matter and not the rest of you, however, as you can see, that is enough for most that fall prey to it to expire." She seemed to enjoy explaining how his near-death experience had come to pass. "I must say, I am surprised that you were able to withstand such damage long enough to cast a spell to save yourself. If you had been a couple levels lower, surely you would have died."

"Thanks for the compliment." He shook his head before adding one of Parker's favorite jokes, "And don't call me Shirley."

"Call you what?" the skull asked before groaning in understanding. "Oh. Clearly, some of that brain-damage stuck."

Alex pushed himself up only to find that the ring had crumbled into dust. "And let me guess, the ring self-destructs if the trap is triggered?"

"Yes, among other things. The only reason that the first ring you worked on is still partially whole is that you haven't removed enough of the mid-layer to set off the trap. So if you think you will be able to get access to the runes engraved on the heart, then you will have to think again."

"That's where you're wrong." Alex placed a hand on the table and leaned down toward the skull. "I don't need to see the runes on the ring's heart layer."

"Yes, you do," she argued back. "You'll never be able to replicate the enchantment to access the world's mana without it."

"Sure, okay." He channeled Digby to give her his most irritating smile. "But that will only stop me from crafting new rings, and I still have a pile of old Guardian rings to repurpose. It won't make an army, but it's a hell of a start. All I have to do is peel off the outer shell of gold to remove the security enchantments that have been locked to a current user. Without that, I should be able to assign a new Heretic and connect them to the Seed. Correct me if I'm wrong?"

Kristen remained silent.

"I thought so." Alex snatched up the first ring that he'd taken apart and tossed it in his pocket. "I'll leave you in here to think about things while I go find a new Heretic. I know being a skull is rough, but it is up to you how rough. With what you could help me learn from these runes, I'm willing to bet we could find you a better afterlife. All you have to do is share what you know."

With that, Alex left the seer behind to stew. She probably wasn't going to come around to the idea of joining up with the people of Vegas, but it couldn't hurt to give her the choice. Either way, Alex had a pocket full of Guardian rings to strip of security enchantments, and he was pretty sure he knew a few people that would make a decent Heretic. That would give them a head start. After that, it would be up to Digby.

CHAPTER TWENTY-THREE

"Oh fuck." Parker shuffled across the ice that one of the fractured sparks had created before Digby had killed it.

The level fifty-eight rogue stood over the corpse of another of the foes, still holding a polite bow in greeting.

"Watch where you are going, Parker." Digby reluctantly caught her shoulder before she fell down, not wanting his companion to embarrass them in front of the new arrival. Especially considering he was around twice the level of the fool they had faced earlier.

Parker responded by grabbing him tighter and pulling herself to his ear. "Be careful."

"What is it, young lady?" Henwick flanked Digby's other side, clearly concerned by the look on her face.

Parker glanced back to the rogue then back to them. "Unless I'm wrong here, which I admit is possible. But if the newspapers from this time called this guy Jack, then there is a good chance he's…" She gulped audibly. "He's Jack the Ripper." She followed the assertion with an awkward laugh. "I kind of wish he was Dracula now."

"Oh good, you've heard of me?" The rogue raised up from his bow. "And by all means, talk amongst yourselves."

"Alright, we will." Digby tried to appear dominant, not liking the air of superiority that surrounded the man. "Who exactly is Jack the Ripper?"

"A serial killer," Parker added with little ceremony. "Murdered women."

Jack's face fell. "Yes, well, I think you'd find that the papers don't always tell the whole story. In fact, quite often, murder can be mercy in disguise."

Not sure I liked the sound of that.

If this man was regarded by historians enough for someone like Parker to know of him, then clearly, he had done some damage in his time. Then again, it was also plausible that the historians got things wrong. After all, he knew better than anyone how easily people jump to conclusions. There was always a chance that there was a misunderstanding in place in regard to his crimes.

Henwick spoke up before he had the chance to determine anything else.

"I shall have nothing to do with a slayer of women."

Digby deflated. It didn't really matter if they wanted to or not. Picking a fight with someone so much stronger than them was out of the question. Sure, it would be three on one, but those still were not odds he was keen to bet on.

"Now, now, let's all calm down here." Digby raised a hand in front of Henwick before giving his attention back to Jack. "What is it you want? Obviously, I have analyzed you, so I know you're friendly, but why? From what I understand, you have more reason to fight."

"Aren't we being a little too demanding? I did just rescue you from this failure." Jack gestured with his hat toward the body of the fractured spark at his feet.

"Failure, you say?" Digby furrowed his brow. "I'd say that spark was pretty powerful for a failure."

"The fractured are usually like that." Jack sounded unimpressed as he placed his hat back on his head. "The Seed takes too much from them too fast. It seems that an incomplete bond can have an enhancing effect in their manifestation here in this realm."

"Incomplete?" Parker spoke up, sounding concerned. "How?"

"Yes, dear, you can't possibly expect that magic treats all who acquire it equally?" Jack clicked his tongue. "No, I assure you not. The Heretic Seed is a fickle mistress. She will take all you have if you let her, and she will reject you if you give her too little."

"What do you mean?" Henwick stepped forward.

"Simple." He shrugged. "If you obtained your power as I have, by tying your soul to one of its shards, then you must accept that power as a part of you. Not an easy task, I'll say. When confronted with something that wants access to the very core of your being, many will simply deny it. Others, like these poor fractured souls here, bend to the Seed entirely, and allow it to take everything until nothing of who they were remains."

"Are you trying to tell me that attempting to connect to one of the Seed's shards is dangerous?" Digby raised an eyebrow, unaware of whatever risks could have been involved.

"Dangerous is an understatement." Jack scoffed. "That sort of bond can be downright lethal. I have seen it happen. If you lack the will to stop the Seed from taking everything, you become a mindless husk. Then again, if you are unable to adapt to the Seed, its connection will unravel."

"What happens if it unravels?" Parker's voice shook a little.

"Then most of the Seed's power will leave you," Jack answered matter-of-factly.

"Okay, that's not so bad." She relaxed.

"But." He smirked. "You can't expect to expel a power like that without it fighting back. No, it will shred your soul to pieces on its way out. You might survive it. Maybe. But the traces of power that remain with you will fester and rot. If you ever tried to use that power again, it would surely land you in an early grave."

"Oh." Parker deflated.

Digby opened his mouth to speak but wasn't sure what to say. The woman's connection to the Seed had only recently become stable. Not to mention she had gained a class that others had not. There wasn't much he could say to reassure her. Instead, he let the subject lie and returned his attention to Jack.

"Alright, that is all well and good, but we don't need a lesson in the dangers of connecting with the Seed." Digby leaned to one side. "Besides, none of us were ever given a choice on whether we formed a bond with the Seed or not. Just happened to be in the wrong place at the wrong time, is all."

"How fortunate for you." Jack grinned at him. "You met the requirements by chance, then. Few can claim to be so lucky."

"Yes, lucky." Digby laughed. "That's what I am."

"I would say so." Jack held out his arms. "After all, you would not have met me had things not worked out in your favor."

"And why would meeting you be lucky?" Digby narrowed his eyes.

"Because Heretics were not meant to fight each other." Jack puffed out his chest. "As I said, I have seen many a fool lose themselves to the Seed one way or another. They might have had plans to do great things with their power, but in the end, it cost them their lives. The sad fact is, not everyone is meant to bond with the Seed's shards, and that sets those of us that are meant to apart from the herd."

"The herd?" Henwick took a step back. "Is that what you think mankind to be? Livestock?"

"Are they not?" He dropped his hands to his sides with a huff.

"No." Parker shook her head.

He blew out a sigh. "Look, I understand how you feel. You must not have had your power long and from what you say, it was thrust upon you. But what you will come to understand is that we Heretics are simply cut from a different cloth. It is not the job of us Heretics to protect the world."

"I am inclined to agree with that last part." Digby nodded.

"Graves?" Henwick snapped his eyes to him.

"Well, he isn't wrong. It is not my responsibility to save the world." He folded his arms. "The only reason I am at war with Autem is because they declared war on me first."

"Exactly, and that's why we Heretics should stick together." Jack grew more excited and stepped closer. "The levels we could gain out there would be limitless. Together, we would be unstoppable."

"Indeed. But that leaves a question." Digby eyed the man. "What do we do about our current situation? None of the souls trapped in this realm were ever supposed to be here. The only reason people formed bonds with the shards of the Seed was because it had been shattered. Now that it has been restored, the souls such as yourself now amount to no more than clutter meant to be cleaned out by the caretaker. As I understand it, that means you would need to be erased so that the Heretic Seed can continue its restoration."

"There is sure to be a way out. We just need to work together to find it." Jack scoffed and stepped closer in an overly nonchalant manner.

Digby raised an eyebrow. That was the second time he had moved toward him.

If I didn't know better, that rogue is trying to get closer.

But why?

To get within range for something?

Digby himself had done the same thing in the past more than once. It was a standard tactic for him to use idle chatter to distract his enemy while getting in range to strike.

Then again, the Seed wouldn't have labeled Jack as friendly if he had an immediate intent on attacking. That could always change as their situation did, but if the Seed was to be believed, the rogue was not yet hostile.

Digby decided to wait and see.

It didn't make sense to provoke the man now. All it would take would be for Jack to cast the same spell as that jester did down below. With that, he could simply kill them all in a heartbeat.

Digby pushed the thought out of his mind. It could just be his suspicious nature cropping up to get him in trouble. Not everyone was as deceitful as he was, after all. Then again, Parker had said something about the rogue having been a serial killer. Not only that but it seemed strange for a man of that sort to be so willing to work together. The fact that he was friendly at all was odd, considering his high level. A man with that much power could surely escape this place on his own.

"Does my offer sound amicable?" Jack inched closer.

Digby held his ground, unsure if he should listen to the voice in his head that said it was a trap. "That depends. What is your plan for when the caretaker catches up?"

Jack merely slipped his knife from his pocket and swiped it through the empty air between them. "We kill it. That should be an easy enough task for four Heretics such as ourselves."

"And when the Seed sends something else after us to whittle down our numbers?" Digby narrowed his eyes.

"Then we kill that too. Honestly, I am level fifty-eight. I can't imagine much that this place could hurl in my direction that I could not end."

"That does make sense." Digby scratched at his chin as if thinking about it. Though, what he was really thinking about was what he might have been missing.

The rogue had mentioned his level as if that alone was the evidence he had to ensure a beneficial alliance. Combined with the fact that he was obviously creeping closer to get into melee range, Digby couldn't help but be suspicious. Hell, Jack had even taken out his knife. Either he was on the up and up, or he was about to try to stab him. Every instinct Digby had told him it was the latter.

That was when Digby sensed mana flowing through the man's blood. He froze in place, fully expecting the rogue to lunge at him in an impossible display of agility. Which was why he was even more confused why that didn't happen. Not only that but Jack's face suddenly fell.

"I'm afraid we have overstayed our welcome here." The rogue raised a hand to point over Digby's shoulder.

"There's something behind me, isn't there?" He furrowed his brow just as Parker and Henwick jumped back and stared in horror at whatever it was.

"More of those fractured sparks." Henwick pointed in the same direction.

"From the alleyways, a dozen of them." Parker followed suit.

Digby's first instinct was to look back before fleeing. Yet something in his deceased gut told him to hold his ground. There was a trick in play. He knew it. He just didn't know what. Then, he remembered something important about the circumstances surrounding how Jack had appeared. Digby flicked his eyes to the rogue and willed the Seed to confirm what he suspected.

Digby suppressed a grin as a line of text ran across his vision.

Remnant Spark, level 24 Illusionist, Hostile.

You sneaky little fiend.

The man was hostile after all.

Not only that, but his level wasn't anywhere near as high as he claimed. Even his class was different. The details fell into place. There had been a corpse blocking Digby's vision when he had tried to analyze Jack before.

The rogue must have held that fractured spark's body in front of himself on purpose to block the Seed's analyze ability. Clearly, Jack had some experience with manipulating magic users.

The trick was actually quite clever.

The first thought for a Heretic would naturally be to analyze a new threat. Knowing that, cast a spell to make it seem like it had worked. Meaning that the message Digby and the others had seen had not come from the Seed. No, it had been a tiny illusion placed directly in front of his eyes to trick them into thinking that the man was a high-level rogue rather than a much weaker illusionist. Not only that, but by showing them a plausible level and class for himself, he ensured that they would not attempt to analyze him a second time, since they believed they already had.

Not a bad ploy. Digby couldn't help but appreciate the con. He even made a mental note to inform Rebecca of it later. The tactic was bound to be useful.

Though, even with that, Digby wasn't sure what this illusionist was playing at. Jack was obviously trying to get close, but not necessarily to attack, or at least, that wasn't his first option.

"I'm afraid we must flee. Those sparks will be upon us." Jack held his ground, now standing close enough to strike. "We must ascend to the next level of this realm."

Ah, that's it. Jack's plan became clear.

The goal really was cooperation.

Actually, it was the same scheme Digby had hatched earlier when they stumbled upon Henwick. Jack wanted their help in surviving the Seed's race and was trying to trick them into following along.

At level twenty-four, Jack didn't have much chance at surviving long enough in the Seed's realm to become one of the last Heretics standing. The alliance he suggested was legitimate. At least until it was no longer needed.

Understanding that, the fact that Jack was getting himself into melee range was just a precaution in case the ploy failed. If Digby and his accomplices were able to see through the ruse, he would probably stab whoever he could and make a run for it.

"Graves, we must make haste." Henwick stared over his shoulder at the fractured sparks that were supposedly coming to kill them.

They were probably an illusion.

"Yes, yes, I know." Digby didn't turn around. The sparks would vanish as soon as he did, and he didn't want Jack to know that he was wise to his scheme. "But first, I do have one question for our new friend Jack."

"That is understandable, but the fragments are coming, and we must move." Jack looked more nervous by the second.

"Dig, this might not be the time." Parker inched away until she was standing a little behind the phony rogue.

"I know, I know, but this will only take a second." Digby swept his eyes across the scene, remembering that there was a corpse of the last fractured spark was still laying on the ground. It rested on the cobblestones several feet behind Jack. He wasn't sure if the Seed would allow him to animate the body, but having a minion would certainly be beneficial to sneak up on his foe.

Focusing on the corpse, he got a message in response.

Corpse, Human, cost to animate: 30 MP.
Animate Corpse?

Digby nodded, glad that the fractured spark counted as human. His new minion twitched, and he made a point to will the new zombie to remain quiet. The last thing he needed was for his creation to moan and tell everyone it was there.

Of course, that was when Parker decided to glance back at it.

Digby cringed, expecting her to say something. To his surprise, she just cocked her head to the side before shaking it off as if accepting that he had some sort of plan. She might not have been the most reliable, but at least she knew when to trust him.

For a moment, he almost dropped all of his minion's bond points into strength but thought better of it. The power would certainly be useful in the short term but considering the lack of corpses within the Seed's realm, it seemed more prudent to invest his points more wisely. He checked his void contents instead.

AVAILABLE RESOURCES
Sinew: 4
Flesh: 4
Bone: 3
Viscera: 4
Heart: 4
Mind: 4

A second thought passed through his head. With what he had to work with, he had the requirement of two flesh and one bone that he needed to activate his temporary mass mutation. The question was, might it be possible to activate it on a minion rather than himself? Considering the fact that he had taken the mutation Mend Undead before being drawn into this realm, there was a possibility that it could work.

It couldn't hurt to try.

That was when Henwick noticed his minion.

"What have you done, Graves?" The color drained from his face.

"I, ah…" Digby struggled to come up with a plausible explanation as Jack spun around to see as well. "I raised a corpse to help us fight. Yes, that's it."

"I assure you we cannot fight that many of the fractured," Jack argued. "There is no time to raise the dead."

"Not to mention it is an affront to God," Henwick added.

"Oh, get used to it, Henwick." Digby groaned, still ignoring the imaginary threat sneaking up on him. It wasn't like Jack was going to let his illusions get close since that would almost certainly unravel the spell. He suppressed a laugh at the comical speed at which the illusionist was going to have to move his creations to accommodate his lack of cooperation.

Instead, he continued his work on his minion, opening his maw and focusing on the zombie as he activated his temporary mass mutation.

His minion let out a howl.

Henwick gasped in horror as tendrils of dead flesh stretched around the zombie to form the necrotic armor that Digby had worn so many times to get himself out of trouble. Even Jack's face fell as slabs of muscle wove themselves together around the zombie. Strangely, the formations were different than usual. At first, Digby attributed it to the fact that he had never seen the mutation from the outside, but then he noticed the hands.

Usually, when he activated his armor, it formed itself using dozens of hands to hold parts of it together. However, now, it seemed to be using them differently, with only two hands reaching across the zombie's shoulders to form some sort of macabre pauldron. It was probably due to the fact that he didn't have as much in his maw to use as building blocks. The armor had to work with what he had, even using bones to literally pin things into place in the back, leaving his new and improved minion looking like some sort of porcupine.

Digby allotted his bond points. Out of the seventeen available, he dropped a third into intelligence, a third into strength, and a third into agility. With that, combined with the power of the armor, he had a solid minion capable of holding its own until the Temporary Mass mutation failed.

Now that is a minion worth raising.

"Oh damn, that's kind of wrong." Parker shuddered as several toes inched their way around the zombie's skull to interlock in a line down the middle, securing a mask of flesh and bits of bone in place. The eye holes were just that, dark holes.

"Abomination," Henwick whispered as if he was a moment away from gagging.

Jack merely looked back to Digby, clearly worried that he had picked the wrong Heretic to try to trick. He could almost see the wheels turning in the man's head. Should he continue his plan or should he just attack and make a run for it? The answer became clear when Jack buried his dagger in Digby's side. His eyes bulged when he didn't even flinch.

"So you gave up on the ruse, huh?" Digby dropped his eyes to the confused man. "I must say, I'm impressed that you went for my side. I think I can feel the tip of your knife in my lungs. If you had gone straight through my chest like most would have, your blade would have been stopped by my bone armor."

"Bone armor?" Jack slipped his blade free from the side of Digby's ribcage, slashing at the underside of his arm in almost the same movement.

Digby felt the blade slice through a tendon, causing his hand to fall limp. Jack tried to jump away but the armored minion behind him moved in to grab his coat. Despite the man's low level, his skill with a knife was impressive. There was actually something surgical about his movements. It was like he knew exactly where to cut to disable someone. If Digby had been a normal person, he might have actually been killed.

The illusionist struggled to get free, stabbing Digby's minion about a dozen times in the chest to no avail.

"I see you have never fought a zombie before." Digby stalked closer, casting a Necrotic Regeneration to repair his arm. "You can't kill what is already dead."

"What?" Jack shook his head before throwing a hand out at the illusions that Digby still hadn't looked at. "The fractured are still coming. They're starting to run."

"You can stop playing at that." Digby didn't even turn around. "I know you're an illusionist. Your continued attempts to fool us are just getting sad at this point."

"What?" Henwick and Parker both looked at the man in unison, clearly analyzing him. Next, they flicked their attention to the illusionary fragments behind him, then they gasped.

"See? Nothing to worry about." Digby waved a hand through the air, assuming that the illusion behind him had just vanished.

"But how?" Henwick looked shocked.

"He blocked our ability to analyze him by holding a corpse in front of himself and cast a tiny illusion of text in front of our eyes to make it look like the Seed had labeled him." Digby reached forward and jabbed Jack in the chest with a cold, dead finger. "That right?"

"How did you realize?" Jack's mouth fell open.

"Simple." Digby grinned. "You can't trick a trickster. Just bad luck is all. It seems our tactics are too similar to be unexpected."

"This changes nothing." The illusionist stopped struggling as if submitting to being captured. "We can still work together. There is no reason to fight. Not until we have progressed further."

"And let you kill us all one by one?" Digby let out a mirthless laugh. "I think not. We would have to be on guard at all times."

"But I can—" Jack started but Digby jabbed him in the chest again.

"Let me ask you one thing before I decide to kill you or not."

"Fine, ask me anything." Jack nodded, clearly trying to be cooperative.

"My accomplice here," Digby gestured to Parker. "She mentioned you were killing people back in your time."

"Yeah, prostitutes," she added.

"Yes, yes." Digby nodded. "Why were you killing these prostitutes?"

"Why else? To get levels." He didn't show an ounce of guilt.

"I realize that." Digby grimaced. "But why did you target prostitutes?"

Jack furrowed his brow as if the answer was so obvious that the question need not be asked. "Because no one would miss them. The authorities barely even look into things. They didn't matter. Their lives were nothing but filth and squalor. Ending their time on earth was a mercy."

Digby frowned, examining the man's outfit. It clearly looked expensive, right up to his stupid hat. There was something about it that rubbed him the wrong way. The idea that this man thought so little of his victims. Even worse, he had admitted as much without shame, meaning his view of the world was so common that he expected Digby and his accomplices to share it.

With that, his fate was sealed.

Digby clapped his hands together and opened his maw. "Well, in you go then."

"Wait, wait!" Jack struggled for a moment before burying his knife in Digby's gut and slipping out of his coat. His hat fell to the ground as he fled.

Digby let out a sigh. "Why do they always run?"

Making a point to keep the man in his sight, he rushed after him. He would have sent his minion, but it still didn't have the agility to catch him. Instead, he ran a few paces and opened his maw in his path to cast Forge. Planting his foot, he sent a post of blood up at an angle and activated his limitless mutation. The combination sent him leaping into the air at least twenty feet.

He cackled in victory as Jack turned to look up. His face was frozen in terror and drained of color.

How many victims had he chased in the same manner?

Digby came down directly on top of the man, slamming him into the cobblestones hard enough to crack a bone or two. A pair of knives clattered to the ground from a hidden pouch in his coat. His prey cast several illusions, each more horrific than the last but they all unraveled in an instant.

"Let me go, you monster!" Jack cast Icicle and drove it into Digby's lower back.

He ignored it and opened his maw. "Sorry, but you're no longer the top of the food chain."

Another icicle plunged into his lower back, then another into his side as he forced the illusionist down. Then, finally, the flailing killer went under. Digby pulled away from the shadowy opening of his maw and closed it shut.

Heretic, level 24 Illusionist defeated. 2,330 experience awarded.

Digby arched his eyebrow at the message that came next.

NEW RITUAL DISCOVERED
Sin Eater: Harness the power of another magic user's spark.
Materials Required: The unfractured spark of a magic user.

Reward: A new spell
RITUAL COMPLETE
MURDEROUS SPARK OBTAINED: By consuming a powerful spark, you have engraved an imprint of it into your mana system.
You have discovered the spell, Summon Echo.
SUMMON ECHO
Description: Temporarily recall the echo of a consumed spark to take action. The actions of a summoned spark may be unpredictable and will vary depending what type of spark you choose to summon. More control may be possible at higher ranks.
Rank: D
Cost: 50MP
Range: 50ft (+50% due to mana purity)
Limitations: The result of this spell will depend heavily upon what spark you choose to summon.
Available Sparks: Murderous Wraith
MURDEROUS WRAITH
When summoned, this spark will manifest and attack a target that is currently hostile to you. Due to the skills of the consumed spark, this spell has a high probability of dealing catastrophic damage to a target.

Digby reread the messages.

Since when can I consume souls?

He had swallowed people whole before in the outside world but never had an effect such as this. Then again, out there was a material space, while the Seed's realm was immaterial. The difference must have impacted his ability enough that he had just discovered and completed a ritual all at once.

Thinking about it, there was a good chance that what he had just done was cheating in some way. There was probably a proper way to absorb a spark out there in the world, but events just happened to have aligned for him to access the ability here. He would have to look into it more when he got back.

"Okay, that is a shitty way to go." Parker caught up, panting.

"I know." Digby sighed as he stood up.

"You just swallowed him whole." She stared at the spot where his maw had been.

"It was a death better than he deserved." Henwick walked up behind her. "That man was as much a monster as any I have seen, as well as a willing user of magic."

Digby nodded, relieved for once that the cleric hadn't declared his actions as evil.

Unfortunately, his relief was short-lived.

Henwick grabbed his shoulder a second later and spun Digby around. He threw a hand out toward the armored zombie that Digby had raised as it joined them in the alley. "I cannot, however, approve of that."

Digby let out a long sigh, a part of him wondering what would happen if he dropped Henwick into his void right then and there. He might actually get another spell. He shook off the thought, recognizing it as what some might call villainous. Something about eating the man, after getting to know his more noble characteristics, soured the idea.

"I know, Henwick." Digby looked him dead in the eyes, getting sick of the constant criticism from the man. "But we have talked about this. My minions are necessary."

"Necessary? You think this abomination is necessary?" He swept his hand up and down in front of the armored zombie. "For god's sake, man, you could have simply asked for my assistance so that you didn't need to resort to creating this sort of horror."

"I..." Digby started to argue but found the words missing.

Henwick wasn't wrong.

He could have said something. There wasn't a need for him to take Jack on by himself.

Henwick didn't let up. "I realized you have a different relationship with morality, and I have sworn to aid you in returning to the world beyond. Yet, I cannot in good conscience do so if you continue to behave like a villain. The fight against Autem is important, but what sort of world will be left if I set you loose upon it?"

Digby considered his words for a moment, then he shook his

head. Things had worked out and he hadn't done anything wrong. Letting Henwick get under his skin was the last thing he needed.

"I'm sorry that you don't like how I do things, but the world will not be saved through heroics and faith." He stomped back to his minion and snatched Jack's coat from its hands to replace his which had been singed in the fight with the fractured sparks earlier. "Out there, we are outnumbered and underpowered. I cannot afford to leave a single scrap upon the table." He finished his declaration by snatching Jack's hat off the street and dropping it onto his head.

Sure, the hat was ridiculous, but it was clearly expensive.

"With that attitude, you will damn the world to hell." Henwick swatted the hat off his head.

"Oh please," Digby snapped back before turning to Parker. "Would you tell him what it's like out there?"

"Nope." Parker blew out a long sigh and picked up the two knives that Jack had dropped before sitting down against a wall in protest. "I'm not even going to bother trying to stop you two anymore. You can just punch each other until you're satisfied. 'Cause I'm out."

That was when a pair of glowing red eyes appeared from the end of the alleyway.

"We will have to continue this later." Digby gestured to the shadowy passage as a fractured spark skulked out of the dark, followed by two more. "I don't think those are illusions this time."

"Very well." Henwick sounded unsatisfied but took up a position at his back regardless. "We will discuss this later."

"Good." Digby picked Jack's hat back up and placed it on his head. "There will be plenty of time to argue later."

Parker pushed herself back up and joined them. "If we survive."

CHAPTER TWENTY-FOUR

"I am what I am!" Digby leapt back as a fractured spark launched a Fireball past him. He willed his minion to tackle the creature just as Henwick fired a cluster of glowing orbs into another.

"That is no excuse for your behavior." The cleric wouldn't let up, even when they were fighting for their very existence.

"Seriously?" Parker shouted at them both. "Are you really going to argue while these things try to kill us?"

"Apparently, Henwick doesn't feel that the fractured souls of dead Heretics trying to murder us are a worthy distraction from his complaints. Never mind the fact that it is the very necromancy that he has such an aversion to that is currently keeping him alive," Digby snapped back as he checked his mana.

MP: 248/298

"Excuse me?" Henwick's tone sounded indignant. "Had it not been for your ridiculous cackling while you chased that miscreant Jack, these sparks shan't have found us."

"He's got you there, Dig." Parker dodged an icicle that shattered a window behind her.

"Whose side are you on?" Digby growled back in her direction.

"I don't even know anymore." She shrugged before diving forward out of the way of another icicle.

Henwick jumped out to catch her as she tumbled past him, slipping his hand around her waist for stability before releasing her. "We are not done talking about this, Graves. You don't just get to declare you are what you are and think that is a good enough reason to behave like a villain."

The cleric stumbled into him as another fractured spark lunged from the rooftops toward him. It hit the ground fist first with a blast of power that pulverized the cobblestones beneath it.

"Too bad, because I am quite finished discussing the matter." Digby leapt at the creature with a hand raised to avoid giving it time to cast its shockwave attack. He cast Forge to send a spike of blood surging from the shadowy opening of his maw at the center of his palm. The point pierced through the foe's throat. He spent the extra mana to reform the blood into a disk within the creature's neck, popping its head off. He caught it by the hair with his other hand.

Fractured Spark defeated. 930 experience awarded.

"I could very well leave you to defend yourself alone." Henwick spun toward the other end of the alleyway as another few sparks stalked toward them, their glowing, crimson eyes sunk deep into their sockets.

"If you feel that strongly about it, you might as well kill me yourself and abscond with my body." Digby cast Cremation to ignite the severed head in his hand and launched it at the oncoming threats. The skull screamed through the air and burst on contact, splashing molten gray matter in the face of one of the fractured sparks. It flailed and collapsed to the street a few seconds later.

Fractured Spark defeated. 930 experience awarded.

The foe behind it simply stepped over its still flaming body. Digby glanced at his HUD.

MP: 203/298

His mana was falling fast. He nodded to his armored minion and sent it into the fray. He had been holding the oversized zombie back in fear that one of the sparks might hit it with that shockwave spell. His minion had only been recently animated. The last thing Digby wanted was to see it blasted into pieces.

That was when a massive beam of pure white light streaked by his head to pour into the threat before his minion could reach it. The fractured spark glowed momentarily, then burst into flames.

Fractured Spark defeated. 930 experience awarded.

"Oh damn." Parker peeked out through her fingers, having shielded her eyes from the light.

The hell was that? Digby stood, stunned by the power he had just witnessed.

Even the skin on his face began to smoke just from being in close proximity to the beam of light. He'd felt that sensation before, back on Autem's base when the sky had opened up to blast him out of existence. Clearly, it was the same spell Henwick had cast then, but on a smaller scale.

The purpose of showing him the spell was clear. Henwick was letting him know that if he wanted to kill him, he could.

Digby turned back slowly with one eyebrow raised. "Been hiding a spell, have you?"

"It's called Smite." Henwick held his hand raised as if he was ready to fire another. "And I would have used it earlier, but it has a high mana cost so it's not one I like to use frivolously."

"Only when you want to make a point, eh?" Digby narrowed his eyes.

"Don't be ridiculous, Graves." Henwick lowered his hand. "I wouldn't do anything as untoward as to murder you and steal your body. In fact, I would go so far to say that is a point that does need to be made here. You are the one suspecting others and making assumptions because that is how you are. I know you think of your lack of honor as a strength, but it only clouds your judgment and makes you expect the worst from everyone, your allies included. You then use that belief to justify your actions."

Digby hesitated, glancing at Parker to see if she agreed.

The soldier answered by holding up a hand and tilting it back and forth. "Kinda."

He frowned and snapped his attention back to Henwick. "I'm afraid the world has only proved me right so far. Besides, right now, I'm the world's only hope out there." Digby defended himself as a pair of red eyes entered the alleyway behind Henwick. He focused on the threat and cast his newest spell to summon the echo of Jack the Ripper.

If Henwick was going to use his spells to make a point, so could he.

A crimson form blinked into existence in the space between them. It shifted and flowed like a still image flickering from one position to another. At times, it resembled the man that had been consumed to create it, while at others it was nothing more than a blur. Digby focused on the fragment behind Henwick and set the echo upon it. The summoned wraith took off in a streak of crimson, a gleaming blade visible in its hand. The magical construct passed Henwick, close enough that it could have reached out and slit his throat just for the fun of it.

Digby couldn't help but notice the color drain from the cleric's face.

An instant later, the wraith met the fractured spark with a slash of precision and violence. Blood sprayed from the foe's neck in an arterial gush that coated the alley wall in a long arc. The flickering form of Jack the Ripper stopped for a fraction of a second then darted back to hit the foe again across the back. The impact spun the fragment off its feet, sending it spiraling to the cobblestones where it bled out.

Digby tried his best not to look stunned by the display. The spell certainly was worth the fifty points of mana that it cost.

Fractured Spark defeated. 930 experience awarded.

A quick scan of the alleyway told him that was the last of the threats.

Henwick didn't look back at the corpse. "Is that you making a point of your own?"

"Maybe." Digby gave him a sarcastic shrug. He sent a mental command to his armored minion to do the same to add to the effect.

"Cute." Parker bent over to lean on her knees for a rest.

Henwick shook his head at the display. "I have a good mind to destroy that abomination before you defile the dead further."

"Oh, don't be such a white knight." Digby groaned. "Destroy my minion and you shall only succeed in slowing us down."

"I can live with that, so long as you learn a lesson about what is appropriate." Henwick raised his hand back up, aiming at Digby's armored minion.

"You wouldn't dare." Digby held his ground, determined to call the man's bluff.

"It is not a matter of my willingness. As I said, I cannot allow you to continue as things are. Not unless you renounce your ways." Henwick began moving mana through his blood. "I think a Smite should put that monster back down."

"Wait, what?" Digby's smug expression fell, realizing that the cleric might actually do it.

"Hey!" Parker rushed in just as Henwick's hand began to glow.

"Wait, stop—" The cleric nearly stumbled as she grabbed his arm. A beam of blinding light poured from his palm to sweep past Digby's minion, just barely missing it before carving a swath up the side of the alleyway.

"Hey, hey, hey, hey! Cut that out." Digby dove behind his armored zombie for cover, only to peek out from behind it to find the pink-haired soldier wrapped around Henwick's burly arm so that he couldn't aim.

"Unless you are going to follow through and kill each other, would you both just stop arguing? It is getting us nowhere and we still have a ways to go." She panted as she let go of the cleric.

"For once, I am innocent in this altercation," Digby claimed as he straightened his new hat on his head. "I barely even antagonized him. Yet this menace's misguided sense of right and wrong gave him a mind to kill my minion."

"Better your minion than you." Henwick stabbed a finger in the direction of the armored zombie. "It isn't right to desecrate the dead."

"That corpse belongs to a fractured spark of someone that lived centuries ago. I assure you that the time to be outraged has passed. I cannot simply swear off the use of my magic simply because you don't like it." Digby clenched his fist. "The world doesn't have time for me to find a more noble method."

"And——" Henwick raised his voice before Parker stepped between them.

"Enough. God. Dig is right. We don't have the strength to take the high road out there in the real world. It would be great if we could work in a way that fits with your values but we're barely hanging on. You can't expect us to change everything just to make you feel better about helping us." She slapped Henwick in the side. "So stop being such a douchebag."

"Well, I never." Henwick shook his head and stepped away, clearly thrown off balance by her intervention. "And what is a douchebag?"

"Ha. That one I know. Hawk taught me." Digby pointed a finger at the cleric as he piled on.

"That goes for you too," Parker snapped back in his direction.

"Me?" Digby pointed to himself in surprise.

"Yes, you." She deflated. "You don't exactly make it easy to not want to kill you, and that's coming from me, a person who generally likes you. So stop being so antagonistic to everyone, and just maybe, Henwick would be more willing to give you a chance long enough to see that your magic can help people. Can we at least agree to that?" She looked back and forth between them both.

"Alright fine." Digby folded his arms. "I can be nice if he can."

"Very well." Henwick did the same. "I can refrain from destroying that walking abomination for now."

"How generous," Digby grumbled before flicking his eyes to Parker. "Since when are you the voice of reason here?"

"Since you left me no choice." She dropped both arms limp at her sides and dragged her feet. "You think I want to be the adult in charge? Honestly, I would kill to go back to napping and making jokes. But no, I'm stuck here with Corpsey McCorpseFace and Sir Chivalry, knight of the grabby hands."

"Grabby hands?" Henwick looked down at his fingers.

"Yes." Parker slapped at him in a huff. "Stop freaking grabbing me. I am a grown ass woman."

"But I am merely trying to protect a vulnerable lady." Henwick looked confused.

"Well stop." She stomped a foot and clenched her fists.

"I always avoid touching people." Digby raised his nose in the air.

"That's just 'cause you're dead and you think you'll gross people out." She hit the nail on the head.

Digby frowned, not appreciating his insecurities being called out so accurately.

Finally she settled down. "In other news, I gained another few levels."

"Really?" Digby's eyebrows climbed up his forehead, glad for the change in subject. "Any new spells?"

"No." She shrugged. "Why? Should I have learned one?"

"Not necessarily." He scratched at his chin. "But I am surprised that the skill link system hasn't granted you something yet. It would be nice if you could at least learn a spell that could actually be used in combat."

"Well, excuse me." She glared in his direction. "I'm sorry getting dropped into this place hasn't turned me into something that suits your needs better."

"Alright, alright." He dropped the subject, catching a level of stress in her voice that hadn't been there before, even when shouting at him and Henwick.

"We aren't through, Graves." Henwick stepped toward him. "Though, in the interest of moving forward, I can set things aside. But if I am to turn a blind eye to things like this." He gestured to the armored zombie. "I need you to swear to me that when Autem has been vanquished from the world, you will do away with the Heretic Seed and abandon the power it bestowed upon you. If you have no enemy to fight, then there will be no reason to continue using this magic anymore."

"I…" Digby started to speak, only to trail off. "I've never actually thought about what I would do after Autem is out of the picture."

"I suggest you start." Henwick remained firm. "I cannot in good conscience assist you if you will simply replace my other self as the ruler of the world. And an undead monster is not much better than a tyrant."

"You have a point. I don't wish to rule the world anyway. In all honesty, my original goal after I was cursed was to find a way to restore my humanity. If I can do that, I would like nothing better than to live out my days in peace." Digby nodded decisively. "Very well. I can agree to your terms. If I manage to win out there and find a way to restore my life, I will gladly retire my power."

"I don't just mean retirement." Henwick grabbed his shoulder. "I mean that I want the Heretic Seed destroyed again and sealed away so that no one may obtain its power."

That part of his request left Digby at a loss, especially considering he would need to give magic to everyone he could to stand against Autem. With that, it would be hard to put magic back in the box. There would be too many people with power, and few would simply give it up. He wasn't even sure if destroying the Seed would have an effect. It might prevent them from creating new magic users, but he had no idea what it would mean for those that already had power.

Eventually, he nodded again and lied. "Fine, I'll do what I can to meet your expectations."

What else could he have done?

"Now come on. We have to keep moving." Digby continued to walk toward the end of the alley without looking back. He made a point to open his maw and consume the bodies of the fragments. He couldn't let that much go to waste.

Henwick, for once, said nothing. The look on his face made it clear he wasn't comfortable with his answer either.

"Wait up." Parker rushed to catch up, his minion plodding along behind her.

Henwick grumbled something under his breath but followed along. Digby couldn't help but keep his focus on the man, just in case he started moving mana to cast another spell. There was no way to know what the future might bring, or what the right course of action was.

It was true the Heretic Seed was dangerous, but at the same time, it could be used to heal and empower the people. There was a part of him that wasn't sure that taking that power away from the world was the right thing to do. The Seed was capable of as much good as it was evil. Who would he be to deny humanity the right to make that decision for itself?

Then again, with Henwick standing behind him, he might not be given that choice. Something told him that the cleric wasn't going to let him lie his way out of the question forever. He would have to find a way to make the man see past his rigid beliefs or they may end up as enemies again.

He pressed onward, unable to resolve anything.

It wasn't long before they saw a stairway in the distance.

Digby followed the twisting steps with his eyes. They reached up to the rough ceiling that hung over the rooftops of the city streets that they walked.

That must be the next level of the Seed's realm. Just how many more spaces did they need to traverse before they found whatever the Seed had waiting for them? Probably many considering how few remnant sparks they had come across. Maybe that was a good thing. Maybe the rest of their opponents would find each other first and thin out the competition. The caretaker was still out there as well. Hopefully it was busy dealing with the other Heretics and not closing in on them.

Digby was getting a little sick of it all.

As they approached the bottom of the stairway, he was relieved to find that at least this one didn't twist over onto itself like the last.

A trickle of debris fell from the opening above where the stairs led.

"Is that... sand?" Parker stared up at the ceiling from beside him.

"Indeed." Digby stepped onto the first step as an out-of-place object rolled down the stairway to meet him. He recognized it instantly, having spent a day in the desert not too long ago.

"A tumbleweed?"

"I don't like the look of that." Henwick nudged the ball of dry weeds off the steps with his foot.

"Nor do I." Digby stared up at the land above.

Parker trotted up the first few stairs before looking back. "At least you two can agree on something."

CHAPTER TWENTY-FIVE

"Having trouble working up the courage?" Jameson asked from the passenger seat beside Becca in the cockpit of a kestrel.

"What?" She glanced at him as Las Vegas appeared on the sun-drenched horizon. It had been a long week of getting things done, but they were almost ready to finalize the transfer of the Hoover Dam's power to the city. With that, Becca's supervision was no longer needed.

Now she was almost home.

"You never gave your guy his hat." Jameson gestured to the cowboy hat that she had left sitting above the kestrel's controls.

"Oh," Becca blew out a sigh. "Mason headed back with the last transport of the dam's people. I didn't have time before he left. I'm sure he'll be waiting when we land, I'll give it to him then."

"Ah. I see." Jameson leaned back in his seat.

"You see what?" Becca glowered at his reflection in the cockpit window.

"Nothing." The old man shrugged in a way that contradicted his answer.

The old vet had been a huge help in everything concerning the dam's power supply and the people living within it. He'd also gotten a little too friendly.

"What do you mean, nothing?" She rotated her head, slowly, until her glower was pointed directly at him.

"Well, it's not my place to say, but it seemed like you had plenty of time before Mason left with the transport." He reached out and grabbed the hat off the console and placed it on his head. "You could have talked to him."

"Yeah, well, I didn't." Becca rolled her eyes.

He was right, she could have talked to him. Actually, she had planned to. There had been a lot of time for thinking the last few days and when everything was considered, she did love him. In fact, her plan had been to give him the stupid hat and slip in a quiet 'love ya' when he inevitably laughed at the gift.

Of course that raised the question, why hadn't she?

Well, the answer to that was she was a giant awkward idiot, and every time she tried, she ended up chickening out. It just wasn't easy to put herself out there. She was so bad off that the only one that might have understood where she was coming from was Digby.

An image of the zombie laying on the floor of the high-roller suite flashed through her head as she thought of the zombie. It was weirdly annoying how much she missed having him around. He might have been a jerk, but he was a reliable jerk, and he meant well. Not to mention he would never have let her indulge the fear that kept her from talking to Mason. No, he would have blurted something out that forced the situation into the light.

Becca chewed on her bottom lip as she shook off the thought.

Of course, Jameson's immediacy brought it all right back.

"So what's the plan? You gonna run into Mason's arms when we land? Maybe give him a kiss and tell him you love him?"

Becca let out a long groan and let her head fall back against the headrest of her seat. "Were you always this nosey?"

Jameson chuckled. "Sorry, got addicted to soap operas the last few years."

"I'm so glad my life has become a suitable replacement now that the world has ended." Becca refocused her eyes on the Las Vegas strip as the craft approached it.

"Sorry, but I have to keep myself entertained somehow without my stories." The old man leaned back and put his foot up on the console.

Becca nodded as if satisfied with his answer. Then she jerked the sticks to the side, causing him to fall halfway out of his seat. The cowboy hat toppled to the floor next to her.

"Hey, I am an old man." He clung to the side of his chair.

She gave a nonchalant shrug. "I would have healed you if you got hurt. Because magic is a thing now, remember?"

"Oh yeah." His eyes widened.

"What's going on up there?" Malcolm called from the back of the craft.

"Nothing!" she shouted back into the passenger compartment without looking back. She would have much rather the man had ridden back to Vegas with Ducky and Sullivan, but things just worked out that she was stuck with him.

Becca pushed her thoughts of him out of her head as she brought the kestrel in toward the parking garage next to the casino. Jameson tensed as she slipped the craft through the narrow opening in the top floor of the structure and followed the ramp down to the one below.

"Relax, I've done this before." She gave him a smug grin and set the kestrel down. "Can't have the aircraft that we stole sitting in plain sight. Don't want a satellite spotting it and giving up our location."

"I suppose not." He waited for the craft to stop moving completely before standing up and heading for the ramp at the back. "Good luck with your whole confession thing."

Becca grabbed the cowboy hat by her feet and swatted him with it. "Yeah, thanks, I'll tell him the moment I see him, if that will get you off my back."

"Sure." He chuckled.

"I mean it." She sighed. "I need to, I know that much."

With that, she shut down the kestrel and stood up. Her foot crunched on a bit of debris laying on the floor of the cockpit as she moved. Becca glanced down at the sound. There was nothing particularly special about the stone under her foot, but it was strangely angular, like a thin chip of rock. She wasn't actually sure why it had drawn her attention. There was just something out of place about it. Her focus was pulled away a second later when Malcolm punched the ramp's open button.

"You coming?"

"Shit, yeah." Becca ignored it and headed to the back of the craft to wait for the ramp to open. If she knew Mason, he would be waiting for her at the bottom, and it was her best chance to set things right between them. She took a deep breath to commit to the plan.

Holding the cowboy hat against her chest, she stood between Jameson and Malcolm as the parking garage came into view.

"Welcome home." Eleanor stood at the bottom of the ramp, alone.

A sharp pain echoed through Becca's chest before settling into her stomach. She nearly asked where Mason was but didn't want to seem distracted in front of Malcolm.

Judging from the look of Elenore, she probably had more important things to discuss anyway. The woman looked a little disheveled. Her hair was a mess, with half of it falling from a scrunchy. On top of that, the dark circles under her eyes told Becca everything she needed to know.

Things had not been easy in Vegas while she had been away.

"Thanks. Sorry to have left you for so long." Becca cringed at the apology and shoved the hat in her hands behind her back.

Elenore and Deuce had pretty much been left in charge to deal with the influx of survivors that they had been sending from the dam every day for almost a week now. That would bring their numbers up to just over a thousand. It was more than four times the amount of mouths to feed than they had previously living within the casino. There would still be plenty of supplies for the time being, but still, keeping everything organized couldn't have been easy. Not to mention they would need to be trained in a variety of skills.

Sure, Alex was there to help, but from the few communications Becca had with him, he was deeply entrenched in his work with the runes they'd discovered. Add to that the fact that Digby and Parker were still doing god knew what in the Heretic Seed's version of a virtual environment, and everyone had to be a little on edge.

"I'm out." Malcolm strode down that ramp straight past Elenore and left them behind, clearly heading back to meet with Bancroft.

Becca breathed a little sigh of relief that he was gone for the moment. He'd behaved fine and listened to her when needed over the course of the week, but he still had a ways to go before she would fully trust him. Then again, she was going to have to meet with the man as well.

"Has Bancroft behaved himself?" Becca dragged her feet down the ramp to meet Elenore.

"Somewhat." She tapped a thumb on a clipboard that she held against her chest. "There have been some problems with his guys in how they have been treating the zombies we've gathered. As for Bancroft himself, he's been helpful in fielding complaints and keeping them in line. Plus, it helps that Tavern has been getting him drunk on the reg."

Becca let out an awkward chuckle. "I'm not sure I want to know what drunk Bancroft is like."

"That's probably the right response." Elenore looked up as Jameson followed Becca down the ramp. She checked her clipboard. "You Jameson?"

"That's what it says on my license." He scratched at his beard.

"Perfect. Thank you for everything you've done with the power supply. That's going to do a lot for this place." She checked her clipboard again. "As long as everything follows schedule today, we should be able to set the lights inside to normal use rather than just emergency systems."

Jameson chuckled. "Should be able to light up the whole strip with what the dam is sending your way."

Elenore looked concerned for a second.

"Not that we would." Becca stepped in. "We might as well send Autem an email to let them know where we are." She paused. "You know, if the internet hadn't mostly failed."

"Eh, the internet's overrated." Jameson frowned. "But regardless, it's a little sad. It would be nice to see this city lit up again."

"You aren't wrong." Eleanor looks out at the strip beyond the parking garage as if picturing what it had looked like before everything ended.

"Maybe someday." Becca tried to sound hopeful. "You never know, maybe with the work Alex is doing with those runes, we'll find new ways of doing things."

"He's definitely figured some helpful things out." Elenore headed back toward the entrance to the casino. She pointed to a pair of posts that bracketed the doors. "None of it's pretty, but he's been making headway."

Becca followed along to examine the posts. They were metal and about as tall as a road cone. Their surfaces were covered in runes and the base of each had been welded to a heavy stand. "Are they for warding?"

"Yeah, they have been keeping the place secure." Elenore poked one with her clipboard. "They don't float and they're way bigger than the ones that you guys took from Autem's base. But between these and the sun goddess statue inside, we don't have to worry about the revenants at all."

"Provided we don't run into a new kind that can break wards and function in high levels of life essence," Becca added. "Speaking of, have you run into any of the sensebreakers in the city?"

"Those the ones that turn invisible?" Elenore furrowed her brow.

"They also deafen the sounds they make," Becca added.

"Nope, none so far." Elenore gave an unconvincing shrug. "Or at least we haven't seen any, which I guess is the point."

Becca didn't love that answer. "Where's Mason?"

"He and Sax got stuck supervising at a power station with some of the engineers from the dam. They're fine and the location is secure with more warding rods, but it might be a day or two before the work is done there." Elenore gestured into the distance. "The timing isn't great, but at least he's getting levels out there."

Becca stopped short. "He's a Heretic?"

She nodded. "Deuce gave him one of the rings Alex prepped as soon as he got here. We need everyone we can get, and Mason headed straight up to touch the Seed's obelisk."

"That's all it takes?" Jameson sounded skeptical.

Elenore started walking again and pushed through the doors. "That's it. And he's a fighter class, by the way."

"I could have called that." Becca smiled, feeling a little more connected to him even if he hadn't come to meet her when she landed. Then she frowned, realizing that she'd probably missed his first spell. It would have been nice to have been there for support. She glanced at Eleonore letting the Seed tell her more.

Heretic, level 1, Fighter.

The woman shot her a knowing look. "You scanned me, didn't you?" She shook her head. "I mean analyzed me. Or whatever it's called."

"You're a fighter too." Becca stated the obvious.

"You can tell just by looking?" Jameson looked surprised.

Elenore gave a half nod. "And I guess fighter fits me. I've always been a bit of a brute when it comes to conflict, so I guess it makes sense. Too bad the ring I used crumbled right after I got my class. We could have reused them."

"So, Alex is well underway with activating new Heretics, then?" Becca continued into the stairwell that connected to the parking garage.

"Yeah. He wanted to get people started as soon as possible so they could start getting levels. I haven't had time to go out yet, though. Not with all the new people you've been sending me. I might as well still be a normal person right now."

"I think we've left normal far behind us at this point." Becca inclined her head. "And sorry about sending you so many people. Couldn't leave them all crammed in the dam."

"The place just wasn't made for that," Jameson added. "It's a miracle everyone got along back there for as long as they did. But, yeah, sorry for sending you everyone all at once."

"Don't be." Elenore glanced at her clipboard. "It puts a strain on things in the short term, but it's better in the long run. Plus, they all seem pretty grateful. Not to mention their experience with Autem has them ready to take up the fight."

"Who do we have now that can use magic?" Becca walked beside her as they entered the casino.

"Well, including Sax and Deuce," she leaned toward her, "we have seven mages. Easton is a fighter, weirdly enough. I kinda thought he would be a back-line kind of guy. We've got a few other fighters as well, including that kid that got in all that trouble with Autem last week."

"Hawk snuck his way in to touch the Seed, huh?" Becca gave her a sideways look.

"Nah." Elenore shrugged. "Alex let him. Said Dig would have approved. Which is probably true, considering that zombie doesn't have the best judgment."

"How much trouble has the kid gotten in so far?" Becca sighed.

"Surprisingly, none." Elenore held up both hands empty. "I don't know what has gotten into him, but he has only gone out when accompanied by the other Heretics and he hasn't taken any risks. Honestly, he's been following orders and doing what he's told. It's like he's turned over a new leaf."

"What about our other problem child?" Becca frowned, remembering that they still had a brainwashed teen in the casino.

"Alvin?" She paused a moment. "He's been fine. Sticks with his sister whenever he's out of his room. Hawk actually keeps an eye on him when she's busy taking care of Parker. I'm not sure if that means he's stepping away from Autem's influence, but it's better than trying to escape or sabotaging things."

"That's good, I think." Becca headed down the hall toward the casino's main floor. "We still have a ring available, right?"

"Yes, Alex has the one that you ask to be set aside for Jameson, here."

"And when do I, ah…?" The old vet's pace slowed as he trailed off.

Becca waited to stay beside him, realizing that he might be having second thoughts. "I was planning on linking you to the Seed as soon as we can. If that's okay with you?"

Jameson paused for a moment before nodding decisively. "I'd be lying if I said it wasn't scary, but I am sure. Might as well get it over with now."

"Okay." Becca gave him a smile before turning back to Elenore. "And where is Alex right now?"

Elenore simply laughed and pointed at a row of slot machines. Becca followed her finger across the room to find the artificer's head traversing the space while peeking over the slots. She cocked her head to the side, noticing something strange but having trouble putting her finger on it. A second later she figured it out.

He wasn't walking.

No, from where she stood, his smug face was gliding across the room like he was floating a few inches above the floor.

Becca rubbed at her forehead. "He made a hoverboard, didn't he?"

"Yep." Elenore nodded. "He hasn't gotten off that thing all morning. But I'll let him explain that. I have things to do, and he can catch you up on anything else."

With that, the ex-showgirl turned level one fighter laughed and left Becca and Jameson to take in the display that followed.

From behind a row of slot machines, Alex glided around the corner, beaming with pride. Beneath him was what looked like a rectangle of iron with a slight angle on the corners at the front. A gap of about five inches was present between him and the floor. A textured panel had been adhered to the top of the iron board where he stood for traction. At his side hung a messenger bag that he wore slung diagonally across his body.

"Welcome home." He held both hands out wide as the ridiculous contraption slowed to a stop in front of her. A stupid grin was plastered across his face.

"This the kid who's in charge of your R&D." Jameson looked down at Alex's creation, then back up to his face.

Alex frowned. "Could I request that you not call me kid? I have been putting up with that all week from Bancroft's guys. I swear Louis is doing it on purpose just to annoy me."

Becca looked up at the artificer, surprised to hear him stand up for himself to someone he just met. Maybe leaving him alone to deal with things in the city was having a good effect on him.

"Sorry, point taken." Jameson nodded as the corner of his mouth tugged up. He dropped his eyes back down to the mana-fueled hoverboard. "That's quite something, though."

"I know, right?" The artificer practically vibrated with the need to talk about his creation.

Becca blew out a sigh. "Okay, go ahead and tell us about it."

Alex grinned like an idiot as he leaned to one side, causing the board beneath him to turn like some sort of gyroscopic scooter. Then he clapped his hands together.

"Well, it has a heart layer of gold that I engraved with all the runes needed to control the flow of mana from the user. So all you have to do is lean and let it draw MP from you."

"Heart layer?" Becca arched an eyebrow.

"Yeah, we made a ton of progress once we figured that part out. It's how the Guardian rings are made. I used the same method Autem did. So there's a heart layer, a mid-layer, and an outer shell." He tapped his foot on his creation. "This one isn't much to look at, but it works. And with what I've learned, I should be able to apply the same effect to other things. If you give us a little time, gasoline might end up obsolete."

"That would be good." Becca leaned to one side. "Wait, who is us? Is Parker awake?"

"No, she's still off on her adventure with Dig. Lana is taking care of her body though. It seems that her Regenerate spell is able to help keep Parker stable and minimize the effects of being out for so long." He shoved a hand into the messenger bag hanging from his shoulder and pulled out the last thing Becca expected. "And when I say us, I'm talking about my new personal assistant."

"Don't call me that." The skull of Kristen the seer groaned as he held her up. He had apparently made some modifications.

What had once been nothing but bone was now partially covered with gold. The metal dripped down its surface in irregular patterns like the wax of a candle. Dozens of runes were engraved across the precious metal.

"You know carrying a skull around in your bag is awfully reminiscent of someone else I know." Becca leaned forward to look at the seer. "So she's actually helping you?"

"Oh good." Kristen's voice settled into a sarcastic tone. "Someone else is here to gawk at my remains. Hooray."

"Okay, that is a talking skull." Jameson pointed at the seer with his mouth hanging open.

"Yeah, things have been getting weirder lately." Alex shoved the skull back into his bag without giving Kristen a chance to insult anyone else. "And I wouldn't say she's really helping. Honestly, she mostly tries to trick or antagonize me. But I have been able to make some progress with what little information she lets slip. Plus, I think she's warming up to me. Hasn't tried to get me killed for a couple days, at least."

"Considering how we've gained allies, that seems par for the course." Becca sighed and started walking again, her thoughts falling back on Digby. "And there's been no contact from within the Seed?"

"None since that first mirror link. Although, if you analyze Parker, she has a class now." Alex hopped off his invention, picked it up, and tucked it under his arm.

Becca arched an eyebrow. "Really? What?"

"Messenger."

"Huh," Becca paused. "Never seen one of those before."

"Neither have I." Alex patted his bag. "I asked my assistant, here, but she wasn't particularly forthcoming."

"It's something rare, then?" Jameson followed along with the supernatural conversation.

"Maybe, but it also worries me considering her connection to the Seed was more invasive than normal. Not to mention its initial instability." Alex slowed as if a weight was holding him down. Becca could relate. Having a friend trapped within the Seed was unsettling.

"Is that something that happens often?" Jameson's tone sounded reasonably concerned.

"No, not at all. Everyone else that has connected with the Seed since it was restored has had no trouble whatsoever." Alex led the way up the stairs.

"I wouldn't worry." Becca tried to sound confident. "I became a Heretic in less-than-ideal conditions, and things have changed a lot for us since then."

"I suppose you're right." The old man nodded. "If I can't take a risk at the end of the world, then when can I?"

CHAPTER TWENTY-SIX

After guiding Jameson through the process of becoming a Heretic, Alex headed back down into his dark laboratory of enchantments. That wasn't his workshop's official name or anything, but that was what he was calling it in his head.

Of course, the old guy became a fighter. There wasn't much surprise there. So far, pretty much everyone that had military or law enforcement experience had either become fighters or mages. Alex had been hoping for another enchanter so that they could get another artificer at some point.

The fact that he and that jerk Louis were the only ones with the Purify Water spell was annoying. Without more people capable of cleansing a zombie or revenant bite, it meant that they both needed to be careful. He hoped Purify Water would become available to Lana since she seemed to be on the path of a healer, but if she was able to learn it, she hadn't yet.

As to why enchanters were so rare, he didn't know.

Autem never seemed to have trouble finding them, considering they had fought enough of the class. Maybe they just had more resources to find people with the right aptitudes. That might explain it. What it couldn't explain was how Parker came to be a messenger.

That one was still a mystery.

Alex glided into his workshop and hopped off his makeshift hoverboard. Placing it against the wall next to the door, he pulled off his messenger bag and tossed it on his workbench where it fell against a box containing some of his past experiments.

The box, of course, started vibrating.

Alex let out a sigh and grabbed Kristen's skull from his bag to place her on the table.

"Oh look, that phallus you crafted is vibrating again." Her mocking tone continued as usual. "What a unique use of the world's magic."

"Shut up." Alex dropped onto a stool next to the table.

"Nonsense. Such an achievement deserves praise, and I simply cannot let you forget what you have created." She didn't let up. Hell, she never let up.

"Thanks." Alex decided not to fight her. There wasn't a point to it, anyway. Besides, the more he did, the better she got at knowing what would annoy him the most.

"You're very welcome." Kristen sounded pleased with herself.

Alex sat quietly for a moment. She was always more likely to let an important detail slip or confess something when she was in a good mood. Now might be a chance to learn something important.

"So why does Autem keep their messengers out of the field? They seem to have an easy enough time finding enchanters, so they must be able to find messengers as well."

"Worried about your little girlfriend, are you?" She didn't even try to lie. No, she just went right on the attack.

"No," Alex snapped back, before adding, "I mean, no, she's not my girlfriend, but yes, I am worried."

"Not your girlfriend? And why not?" The skull's ghostly tone turned shrill. "She seemed to be a lovely young lady. A little slow, but lovely, nonetheless. And you—"

"And I, what?" He eyed the Skull.

"You are... How do I put it?" She made a noise that sounded like clicking her tongue despite not having one. "You are one of the few options available. I'd say that makes you highly desirable."

She paused for impact. "You know, because most of the other men in the world are dead."

"I got that, thanks." He chuckled. Her delivery was actually pretty funny. She almost seemed to be getting better. "But again, I'm not really interested in her like that. Not really interested in anyone. So, sorry to disappoint."

"Eh, my existence is mostly disappointment, so one more won't harm me." She sighed. "Well, let the poor girl down easy then. Wouldn't want you to break the poor messenger's heart."

"Maybe she's got a spell for that. One to heal a broken heart," he joked while also trying to pry some information from the skull.

The skull groaned at the corny line. "I doubt that broken hearts are her class's specialty."

Alex immediately jumped up from his stall and pointed at the seer's skull. "Ah ha!"

Kristen scoffed. "Ah ha, what?"

"You said you doubt that is her class's specialty." He grinned down at her gold-coated visage.

"And?" Her tone grew annoyed.

"And you didn't say it's *not* her specialty, only that you doubt it is." He picked her up and placed her back down on top of the box containing the vibrating magic dildo he'd made days ago. "From your wording, I assume you don't know what the messenger class does."

"Of course I do." Her voice came out like she was speaking into a fan, disrupted by the vibration of the box the skull sat on. "It sends messages, obviously."

"Really?" Alex channeled Digby as best he could to give her the smuggest face possible. "Because it sounds like you just guessed."

"Fine! Autem doesn't have any messengers." She pouted as best as she could. "Now would you take me off this idiotic vibrating box?"

"Oh sure." He picked her up and placed her down a few feet away. "So Henwick has kept the messenger class secret from you?"

"No, he wouldn't do that," she snapped back. "He told me everything, and Autem never had a messenger before, so whatever that stupid class is, it's something new that the Heretic Seed just created."

"Oh, that is interesting." He tapped her on her gold-plated forehead. "Now, isn't it easier to just tell me what I want to know instead of annoying me all the time?"

Before she could make a comment back, the door to the workshop swung open.

Alex spun toward the disturbance only to let out a sudden, "Yeep," as Bancroft practically staggered into the room.

"There you are, Mr. Sanders." Bancroft stopped as soon as he made eye contact. "Sorry, I mean Alex." He sighed. "Old habits and all."

Alex could smell the alcohol almost as soon as he'd entered. The man had clearly seen better days. His complexion carried a sickly pallor along with the dark circles under his eyes. There was even a sheen of sweat coating his forehead.

"You're drunk." Kristen's skull blurted out the words that Alex was already thinking.

Bancroft winced before pulling a handkerchief from his pocket to wipe his forehead. "Not quite, but you are correct to assume that Tavern has their own ideas about how to spend the night. We have reached a somewhat functional compromise, but honestly, I don't think I have come out on top."

"Compromise?" Alex folded his arms, asking himself what Becca would do. Normally she would try to act authoritative. Then again, maybe he should be concerned about the man's health. In the end, he sat awkwardly at the edge of his stool.

"Yes." Bancroft shoved his handkerchief back in his pocket. "Getting Tavern to cooperate has not been easy. Honestly, it's like the entity has somehow taken on some of their master's more disagreeable properties." He rubbed at his temples for a moment. "The agreement has been that Tavern allows me most of the day without disruption and I will ensure a supply of alcohol when we have downtime. Unfortunately, I had not foreseen the quantity that Graves' minion would require to be satisfied. If it weren't for the fact that I have the constitution of a high-level Heretic, I would be dead of alcohol poisoning. As it is, I have had a near continuous hangover for days."

"How much do you have to drink to get drunk anyway?" Alex arched an eyebrow. "I've never been that much of a drinker, so I haven't tried."

"Well then be glad that your skeleton is not inhabited by an infernal spirit that can drink an entire bottle of whiskey every night." Bancroft flinched as his mouth opened to add a twisted sounding, "Thanks, bruh," in a voice that clearly did not belong to him. He immediately grimaced. "That wasn't a compliment, Tavern."

"Okay then. I'm glad you have found a way to coexist." Alex nodded, imagining how difficult it would be to operate like that every day. On the up side, Bancroft couldn't organize any form of mutiny even if it was his top priority. Actually, if he wasn't a Heretic, he'd be dead of liver failure within the month.

Alex fought the urge to laugh.

It really wasn't funny, but there was something about the man's ridiculous predicament that made him feel like there was a chance he might fit into their party of misfits.

The idea of them getting along crumbled the instant Bancroft spoke again.

"I'm glad I caught you before you turned in for the night. I think we should discuss the free ride that you have been giving everyone here."

"I'm sorry?" Alex stood up from his stool. "What about a free ride?"

"It should be obvious." The sweaty man shook his head like he shouldn't have needed to explain. "You have been feeding, sheltering, and providing for every survivor that you come across. I don't think I have to tell you that there is a limit to how long we will be able to keep that up. You can't simply let people sit in their rooms upstairs and play games while others do all the work."

"He is not technically wrong," Kristen chimed in. "Even if he is overly sweaty."

Alex snorted at her comment, appreciating that she had aimed her jabs at Bancroft and not him. "True, you aren't wrong. But right now we have enough supplies to cover the people here for the time being. In the long run, we will need to work toward building a sustainable system, but with Autem out there, now doesn't seem like the time to really worry about it."

"A solid point. It is likely you will all be killed long before you run out of supplies." Kristen continued her commentary.

"That is less helpful." Alex turned to glare at the skull. "But you aren't wrong either. As much as I don't want to think about it, there isn't much point in setting up a full-blown society when the future is so uncertain. Besides, we have a war to focus on."

"I understand that." Bancroft let out a long sigh. "And I realize that what I am about to explain is going to make me sound like the villain, so I will preface it by saying that I am only trying to be pragmatic. But it will be much easier to get people to accept a higher degree of structure to their lives the earlier you start. The longer you wait, the harder it will be to impose new rules. Especially considering there is a fair amount of goodwill toward Graves amongst the people here. That is a powerful tool that can be leveraged, but it also has an expiration date. Depending on a number of factors, that influence will not last forever, meaning it is best to get this place under control before that happens. Not to mention, your people are the only ones with magic right now. What do you think will happen when Graves comes back with a way to give magic to anyone that wants it? You will have lost the one shred of leverage you have now."

Alex fell silent for a long moment before Kristen spoke up. "You're right. That does make you sound like a villain."

"I'm not sure the people here will still want to help us fight Autem if we start ruling them with an iron fist." Alex sat back down on his stool. "I've had enough crappy bosses in my life. I don't really want to become one."

"I realize that." Bancroft remained calm. "But I need you to accept two facts here. One, I really do want this city to prosper. And two, I am older than everyone currently involved in its leadership combined. I have experience in setting up organizations that no one here shares. I have no intent on trying to take control of anything. No, all I want is a seat at the table and the opportunity to make use of my experience when applicable. All I ask is that you use me to make this city stronger. So please, hear me out."

"I usually run this kind of thing past Becca." He scratched at the back of his neck.

"Oh, of course." Bancroft nodded. "That is completely reasonable. If you need Ms. Alvarez's approval, I will speak to her as well. If she's not in agreement, then I'll go back to the drawing board and find another way to help."

Alex glanced back to Kristen as if she might have something to add.

"Don't look at me. I couldn't care less what happens to this city."

Alex groaned and turned back to Bancroft. "What do you suggest? 'Cause we can't act like Autem and demand combat service from everyone we take in."

"No, no." He waved his hands from side to side. "Nothing that extreme."

"Then what?" Alex held his hands out empty.

"Money." Bancroft held his ground.

"What?" Alex frowned.

"Currency." Bancroft nodded. "This city needs a currency so that goods and services can be assigned a value. That is the only way that we will be able to remain in control of Las Vegas as this city continues to grow."

"Um, okay." Alex gestured to the forge. "I'll go set up a mint and start minting coins."

"Is that sarcasm?" Bancroft eyed him sideways.

"I believe it was." Kristen helped out.

Alex smirked. "Not to impersonate Dig, but yes, of course, it was sarcasm. I have other things to do. I can't be setting up a printing press or whatever you are expecting."

"And it's not like we can use money that was already in circulation." Kristen sighed. "There is simply too much of the useless stuff laying around. It's no better than toilet paper now. Not that I would require any at this point, on account of my not having a butt to wipe."

Bancroft's mouth fell open as if shocked by her comment.

"Sorry, she's been hanging around with me for the last few days and this is her thing now." Alex shrugged as if there was nothing that could be done.

"Clearly." The man groaned before returning to his point. "Regardless, there is still a way to make use of some of this city's pre-existing resources. Of course, we will eventually need to produce our own metal coins. But for now, we can use something that we have plenty of." Bancroft reached into a pocket and tossed a poker chip to him.

Alex caught it. "You realized that these things are all over the strip." Alex pointed at the chip with a finger. "What would stop anyone from just picking them up?"

"Yes. But with what you have been learning through your experiments with rune engraving, you might be able to find a way around our problem." Bancroft stepped forward to the work bench as if Alex had already agreed to his proposal. "Henwick had always been quite shrewd with what abilities he allowed the Guardian Core to teach his men. As far as I know, it was only the research and development division of Autem that was allowed to handle rune work."

"That makes sense." Alex's sarcastic tone faded as the mention of runes entered the conversation, finding the opportunity to learn more. "From what I've seen so far, they're definitely something that Henwick would want to keep to himself. The runes could actually replace some of the modern tech that we can't use anymore."

"Yes, and the same goes for transaction systems." Bancroft placed another few poker chips down, each valued at different increments. "With a little experimentation, you should be able to create an enchantment plate that can encode one of these chips with an identification marker. It's the same process as the security system that Autem used back on the base. The only difference would be that we would be using it to authenticate currency. As long as no one is given access to the original enchantment plate, there will be no way to counterfeit it."

"Hmm." Alex ran a finger over the chip in his hand. "We could actually destroy the original plate and store the rune work needed in an image format or something. Becca would be able to help secure or encrypt it."

"Exactly, and once you engrave an enchantment plate," Bancroft continued. "We can gather all the chips in the casino and encode them with the marker."

"That still leaves the question of if we should." Alex brought the conversation back to the ethics of the situation.

"I'm not suggesting we throw people out who can't or won't lend a hand." Bancroft shook his head. "That wouldn't help anyone, considering they could easily leak our location once they no longer needed our protection. What I propose is that, for now, we get the system up and running, and assign values to the goods and services that matter. That way we can start by giving everyone a stipend without asking anything in return. That would be a way to test the waters and get a little more organized. We will have to transition to a more structured society at some point and this will make the process as painless as possible."

Alex chewed his suggestion over. "Fine. If you can get Becca to agree, we can implement a standardized currency and set up a system of basic income."

"Thank you." Bancroft inclined his head, looking a little green. "Now, if you'll excuse me, I think I am going to throw up."

"Oh, ah. Okay." Alex stepped away from him.

The man immediately did an about-face and walked briskly toward the door as if he had barely been holding himself together the entire time.

Tavern's voice could be heard as he left. "Lightweight."

"Shut up, you." Bancroft's footsteps broke into a run as he closed the door.

Alex shook his head and looked down to the poker chip in his hand. It was actually an interesting project. He glanced back to Kristen. "You think it's the right thing to do?"

She let out a ghostly sigh. "I still don't care."

CHAPTER TWENTY-SEVEN

Becca blew out a long sigh as she closed the door of her hotel room.

She immediately leaned her back against it, fighting the urge to just slide down to the floor and take a nap. The last few days had been long as hell and just as stressful. She placed the cowboy hat she'd brought back from the dam on the table by the door.

Without turning on the lights, she headed straight for the bathroom. A shower would hopefully help her see the world a little clearer. She flicked the switch on the wall as she passed by and reached for the shower curtain.

Then, she stopped and leaned back out of the bathroom, catching something in her periphery.

"What is that?" Becca arched an eyebrow at a white box sitting on the bed. The light spilling from the bathroom framed it in a sharp, angular shape. A crimson ribbon wrapped the pristine cardboard and was tied off with a bow on the top. The packaging looked like it had been taken from the shopping center down stairs.

Becca inched away from the bed, feeling a little uneasy. Obviously, it was some sort of present.

"But, from who?"

At first, she assumed it was from Mason, but he was still at the power station, keeping guard for the workers. Plus, he was more of an upfront kind of guy. Mason wasn't really the type to sneak into her room like a creep. The fact that he respected her privacy was something she appreciated, considering she used to live under surveillance.

Granted, it wasn't like she owned anything that she needed to keep private. No, all she had was a few pairs of leggings and some random t-shirts, most of which were either plain or featured cheesy puns involving Vegas or gambling.

As she approached, Becca cautiously reached for an envelope that was tucked under the ribbon as if it was a bomb. A paranoid voice in her head told her it was a trap. Some kind of attempt by Bancroft's men to blow her up or something.

The envelope came free with no sign of exploding. She tore it open. Hopefully the note would shed some light on the suspicious package. Becca relaxed as soon as she saw the handwriting. It was messy and rushed, but she recognized it easily.

"Alex."

He wasn't exactly someone she expected to receive a present from. She shrugged off the question and read the note.

Sorry for sneaking into your room, I know that was weird. But I didn't want to give you this in front of anyone or even make it known that I wanted to meet you about anything. I just figured that, with Bancroft and his guys around, it seemed like a good idea to keep a few things secret. I will be alone when you find this, so project yourself to me and I will explain it.

-Alex

"Umm, okay?" Becca tossed the note to the side and went to untie the bow that held the box closed. It turned out to be stapled together and attached to the lid, which explained things a little. She'd thought it strange that Alex would go out of his way to add a bow. He must have just grabbed the box from the shopping center without thinking about it. That sounded a little more like him. The artificer was probably more concerned with the runes he had been working with than packaging.

Tossing the lid to the side with the note, she stared down at the folded, black garment inside. At first glance, it was made of a soft but sturdy canvas. Lifting it up to let it unfurl, she furrowed her brow.

It was a poncho, like something out of a cyberpunk movie. There was an asymmetrical, cowl-like collar with a zipper that when fastened could turn it into a hood. Another zipper ran down the length, forming the neck at an angle to close it. A row of modular loops bisected the front from one shoulder down to the opposite waist so that pouches could be attached.

"Okay then." Becca tossed the garment over her head, finding a pair of straps that looped under her armpits to ensure it didn't move around too much. The inside was soft, lined with some kind of red fabric. There was even a face mask in the collar that could be pulled up to cover her nose and mouth.

"I'll be all set if I need to rob a train." She nodded and stepped into the bathroom.

Looking at it in the light, it was more of a cloak. It was certainly nicer than the army rain poncho she had been wearing. Plus it was light enough not to get in the way of her movement. She let out a small laugh. It was easy to see why Alex had picked the design.

"I look like something out of Ghost in the Shell."

That being said, she wasn't sure why he had made such an effort to maintain secrecy. She focused on the garment and willed the Seed to inform her of any enchantment that Alex had placed on it, but it came up with nothing. There weren't any runes on the thing either.

"That's weird. Maybe he wants me to donate some mana to imbue it like my crown."

Becca shrugged and laid down on the bed to project herself to him. Her stomach lurched for a second as the sensation of shifting from her physical body to a mana-formed illusion fought with her senses. Then she found herself in a dark room.

"Great, you got the package." Alex flicked on a light, standing by the switch on the wall.

Becca found herself standing in a hotel room just like her own. "Yeah, now what's the big secret?"

"You haven't seen the enchantment, then." He smiled wide like he'd just confirmed a theory. "Perfect."

Becca looked down at herself, having manifested in the same garment. "No, I didn't see an enchantment."

"How close did you look?" He stepped toward her to admire his handiwork, clearly excited.

"I put it on and focused on it like I would when I try to analyze anything." She arched an eyebrow.

That was when he pumped a fist. "Yes!"

"Yes what?" She narrowed her eyes, beginning to get annoyed with his cloak and dagger shit.

"Okay, so remember those two cases we stole from the moon along with the Heretic Seed's shards?" He walked across the room to grab a notebook from a pile of about fifteen of them.

"Yeah, you were going to go through them while I was away." She watched him flip through a few pages. "I take it you found some—" Her mouth fell open as she remembered the red fabric that had been in one of the cases. She immediately grabbed her projected representation of her new cloak and flipped it inside out to find a bright crimson lining. "Holy shit, you covered it to keep anyone from analyzing it."

He placed his notebook to his chest and took a slight bow. "Pretty cool, huh? I figured using it as a lining would ensure that no one could see enough of that cape to analyze it."

"Okay." She nodded and stared down at the cloak. "That is a little genius."

"I know, right?" He beamed with pride.

"What's the enchantment?" She snapped her attention back to him.

"That is," he held up his note book to read something, "the cape of steel. It's a legendary item with a mass enchantment. It absorbs life essence to maintain its own mana system. Then it uses that power to create a semi-permanent barrier around whoever wears it. It will fail if you take enough damage just like a normal Barrier spell, except this one has a much higher threshold. So it lasts until the cloak's mana system runs out of MP. Though the barrier will reform as soon as the cape absorbs more mana. You're not full on invincible, but you're damn close."

"And no one but you and I know about it." She followed his line of thought. "Because we never told Bancroft and his men that we stole more than the Seed's shards from the moon."

"Exactly." He tapped a finger on his notebook.

"Wait." She stopped short. "What about those shoes we found?"

Alex glanced to the space beneath his bed, making it clear where the slippers they had stolen from Henwick's vault on the moon were. "I'm not sure anyone should touch those."

She arched an eyebrow at him. "You afraid someone is gonna try them on and click their heels together?"

"Maybe." He blew out a heavy sigh. "Let's just say that there are more dangerous spells than 'there's no place like home.'"

CHAPTER TWENTY-EIGHT

"Looks like this here Heretic Seed ain't big enough for the three of us." Parker spit on the dusty ground next to Digby's foot.

"Did you just spit at me?" He stared out at a strange desert village.

Though smaller than the city street in the area below, this space was also populated by buildings that stretched out on either side, separated by an unpaved street. Though that was where the similarities ended. The structures below were stone and brick, yet these were merely wood, just two stories tall. The crimson moon hung in the sky as dust swept across the land in the distance.

"Get it?" Parker tried again. "This town ain't big enough?"

"I don't understand the reference." Digby glowered at her.

"My condolences, pardner." She spat in the opposite direction, this time hitting Henwick's leg.

"Would you please refrain from spitting everywhere, young miss?" He stepped out of range, leaving her to spit on Digby's armored minion that was trailing behind.

"Sorry." Parker ducked her head. "But it's a ghost town, you can't expect me to not make the obvious joke."

"Ghosts?" Henwick's eyes darted around. "I see no spirits."

"It's an expression." She waved a hand back and forth. "'Cause it's abandoned and such."

"Oh." Henwick relaxed.

"At least this place is smaller than the one below. It shan't take us as long to locate the owner of this memory." Digby started walking as a tumbleweed rolled between him and his oversized minion. He checked the number of Heretics remaining within the Seed's realm.

36/2

The population had decreased a lot since last he looked. The rest of the Heretics had to have been encountering each other more frequently. Digby squinted into the distance, catching the silhouette of other landmasses floating further away. There must have been multiple paths to reach the top with more areas that they hadn't passed through. That explained why they had only encountered a few of the Seed's inhabitants so far. Hopefully that trend would continue. The thought reminded him that Sybil was probably still down in the castle below. He wondered if they were going to have to travel back down there to kill her in order to clear the ridiculous death game that the Seed had placed them in. Then again, there was a good chance the caretaker had already found her and removed her from the board. There was no way to be sure until the population of the realm dropped lower. Maybe there was a way out without having to go through such lengths.

Henwick brought his attention back to their surroundings. "Let us pray that the fact that this place is smaller than the ones before means that there are fewer remnants or fractured sparks here."

"I'm not sure Parker will do much within the Heretic Seed's realm, but yes, I hope you are right as well." Digby marched onward, figuring that whoever was lurking in the sleepy little town might show themselves.

Before he could take another step, the unmistakable bark of a gunshot shattered the silence.

Digby's minion acted fast, throwing its bulk in front of him as

Parker dove to the ground beside him. Henwick remained standing, clearly unaware of what the sound meant. A bullet thumped into a slab of necrotic flesh that covered Digby's armored zombie.

"What, where?" Henwick spun as another shot rang out.

"Get down, you fool." Digby crawled toward a barrel that sat to one side of the street. His zombie moved with him to provide cover as a second bullet tore into the monster's armor.

"Why, what is that sound?" Henwick dropped to one knee.

"Someone is shooting at us." Parker rolled past Digby in a messy somersault that left her mostly behind a trough full of water near Digby's barrel.

"But I see no arrows." Henwick flattened himself to the dusty ground. "Nor do I see a foe in range."

"Just get out of sight." Digby rolled his eyes, not wanting to explain firearms to the man. The devices had been hard enough to understand when he had found out about them. Then again, the cleric's second point did merit consideration. Judging from where his minion had been hit in the back, their trajectory didn't make sense. Their attacker should have been standing somewhere in front of them. He swept his eyes across the rooftops.

There was no one there.

Digby reached out with his blood sense but felt no mana moving anywhere. He checked his HUD.

MP: 298/298

He'd gained back everything he'd used down below, leaving him plenty to work with, yet there was no target in sight.

"At least this Heretic decided to cut to the chase, right?" Parker ducked down against the water trough before inching her way across the wooden walkway in the front of the building and taking a long look at one of the windows.

"Indeed," Digby grumbled.

That was when a third gunshot barked from somewhere in the area. Ducking his head, he expected to hear another projectile thump into his minion. What happened instead sent his mind into a spiral.

A bullet streaked between him and Parker only to come to a dead stop mid-air. It remained there just long enough for him to notice a ring of crude runes engraved around the glowing piece of hot lead. An instant later, it flicked its tip in his direction and launched forward.

"Gah!" Digby fell over as the projectile slammed into the bone plate that covered his heart. Rolling with the impact he tumbled back, out of cover. Stunned, he rolled over into a stable position and snapped his eyes to his minion. "To me!"

The armored zombie marched over and crouched down in front of him as Henwick shouted from his place still in the street. "Where are they?"

Before Digby could open his mouth, their attacker answered for him. "I reckon that round should have gone clean through your heart." The voice was feminine and vaguely antagonistic. "I am harder to kill than most." Digby peeked over the back of his minion, finding the ghost town's main throughway empty.

"We'll see," the voice added.

Digby rolled his eyes, wondering why every Heretic he came across so far was so irritating. Present company included. He was especially annoyed by this one and their shoot first, ask questions second mentality. At least Jack had the manners to try to trick him first before attempting to kill him. Then again, there were plenty of times that he'd asked Rebecca to conceal their presence. So the tactic wasn't bad. The thought added a bit of clarity. His opponent was a Heretic with magic and clearly thought a bit like him. If that was the case, the answer was simple.

Where would I hide?

Still in the street, Henwick started to stand as if preparing to cast a spell in a random direction. Clearly, he lacked a better idea. Digby held up a hand to stop him.

"Wait. No sense wasting your mana."

Digby flicked his vision around their dusty surroundings.

"They have to be an enchanter," Parker whispered from behind her water trough. "Or an artificer."

Digby nodded. She was right. That was the only explanation for the engravings on the bullet and the fact that he hadn't felt any mana moving. The only explanation was that the Heretic in question had been prepared in advance. He added that to the equation.

If he could fire a projectile and change its direction so he could attack from anywhere, where would he attack from?

Obviously from wherever is safest. Probably inside.

A quick glance showed him that none of the doors or windows were open, and he hadn't heard any breaking glass. Then he caught one building that fit his requirements. It was the tallest, with two partial doors that only covered the middle portion of the entryway. The word saloon was painted on the window.

"There you are." He eyed the building.

"What?" Henwick shot him a sideways glance.

Digby prepared to move. "When I say now, I want you to unleash whatever you have at that building."

"Very well." Henwick nodded.

"Good." Digby debated on giving him a count of three to get ready but then decided the hell with it. Another gunshot could go off at any second. "Now!"

With that, Digby leaped up and summoned his wraith, calling Jack back into the fight. He wasn't sure if the echo could find the target, but it was worth a try.

A swell of power flowed from his mana system as he thrust a hand out toward the door of the building. The crimson silhouette of a man flickered through the air. At first, it seemed to be running, but then it simply streaked forward with a blur and the shining edge of a blade. The sound of glass breaking and wood splintering struck the air and for an instant, all went still.

Then, almost all at once, a slash over a dozen feet long exploded from the saloon like it had been struck with a blade the size of a truck. Digby's eyes widened. The wraith had attacked the building itself, rocking it right down to its foundation.

Henwick followed suit, raising his hand to pour a beam of light into the entryway. That was when a woman leaped through the shattered window. Glittering shards of glass showered the ground as she rolled into the dusty throughway between the buildings. A coat of dingy leather swooped around her like a cape as she stabilized on one knee and raised a short rifle. The gun was strange, all wood except for a metal barrel and an engraved plate running down the length of its underside.

She fired.

"Damn!" Digby jumped back as the bullet shot off at an angle that sent it veering to one side before coming straight back at him to get around his minion. It slammed into the exact same spot as the last bullet he'd been shot with, this time cracking his bone plate. He ignored it. After all, it hadn't been aimed at his head, nor did he have to worry about the Seed's fragment while within its realm. A bullet to the heart meant nothing.

He rolled backward and summoned his wraith again the moment he got the woman in his focus.

Heretic, level 51 Artificer, hostile.

The crimson echo darted forward in a blur, streaking past his target. It vanished a moment later just before a spray of crimson burst from the artificer's side. The spell was powerful indeed. The strike hadn't been as devastating as when he'd used it in the area down below, but the woman's attributes were bound to be higher than the fragments they'd fought before.

The woman let out a shriek and dropped the strange rifle she had just fired. Falling to her knees, she reached for a glass bottle of what looked like liquor that hung beneath her coat. Mana flowed through her body as the vessel glowed in her hand. She downed a mouthful before throwing it in the direction of Digby and his minion. As it tumbled through the air, she drew a revolver from a holster and fired. The bottle burst in a shower of glass and liquid.

"Blast!" Digby ducked behind his minion again as the fluid showered the oversized zombie. Its necrotic armor sizzled and popped. She must have cast Purify on the bottle to heal her wound then used the remainder as an improvised weapon. Digby winced as a spattering of droplets landed on his arm to remind him of the long-lost sensation of pain that he so rarely felt.

Henwick leaped forward to attack, only to take a bullet in the gut from her revolver. Clearly, he still didn't understand quite what a firearm could do. The woman had been ignoring him up until now, but it seemed he had finally merited her attention. She fired twice more in Parker's direction. They didn't hit anything, but they certainly gave the soldier enough reason to stay down. From where Digby ducked, he caught Parker in his periphery. She was laying with water pouring on her head from a pair of bullet holes that had been punched in the trough she hid behind.

With a grunt of pain, the wild artificer holstered her revolver and slipped the tip of her boot under her rifle to flip it off the ground. Dust and sand blew past her as she caught the weapon. She pushed back up into a standing position, the wound on her side beginning to heal.

Digby cursed the woman's level. Clearly, she must have ranked up her purification spell to a point where its healing property was strong enough to repair the damage she'd taken. That, combined with her heightened defense attribute, must have minimized the effectiveness of his attack. It would take more than a single slash from a wraith to take her down.

"You alive over there?" Digby glanced at Henwick.

"I shall persevere." The man rolled to safety behind a post on the other side of the street. Clutching the wound on his stomach, he cast an unfamiliar spell. For a moment, his palm began to glow just before the bullet popped out of his abdomen. He caught it in his hand and cast a regeneration spell to heal the wound.

Interesting. Digby watched as the hole closed. Apparently, the cleric class could remove foreign objects to allow healing. He shook off the observation and returned his attention to the artificer as she snapped open her rifle and retrieved another engraved bullet from a belt on her hip. She slid it into the barrel and closed the chamber with a flick of her wrist.

The woman raised the gun to fire just as Henwick blasted another Smite in her direction.

"No, you ain't!" The artificer flipped her rifle upright to hold it vertical as the spell hit. The runes engraved on the underside of the weapon glowed.

How? Again Digby couldn't believe his eyes as the spell's

energy poured out in all directions, like water being diverted by a stone, leaving the woman unharmed. The instant the light faded, she flipped the rifle back in his direction and fired. Digby shouted a command to his minion, "Guard!"

The oversized zombie spread its arms out wide in an attempt to take up as much space as possible. Digby struggled to sense what direction the bullet might come from only to be caught off guard when it struck him in the back. He gasped as the projectile cracked another bone plate.

Stabilizing himself, he was just glad that he was within the Seed's realm where he didn't have to worry about the shard that was lodged in his heart back in the outside world. There wasn't much she was going to do to him by repeatedly shooting him in the chest. That was when an obvious question struck him. Why the hell was she aiming for his heart anyway? For that matter, why hadn't she aimed for anyone else with her rifle? Why did she have it in for him?

Maybe the runes have a limitation.

The thought made sense. After all, the heart held a significant value to his mutations, so it stood to reason. Maybe the runes weren't targeting the organ itself and instead, were focused on whatever quality the heart held that made it unique. He shook his head. Whatever the reason, if she was going to keep it up, he had nothing to fear.

Digby tapped his minion's shoulder and pointed forward. "Charge."

The armored zombie started moving. He ducked behind to use it as cover while he closed the gap.

"Hey, what are you—" The woman's words were cut off as Henwick cast another Smite. "Now cut that out, you hear!" She blocked the spell with the rune work on her rifle before reaching for her revolver and firing off a shot in his direction before it clicked, empty. The cleric let out a yelp, but Digby didn't look back. With his healing magic, Henwick would be fine. Instead, he continued the charge, opening his maw on his hand to forge a short sword. He summoned another wraith halfway there.

The echo of Jack the Ripper blurred into existence, streaking toward the artificer. She twisted her rifle to deflect, taking a slash from the vengeful spirit to the metal plate of glowing runes. An explosion of crimson power erupted from the impact, leaving her unharmed. Then again, the hit might not have hurt her, but it did succeed in throwing her off balance. She fired her rifle regardless, not even bothering to aim.

The bullet shot off into the sky.

Digby kept moving. As long as he stayed behind his minion to keep her from getting a clean line of sight at his head, she had to keep using the runes to land her hits. He assumed that meant that her bullet would target his heart again. Sure enough, something struck him in the back, this time making it through his bone armor to bury itself in his unbeating heart.

"Think that will stop me?" He pushed forward, letting out a cackle.

"Shit, you're already dead!" The woman's jaw dropped as if she had only now realized it. She must have analyzed him already, but like Jack down below, she must not have known what a zombie was. That was when her tactics changed. "Fine. We'll do this the hard way!"

"No, we won't." Digby and his minion reached her just as she lowered her rifle and reached into her coat to draw a second revolver much larger than the first.

A barrel the length of his forearm flicked toward his armored zombie as she began to push mana through her body.

"Grab her!" He willed his minion to lunge.

The zombie's shoulder exploded a second later.

"What?" Digby dove to the side as chunks of necrotic flesh peppered the sand, the bullet tearing through the zombie's armor like it had been made of paper. A red-hot projectile kept on moving until it slammed into the ground. Dirt and sand sprayed Digby's side as he rolled away from the impact.

The woman flipped the massive revolver to the side and fired again, this time detonating his minion's head in an instant. One second it had been there, the next it was gone. The oversized body of the monster hit the sand with a damp thump.

"Holy hell!" Digby cried out, throwing up a hand to send another wraith in her direction. His jaw dropped when nothing happened. He reached for the mana but came up short. Flicking his vision to his HUD, he saw why.

It was gone.

No, not gone. Just hidden.

He had been silenced.

How?

He panicked for an instant before he realized the cause.

The bullet! Digby slapped a hand to his chest where the leaden projectile was lodged. He cursed the item. It was going to take time to dig out. Time he didn't have, as the woman spun to level the revolver at him, giving him a close look at a barrel covered in engraved runes.

"Damn." He tensed, unable to move fast enough to get out of the way. That was when Parker's voice called out from behind him.

"Run, Dig!" A small knife, looted from Jack the Ripper, spun through the air in the artificer's direction only for her to whip her revolver to the side to swat the blade out of the air. It was enough to buy him a precious second.

"Get behind something!" Henwick unleashed another Smite to grant him a few moments more.

Digby scrambled to the nearest building, making it just as a gunshot went off. He dove forward into a roll, making use of his agility as a window behind him shattered. For an instant the glass remained in the pane, then it exploded outward from the power of the bullet's impact inside. She must have been enchanting each shot and using the runes engraved on the revolver to amplify the spell.

Digby rolled back to his feet and kept running.

I have to get behind something substantial.

Leaping for cover, he made it to a thick wooden pillar that held up the overhang of the buildings that covered the walkway. He pressed his back against it as soon as he was safe.

"Hey." Parker waved to him from behind a barrel nearby.

"Since when do you know how to throw knives?" He gestured

back at the blade that was resting in the sand back near the artificer.

"I don't, I just kinda chucked it. But I've been putting my points in dex so maybe that helped." She shrugged.

Digby rolled his eyes and turned to his other side. "You alive, Henwick?"

"I'll survive," his voice called back from someplace out of sight. At least he'd had the sense to get back into hiding. A second later, Digby caught him peeking out from behind a pillar on the other side of the throughway.

"I could use another Smite aimed at our foe right about now." Digby tried to push a finger into his chest to reach the bullet that was silencing his magic.

Henwick said nothing in response, but instead shook his head. Clearly, he was staying silent to avoid telling their enemy anything that might give them an advantage.

Damn. Digby groaned. The cleric must have exhausted his mana supply already. That was why he was being secretive. He had mentioned that his Smite was costly, after all.

"You gonna keep hiding, dead man?" The sound of the woman's boots stepping up onto the wooden walkway somewhere further back accompanied her taunt. "Not sure how you managed to exist as a walking corpse. Well, no matter. We'll put you down six feet where you belong one way or another."

Digby resisted the urge to shout something irritating back in the hope that she might have lost track of where he was. Instead, he tucked in his arms to make sure he was concealed by the post he hid behind. He slid down a moment later when he heard the click-clack of her rifle's chamber snapping open and closed to load another bullet. The following shot reverberated like a cannon, vibrating the glass in the surrounding windows as every support pillar between him and her detonated in a shower of splinters.

Why me? Digby covered his head with his hands as debris fell all around him and the buildings creaked at the loss of their supports. Why the artificer was so hellbent on killing him first was beyond him.

Perhaps because he was the highest level and the most dangerous?

As much as he hated to admit it, until he could dig that engraved bullet from his chest, they didn't stand a chance. That only left one option. He snapped his attention to Parker then to the unbroken pane of glass closest to her. "Alright, use the window next to us to open a Mirror Passage. I don't care where."

The pink-haired woman looked up from where she hid behind the barrel. "I can take us back down to the castle, I saw a mirror there."

Digby thought back. He had smashed the mirror back in the castle's hall, but the one in the upper chamber should still be intact. He grimaced. Returning all the way back down there was less than ideal. The sound of that gunslinger loading another bullet made the decision easier. He gave Parker a nod and beckoned to Henwick. Digby wasn't sure if the cleric would make it to the window, but if he and Parker waited, they would all be lost. They would have to take their chances.

Henwick got into a runner's stance, ready to sprint for the passage as Parker inched her hand toward the window.

Then, she stopped.

"What are you waiting fo—" Digby furrowed his brow as he realized she was looking back at the gunslinger. He peeked around what was left of the pillar he'd been hiding behind.

"What the—" Digby's mind locked up as a man dressed as a literal wizard, straight out of a board game, walked toward the gunslinger from behind like he had nothing to fear. His robes were bright blue, with stars and moons embroidered here and there, and he wore a matching, pointed hat with a wide brim. The artificer clearly didn't know he was there, at least, not until the man cleared his throat.

Is he insane?

Digby watched as the woman spun to meet the strange man. She froze for an instant as she experienced the same bewilderment that he was feeling. Then she raised her weapon to point it directly in his face. Digby arched an eyebrow. Then he analyzed the man.

Nothing came up. He immediately forced himself to stop thinking about it, realizing the reason why.

Everything suddenly made sense. Well, except for the wizard outfit.

He'd had enough experience working with Rebecca to know an illusion when he saw one. If he let himself doubt what he saw, it would unravel whatever this wizard fellow had planned. There was no way to know if the illusionist behind the spell was friendly, but he was willing to put his trust in the hope that he was.

That was when the wizard's body exploded into thousands of tiny bits of colored paper. The woman with the rifle jerked back in surprise, clearly not expecting it. The illusion unraveled an instant later. She must have realized it was a distraction.

Then the real attack started.

Again the man dressed in the bizarre robes appeared, but this time just off to the side of the artificer. A quick analyze labeled the new arrival.

Remnant Spark, Heretic, level 22 Illusionist.

He raised a hand as if to cast a spell directly in her face.

That's it! Digby expected an icicle or something to explode out the back of the woman's head or something equally as gruesome. Yet, that wasn't what happened. Instead, the wizard simply opened his fingers to release a handful of sand.

What? Digby couldn't believe the stupidity.

Then again, the artificer reeled back and dropped her revolver so that she could rub at her eyes. "You god damn, son of a—"

"Oh wow, pocket sand." Parker nodded as if approving of the insanity.

Frantically, the gunslinger rubbed at her eyes with one hand while reaching for her other revolver with the other. She emptied it in a random direction as the wizard ran like hell. A torrent of foul language was hurled after him, but no more.

"Come with me, damn it!" The strange man, dressed as a wizard, rushed past Digby, urgently beckoning to all three of them as he ran. "Quick, before she recovers." He darted off to one side before ducking between two of the wooden buildings.

With few options, Digby shrugged and followed. Parker and Henwick did the same. The gunslinger reloaded and fired off a few more shots from her revolver, the bullets punching into the wood behind them. Her voice echoed as they fled.

"I will find you, necromancer! I have a bullet with your name on it. Literally."

CHAPTER TWENTY-NINE

"Hurry!" The strange wizard rushed along the side of the buildings until they reached a structure that resembled an old barn. The sound of the gunslinger shouting echoed behind them.

"Who in the hell are you?" Digby grabbed at the man's robe, frustrated that he had been forced to flee.

"And why are you dressed as Gandalf?" Parker flicked the brim of his hat.

"I, umm…" The illusionist's eyes darted between them.

"Who is Gandalf?" Henwick caught up, after taking a moment to claim an ax that was leaning against a building that they passed. Digby nodded to him. It was prudent to bring a weapon wherever they were heading, just in case things went south.

"My name is Thorn, and please unhand me." He struggled to pull his robe from Digby's fingers. "I will explain everything once we reach somewhere safe."

"Alright." Digby eyed the man for a moment, catching him tremble. A bead of sweat ran down his forehead. He was definitely hiding something. Level twenty-two wasn't much to speak of. If he were to turn out to be hostile like the last illusionist that they had fought, the strange wizard would not stand a chance. Either way, if they had somewhere safe, it was worth investigating.

Thorn straightened his robes before turning toward the barn and pulling open the door. What sat inside caught Digby off guard. A box that resembled an elevator hung a foot above the floor from a gaping hole in the ceiling. A heavy cable extended upward. It swayed back and forth slightly, a metal gate covering its entrance like a door. At first, the sight of the modern feature within the old barn was jarring, yet with the way the Seed's realm had been patched together from the memories of every Heretic that had wielded its power, the mismatched features made sense.

"Get in." Thorn pulled the gate to the side, causing its diamond pattern to fold in on itself to let them through.

"Okay." Parker hopped inside, sending the elevator swinging a few feet toward the back of the barn.

"What is this chamber?" Henwick crept toward the lift as it swung back in his direction.

"It's an elevator, climb aboard." Digby shoved him forward, chuckling when he tripped and tumbled inside. He cringed a second later when he remembered how foolish he had looked the first time he had ridden in a lift back in Seattle.

Henwick glanced back, his eyes burning with indignation as he supported himself on the inside wall of the lift. His new ax fell to hit the floor of the swinging box with a heavy clunk.

Thorn climbed in behind him and closed the gate, not giving the cleric time to argue. Once everything was secure, the illusionist pulled a lever. Digby braced himself as the lift began to rise into the sky. Looking up through the gate, he had trouble seeing where they were heading.

"Where are you taking us?" Henwick pressed himself up against the wall furthest from the front.

"Up." Thorn avoided eye contact.

Now that he had a moment where no one was shooting at him, Digby fished through his pockets to find the pair of shears he'd taken from the shop down below where he'd looted some clothes. Thorn immediately stepped back as if expecting to be stabbed. Digby put the man's fears to rest by turning the blade on himself and digging it into his chest. "There's a silencing bullet lodged in my heart."

"Ah jeez." The illusionist turned away and covered his mouth.

"Oh relax, none of this place is even real." He continued to look for the bullet, having trouble ignoring the fact that Thorn reminded him of Alex from back when they had first met. Back when his apprentice had been far less capable. He shook off the thought and shifted the shears to one side. "Where is this blasted thing?"

"That's a Mage Killer Round," Thorn added. "It's designed to lock on to a Heretic's heart and silence them once inside their body. The result stops a mage from being able to cast a spell to remove the bullet or heal the wound. It's usually a death sentence. If you weren't already dead, you wouldn't have survived."

"Good thing for small blessings." Digby shoved a finger into his chest when he felt the tip of the sheers hit something solid.

"Can you please wait to do that until we are not confined to an enclosed space?" Thorn gagged and closed his eyes.

"Yeah, this might not be the time." Parker flailed her hands about. "Otherwise, I'm going to have to steal Merlin's hat to hurl in."

"What does hurl mean?" Henwick asked just as the elevator lurched to the side. A column of grit and stone surrounded them a moment later, the lift still rising into some sort of landmass.

"She means throw up. And need I remind you all that there is still a caretaker somewhere down below that is still stalking us. What do you all think will happen if that monstrosity catches up while I am silenced?" Digby felt the bullet with his fingertips only to lose his grip on it when he tried to grab it. "Damn it."

"Caretaker?" Thorn asked as the elevator's surroundings changed from rough earth to a shaft of more familiar construction.

"Yes." Digby eyed him. "Have you encountered it?"

"No, I have kept myself hidden. Other than a few of those fragments, I have avoided anything and anyone. Especially since that gunslinger has been killing everyone that has come to her level." He glanced in Digby's direction. "Illusionists aren't exactly built for fighting, and it's easy to stay hidden. We should be safe where we're going. There are plenty of paths to take within this place and with the elevator raised, no one will be following."

Digby furrowed his brow. The man was right about the second point, but as far as an illusionist's fighting potential, Jack the Ripper would have disagreed. Not to mention Rebecca had certainly proven herself a deadly combatant. He considered the error. This Thorn person might have been a bit of a coward.

Finally, getting a grip on the bullet in his chest, Digby ripped it out with an unsettling squelch. He chuckled when Thorn winced. "And just what made you decide to come out and assist us during our fight with that artificer?"

"Easy. Two of you show up as regular Heretics when I analyze you, not a spark like me. So I assume that you still have a body out there in the world. That means that you must know the most about what is happening here and that you will have the best chances of fixing whatever is wrong with the Seed." The illusionist looked up as they began moving mana through their blood.

Digby arched an eyebrow, expecting an illusion of some kind to manifest. He immediately suspected a trap when none did.

I am really getting sick of everyone trying to kill me. He rolled his eyes. *I'm starting to feel that the Heretics of the past had no honor among them.*

The elevator rose up to an opening in the shaft, through which a large wood-paneled room filled the view. Thorn pulled the gate open as soon as the lift came to a stop.

"Come, you will be safe here."

"I'm sure." Digby stepped inside, looking up at the vaulted ceiling above. It was an extravagant space, much like the castle that they had claimed back in California. He kept his eyes peeled for anything that seemed out of place. Whatever illusion had been cast had to be somewhere. All he had to do was doubt it and whatever trap Thorn had planned would fall to pieces. "I suppose you won't be attempting to outlast me and steal my body then?"

"What? No." Thorn seemed surprised by the idea of it.

Or he's a better actor than he is a fighter. Digby debated on lunging at the ridiculously dressed man just to tear through all the pretenses.

That was when the last person he expected to see through the situation stepped forward.

"Okay, who are you?" Parker reached for the illusionist's hat as if she was going to use it to throw up in as she had previously mentioned. She refrained, opting to pull it off his head and examine it up close. "You know, the stitching is actually pretty good. Did your mom make it for you?"

"Give that back. I have no idea what you're talking about." Thorn reached out to snatch the hat from her, but she yanked it away.

"Hey, I worked a ren-fair for a few summers, I know cosplay when I see it."

"Cosplay?" He screwed up his eyes.

She did the same. "Okay, good to know. You're from a little before my time then if you don't know the word."

"What are you—" he started to ask, only to be cut off when she thrust a finger in his direction as if declaring victory.

"You reacted when I said Gandalf!"

"What are you on about?" Digby stepped forward, unsure what to make of the ridiculousness.

"He's not a wizard, just a big nerd!" She laughed.

"Oh, you mean like Alex." Digby nodded, starting to understand.

"What is a nerd?" Henwick's eyes drifted between them.

"This guy." Parker gestured to Thorn, demonstrating the term by example. "If he recognized the name Gandalf, then he's gotta be from some time after the fifties. Which means that his whole wizard persona is just as fake as his costume. And there is no way in hell his name is really Thorn. It sounds like a nickname that he came up with in school but could never get it to stick." She stepped a little closer to him and poked him in the chest. "So why the misdirect? Huh, buddy?"

"Yes, why indeed?" Digby stepped closer to stand shoulder to shoulder with Parker as she accused the man. At least she was making some progress.

Thorn backed up, stopping a second later despite having a few more steps before running into the wall. Digby flicked his eyes to the wood paneling, realizing the trick that was in play. He had been thinking too small. Thorn wasn't hiding a trap, he was altering their surroundings entirely.

The moment the thought passed through Digby's necrotic gray

matter, the entire room shimmered and faded to reveal a drab and somewhat messy room with no windows. The vaulted ceiling above vanished, only to be replaced by a much lower one that hung just a foot above their heads. A set of unfinished wooden stairs took up the wall behind the illusionist. That was why he stopped backing up. He would have tripped if he had kept going.

"Well shit, I was right." Parker's mouth fell open as if she was only now gaining confidence in her theory. "We're in a basement."

"Fine. Yes. You caught me. I saw all of you dressed in outfits from the past, so I assumed that's where you were from originally. I wasn't sure how that was possible since you still have bodies in the real world, but I was afraid you wouldn't take me seriously since I am a lower level." Thorn snatched his hat away from her and threw it on the floor before tearing off his robe and throwing that down as well. Underneath, he wore a pair of ripped jeans and a black shirt bearing the image of a strange creature with a long snout. The words 'no problem' were written underneath.

"The Alf shirt doesn't help." Parker wrinkled her nose.

"Don't you think I know that?" he snapped back. "You think I wanted the Seed to manifest me in this outfit? No, I didn't. Fortunately, it also gave me my DM robes. So yeah, I threw on a wizard hat and tried to play along."

"That makes sense." She dropped her hands to the side. "And what is your name by the way?"

"It's Gary." He dropped himself down into a beat-up sofa at the edge of the basement.

"Alright, well, Gary, is it?" Digby stepped into their exchange to try and make some sense of things. "I gather that you are somewhat intimidated by everything happening, but in all honesty, we don't have the luxury of caring. I may be eight hundred years old, but I assure you, this is not the first time I have met a nerd. Now, if you have information about what is happening here in the Seed, then I suggest you spit it out. "

"Eight hundred?" Gary raised his head suddenly. "Wait, that would make you one of the first Heretics. Were you there for the fracture?"

"The fracture?" Digby leaned his head to one side.

"It's what the fools call the time when the Seed was destroyed."

"The fools?" Digby glanced around, finding a plastic crate to sit on.

"Yes. Do you not know who they are?"

"Wait a second." Parker sat down as well. "Didn't Jack say something about fools?" She slapped her hand down on a couch cushion. "Shit, was he talking about an organization? I thought he was just being an arrogant ass."

"What?" Digby frowned. "But I call people fools all the time."

"Yes, and you sound like an arrogant ass when you do," Parker added.

"I can't argue with that," Henwick grumbled under his breath.

Gary's face went through several expressions, clearly having trouble following the sudden tangent. Eventually, he just pushed it aside and continued.

"Yes, the Fools refer to the time when the Seed was destroyed as the fracture, and they have been working to find the shards ever since."

"I suppose that jester we faced was probably a member of this organization as well." Digby scratched at his chin, drawing a conclusion from the man's costume.

"Yes. And he was the one that witch, Sybil, had sent the Seed's shards to." Henwick remained standing.

"Indeed." Digby connected the dots. "Which means that she was a part of it as well."

"So these Fools were behind everything, then." Henwick folded his arms. "Had it not been for them, none of this would have happened."

"Well, yes." Digby shook his head. "But as much as I might dislike that old crone, from what I understand it, her, and these Fools, were not the original root of the problem. We seem to have Autem to thank for that, since they were the ones that were originally exploring the Seed's power. Sybil was only there as some sort of spy. She might have killed you and I, but she wasn't the one that had been causing the disappearances back in our day. Apparently, that was from Autem's attempts to create a system of magic they could control."

"Yes." Gary nodded. "The Fools only got involved because they feared what Autem might do if they figured out a way to harness the Seed's power."

"Indeed." Digby traced a finger around the tiny runes on his hand. "It seems that the ring I found back then was a part of an experiment to seize control over magic. As well as anyone who they granted access to that power. I don't think it was successful, since I am unable to do any of that, but it seems that Autem figured it out eventually. I don't know how many versions it took, but at some point, they created the Guardian Core." Digby snapped his eyes back to Gary. "But I must ask, how do you know of these Fools and their fight with Autem?"

"The Fools are not an organized group. They're more like a network of people working for the same goal in their own way. I learned about them shortly after I found a shard of the Seed at a garage sale of all places. It was tied to a bag of dice that I purchased." He reached in his pocket and pulled out a handful of polyhedral game pieces. "I used these to DM for years. Apparently, that was enough for the Seed to recreate them here as part of my memory."

"Oh, wow!" Parker slapped a hand against her head. "It makes sense now."

"What does?" Digby eyed her sideways.

"The similarity between the way the Heretic Seed works and how modern games do." She let out a laugh. "Alex and I talked a ton about it but couldn't come up with anything that made sense until now. It isn't that the Seed functions similar to our games, it's the other way around. If the Fools and the Heretic Seed have been a part of history since your time, then they could have influenced gaming from the beginning."

"That was always my theory as well." Gary nodded. "As a DM, I couldn't believe how similar the Seed's system was to the games I'd grown up playing. There was no way it was a coincidence. Plus, it added an extra layer of cool for me when I first bonded to the shard I'd found."

"I'm sure." Digby failed to share in their excitement. "But how did a piece of the Heretic Seed travel from England all the way to America?"

"It's a long story, but I can try to summarize." Gary stood up and held a hand out as mana flowed through his body. At the same time, the room they sat in was again replaced, this time by the main hall of a castle. At the center stood a jester. Gary continued, "The Fools got their name because that was how they started, literally using the occupation as a cover to infiltrate the highest reaches of society. Not only that, but everything they stand for is a contradiction. To them, the most precious thing in the world is free will, but at the same time, they understand the chaos that it can cause. Essentially, free will is a double-edged sword. People don't always act in the best interest of others. They can be greedy, selfish, and irresponsible. Sometimes even worse."

Digby couldn't help but notice Henwick glance in his direction as Gary listed humanity's flaws. "Oh, don't look at me. I never claimed to be a saint."

Gary ignored him and gestured to the other end of the illusionary hall where a man in a crown appeared, sitting atop a throne. "The main problem is that as people gain power and influence, their free will often becomes a liability. It's the old adage that power corrupts. Through history, royalty, merchants, even the church has exercised their free will to harm those that lack that same power and influence."

"And that's where the Fools stepped in." Digby nodded.

"Exactly." Gary flicked his eyes to the jester at the center of the hall as they pranced up to the king sitting on the throne. They leaned close and whispered in his ear. "No one suspected the Fools. Sometimes all it took was the manipulation of information. The right rumor here, the right lies there. Other times, it took... more."

With that, the illusionary jester pulled a dagger and raised it to strike the king down before freezing in place.

"The Fools aimed to balance the scales." Digby scratched at his chin. "Free will versus mankind's ambition and thirst for power."

"Yes. If things got out of hand and threatened the world, the Fools put things in check while making sure to preserve the free will of the people. They were like a gardener, pulling the weeds so the rest of the plants could flourish. Though, they only intervene as a last ditch option." Gary waved a hand as the king and jester vanished only to be replaced by a man standing at an altar surrounded by the statues of nine angels. Another three men appeared, kneeling before him. "Autem stands for the opposite. They believe that people cannot be trusted with free will. That it creates too many differences. They think that, if left to their own devices, humanity will destroy itself. To them, existence is about control."

"That sounds about right." Parker sighed.

Gary nodded. "Ultimately, Autem's end goal is the same as the Fools in that they wish for the continued survival of the human race. The difference is that the Fools will risk the future of the world to maintain everyone's free will, to the point where they would let us teeter on the brink of annihilation. Autem will not take that risk, and instead seeks to ensure humanity's survival at all costs, by removing our free will. Sometimes that just means convincing people that they don't have a choice, and other times it means removing our choices from the board altogether."

"Jeez. The Fools and Autem are just two sides of the same coin." Parker blew out a sigh and sunk into the sofa. "That one small difference creates a massive change in the outcome."

"Exactly." Gary held out both hands to represent them. "Both groups want to protect humanity. On the one side, you have the Fools, who are basically chaotic good, and on the other, you have Autem, the lawful good."

"Good?" Digby scoffed. "What part of what Autem has done do you think is good?"

"Sorry, it's complicated. Obviously, what they've done is terrible, but if you twist things around to see it from their perspective, their motivation is good." He dropped his hands to his lap. "I mean, technically, their approach is more likely to ensure the survival of the human race. The problem is that the world that they create will only represent a fraction of humanity. In exchange, the Fools might not be able to ensure our safety, but at least they will leave the future in our collective hands."

"Yes, yes, that is all well and good, but that doesn't explain how you know any of this." Digby slapped a hand to his thigh.

"Yes." Henwick's tone grew concerned. "That jester was hunted down by Autem. I was there. Even if there were more after him, Autem would have tracked them to the ends of the earth."

"That's true, but as I said, the Fools were never an organization. They never had any sort of membership. Most weren't even aware of how many there were. Operating like that kept them safe. So you are correct when you say Autem hunted them down, but that was only the ones that were active at the time. There are always more. Sure, they might lay low for decades at a time, but they never failed to step up when needed. Even if Autem managed to kill them all, their story would remain. Someone would take over where they left off. That's just how people are. There's always someone willing to fight."

"I see." Digby nodded. "So there is always a loose end."

"A loose end that multiplied, died off, and returned several times over the centuries." Gary waved a hand and the scene changed to show a group of jesters leaping from the rafters down upon Autem's people. "If it hadn't been for their intervention, Autem would have won back then in your day."

"Then why didn't they wipe Autem out once and for all?" Digby pressed a fist into his palm.

"As a general rule, they only intervened when needed. Their people hit targets surgically and aimed to impact as few people as possible." Gary snapped his fingers, causing the scene to fade away. "Plus, the Fool's disorganization did limit their effectiveness. Sure, it kept them from being wiped out, but against Autem, whose forces thrived on rigid control, the lack of organization hindered the Fools' ability to fight."

"They failed then." Digby grimaced.

"Maybe." Gary leaned from one side to the other. "But the Fools acted as a thorn in Autem's side for centuries, always cropping up and hitting them when they least expected. After I connected with my shard in the nineteen-seventies, I was contacted by someone claiming to be a Fool."

"They were still around in the seventies?" Parker leaned forward.

"Yeah. They had been killed off several times by Autem throughout history, but the Fools always seemed to have someone to relight the fire. From what I know, they were involved at least in part with several important moments over the centuries. World Wars, revolutions, rebellions, things like that. Most didn't even have magic, but they did what they could."

"What did you do when they contacted you?" Henwick scratched at his beard.

"At first, they kept everything secret and sent me to a facility to study the shard of the Seed I had and to give me some training. I never saw the extent to which their operation ran." He placed a hand to his chest. "I was just a kid at the time, with fantasies of being a spy. It was exciting, so I did everything I was told. Eventually, they started sending me on… quests." He raised his hands to make air quotes around the word. "Mostly they were little things like paranormal investigations. Dealing with lingering echoes and stuff like that. There wasn't much to gain in XP, but I got a few levels out of it."

"Echoes?" Henwick turned a little pale. "You mean ghosts?"

"No." Gary chuckled. "But when a person dies, in rare cases their spark can leave an imprint on the essence in the area that creates its own mana system. It's not a ghost, but it can act like one."

"Ah, like the lingering traces of the dead that I used to create Tavern." Digby tapped a finger on his chin.

"Tavern?" Gary stared at him.

"That's his dude bro minion that he pieced together from the traces of a busload of frat guys." Parker shrugged.

"That sounds," Gary paused before adding, "irritating. But I guess a necromancer is powerful if you can call back the dead in such a way."

"Yes." Digby extended a slightly accusatory finger in the illusionist's direction. "But what did you gain the rest of your levels from? Surely you must have gotten up to some actual killing to have reached level twenty-two."

Gary shrank back and let out a long sigh. "You would be surprised what kind of things lurk out there in the shadows of the world. I learned that when I was sent with a few other Fools to investigate a rural town in Germany. Not only had the whole place been overrun by some sort of modified monster cooked up by the Nazis in World War II, but Autem was there."

"Nazis?" Parker looked nervous.

"Yes, they had their fair share of supernatural projects." Gary frowned. "And as you can imagine, Autem was more than happy to help them, considering their goal of control over free will."

"Gross." Parker wrinkled her nose.

"Yes, very." Digby ignored her and probed for more information, glad to finally have someone willing to answer his questions. "What about these monsters?"

"Yes, the creatures must have been trapped for decades, before infesting the town I was sent to. Autem was there trying to capture them." He shrugged. "The Seed called them revenants."

"Revenants?" Digby sat up straight. "There were revenants back then?"

Gary's eyes flicked to meet his. "You mean there are still some around in the time you come from?"

"Yes." Digby frowned. "Autem set them loose on the world."

"No, that's impossible." Gary shook his head frantically. "I died to make sure none of those things survived and that Autem left empty-handed."

"Apparently, that wasn't enough." Digby groaned. "Autem was able to twist the curse that created me in a way that brought the revenants back from extinction."

"Damn it." Gary slapped his thigh. "If that's true, then the Fools failed. Autem won in the end."

"Not quite." Digby held up a finger. "I and a handful of other Heretics are doing what we can to stop them. That's why we restored the Heretic Seed. We need to find a way to create more magic users to win."

"And what about the Fools?" Parker leaned toward Gary. "Were they killed off by Autem, or are there some still out there that we could maybe ally with?"

"I'm not sure if any of them survived, but…" Gary shook his head. "There is still the potential for them to return."

"How?" Henwick arched an eyebrow.

Gary looked up at him with excitement in his eyes. "Why do you think I helped you all with that gunslinger?"

"Umm…." Digby drew a blank. "To help you find a way out of this realm?"

"No." Gary shook his head. "I know I am thoroughly screwed. As are the rest of us sparks in here. The only reason the Seed hasn't absorbed us is that it's incomplete and is having some kind of error. I helped you because you still have a chance to help the world."

"Well yes, we are doing what we can—" Digby started to explain before being cut off.

"I see that, but you need to do more." Gary slapped a hand on the cushion of the beat-up sofa he sat on. "Don't you get it? I may be dead, but I am still a Fool, and now so are you."

"What?" Digby's face fell.

"I am the loose end left to pass on the mission. I want you to pick up the cause." Gary stood up. "That is why I helped you. I want you to complete the Seed's restoration and give its power to everyone you can. You can stand up and protect the world from there to keep it from losing its way."

"Now wait just a minute." Digby stood up as well. "I am all for stopping Autem, but protecting humanity is not exactly the kind of undead necromancer I am."

"Why not?" Gary pointed a finger back at him.

"Umm…" Digby trailed off, unable to think of a good excuse. Ultimately, he only wanted to stop Autem because they were a threat to him. Well, that and spite.

That was when Henwick decided to step in and argue for him.

"I cannot abide by this lunacy."

"I'm sorry?" Gary's face fell.

"The Heretic Seed is too dangerous to grant its power to everyone who wants it." Henwick swiped a hand through the air. "I agree that Autem must be stopped, and that magic will be needed to ensure their defeat. However, that power is a blight on this world. It should only be given to those necessary in the war. Most of all, the Seed must be destroyed again afterward."

Digby glanced between the two of them, not sure who to side with.

Gary answered the question for him. "You are right that the Seed offers a power that can hurt people. But you're wrong if you think that is all it can do. The Seed isn't a weapon, it's a tool that can lift and enlighten humanity. It can heal the injured and strengthen others. Magic belongs to the world. It is not up to any one person or group to say who can and can't use it."

"Yes, well, one thing at a time." Digby nodded, struggling not to commit to anything. "What matters most is that we figure out how to access the Seed's full power. I will figure out what to do with it after we have dealt with Autem."

"What do you mean?" Gary cocked his head to one side. "Do you not know how to get out of here?"

"No, do you?" Digby did the same.

"Umm, I don't know for sure, but I think I know where you need to go." Gary looked up toward the ceiling. "Or at least, I know where the finish line for the Heretic Seed's race is."

"Well, what are we waiting for?" Digby squawked.

"Nothing. You were asking questions, so I answered them." Gary shrank back.

"No one cares about that; we need to get moving." Digby spun toward the stairs in a huff, looking back as Gary followed.

"You're forgetting this." Parker tossed the illusionist his wizard hat before picking up his robe. "Gotta look your best."

Henwick rolled his eyes, clearly not appreciating that they had gained a new member to their merry band of Heretics. "Fine, we must be done with this."

"My thoughts exactly." Digby tried his best to pretend that everyone could get along. "With the four of us, we should be able to figure everything out in no time."

"Really? You going to invite disaster, just like that?" Parker cringed. "Because last time you said something optimistic, things did not go well."

Digby rubbed at the bridge of his nose and deflated. "Shut up, Parker."

CHAPTER THIRTY

"What was that about us being able to figure everything out in no time?" Parker stood with both hands out wide to gesture to the top of the stairway.

"Shut up, Parker." Digby stomped his way up the steps behind her. "No one likes to be told I told you so."

Henwick and Gary followed behind, though the cleric didn't seem happy about it.

Ahead of them floated a circular structure of stone bathed in the crimson light of the moon. The outside was surrounded by ornate stone carvings and archways, making it look like some sort of coliseum. There was no way to tell what it was inside.

Looking down, Digby saw more stairways reaching up from landmasses below, all joining together to reach various entrances that surrounded the outer wall of the structure above. There were many more floating areas than just what they had passed through. Seeing it all from the top, there must have been several paths and starting locations for each of the heretics that had been set against one another.

Pushing the thought out of his head, he glanced up. There were no pathways reaching out from the coliseum. Whatever the structure was, it was the apex within the seed's realm.

Considering the situation, maybe a coliseum was an appropriate choice of design. After all, they were expected to fight each other until there were only two left. The coliseum must have been placed there as a final battleground for the Heretics that made it up from the levels below.

Digby checked the number of rivals on his HUD.

24/2

The population of the realm was falling faster. It must have taken a bit for each of the heretics to figure out what was happening. After that, it was just a matter of finding each other. There must have been fights breaking out through the realm by now. Not to mention the caretaker was down there somewhere to kill off anyone it came across. Digby shuddered. It wouldn't be long before the population fell to just a few remaining. Hopefully he and Parker would survive.

A pang of guilt jabbed at his chest at the thought of the inevitable. Henwick didn't have much time left. For that matter, they had only just met Gary, and his existence would be on the chopping block soon as well. They both might have come to grips with their fate, but that didn't make Digby feel better about sacrificing them. It was one thing to step over the corpses of his opponents or those that he'd never met, but something else entirely to snuff out the souls of people that had stood by him.

The idea that his body was one of the prizes on the table didn't sit well either.

Stepping through the archway brought them to a long corridor. It seemed to wrap around the outer edge of the structure to meet the other entrances.

"It's like a representation of time itself." Parker ran a hand along the wall, her fingers exploring a complex design of carved images.

"I don't recognize most of this." Digby placed his hand against the wall as well.

"I do." Gary pointed out a number of elements. "It shows everything from the knights of old that you may have seen, to," he laughed, "the ghostbusters." He pointed to a carving of four men wearing backpacks of some kind.

"Neat." Parker leaned closer.

"Yes, very." Henwick pushed past them and headed further down the hall.

"I don't think he likes me." Gary fidgeted with his hat.

"You think?" Digby stated the obvious as he followed after the cleric.

That was when Parker stumbled into the wall.

"Are you alright?" Digby stepped closer.

"Yeah, I'm fine." She regained her balance and placed her hands to her temples while opening and closing her mouth as if trying to relieve pressure in her ears. "It's like the air is thinner here."

"I haven't noticed anything." Gary furrowed his brow.

"You sure it's the air pressure?" Digby stepped back again to give her room.

"I..." She trailed off. "I don't know. It's like everything is thinner here. Like it's all just barely hanging by a thread." She reached a hand into the air. "It feels like I could slip right through."

"I wonder if that has something to do with your messenger class." Digby arched an eyebrow. "That old witch did say that the Seed doesn't do things at random. Maybe it gave you that class because it will be needed here."

"Oh good." Parker groaned.

"Do you sense anything?" Gary passed his hand through the air as well.

"Not really. It's more like I feel the possibility of something." She shook her head. "I don't really know how to explain it. It's like there are places out there but they either don't exist yet or have already ended. Or they're just out of reach." She lowered her hand to her side. "I don't really know what I'm trying to say."

"Well, we should catch up to Henwick regardless." Digby continued walking but kept the soldier in his periphery to make sure she was stable.

Heading further down the corridor, he came across an archway on the inner wall. When he rounded the corner, he found Henwick standing still just a few feet in. Digby stopped short as well to take in what was inside.

A large area the size of a coliseum's combat pit lay before them, but instead of sand, it was solid stone and covered with more carvings. Torches lined the outer walls to bathe the place in a warm orange glow. At the center stood an elevated platform a few inches high that held a chamber of gray stone. It reminded him of a mausoleum. A pair of heavy doors barred the entrance. They look too heavy to move.

"I guess that's the finish line." Parker stepped into the archway behind Digby.

"Seems that way." He swept his vision across the open space that surrounded the chamber, Digby found the area filled with statues of obsidian, just like the Seed's obelisk. Walking up to the nearest of the glossy black statues he couldn't help but notice something familiar about it. "Is this... me?"

He stepped away in shock.

"Shit, this one is me." Parker ran up to another one not too far away.

Digby took a count of the statues, finding twenty-four, the same as the number at the corner of his HUD. That was when Digby noticed the pieces of broken obsidian that littered the rest of the floor.

"What the...?"

Before he could finish his question, one of the statues that he'd yet to examine crumbled to pieces, leaving nothing but a black pedestal at its feet. The number on his HUD ticked down to twenty-three at the same time.

"What just happened?" Parker spun around.

"I think these statues represent the souls that remain?" Digby walked between a few, finding one of Henwick.

"Then that statue breaking means that—" Gary stepped in.

"Yes, a Heretic just perished down below." Henwick nudged a piece of obsidian at his feet.

"Indeed." Digby looked over the handful of statues that were left. "I was just noticing that the population within this place has been falling faster."

Gary let out a sigh. "Well, that's to be expected. It won't be long now."

"Sorry." Parker gave him a sympathetic nod.

"It's okay." He shrugged. "I lived my life and made my decisions."

Digby shook his head. "Don't just give up."

"What?" Gary sounded surprised.

"Obviously it's unlikely, but we are here now, and I don't see anyone present to get in our way. So we might as well try to find another way. It wouldn't be the first time the Seed left a loophole open, and I am never opposed to taking advantage of an opening when I see one." Digby turned to Henwick. "Right? You're not ready to give up yet."

The cleric remained silent for a moment before giving a noncommittal nod.

The pain in Digby's chest swelled. He wasn't sure why he suddenly wanted to help the two men, but something just didn't feel right about letting them go. It was like a weight hanging around his neck.

"Okay, sure." Gary stepped forward. "We can try."

"That's the spirit." Digby ignored the voice in the back of his mind that was telling him he was wrong. He pushed the thought aside and added, "Besides, eventually that gunslinger or the care-taker will come up here after us, and then things might get complicated."

"Maybe we can break into that chamber before anyone else gets here." Parker pointed to the mausoleum in the center of the space.

"That sounds like cheating." Henwick eyed her.

"It's not cheating, it's taking advantage of a loophole." Digby waved away the concern.

"Is he always like this?" Gary hooked a thumb in his direction.

"Yep." Parker nodded.

"Oh, stop acting so honorable." Digby gave the three of them a sharp look. "We're cheating to save you, so shut up and let us try."

"I thought it wasn't cheating," Henwick commented.

"Oh, whatever." Digby threw up his hands and continued toward the center of the coliseum. As he stomped his way forward, Parker called his attention back from beside one of the statues.

"Look who's still alive down there." She pointed to a figure of an old crone.

"Good god." Henwick stopped to stare. "It's Sybil."

"Looks like that old witch is harder to kill than we thought. None of the other heretics have taken her out. Or she's still hiding down in the castle away from everyone." Digby kept walking. "Surprised the caretaker hasn't found her."

As he neared the chamber at the center of the space, he stepped up onto the platform that held it. Parker stepped up behind him.

"I came up here before. Couldn't find a way in though. Figured the requirements for the door to open hadn't been met yet," Gary chimed in as he stepped up as well.

The instant he set foot on the raised section of stone, the entire place began to rumble.

"What did you do?" Digby froze in place just as a familiar scream echoed from somewhere below.

"Oh shit. That was the caretaker. I think it's responding to this platform." Parker glanced back at Gary's foot. He jumped back, removing his shoe from the raised portion of the stone. The rumbling stopped the second he did.

"Okay, looks like that is as far as I go." Gary sighed. "The Seed must only allow two sparks to stand within the center."

The caretaker cried out again from somewhere below.

"From the sound of that, the Seed is coming to make sure we follow the rules," Henwick spoke up from further back.

"Well, it's too late to go back now." Digby pressed on the doors. "Let's smash our way through and get inside."

Parker ran to throw her weight against the door beside him. They both strained, but even with the attributes of a Heretic, nothing budged.

"I don't think we're getting in." Parker let out a grunt of effort.

"Nonsense." Digby raised his hand and started casting Decay on the stone. "One way or another, these doors are opening."

Digby checked his mana as he cast another Decay.

MP: 278/298

Dust trickled from the surface as the carved pattern on the doors faded to a smooth indent. Even with the spell's advanced rank, it would take at least half of his mana to get through. Provided the doors weren't too thick. Digby glanced back over his shoulder. Good thing that the caretaker wasn't particularly fast. He shuddered to think what would happen if it caught up while his mana was low.

Shifting his attention, he beckoned to Henwick who was still standing further back. "Get over here. I want you and Gary ready to run inside behind us once I'm through these doors."

The cleric turned away to face the outer wall of the coliseum. "Someone has to make sure the caretaker doesn't catch us off guard. Just promise me that when you get back to the world and stop Autem, that you will do what is right and destroy the Seed."

Digby's mouth fell open, at a loss for what to say.

The bottom fell out of his stomach when his mind processed what the cleric was asking. Henwick was really ready to give up his existence to help him, but no matter how much Digby thought about it, he couldn't make that promise. It wasn't the first time that the cleric had asked for his word to destroy the Seed, but he had always dodged the subject. Now, with Henwick ready to give up his existence, there was no way to evade it.

Of course, that left one obvious choice left.

He could always lie.

It would be so easy. Just like always.

Digby stepped forward, opening his mouth to speak. He closed it again just as fast.

No, I can't.

Not now.

Not when Henwick is ready to sacrifice everything.

The weight around his neck grew heavier. So heavy it seemed unbearable.

That was when all the torches in the colosseum went out all at once.

The cry of the caretaker followed.

"No!" Digby spun, in search of the monstrosity that spoke in his father's voice.

Gary held out a hand as a Fireball formed in his palm to chase away the darkness. Digby glanced at the spell, then quickly looked away. It was obviously an illusion, considering it hadn't burned the false wizard's palm. He pushed the thought out of his mind and returned his attention to the doors to cast decay.

Parker winced before shaking off whatever she was feeling. "What do we do?"

Digby glanced for a moment in Henwick's direction as the man stood, still waiting for an answer. He forced the question out of his mind. He wasn't dodging. There wasn't time for them to debate the future. The caretaker was already there.

"Alright! We do the same as before." Digby gritted his teeth and turned away from Henwick. "I'm going to cast Flare and try to blow that monstrosity to hell. Just be ready to run if that fails."

That was when the world went white.

Pain, real and excruciating, surged through his body.

Digby collapsed to the stone, his skin blistering and flaking away as smoke filled his nose. He was burning. Even worse, he recognized the feeling.

It was a Smite spell.

Why?

The only thing he could make out through the blinding light was Henwick, standing with his hand outstretched in his direction.

Why?

Digby's skin still sizzled as the spell that the cleric had just blasted him in the chest with faded. He tried to move, but his limbs refused to cooperate. It was like the curse that animated him had been purified from his body. All that was left was a seed of death essence, clinging to his body. He checked his mana.

MP: 198/298

He cast Necrotic Regeneration, hoping it could force the curse back into his limbs.

"Stay down, Graves!" Henwick stood over him, ready to blast him again.

Digby struggled to form the word 'why,' unable to make the syllable work in his mouth.

"What is wrong with you?" Gary slid into the space between them, still holding his illusionary fireball in his hand to light the cleric in a flicker of orange and red.

"Get out of the way, boy." Henwick moved his hand in the illusionist's direction. "If I can't trust Graves to do what must be done, then I cannot allow him to leave."

The voice of Digby's father, mimicked by the caretaker, echoed through the corridor just outside. It would be there in moments.

"I will not step aside!" Gary shouted back. "Graves is the only one that can fight Autem. I won't let you snuff out the only chance we have left in the world. He must carry on the fight."

"We don't need Graves." Henwick took a step back toward the platform where Parker was standing.

"You traitor!" Digby shouted, his speech slurred as the curse struggled to reassert itself within his body. "You dirty rotten traitor. All that talk about honor, and you try to steal my body anyway."

"This is not what I wanted." Henwick shook his head. "The world still needs a savior. I would have liked for that to be you, but if you won't destroy the Heretic Seed when you are finished with it then I have no choice. I must step in to take your place. I can bear the reality of damning myself, but I won't allow you to damn the world."

"And I still won't let you." Gary moved to get in his way.

"You fail to realize that I cannot let a Fool like you leave this place either." Henwick began moving mana through his blood.

"But you won't kill me!" Parker slid in front of Gary just as a beam of white light exploded from Henwick's palm.

"You foolish woman." The cleric jerked his hand to the side, firing the blast to the left of her. The air crackled as the beam hit the stone wall of the coliseum.

Digby cast Necrotic Regeneration again to push his curse back through his system. It felt like pumping mud through his veins, but he gained a small amount of sensation in his limbs.

That was when a hulking form entered the space from the entryway.

"Digby!"

The voice of his father accompanied the caretaker's oversized skull as it ducked its head to fit through the archway.

"Shit." Parker held her ground as Digby struggled to regain feeling in his body. Little by little, sensation returned, almost enough to crawl.

"It is not too late, young miss." Henwick held out a hand toward Parker as he stepped toward the platform behind her. "You need not perish here. I have no quarrel with you. You may return along with me once the caretaker has dealt with the rest of the Heretics."

"Yeah, no. I'm not leaving without this jerk." The pink-haired soldier moved to keep herself between the cleric and Digby. "And I have a name, you sexist dick."

Digby pushed himself up onto one elbow, still struggling to move.

Gary looked to her as he remained in Henwick's path. "Get Graves out of here."

"What about you?" She dropped to a knee next to Digby.

The illusionist threw a hand out to his side as several identical images of himself appeared. "Just go, I'll cover your escape."

With that, the false wizard darted to the side, making it hard to tell which one of his decoys were real. Some of his illusions headed for Henwick, while the rest headed straight for the caretaker.

"You heard him." Parker grabbed hold of Digby's shoulder and started dragging him away from either of the threats.

"Where are you taking me?" Digby stuttered as his jaw regained its function.

She kept dragging him. "We need to get around the caretaker and make for the stairs. We'll get away and regroup."

"Fine." Digby managed to get a foot under himself.

"Graves!" Henwick shouted after him as he threw a punch through another of Gary's copies. "You can't run from this, Digby. Please understand, this is the best way."

Digby struggled to maintain his footing. "Never!"

"You are a monster, Graves! By your own admission, you understand that." Henwick raised a hand toward him, but Parker made sure to keep her body in the way to block his shot. He cursed her and lowered his hand. "You can't possibly think yourself capable of creating a future that the world wants."

"You might be right." Gary looked back, just as the caretaker took out the last of his decoys. "But it's not always about creating the world that people want. Sometimes it's about creating the world that they need."

A choking cough punctuated his sentence like a period at the end as the caretaker snapped a clawed hand around his throat. Digby turned back for a moment, as the monster impaled the illusionist with the claws of its other hand. The finality of Gary's words cut straight into Digby's chest.

"Come on, come on." Parker dragged him back into the hallway that surrounded the colosseum.

"He's dying!" Digby struggled to go back, not even sure why leaving the fake wizard behind tore at him so.

"Yes, and there's nothing we can do." Parker yanked him down the hall just as the caretaker stepped into the archway behind them. It dragged Gary's corpse at its side. Parker looked back and let out a whimper. "We have to keep going."

"Keep going where?" Digby struggled to walk normally. "I won't make it down the stairway in my condition."

"I don't know where, damn it," Parker growled as they reached the entrance that they had come from. "But I am not about to let you get murdered now."

"That doesn't instill me with confidence." Digby reached for the railing to the side of the stairs to support himself as he stumbled down a few steps.

"Shit, hey." Parker lost her grip on his shoulder. "You can't just fall the whole way down." She paused as soon as the words left her mouth. "Actually, maybe we can."

"I can't help it. That Smite spell screwed up my entire body." He reached up and grabbed the railing to pull himself back onto his feet as his mind processed that last thing she'd said. "Wait for a second, what did you say about falling?"

"Do you trust me?" Parker jumped down the steps to land beside him.

"Umm…" Digby stared at her for a second.

"Do you trust me?" she repeated, this time louder.

"Fine, fine, whatever. I trust you." Digby kept his balance long enough to let her slip between him and the railing.

That was when the caretaker dropped Gary's body at the top of the stairs. His corpse flopped onto the stone upside down with his head lolling at an unnatural angle.

"Whatever you're planning, you better do it fast." Digby trembled as the caretaker stalked down the stairs toward them.

"Okay, just don't bite me on the way down." She wrapped her arms around his waist and clasped them together at his back. "We're gonna have to get a little close."

"Wait, what are you—" Panic filled Digby's mind as she leaned back with her rear against the railing. For an instant, he nearly fought back, but then he remembered her question.

Do you trust me?

Instead, he let her pull him over the side with her. Dread rolled through his gut as gravity asserted its dominance and the sea below filled his view.

The caretaker's oversized hand swiped through the air. One claw scraped the bottom of his boot as they went over the side.

Then, they fell to their doom.

CHAPTER THIRTY-ONE

"That'll be thirty chips." Campbell placed a plate of food down on a tray at the counter of the buffet in the casino's dining area.

"Thirty?" Becca looked down at the enchanted poker chips in her hand. A neon green skull with the words 'Sin City,' glowed on the surface of each as she held them. "Isn't that a little steep?"

"Umm, I don't really know." He shrugged. "Five chips convert to about a dollar if you do the math, so I guess thirty is the equivalent of six bucks. That's about right for a lunch out."

Becca sighed, unsure if the value made sense for everyone.

It hadn't taken long for Bancroft to get his currency system up and running. Just a couple days. With the access to the dam's power, pretty much everything had started to move faster.

Unfortunately, once Alex had figured out how to set up the enchantment plates to encode the chips with a marker, Bancroft's artificer took over the process. The result was that whenever a person touched one of the chips, the enchantment skimmed a little mana from them to illuminate a design on the surface.

Hence the ridiculous skull icon.

Apparently, that was what you got when you outsourced the illustration work to Hawk, who had scribbled the logo onto the enchantment plate. Becca was pretty sure Alex had put the kid in charge of the design to annoy Bancroft, so she couldn't completely hold the artwork against him.

Once the system was worked out, it wasn't long before they had a bank set up in one of the casino's cash-out areas. She'd worried that the survivors would have trouble returning to a currency-based system but surprisingly they accepted the new rules pretty quick. As much as it pained her to admit it, Bancroft's theory that the people would appreciate the return to normalcy seemed to be right. Not to mention the new system had made things easier to organize overnight.

A basic allotment was set up for everyone regardless of their role, as well as an additional amount based on the tasks that they contributed to. As one of the city's leaders, Becca had been given what seemed like a fairly high salary, so thirty for lunch didn't seem like a problem. Despite that, the idea of implementing the currency system still made her feel uneasy.

She couldn't help but feel that she had made a mistake when she'd given Bancroft the go-ahead.

So much was changing so fast, and she didn't have anyone to lean on. She sighed. Mason had gotten held up at the power station. Apparently there was more work for the engineers. They had the power connected but were making some adjustments to ensure the systems were stable. The situation left her feeling a little down. She had a good mind to take a kestrel out there and surprise him, but with Bancroft here, she didn't dare leave him alone.

Of course, she could also go to Alex for a little support, but with the work he was doing, it was best not to interrupt him. The runes he was studying were important, and he was making progress every day. Progress that could actually play a hand in the war to come.

In the end, she couldn't help questioning everything she did. Maybe it was just because she had spent so long living in an apartment with Skyline deciding every aspect of her life. After that, making choices that affected hundreds of people seemed like more responsibility than she could handle.

Everything had been so much easier with Dig around.

Becca sighed and handed over the poker chips to pay for her

meal, then brought it over to a table near the edge of the dining area to stress eat. On her way, she couldn't help but notice a few groups of people. Strangely, their trays held nothing but soup.

Not more than a minute after she sat down did someone sneak up behind her.

"Hey, Becca?"

"Jesus fuck!" She spat a bite of bread from her mouth and launched the rest of a roll several feet in the air.

"Sorry." Hawk caught the falling dinner roll before it hit the floor. "I forgot my stealth was on."

"God damn it, don't do that." She panted a few times to gather herself. After getting used to hearing literally everything, having someone sneak up on her was unsettling, to say the least.

"Sorry," the kid repeated and ducked his head. "I'm trying to get the Seed to give me Conceal. Was hoping I might get there faster if I snuck around a lot."

Becca eyed him sideways and snatched her roll back. "Are you really sorry?"

"Okay, yeah, I'm not that sorry." He shrugged. "I have to get stronger somehow, since I can't get myself on a team to help clear the revs outside."

"Well, you are a kid. I'm sure you will get your chance eventually." She bit into her bread glancing in his direction out of the corner of her eye.

Heretic, level 3 Fighter, friendly.

"No, it's not just me that's having trouble. I get that I'm a kid and I'm trying not to be a pain in the ass to everyone, but the guys from Skyline are hogging the XP."

"What?" Becca's ears pricked up.

Hawk dropped into the chair beside her. "They have been leading most of the teams that go out and they include at least two of their guys on every trip. The rest of us get rotated out so we just don't get as much opportunity to do anything. Not to mention the Seed doesn't like to give points to the rest of us if they take a kill, and they don't really hold back."

"Okay, that is a problem." A part of her relaxed, despite the fact that the issue was significant and that she had no idea how to fix it on her own. Though, having the knowledge that what she had been dreading for so long was finally happening gave her some comfort in the fact that she had been right to be worried in the first place. "Is there anything else you want to report?"

"Umm." Hawk's eyes widened as if having his input taken seriously was something new to him.

"It's okay." Becca smiled at him and nodded. The kid may have acted like a bratty little brother most of the time, but he had been working hard. That was worth a little trust.

He nodded back and leaned on the table, looking more comfortable. "Well, I heard some of the other kids complaining that they were hungry. A lot of them are like me, so they don't have parents, but most have been taken in by other survivors. I guess a lot of people lost kids too, so it kind of worked out. But Bancroft's whole money thing hasn't been adding enough for the kids that are living with some of the adults."

"Oh." She sat up straight. "That will definitely need to be adjusted. I'm seeing a problem with it too. Not everyone can do something vital here, especially since we are stuck inside. And it looks like the basic income being given isn't enough to afford more than the bare minimum."

"Yeah, that sucks." He shrugged. "The only reason I have gotten enough to eat and stuff is because I'm a Heretic, and I get to help with more things. But not everyone can get magic yet, so that's not an option for everyone else."

"Sure." She snapped her head to the side. "Wait, who are you living with?"

He opened his mouth to let out a long, 'ahhhhhhh,' as if no one had asked him that question before. "I've been sort of staying in Parker's room while she wasn't there."

"What?" Becca slapped a hand down on the table. "Why?"

"I don't know." He shrugged. "She let me stay when we first took over this place, and I didn't really know what to do when she passed out with Dig. It's not like she was taking care of me or anything, so I figured I was on my own."

"Aren't you twelve?" Becca shook her head at him as well as the fact that Parker had failed to mention the homeless child staying in her room the last time they had spoken. Considering the fact that she had been separated from her parents when she was thirteen, she didn't like the idea of the same thing happening to Hawk.

"I can take care of myself." He pouted, making himself look younger.

"I'm sure you can, but that's not the point." Becca jabbed him with a finger the way Dig might do when he was annoyed. "The point is you're a kid and you shouldn't have to take care of yourself."

"Well yeah, but I don't really know anyone else here." The child continued to sit with his arms folded.

Becca hesitated for a moment. He had a point. Other than Dig, herself, Alex, and maybe Lana, he hadn't really warmed up to anyone. Obviously, Digby was too busy to adopt a kid. Not to mention living with a zombie would probably present some problems. Hell, the necromancer didn't even sleep. Her next thought was Lana, but considering that she was only nineteen and had her hands full with her traitor of a brother, that was probably out. Alex wasn't much better, since he had been working on his various projects so much lately that he had barely been up to his room.

That just left her.

Becca's mouth fell open. It wasn't like the kid needed much supervision. Just a place to stay where he wasn't completely alone. Plus, when Mason got back, having him around would probably be a better influence on Hawk than Dig or Parker. It wasn't like she was about to move in with the soldier, not yet at least, but she did love him and he probably wasn't going anywhere.

She winced. "Okay, I can't believe I'm saying this, but why don't you stay with me until we figure out a better place for you?"

"Seriously?" A confused expression filled his face.

"What?" Becca couldn't help but feel self-conscious.

"I don't know." He shook his head. "I didn't think you liked me."

Becca flinched, not sure what she'd done to give the impression. "Oh, shut up. You're a pain in the ass, but I'm used to that after dealing with Dig for the last month. I like you fine." She cringed as she listened to herself. "Besides, I'd be kind of a shitty adult if I just left you on your own."

"'Tis true. I am a mere helpless child." He switched on the terrible accent he used to taunt Digby.

Becca rubbed at her temples. "Yeah, this is going to be a mistake."

"So what are you going to do about those Skyline guys?" His face looked a little more serious as he changed the subject.

Becca's heart sped up a little at the realization that she would have to deal with the problem. Again, she wished Digby was there to help. It wasn't that he was better than her at these sorts of situations, but his lack of shame and bull in a china shop approach to everything always seemed to work in the end.

That was when she remembered that the zombie wasn't the only one on her side. As much as she didn't want to interrupt everyone's work, it sounded like dealing with Bancroft was becoming a priority. She glanced around for a moment, then looked at Hawk.

"Think you can help me out?"

"Yeah." He nodded as if he was just glad to be asked.

"Okay, I don't want to announce a meeting over the radio since Bancroft's men would hear it, so could you go find Deuce and Sax? They should be in the armory. Tell them to get Elenore and meet me up at the obelisk. I'll go grab Alex. We'll come up with something."

"Got it." The kid hopped up and headed off toward the armory.

With that, she leaned forward and put her head down on the table, as if taking a nap, and cast projection. The world blurred around her for a second before coming into focus again with the parking garage surrounding her. Sure, she could have just walked around until she found the artificer, but using magic was faster and quickly becoming her first response to most problems.

"Okay, why would he be in the garage?" Becca glanced around at the empty structure. It may have been warded against revenants, but it was dark out and working out there felt a little risky.

Even stranger, she didn't see Alex anywhere and her projection spell usually brought her straight to whichever member of her coven she wanted to speak to. That was when she heard the sound of someone shuffling around beneath a nearby car.

Becca strode over to the vehicle and crouched down to look underneath, only to come face to skull with Kristen's gold-coated visage. "Whoa, hey, there."

"Oh good, it's you." The deceased seer tilted to one side as if gesturing behind her where Alex jumped at the sudden noise.

"Shit." The artificer slammed his head into the underside of the car. "Ow, damn." He rubbed at his nose. "Hey, Becca."

"Should you be hanging out under a car in the middle of an empty parking lot while revenants roam the city?" She didn't apologize for startling him.

"It's fine, I warded the whole structure." He shoved his way out and grabbed the seer's skull. "Besides, if one of the revs got in, I'm sure Kristen would warn me."

"No, I wouldn't." The skull scoffed.

"Yes, you would." He set her down on the car's hood. "You're warming up to me. You haven't even tried to get me to kill myself all day."

The skull simply groaned in response.

"Well, could we maybe leave her head here for a bit so I can talk to you inside?"

He glanced down at his deceased assistant. "You mind?"

"I am not your keeper." There was something about her tone that sounded annoyed.

"Fair enough." Alex wiped his hands on his pants. "Give me fifteen minutes to get my stuff cleared up here, and I'll meet you in the high-roller suite."

"Great, I'll see you upstairs." Becca released her projection, leaving him alone while she returned her mind to her body back in the dining area.

Raising her head from the table, a nagging feeling pulled her thoughts back to the parking garage. A memory of that weird piece of debris that she'd found just after they had landed a couple days before. She'd forgotten about it until now, but with the suspicious actions of Bancroft's men, she couldn't shake the feeling that it was important. She wasn't sure why, but the more she thought about it, the more it seemed possible that her heightened perception was cluing her into something that her mind hadn't fully worked out.

If Alex had warded the parking structure, then there was nothing stopping her from heading up to the kestrels to investigate.

"Why not? I've got fifteen minutes to kill." Becca shoveled the last of her meal into her mouth and cleared her tray.

A couple minutes later, she was slipping into the garage. The entire structure was dead silent.

"Hope Alex's runes will keep out those sensebreakers." The last thing she needed was to have a few of the invisible revenants sneaking up on her.

The artificer's wards seemed to work when she reached the kestrels without a problem. She hit the ramp button as soon as she could. There was no sense waiting around.

"Okay, where was that weird rock?" Becca headed inside and crouched down by the pilot's seat. "There you are."

Reaching under the console, she scooped up the slender fragment. It wasn't until she took a good look at it that she realized why it had stuck in her mind. It wasn't a chip of stone, like she had assumed. No, it was a piece of a seashell.

"What?" Becca sat in the pilot's seat and stared at the triangular piece of calcium.

The kestrels had been cleaned a few times since they had been stolen and they hadn't gone anywhere near the coast. The facts raised the question, "Where did you come from?"

Becca set the shell aside and switched on the kestrel's computers. They weren't good for much since the internet was mostly unusable, but they still had flight records, even if they could only be accessed from inside the craft. She hadn't been able to keep tabs on all of Bancroft's guys with everything that had to be done to get the dam's power supply connected, but it was possible that Malcolm had taken a detour.

After scrolling through the map, she had an outlier. Most of the points that the craft had traveled to made sense, but there was one that was way out of the way.

"California?" She furrowed her brow at a beach on the coastline. "Why would you be there?"

Becca shut down the kestrel's system and stood up. There was something else to add to her list of questions for Bancroft.

She blew out a long sigh.

"I am so not looking forward to this."

CHAPTER THIRTY-TWO

"What seems...?" Bancroft trailed off as he walked into the high-roller suite.

"We need to talk, Charles." Becca stood with her arms folded to greet him as she did her best to hide the fact that her heart was racing.

Alex, Sax, Deuce, Elenore, and even Hawk stood at her sides to back her up. Together, they surrounded the poker table in a unified front. The only member of the city's leadership that was missing was its newest, Jameson, who had gone back to the dam.

Bancroft stopped in his tracks and swept his eyes across her group as he finished his question. "...to be the problem?"

That was when everyone around Becca spoke up at once.

"The income you're giving isn't working out, and families are hurting." Deuce slapped a hand to the table.

"They have been way too rough with the zombies and Clint," Alex added.

"Plus they aren't very respectful of the non-magic-capable survivors." Elenore folded her arms.

"And I told you I didn't want my enchantments used to create a financial hellscape." Alex tossed a few poker chips to the table.

"You went right back to business as usual the moment you got money."

"Your guys are hogging all the XP," Hawk finished, sounding a little like a kid getting salty about a game.

Becca threw a hand out to silence the group. "I think it's time you stopped the act, Charles."

"What act?" Bancroft shook his head, still looking hungover or a little drunk. She wasn't sure which. Either way, his speech was slower than usual.

Becca eyed the man and cast Veritas in case he tried to lie his way out of the confrontation. "This whole act of you trying to help while using every bit of wiggle room you have to take advantage of us. Dig might not be here right now to give Tavern commands, but that doesn't mean the rest of us are going to just sit back and let you and your men take over the city."

A flash of anger streaked across his face, making him resemble the man they had fought not too long ago. "Now you listen here, I have put up with just about enough hostility from your people."

Becca scoffed. "Excuse me, but I think you earned that."

"I most certainly have not." He swiped a hand through the air. "Yes, we used to be enemies, but things change. I am not the villain here; it is all just business. There is no need for things to get emotional or for everyone to hold grudges. Do you think I am not still angry that my very skeleton has been stolen from me? Of course I am, but I am not running around accusing you or your people of working against me."

Becca shook her head at the disbelief of his statement. It was like he was somehow trying to make her out to be the bad guy. She eyed her HUD to make sure he wasn't lying.

True

She considered his words. Technically he hadn't said anything that she could take issue with. "Okay, sure, you haven't accused us of anything, but you can't deny that everything you have been doing is causing problems. Just the fact that your men are making sure they get more kills than everyone else is enough to question your motives. I shouldn't need to explain why we would be uncomfortable with them being the highest-level Heretics in Vegas."

Bancroft slapped a hand to his leg. "That is exactly what I'm talking about. You are seeing what you want to and making accusations instead of asking me why."

Becca glanced to her HUD, finding that he still hadn't lied. "Okay then, why?"

"Because my men are trained mercenaries." He sighed as if frustrated that none of them were getting his point. "It is literally their job to take on the majority of the risk. They belong on the front line so that our newer Heretics are able to gain strength in the safest manner possible."

"Hey, I can take care of myself," Hawk called out from behind her.

"Of that I have no doubt, child." Bancroft let out a chuckle. "After the ruse you pulled a week ago, I would agree you are more than capable. But the sad fact is that we do not have enough magic users and we don't even know if Digby will wake up with a way to create more." He held out an open hand. "We literally can't afford to risk Heretics without a good reason. So yes, it will always make sense to let our most capable personnel take on the majority of the risk."

"How are the rest of us supposed to get any levels?" Deuce leaned forward.

"The same way we handled this problem in Skyline." He dropped his hand to his side. "You all seem to think I have something nefarious in mind, but I'm following the tried-and-true procedures that my forces have followed since this apocalypse started. The point is for the higher levels to handle the heavy lifting while the rest grow stronger at a safe pace. Once the rest of our Heretics reach level fifteen and access their next class, they will be cleared for more."

True

Becca frowned at her HUD. He wasn't wrong. From his

perspective, he was just following the same tactics as before. "What about the miscalculation of incomes, then?"

"It's exactly what you said, a miscalculation." He folded his arms. "With everything that has happened between us, I think you forget that I am used to running a private military company. I am good at this sort of thing, but I am not perfect. Organizing budgetary finances for families and children is different from funding squads of mercenaries. So yes, I do occasionally make mistakes. But you have to realize that speed bumps will happen from time to time."

"But what—" Becca tried to interject but he talked over her.

"We are trying to build a literal society from the ground up so that it can grow and flourish, rather than devolving into anarchy the first time something goes wrong." He shook his head. "That doesn't happen easily. Believe me."

The continuous 'true' being displayed across her HUD grew increasingly irritating. She let out a frustrated growl. "Okay, fine. But none of that explains why your men would have taken a kestrel out to the coasts without telling anyone."

Bancroft's face fell an almost imperceptible amount.

"Huh?" Becca added, "No explanation for that one, is there?"

"How did you…?" He shook his head. "No, it doesn't matter how you know." He took a deep breath. "You are correct, I sent Malcolm on a detour to check a theory of mine. It was a long shot, so I didn't put too much thought into it. Though, if it had paid off, it would mean gaining an upper hand on Autem that could drastically impact this war."

"That sounds like something you would have wanted to mention to the rest of us." Becca gave him a smug look.

He lowered his head. "You are right, I should have said something. At least to you, Rebecca. I have a habit of compartmentalizing information, and I should have included you in some decisions like this."

"That's a little better." She relaxed a little now that something had stuck to the man.

"Very well, I will continue to send my men to investigate the coast and I will compile a secure report with their findings once I am ready. We can discuss what to do from there." He glanced around the table at the rest of her group. "I would say more now but some things really do need to be kept quiet. I may not always make the right decision, but I do know how to handle information."

"This isn't Skyline, and you don't have Autem lurking behind you anymore. There is no need to compartmentalize information. So spit it out." Becca groaned at his continued resistance. "I'll give you the benefit of the doubt that you aren't trying to overthrow us or cause trouble, but that doesn't mean that you can keep doing things without involving us. We are supposed to be working together."

He nodded before betraying the gesture with an added sigh. "I know. I realize that."

"I'm sensing a but coming." She folded her arms.

"There is." Bancroft nodded again as his face softened. "But there is a problem that I haven't brought up with you that impacts the situation."

"Okay, then you can bring it up now." She locked eyes with him.

"Some things are not quite that simple." He looked away. "With the way that you clearly feel about me, I was hoping to gain a little trust before mentioning anything, but since it has come to this, I don't see that I have a choice." Bancroft brought his gaze back to hers. "Just for a moment, I want you to forget about every-thing that has happened between us and just ask yourself who is more qualified to lead a settlement in a time of war."

Becca opened her mouth to speak but found the words missing.

Bancroft answered for her. "I understand that you have been doing things on your own so far. And you have done incredible, considering where you all came from. But I have to put an emphasis on that because it is where you all came from that matters." He held his hand out, moving it from left to right. "Alex, you were an average salaryman, recently fired from a job if I have heard correctly. Deuce, you checked IDs on the casino floor to make sure no one underage was drinking. Elenore was a stripper."

"Showgirl," she corrected with a harumph.

"Yes, a showgirl." Bancroft nodded as his hand swept to Sax. "You have military experience."

Sax stood a little taller as he continued.

"And you are a valuable asset in that regard, but a rank of Private or even Private First Class does not equate the skills or experience needed of a General. The same goes for Mason and Parker, provided she isn't off napping somewhere." That was when his focus returned to Becca. "And that brings me to you, Ms. Alvarez. You were a member of Skyline."

"I was, until you all decided I wasn't worth rescuing from Seattle." She glared daggers at him.

"As cruel as it is, that fact reinforces my point." He lowered his hand. "As a Heretic, you are valuable. But as hard as it is to tell you this, the fact is that your experience as a drone operator doesn't add up to much when it comes to leading a settlement. Especially one in war time."

"Now you wait just a damn second." She took in a lungful of air, ready to rip into him.

He held up a hand to stop her. "I know how this sounds, and this is why I haven't brought any of this up. It's difficult for people to hear when their shortcomings are brought to light, but you can't tell me I am wrong. I'm sure you have been checking to see if anything I have said is a lie, right?"

Becca glanced at another 'true' listed on her HUD. At the very least, Bancroft believed every word he had said. He hit her with another truth for good measure.

"You aren't a leader, Rebecca." His tone sounded sympathetic. "One day, you will be. If given the time, I'm sure you'll be one of the greatest leaders the world has seen. But right now, you're a drone jockey without a drone. Even you have to see that. Up until last month, you didn't even have to decide what to eat for dinner, much less how to allocate forces and resources."

Becca closed her mouth as anger bubbled from in her gut. She thrust out a finger at his throat. "Listen, you fucking piece of shit! It was your leadership that caused Skyline to steal a teenager away from her parents. And it was your leadership that blocked every attempt they made to get me back. It was your fucking leadership that hid their letters from me so that I grew up thinking they had abandoned me! I had a god damn adoptive brother that I never fucking met."

Bancroft flinched. "I admit that while none of that was under my direct orders, I was aware of the practices that Skyline's acquisitions department carried out."

True

"There is nothing I can do to change that now."

True

"But the fact is that holding a grudge against me will not do this settlement any good."

True

Becca took a few deep breaths as she realized she had done exactly what she had been trying to avoid. She had let her personal grievances mix with her complaints. She cringed, feeling the eyes of everyone around her staring. She could see the pity on their faces without even needing to look.

None of them spoke up, causing the moment to drag on even longer.

What hurt even more was that Bancroft was right. She wasn't cut out to be a leader. She knew that much. As much as she hated the man, his experience did make him the better choice.

Bancroft broke the silence. "I didn't want to say anything but —"

"I get it." She deflated, completely losing the position of strength that she'd had. "Just tell your men to start prioritizing the other Heretic's growth, redo the math of your whole income thing, and adjust the amount people are getting. I want a report of whatever you are doing in California too."

"That's entirely fair." He nodded.

"Good, then get out." She dropped into a chair and sunk her face into a hand.

"Ah, yes. I can do that too." He turned toward the door only to glance back. "I will earn your trust; I promise you that."

True

Becca actively avoided looking at her HUD.

"I know." She made a point of breaking eye contact to make sure he left without adding anything else.

"Have a pleasant evening, then." He gave her a sympathetic smile before pushing through the door.

Everyone remained silent for a long moment after he left.

Becca sunk back into her chair and groaned.

"Holy crap. I wish Dig would wake the hell up."

CHAPTER THIRTY-THREE

Becca stood in the middle of the high-roller suite, her forehead still burning with embarrassment. Silence filled the room now that everyone had gone.

Of course, Alex and the others had tried to talk to her about how the conversation with Bancroft went, but she had shooed them all away. Now that they were gone, she realized how stupid that had been. Being alone with her thoughts wasn't great either. She let out a long continuous groan, wishing Mason had gotten back from his mission. Becca let out a second groan that she'd left things unsaid. The more she thought about it, the more it weighed on her.

She had never fallen for anyone before.

How could she?

She had been locked in her apartment until the world ended. It wasn't like she had been able to play the field. Even worse, she had literally jumped into bed with one of the first guys she'd met that wasn't already dead. It was what she needed at the time, and she sure as hell didn't feel bad about it. But now that she had started something, she didn't want it to end.

With the amount of pressure she was under as the temporary leader of Las Vegas, the added tension made it worse. She tried to shove it out of her head. There were other things to worry about, considering her actions could affect the outcome of a war. Maybe someday she would have more freedom and time to deal with her problems in a healthy and mature way, but today was not that day.

With that, Becca strode over to the bar and snatched one of the few bottles in the casino that Tavern hadn't yet poured down Bancroft's throat. Some kind of low-grade gin. She didn't bother to grab a glass.

Bottle in hand, she wandered back over to the Heretic Seed's obelisk and leaned against it to let herself slide down to the floor. She tipped back the bottle, only to immediately grimace and set it back down.

"Ack." She groaned. "What the hell am I doing? I don't even drink."

In truth, she had seen people hit the bottle in the movies when they were feeling down and thought it might help after how badly she had just embarrassed herself.

"Stupid Bancroft." Becca snapped her fingers and cast Ventriloquism without even thinking of a sound for the spell to play. What she got was a sad piano that she vaguely recognized. "Yeah, that sounds about right for how I feel."

After all the progress she'd made recently, Bancroft had shrugged off everything she had to say until she lost her temper and dredged up things that had nothing to do with the current issue. It wasn't a good look.

"Why the hell aren't you here, Dig?" She dropped her head back against the Seed's obelisk. "I could really use some help."

Digby wasn't there to answer.

She stared up at the ceiling. "I just feel like everything I do falls short."

A part of her could imagine Digby's response, leading her to add his half of the conversation for him. She made a point to add Hawk's terrible British accent as another imitation. "Least you've stopped hiding in closets and vans."

The slow piano droned on as her spell filled the room with depressing tones.

"I thought I could handle things here without you. I thought that I could take charge of things." She shook her head. "Bancroft just has so much more experience, I can't compete. He might be genuinely working with us, or he might be plotting our deaths. I just can't tell when everything he does ends up having a reasonable explanation. My gut tells me not to trust him, but in all honesty my instincts for dealing with people tend to be wrong. There is a good chance that I am making things difficult for everyone simply because I have a hard time trusting, or even being honest about my feelings. I mean, am I holding Vegas back?"

The sad piano answered back in Digby's place.

"I bet this is how you felt that time you called out Rufus back in California. You went all in and accused him of everything you could think of only to have it backfire and leave you with both of your feet in your mouth." She blew out a long sigh. "God, we are more similar than I ever care to admit."

She shook her head as a dull ache settled into her chest. Not having Dig around was beginning to take its toll. She probably wouldn't admit it, but she was pretty sure he was the only one that actually understood her. Sure, Mason was trying, but the eight-hundred-year-old dead man was just as broken as her. They might have bickered non-stop, but he was the first and best friend she'd had.

"What should I even do now, Dig? I could really use your no fucks given attitude. You know, when you completely disregard whatever sense of shame you have and just bowl through the world like a runaway train. I mean, I know it's mostly all talk, but I could use a little of your confidence."

That was when a knock came from the door.

"Ah, Becca?" Hawk poked his head in the room.

"What do you want?" She groaned, channeling Digby to express that she didn't really want to deal with kids at the moment. Then again, she didn't really like being alone either.

"Sorry, but I am kinda locked out of the room upstairs. And you said that I should stay there." He glanced around the room clearly wondering where the piano music was coming from.

"Oh shit." Becca slapped a hand to her face, realizing she had forgotten about her random ass plan to take the boy in temporarily. "I suck."

"No, I get it." Hawk crept in. "There's a lot happening. You don't suck."

"I mean, I kinda do, but I appreciate you saying so." She fished around in her pocket for her room key as Hawk walked into the suite. She held it out as he reached her.

"What are you doing in here?" He glanced down at the bottle of gin sitting on the floor with a concerned expression. "You getting wasted or something?"

"Ha, no." She pushed the bottle away. "I don't drink and that stuff's nasty. So no, I'm just hanging out with Dig here." She reached back to slap a hand against the Seed's obelisk. "Figured if I was going to wallow in self-pity, this was the place to do it."

"I get that." He fidgeted with the keycard in his hand, then he dropped down to the floor to sit beside her.

She leaned to one side. "Do you need something else?"

"Umm, no." He let a long pause go by before adding, "But you said some stuff to Bancroft that—"

"Ugh." She let her neck go limp, so her head lolled to one side. "I get it. I embarrassed myself and made us all look bad. I don't need to talk about it. Everything I say just shoves my foot further down my throat. If I don't get my shit together, I'm going to have to storm off into the night like Dig did back in California."

"That's not why I'm…" Hawk trailed off before adding, "Well yeah, things didn't look that good, but I'm here for something else."

Becca groaned. "Yeah, the room key. And you got that. So, to quote Dig, scram."

"Dig never told me to scram." Hawk smirked. "He's told me to go away and to stop bothering him before. But never scram. I don't think he knows the word."

"Argh." Becca clawed at the air. "What do you want?"

The next words out of his mouth might as well have been an iron spike through her heart.

"Were your parents named Maria and Jose?"

"What?" Becca's face fell as the ache in her chest climbed into her throat. "How do you—"

"Bancroft said your last name was Alvarez and you said that you were taken from your family." He shoved a hand into his pocket to pull out a folded photograph that he handed to her. "I know I don't say much about the shit I've been through, but I was adopted. Not that long ago. They mentioned you. I don't know the details of everything that happened, but I know enough for the story to make sense."

Becca's mind raced to connect the dots as she took the photo from him.

It wasn't possible.

It couldn't be.

The world was so big.

Her hands trembled as she stared down, too afraid to unfold the picture. She already knew what it showed. Her eyes welled up to the brim.

"Sorry I'm dumping this on you now." Hawk's expression wavered between fear and hope. "I just have to know."

Without another word, she threw her arms around the kid.

"Whoa, hey." Hawk struggled for a moment.

Becca choked out a few words and burst into tears. "Shut up and hug me."

"Oh fuck, hey, don't cry." Hawk's voice wavered on the verge of tears as well.

She squeezed him tighter, unable to hold back. "You're alive. I just found out last week that they adopted some klepto, but I thought they were dead." She cried into her brother's hair, unable to help herself.

"I know." Hawk clung to her as well, soaking her shoulder with tears of his own. From the sound of him sniffing, there was probably a fair amount of snot in the mix. She didn't let go.

The sad piano continued on as they both shared in the trauma of losing everything and the shock of finding a scrap of something remaining. Technically they were strangers, but it didn't matter. Even if only connected by paperwork.

That was enough.

That was plenty.

Finally, after a solid minute of sobbing, Becca got herself under control. "Sorry, I'm... I don't really cry much, so I sort of lost it there. I'm not really the emotional type. It was just that..."

"I get it." He wiped his face with a sleeve. "I'm not either. But I have a sister, kind of."

"No kind of about it." She punched him in the shoulder. "I have been alone for so long, I'm not going to push you away. Even if I am an emotionally closed-off jerk. The world has changed too much for me to let my bullshit get in the way. I've learned that much."

"I know." He looked down. "If I had said something about myself earlier, instead of staying quiet, I might have figured it out weeks ago."

"Holy shit." She slapped a hand on the floor. "If I hadn't gone off on Bancroft and embarrassed myself, we still wouldn't have known." She reached for the photograph he'd handed her and unfolded it. A new stream of tears started the instant she did.

"That was the day they signed the papers to officially adopt me." Hawk leaned closer to look at the picture alongside her.

"I barely remember them." Becca studied every inch of the photo.

Hawk stood in the middle of the picture while her mother and father leaned down to hug him. They looked so much older than she remembered, like they had been through hell and back in the time since she'd left. Despite that, everyone looked happy.

A pang of jealousy stabbed at her heart at the fact that she had been robbed of the same comfort. She ignored it as the truth of the photo settled in.

Her parents really were dead.

Sure, she had already assumed that, but it was something else to know it for certain. Becca threw one arm around her brother.

"They didn't talk about you much." He wiped at his eyes as the tears started up again. "I think it was because they didn't want to freak me out or something. But I could tell they missed you. It was in their voice whenever you were mentioned."

"I hated them for so long." Becca handed the photo back. "I thought they had forgotten about me."

"No way. I saw some pictures of you. They were old photos and you looked like a kid, but they looked at those pictures every day."

"Thank you." She dried her eyes. "I still don't know how I'm going to deal with everything here, but thank you for being here with me."

"Like I have a choice." He shrugged. "'Cause the apocalypse and stuff didn't leave much of an option. But yeah, I'm glad you're here too. I don't feel so alone." He hesitated. "What's with the sad piano music by the way?"

"Shut up. I was feeling down and cast Ventriloquism." She gestured to the air around her. "I don't even know where I heard this song."

"You might want to switch to something more upbeat." He wrinkled his nose at her. "You can't just hang around on the floor being emo all night."

"That's true." She canceled the spell and waved her hand to recast.

"What you changing it to?" Hawk eyed her.

"Some songs you can't go wrong with." She shrugged.

"Like what?"

"Oh, little brother." She smirked. "I have so much to teach you."

Alex entered the room just as the opening to *Don't Stop Believin'* filled the air.

"I take it from the Journey you're playing that you're feeling better?"

Becca wiped at her face with her shirt. "How long have you been waiting down the hall?"

"A while. I figured you could use some cheering up once you cooled off." He gestured to a box under his arm. "Board game?"

"Why not?" She pushed herself off the floor.

Alex tossed the game box onto the poker table. "I asked Campbell to run up some popcorn from downstairs."

"I'll go get Alvin." Hawk stood up and headed for the door. "He needs people around him right now."

"I'll come with you." Becca followed. She had lost too much time with her brother already.

Hawk nodded and fell in step beside her.

It was hard to believe he was the same bratty kid that was such a pain a few weeks ago.

Warmth filled her chest.

He was a good kid.

No, he was more.

Hawk was a good brother.

CHAPTER THIRTY-FOUR

"What?" Confusion chased every thought out of Digby's head as Parker pulled him over the railing of the stairway at the highest point of the Seed's realm.

"Digby!" The caretaker screamed his name as its claw came just sort of reaching them before they fell.

The sound of a piano drowned it out.

"Is that Journey?" Parker held tight to his chest as they plummeted, head first, past a twisting stairway on their way down to the sea below. "Everything still feels thin. The music must be bleeding through. I think someone is playing it back in the real world."

"What in the bloody hell is Journey?" Digby shook his head, remembering that there were bigger questions. "Never mind that. Why are we falling?"

"I told you to trust me." Parker angled her head so she could look down.

"Fine, I trust you, but whatever you do, do it fast." Digby's eyes widened as they passed the landmass that held the ghost town where they had fought that gunslinging artificer earlier.

"Don't worry, I have a plan." Parker let out a laugh. "Just don't stop believing."

Digby rolled his eyes as the song bleeding through from the

outside repeated her words. His mind scrambled to understand what Parker could possibly be thinking. Even with her messenger class, she didn't have any spells that could save them.

That was when he caught a glimpse of her eyes.

The pink-haired soldier was serious. More serious than he'd ever seen her. He followed her gaze to the point below that she focused on.

There was nothing there.

Nothing, but the sea.

Digby's thoughts screeched to a halt as he realized what she was thinking. The water was reflective.

"Are you insane?" Digby squeezed her tighter as they plummeted past the twisted stairway they had fought the caretaker on.

"Maybe." She stretched her fingertips out toward the sea. "I just have to concentrate."

Digby's first instinct was to jab her about concentration not being her strength, but he kept his mouth shut and locked his eyes on the water. There was no way to know that its surface would work for a Mirror Passage, but it was too late to do anything else.

No, all that was left was to believe.

Together, they plunged into the sea, the music swelling as reality bent around them into a moment of infinite possibility. The Mirror Passage formed around them, giving him a look behind the curtain of how the spell worked. It wasn't just a portal. No, it was so much more. It was as if everything everywhere had suddenly come into existence all at once. A flood of worlds and realms both real and unreal. Light shined from every angle, reflected off a million glittering fragments of glass.

Then, it all snapped into a single point.

The lyrics of the song behind them faded to a faint echo as they tumbled from a window pane.

"Ow, shit!" Parker let go of him as they hit the ground.

"Wait no!" Digby slammed into a wooden walkway before tumbling into a dusty street. He spit out a mouthful of dirt as his body skidded to a stop.

"You okay?" Parker called out from nearby just as Digby turned over to find the barrel of a rifle pointing in his face.

"Oh no." He followed the weapon to find a woman that he recognized. Digby flicked his eyes to the side, catching a reflection of a familiar ghost town in the window of a building. He repeated his previous, "Oh no."

Of the reflective surfaces that Parker could have connected her passage to, she had thought of the worst. She had gotten them out of the frying pan and dropped them straight back into the fire.

"I don't suppose you would just let me saunter my way out of here?" Digby stared up at the gunslinger that had recently fired a mage killer bullet into his heart as she placed her rifle against his forehead.

He debated summoning his wraith.

Sure, she was sure to detonate his skull all over the dusty ground before the echo of Jack the Ripper could tear into her, but at this point what could it hurt?

That was when a raspy voice came from behind the heavily armed woman. "Looks like you've had a rough time of things."

"What?" Digby leaned to the side as the gunslinger readjusted her aim to keep her weapon against his head. "Who's there?"

A familiar old crone sat in a chair on the other side of the street. "Surprised to see me again, are ye?"

"Sybil?" Digby's eyebrows climbed up his forehead as the witch from the castle below gave him a casual wave.

"How are you here?" Parker sat up a few feet away.

"I should ask you the same thing." The old woman gestured to the window they had just tumbled out of. "That was an interesting trick with the glass there. Haven't seen that spell before."

"It's called—" Parker started to say before Digby cut her off to keep her from spilling any of their capabilities.

"Indeed." Digby glanced back to the gunslinger standing over him. "But as you can guess, we are less inclined to answer questions with a rifle pointed at my skull."

"Oh, yes, of course." Sybil waved a hand.

The gunslinger pulled her rifle away from his head in response before stepping back. Digby eyed her, noticing a slowness to her movement.

Zombie, common, neutral.

She was dead?

He snapped his vision back to Sybil. The old witch must have made her way up from the castle below and killed the gunslinger on her own. Now the menace was just a minion. Digby shuddered, realizing that Sybil might have been more powerful than he realized. After all, she had beaten a foe that not even he and Henwick could defeat working together. He might actually do well to try to learn something.

Then again, she could have just gotten lucky.

"I see you had a run in with this gunslinger as well." He pushed himself up.

"I did." Sybil let out a mirthless laugh. "I hazard a guess that my encounter went measurably better than yours."

"Yes, but I see you found yourself a minion." Digby stood up.

"Yes. She thought me easy prey on account of my elderly appearance." Sybil pushed herself out of the chair she sat in. "In the end, I was forced to kill her and take her corpse into my service."

"And what persuaded you to leave your workshop down there in the castle?" Digby arched an eyebrow. "I thought you were satisfied where you were."

"As much as I regret to admit it," the old witch grumbled to herself for a moment, "I came in search of both of you."

"Us?" Parker pointed to herself.

"Yes." Sybil marched toward them. "I have not changed my mind. My work is still my priority. However, I realized that finishing my work might not be a job that I can do. After taking some time to understand our situation more, I have concluded that I must leave the task to you. After all, that is the way the world works. Where one story ends, another will always take its place. Thus is the life of a Fool."

"Yes, we know all about you Fools." Digby eyed her. "We've met one or two on our travels through this realm."

She took a step back with an arched eyebrow.

"Oh, don't look at me like that." Digby rolled his eyes. "I did not harm your conspirators. They fell to the caretaker. But they did open our eyes a bit to what your goals were back in our time and why you were meddling with the Seed's power. Unfortunately, it has left me no more capable of escaping this place, thanks to that traitor Henwick."

"Ah, yes. Henwick would be here, wouldn't he?" Sybil scratched her chin.

"Indeed." Digby gave her a brief summary of the man's treachery. "I had thought for a time that he might be capable of reason and working toward a common goal, but it seems he is just as blind as ever. It's no wonder an organization such as Autem was able to twist him into something destructive."

"I see." Sybil paced for a few steps. "Then I'd say what ye must do is bend him back to your side."

"What?" Digby scoffed.

"If he be blind, then you need to open his eyes." She gave him a smile full of blackened teeth.

"That didn't work so well for you back in your time." He stared at her.

"He does have a point." Parker patted dust from her pants with her hat.

"True." Sybil deflated a little. "But back in my day, Autem had its hooks deep in him and that is no longer the case. He has at least seen that trusting them was a mistake."

Digby threw up his arms. "That may be, but I have tried—"

"Did ye?" The old crone stomped toward him with a sharp look in her eyes. "I dare say, I find it hard to believe that you have given him much reason to trust you. Nay, I assume you have lied and insulted your way through any disagreement that you have had."

"Hey, now, that's—" Digby started to argue before deflating. "Alright, that's a fair judgment."

"Yes, I think so." She jabbed a finger at him. "I'd say that it's time for another approach."

"Why don't you try?" Digby narrowed his eyes. "You could march your way up the nearest set of steps and try your hand at convincing him."

"Have you not listened to a word I have said?" She threw up her arms. "Of course, I could take on the task myself, but then how would you learn anything?"

"Bah." Digby shook his head. "Why must I learn anything?"

"You must learn so that you might become someone worthy," she snapped back. "You must understand why Fools like us do what they do, so that you can carry on in my place."

"In your place?" He avoided eye contact.

"As much as I may not care for your attitude," Sybil blew out a sigh, "you do stand the best chance of stopping Autem out there in the world."

Digby folded his arms, not liking the pressure that she was placing on his shoulders. Sure, he was already committed to fighting Autem, but that was more out of survival. Besides, there was nothing stopping the witch from taking on the task herself. As to why she thought he should do it, he was at a loss. Then again, he probably shouldn't go question people that could just as easily decide to kill him.

Despite that, he argued anyway.

"What makes you so sure I am the right person to do this?"

The old witch threw a hand out toward Parker. "Because of her."

"Me?" The pink-haired woman flinched.

"Yes." Sybil locked eyes with Digby. "Lord knows why, but you have found people like her that believe in you. And if I were to kill you now and take your place out in the world beyond, I would have a difficult time winning the hearts and minds that have gathered around you. I may not see a good man in you, but they do. And I am willing to give them the benefit of the doubt. Not to mention, you have the raw magical potential to become more powerful than I. I dare say the only thing you need is a true direction and proper resolve. With that, I believe you will do more good than a dozen Fools."

"But what about you?" Parker asked before Digby had the chance to say anything else. "Doesn't that mean you have to die here?"

Sybil merely blew out a sigh. "I'm afraid the sun set on my

time long ago. Even now, I am nothing more than a remnant spark. It would be arrogant to think myself more. Like Henwick, I am currently standing in the way of the Seed's restoration. To that end, I cannot justify my existence."

Digby stumbled backward at the woman's willingness to sacrifice herself. If it had been him in the same position, he would have dug his claws in and clung to survival. Hell, if it was him, he would have made a deal with the devil himself if he thought it would buy him some time. An ache rose in his throat, but he swallowed it back down.

It was the same with that illusionist, Gary. Digby struggled not to think about the man's gruesome death. They had only just met, yet still, the fact that he'd died while placing his faith in him was too much. He knew that the other souls within the Seed's realm had to be snuffed out for him to return home, but the idea that they would willingly step aside for him sent waves of revulsion through Digby's core. It didn't make sense to stop Sybil from following her fellow Fool's example, yet everything inside him demanded he argue.

"Listen here, you old crone——"

"And there it is." Sybil cut him off. "Have you ever considered that this need you seem to have to be an absolute ass every minute of every day might just be because you're afraid that if you were decent for one second, people might begin to trust you?"

"What?" Digby fidgeted with his coat.

"That sounds about right." Parker nodded from the side of the conversation.

"I shan't be giving you a choice." Sybil put her foot down. "Clearly you are uncomfortable with the idea of anyone believing in you. That way if you fail, you can simply point the finger and say, see, you never should have trusted me."

"Of course you shouldn't trust me!" he shouted back.

"Too bad. If anything, I can die happy knowing that my trust is kicking you in the ass to do what needs to be done." Sybil stomped toward him and slapped a hand to his chest. "I may not be able to do more, but I can leave a piece of my spark right here in your mana system."

"What?" Digby recoiled.

"You know what I mean." She laughed.

"You wish me to eat you?" His mouth fell open.

"I can't say it would be my first choice, but I understand necromancy." She gripped his lapel and yanked him down to her level. "If I am consumed by your maw, I can place my trust in you. Literally. I will be that nagging feeling inside your heart telling you that running away solves nothing. For that, I will gladly drown in the darkness of your maw."

"That's awful." Parker shuddered.

"Is it?" Sybil let out an elderly cackle. "Death has always been my fate. This way, my echo will continue to fight on long after my demise. In terms of a dying wish, I feel that is adequate."

"Now you wait just a bloody minute. I don't suppose I should be given a say in this." Digby struggled to come up with a valid argument.

"No, you shan't." She jabbed him in the chest with a boney finger.

"Too bad." He slapped her hand away. "I won't do it."

"Yes, you will," she snarled back.

"Will not." He folded his arms.

She swiped a hand through the air. "I shall not have my sacrifice thrown back in my face by a common hoodlum such as yourself."

"And I shall not be tainting my mana system with the spark of a rotten old crone," he snapped back.

"This is a very weird argument." Parker stared at the pair as Sybil pushed him.

"Eat me, you coward!"

"Yep, definitely the weirdest argument." Parker nodded to herself.

Digby ignored her and tried to walk away. "I will not stand here and let you call me a coward."

"Why not?" Sybil scoffed. "It be true."

He spun back around. "Can you fathom the pressure that is placed on me? Hell, the only reason that I am here is because I was in the wrong place at the wrong time."

"That changes nothing. You—" She stopped short and took a few breaths, as if trying to calm down. "This is getting us nowhere and only serving to frustrate me further. You are a maddening creature, do you know that?"

"I do." Digby placed a hand to his chest. "I dare say my ability to irritate is one of my strengths."

She grimaced. "That isn't something to be proud of."

"Yeah, but he's not going to change." Parker shrugged.

"Indeed." Digby puffed out his chest.

Sybil deflated. "I suppose that can't be helped. But that doesn't mean you can simply remain a victim of your own cowardice. Heavy may the weight on your shoulders be, but that is no excuse to set yourself up for failure. You only be lying to yourself."

"Sometimes lying to yourself is the only way to keep moving forward." He eyed her. "I never claimed to be strong enough to carry your burden."

"Aye, that's true." She nodded. "How about we make a deal then?"

"Maybe?" He tapped a finger on his forearm.

"Allow my spark to become part of your strength, and you can forget about everything the other Fools told you. You do not have to bear the weight of their legacy. Nor do you need to carry mine." A sympathetic tone entered her voice.

"And?" He waited for the other shoe to drop.

"And that's it." She grinned. "Just do as you see fit. No obligations attached."

"But then you get nothing." Digby turned away from her. "Why would you agree to that?"

"Because I have faith." She placed a hand on his shoulder.

"In the Seed's will?" His body tensed.

"Yes, but also in you." She squeezed.

"Why? You don't even like me." Digby clenched his jaw.

"True, but I'm beginning to understand why it must be you." She let her hand slip from his shoulder. "You may be weak and cowardly, but that is precisely your strength. Besides, you are a bringer of chaos, and against something as rigid as Henwick and Autem, I don't think you can stop yourself from butting heads. You are oil and water. You simply cannot coexist. Eventually, you will live up to everyone's expectations, one way or another."

His throat tightened. "And what if you place all your hope upon me, and I fail?"

"Then you fail." She slapped him on the back. "I don't expect you to be infallible. No one is. Believing otherwise is how people like Henwick lose their way. If anything, the fact that you are afraid ensures me that I can trust you."

"Why would something like fear give you faith in me?" He rolled his eyes.

"You truly are a fool in every sense of the word." She let out a cackle. "Sure, a man of pride and courage might feel they are up to the task of deciding the fate of the world. Yet that is precisely why so many go wrong. After all, a leader is supposed to have doubts. Oftentimes, that is all that prevents one from becoming a tyrant."

Digby remained quiet for a long moment, trying to forget her words so that he could laugh them off or tell himself she was wrong.

How can she be so sure?

He forced a grin on his face.

So be it. If she wants to throw her existence away, who am I to turn down an increase in power? Hell, I should take her for all she's worth.

His mouth sunk into a frown, unable to lie to himself so easily. He couldn't simply write her off like so many he'd taken for granted before. What she offered was too precious. Yet, he couldn't find the flaw in her words. In the end, she was right.

Digby gestured to Parker with one hand. "Could you come and stand by me?"

"Okay." For once, the soldier refrained from making a comment or joke and stood next to him. Digby held still and stared out at a stairway in the distance that headed up. Parker did the same, leaving the old witch standing behind them.

Digby spoke without looking back and opened his maw on the ground. "I can't make you any promises."

"And I shan't ask you to." Her voice fell to a kind whisper that was entirely out of character.

He left his void open on the ground behind him for a long moment, too afraid to turn around. Parker remained facing forward as well, her eyes welling up for the old witch.

No, not witch.

She had a name.

Sybil.

Digby held her name in his thoughts as he closed his maw.

I'm sorry.

Remnant Spark defeated. 3,430 experience awarded.

CHAPTER THIRTY-FIVE

Becca immediately froze at the sound of footsteps coming down the hallway outside her hotel room. They were unnecessarily heavy. She knew who it was immediately.

Malcolm.

Bancroft must have sent him.

"Damn." She blew out a sigh as the sun rose over her window's view of the city.

It had been a day since she'd embarrassed herself and she hadn't seen Bancroft, except in passing. As for everything they had talked about, he had been living up to his side of the bargain. Sure, he was still working the kinks out of his currency system but overall he did seem to be trying.

He'd even submitted a report on the actions of his men and their secret mission to the coast. Apparently, they were looking for one of Autem's properties in hope of raiding the place. They hadn't found it yet, but he wanted to keep looking. Beyond that, he was holding back the details until he was ready to organize a formal mission.

The footsteps in the hall grew closer.

"I guess Bancroft found what he was looking for." Becca glanced at Hawk.

The kid, no, her brother was still fast asleep in his bed. She pulled the hotel's stationary out from a drawer and jotted down a note to tell him where she went. Tossing it on the nightstand, she went to the door and pulled it open to find Malcolm there in mid-knock.

"Hey." Initially he looked surprised that the door was open, but he quickly reverted to his normal overconfident self. "The big guy has a mission for everyone."

"Oh good." Becca remained standing in the doorway.

He stared at her expectantly without saying more.

"I'll head down in five," she added when it became clear he was going to wait for her.

"Say no more." He held up a hand and did an about face. "See you in five."

Becca watched him go, then closed her door. They had been getting along better after working together at the dam, but still, she didn't really want to walk down to the high-roller suite with him. At least not first thing in the morning. She needed coffee first.

Before heading down, she dropped into a chair and cast Spirit Projection. She wasn't sure if Bancroft would send one of his guys to get Alex, but she wanted him present if they were to be discussing anything of importance. The way her judgment had been lately, she wanted a second opinion that she could trust.

The world blurred as mana moved through her body, then she was standing in a bathroom the same as the one in her room.

"That's weird." Becca turned around to find Alex sitting on a toilet with his mouth hanging open.

A moment of devastating silence passed before they both screamed.

"What the hell, Becca?" He scrambled to cover himself as she spun around again. "Can't a guy poop in peace?"

"Shit, shit, sorry." Becca slapped a hand over her eyes to avoid looking in the mirror.

The sound of Kristen, the deceased seer, laughing could be heard from the other room. "I have been waiting for that to happen."

Becca blew out an awkward laugh. "Bancroft wants to talk about a mission in five minutes down in the high-roller suite."

"Fine, sure, I'll be there, just get out," Alex shrieked, clearly not finished with his current business.

"Yep, fine, I'm out." She released her spell, finding herself back in her hotel room with Hawk snoozing a few feet away. She cringed at what had just happened. "Well, that was awkward."

After sitting for about a minute to process things, she hopped up and headed downstairs.

Bancroft was waiting for her with Malcolm standing at his back.

"Charles." She gave him a nod in greeting.

"Rebecca." He returned it as she avoided eye contact.

She cringed for the second time in a few minutes at the tension that still hung between them. Of course, that was when Alex walked in to make everything worse. A memory of him shrieking while sitting on the toilet flashed through her mind the moment their eyes met.

"Good lord, what is wrong with me?" she muttered to herself.

"What was that?" Malcolm asked.

"Nothing." She rubbed at her temples as Alex stood awkwardly with his hands in his pockets as if he was trying to act natural. Kristen's skull was tucked under one arm. A ghostly chuckle came from her direction.

Bancroft looked down at the skull, then back up to Becca. "Thank you for coming. I think you'll be happy with what we've found."

Becca cast Veritas on instinct, immediately feeling guilty about it. After creating so many problems by not trusting anyone, it wasn't a good way to start out. She shook off the thought and tried to move past it all. "Tell me what you have."

"Yes, thank you." Bancroft stepped forward as a prideful smile took over his face. "I have a way to win this war with Autem before it gets any further."

"Really?" Becca raised a skeptical eyebrow.

"Really?" Alex asked, a second time. Though his tone sounded more hopeful than hers had.

"As a certain deceased zombie would say, indeed." He gestured to Malcolm. "Show them."

"You got it." He cleared away a board game that had been left on the poker table so that he could unroll a large map.

Alex winced. "Careful with the game pieces."

Malcolm shot him a judgmental look.

"What? There is no way to replace some of those miniatures."

Becca shook her head and leaned on the edge of the table to stare down at a map of Southern California. "Okay, what are we looking at?"

"As you know," Bancroft smoothed out the paper, "I have been searching for resources that we could potentially confiscate from Autem while they are still in disarray."

"You want to pull another heist?" Alex leaned on the table as well, placing Kirsten's skull down at the corner of the map.

Bancroft shook his head. "Nothing that flashy, but possibly far more advantageous."

"You found the ghost ship, didn't you?" Kristen asked.

"I think so." Bancroft looked a little smug.

"I'm sorry, what?" Becca furrowed her brow. "What's this about a ghost ship?"

Bancroft chuckled. "Autem has been working on many things behind the scenes of the world for quite some time, and they used Skyline to handle a lot of the dirty work prior to the apocalypse. Obviously, my position kept me better informed than most. One such thing I became aware of was a cargo ship."

"Okay, and what was on it?" Becca finally made eye contact with him.

"Some sort of weapon that Henwick was keeping for a rainy day." He folded his arms. "The man was never one to let himself get backed into a corner, but in the old world, it was harder to make the kind of big moves that he does now. That was why he set up a cargo ship to store things that he wanted to keep hidden."

"What kind of weapon are we talking about? Something like the runes?" Alex looked down at Kristen's skull, clearly hoping she might know more.

"Don't look at me, I have no idea." She paused. "I was not involved in any weapon that Henwick might have acquired."

"That's not surprising," Bancroft added. "He was secretive about it even with me. Technically, I don't know any of this for sure. I only put two and two together when I helped arrange for the vessel. Basing my theory off some documents I've glimpsed, the weapon is something powerful enough to turn the tide of this war." He nodded decisively.

"What would Henwick need another weapon for?" Becca eyed him, trying her hardest not to sound like she didn't trust him. "Can't he just blast us off the planet with that sky beam ability he has? Actually, he doesn't really have to, considering he did nuke Seattle. Can't he just do that if he finds out where we are?"

"Yes and no." Bancroft tilted a hand back and forth. "Henwick's sky beam is an advanced version of a spell called Smite. I know that much. But as far as I am aware, it can only take out a moderately sized building. As for his missile strike capability, he still has a limited arsenal back on the east coast, but he lost the ability to nuke us when he killed off the world's militaries. Even before that, he would need to leverage a lot to get it done. Honestly, the red tape was a nightmare. Now, he simply doesn't have access to that kind of firepower within Autem's current arsenal. Hence why he's squirreled away a weapon. He knew this day would come and wanted something strong enough to secure his reign."

"I don't like the sound of that." Alex tensed up.

"Neither do I." Becca couldn't help but agree. "But none of that tells me why we are looking at a map of California's coast."

"Simple. Because that is where this cargo ship is." Bancroft tapped the map a few dozen miles offshore. "This is where things start going in our favor. The ship went missing a week or so after the world ended. Lost contact entirely. Initially, Henwick was concerned that the ship had fallen into the wrong hands, since we couldn't find it, but just before you all attacked the base, the satellites located it. The footage confirmed it was revenants that took the vessel. They got on board somehow and killed everyone."

Becca chewed on her lip. "How do you know Henwick hasn't already sent a team to retrieve this weapon of his?"

"An operation was on the books to do so, but with what you did to his base, the schedule has certainly slowed down. Not only that, but he is not aware that I know what I know. Ultimately, he has no reason to think his weapon is in any danger." Bancroft grabbed one of the game pieces from the edge of the poker table and placed it on the map to indicate the ship's location. "That being said, it won't be long before he does. Technically, he could send a team out anytime."

"So time is a factor." Becca nodded.

"Exactly." Bancroft tapped his nose. "Now that we have found it, we have to move. The ship has drifted away from the area it was in when Skyline's satellites found it last, so we have an advantage but not much of one. I think you can agree this is an important opportunity. Not to mention, if Digby is going to save the world by stealing things, then why stop now? We might as well take this weapon out from under Henwick too."

"That's true." Alex laughed.

"I'm surprised you didn't have your men head in and take this weapon the moment they found the ship," Becca added, trying not to make her comment sound like an accusation.

"We would have." Malcolm chimed in. "But when we approached, a number of large revenants, bloodstalker types, all came out to attack. With a kestrel, we can take a few out but there are bound to be more of them, as well as the little ones further into the ship. Going in with a small team would be suicide."

"So a group effort then." Becca sighed at the realization that they were going to have to work together again so soon.

"With what we know," Malcolm grabbed a few more game pieces and placed three around the ship, "there's three winged bloodstalkers that will attack anyone that gets close. And we spotted another two on the deck that didn't take off. We will need to take them out first, then head in."

"That's right." Bancroft nodded. "And we will do this together. Meaning all of us, including all of your Heretics that are capable of fighting."

Becca nodded, unable to deny that it was the right choice. After all, Digby was still out of commission, and they couldn't wait for him to wake up. She wasn't sure if they were strong enough to take out multiple bloodstalkers, considering how much trouble one had been the last time she had faced one, but considering how far they had come, there was a chance. Not to mention they had the advantage of attacking during the day.

Becca raised her eyes back up to Bancroft. Every fiber of her being told her not to trust him.

She had been wrong before.

Hell, she hadn't trusted Digby back when they first met, and he had turned out to be her strongest ally. It was true that there was a past between them that made it hard to see him as anything but an enemy, but maybe it was time to let things lie and move forward.

She glanced at her HUD to again find that he hadn't lied once in their entire conversation. Was it actually possible? Could he be trusted? Were her instincts wrong?

"I know how you feel." Bancroft's face softened. "But we can do this if we can learn to work together."

True

Breathing out the heaviest sigh of her life, she gave in.
"When do we leave?"

CHAPTER THIRTY-SIX

Digby glanced at the line of text on his HUD that he had been avoiding looking at as they ascended the twisting steps that led to the top of the Seed's realm.

ECHO OF THE CRONE
When summoned, this spark will call upon the remnants of the lingering dead to grab hold of a target and prevent movement. This spell will last until the target is either able to break free, or until canceled.

The addition of the summon was a significant boon, yet he still felt the weight of how he'd gained it. He tried not to think about it as he dragged his feet up the steps toward the coliseum. The climb had taken hours without the use of the elevator that they had ridden before. They made a point to stay away from the larger land masses, hoping to avoid the clash of other Heretics as the population counter continued to fall. They passed through one area that Parker had said reminded her of a mafia movie, but the only thing they found there was a charred corpse laying at the foot of one of the stairways. Other than that, they had found no one in their path.

There had been no sign of the caretaker so far, either. It must have traveled down one of the other pathways or it was waiting up there for them. There was no telling if Henwick was there as well. It was always possible that Henwick had already been killed, but somehow, he didn't think he was that lucky. Besides, that platform at the center of the coliseum seemed to be some kind of finish line with room for two. Henwick had probably waited there. If so, the caretaker would have no reason to kill him since he was in the safe zone. The creature would just head off in search of someone else to kill in one of the other areas.

Digby glanced to the population number at the corner of his vision.

5/2

It was down to the last few Heretics.
The number ticked down a second later.

4/2

Then, it ticked down again.

3/2

Digby stopped short. One more opponent left. Whoever remained standing would be released along with the power to create more Heretics as they saw fit. Even if it wasn't Henwick waiting for them up there, they were going to have to fight some-one. The pressure in the air was palpable.

At least the fact that two Heretics had just perished implied that the caretaker had left the coliseum, otherwise there would have been a survivor.

Good thing it didn't stumble across us. Digby started walking again, realizing how lucky they had gotten. He was just glad they were almost back to where they had fallen from. Looking up, numerous stairways coiled upward to meet the archways that covered the outer wall of the coliseum.

Digby glanced back at his HUD.

MP: 298/298

He'd only gained one level since entering the Seed's realm. If it hadn't been for Sybil and Jack, he would have had nothing to show for his climb up from the sea. The thought dredged up the memory of that witch's final moments. His shoulders sunk under the weight of it all.

"Stop that," Parker snapped at him abruptly from her place climbing the steps beside him.

"Stop what?" Digby recoiled at the sudden attack.

"Stop sulking or brooding or whatever it is you're doing." She groaned. "I swear, you're gonna get me all depressed just by proximity. And considering we probably have to fight Henwick when we reach the top of these stairs, I don't want you sulking when you should be kickin' ass."

Digby stared at her, unsure what to say.

"I get it, you're all freaked out that you won't live up to everyone's expectations, but let me tell you, I get you way better than you think."

"What do you mean, you get me?" He hesitated before taking another step.

"I mean, look at me." She threw her hands out at her sides. "I'm well aware I'm the last person you wanted to be stuck in here with. And yeah, I'm not that responsible. In short, I am aware that I'm a fuck up."

"I never said that." Digby tried to deny the comment.

"Yes you did. Like, a bunch of times," she growled. "Maybe not in those exact words, but you haven't kept your feelings hidden."

"Alright then, I apologize," he spat back with more hostility than he meant to.

Her face dropped in response. "Holy shit."

"What?" Digby winced.

"You just apologized." She pointed an accusatory finger at him.

"And?" He frowned.

"And I have never heard you do that before." She dropped her finger to her side where she let it hang limp.

"Don't be ridiculous, I…" He trailed off, having trouble remembering the last time he'd apologized. "Alright, you may be right. I might not have considered you to be capable when we first set out to explore this realm. Not that you can blame me, considering your past behavior. Yet, I am not so small-minded to fail to see that I was wrong. You may have a unique way of doing things, but you have saved me on a few occasions and figured things out when others have struggled." He sighed and softened his voice. "You are not a… What was it you said?"

"A fuck up?" she offered.

"Yes." He nodded. "If anyone has been messing things up, then it was most likely me."

"And that's my point." She jabbed him in the chest with a finger.

He narrowed his eyes. "That I'm a fuck up?"

"No." She shook her head. "What you said before, about me being a genius, reliable, and saving your ass so many times."

"I don't think I said that you were a genius." He furrowed his brow. "I said that you were not a fuck up."

"Same thing." She hopped up a couple stairs and turned back to look down at him.

"Is it though?" He stared up at her.

"My point is that you had low expectations for me, and I proved you wrong. I might have been kind of a screw up in the past, but I got my shit together to a point where I am at least somewhat reliable. And you are pretty much the same. Except that you don't even believe in yourself. So stop being all mopey about the pressure that everyone has put on you. You'll get your shit together and get through things just like I always have." She folded her arms and nodded as if she had just bestowed some sort of important wisdom.

"Alright, fine. I suppose I can try and look at things that way." He blew out a musty sigh.

"Damn straight." She placed a hand on his shoulder. "You're

still kind of a dick, but you get shit done when you need to. So stop looking at the future as an impossible mountain to climb. Just have faith in yourself."

"Is that how you get through the day, just telling yourself that things will work out?" Digby grumbled.

"Pretty much. So let's go mess up Henwick for not having the faith in us that we deserve." She hooked a thumb over her shoulder at the archway that awaited them.

Digby shrugged off a little of the weight he'd been carrying. "It's not much of a battle cry, but fine, let's go mess him up."

That was when the familiar sensation of mana moving through blood met his senses.

"Get down." Digby grabbed Parker by the jacket and yanked her toward him. Throwing one arm over her head, he thrust out his other and cast Absorb just as a Smite poured into it. He wasted no time, immediately tossing the magic right back attached to a Flare spell.

Henwick stood in the archway with his ax in hand as emerald energy streaked through the air toward him. Digby ducked as ribbons of white light coiled around the epicenter of the spell. The stored power of Henwick's Smite blast twisted and merged into the flare before detonating in an explosion of power. Chips of stone flew from the archway in all directions like shrapnel, showering the steps. The sound shattered the air like a crack of thunder.

"Did you get him?" Parker shoved out from under Digby's arm as the blast echoed through the sky.

Flicking his eyes to the top of the stairs, Digby found the spot where Henwick had been empty. Only the damaged archway remained. "I assume not."

He glanced at his HUD.

MP: 238/298

"Come on, we have to move." Digby kept his head low and skulked up the steps.

"I'm right behind you." Parker crouched at his back.

Together, they made for the coliseum. Digby opened his maw

and cast Blood Forge on his way to form a pair of short swords. It wasn't much, but he didn't want to take on Henwick barehanded. After passing one of the weapons to Parker, he dove through the open archway. Another blast of cleansing power came from further down the hall.

Digby caught it with another Absorb and ducked back into the shelter of the archway. He peeked around the side to catch the cleric standing in the middle of the hall. "Hey, Henwick, how about you just throw yourself off the side and let Parker and I go about our business?"

"It is comical that you should suggest that, because I extend the same offer to you."

Henwick held his ground. "The young lady has done nothing wrong and still has a chance at life."

"He could at least call me by my name. I know damn well he knows it." Parker crouched beside Digby.

"Send her to me and I will ensure that she is taken care of once we return to the outside world." Henwick sounded sincere.

"Okay, I'm gonna go stab him." Parker started to make her way into the hall to do the aforementioned stabbing, but Digby grabbed her jacket.

"Get back here. You want to get Smited?"

"Oh, like he'll attack me." She shrugged. "I'm just a poor, defenseless woman."

Digby hesitated.

She might be right. Henwick probably wouldn't attack her if he didn't have to.

"What do you say, Graves?" Henwick called back.

Digby tried to keep him talking while he thought of a plan, gaining a few points of mana in the process. "If I let you and Parker go, that would mean you would take possession of my corpse. Your existence would become that of an undead monster. Are you really prepared for that?"

"It would allow for me to set things right with Autem." Henwick's tone grew serious. "That is all that matters. I shall not need to continue on after that."

"So you intend to destroy yourself when you're finished?" Digby peeked around the archway. "That it?"

"I see no problem with sacrifice." Henwick stepped closer.

"Well I do!" Digby cackled back. "If you are so comfortable with sacrificing yourself, then why not just throw yourself to the caretaker and let me handle things from here?" He hesitated before looking down to Parker and adding, in a whisper, "Think you can run in as a distraction? I'll rush in behind you."

"Got it." She nodded. "You want to use a woman as a human shield. Say no more."

"Don't say it like that." Digby rolled his eyes as Henwick continued to drone on.

"I honestly wish I could leave things to you, Graves. Yet I cannot trust you to do what must be done. If you will not destroy the Seed when you are finished with Autem, how will you resist the temptation to use its power for your own gain? I know you, Graves. With that power, instead of the Autem empire grinding the world beneath its heel, you would merely be a dark lord doing the same. Power corrupts. That's why God did not grant us magic in the first place."

"Now you sound like Autem. Like one of their zealots regurgitating scripture from their imaginary angels." Digby glanced at Parker to make sure she was ready. Then, he shouted one last jab at Henwick. "You have backed the wrong side before. Yet you are still so sure of yourself. If you can't see your own flaws, then you have already lost your way. And I can't afford to give you a second chance."

With that, he gave Parker a nod.

The pink-haired soldier's boots squeaked against the stone floor as she leapt forward into danger, ready to do some stabbing. "Surprise, motherfucker!"

Digby darted out to stay behind her, so he didn't get Smited.

"What the—" Henwick stepped back as Digby closed the gap and summoned his wraith.

The crimson echo of Jack the Ripper materialized, already streaking toward the man, a narrow blade of spectral energy at the ready. Henwick reacted fast. Flipping his ax to the side, he blocked the blow as blood red streaks of power erupted from the head of the weapon at the center of the impact.

"Good effort!" Digby summoned his wraith a second time, dropping his mana down to half remaining.

It was worth it.

The spell hit like a truck, the first strike throwing Henwick off balance. The second sent a glinting silhouette of the murderous wraith slicing across the cleric's back. Blood splashed against the stone as Parker skidded to a stop behind him.

Digby sprinted toward Henwick as he fell forward and struggled to keep his insides from spilling out. The mana of a spell began to flow through his blood. Digby braced. The cleric would either try to heal or counterattack.

Henwick gave away his intent by baring his teeth and shifting his weight.

A counterattack!

Digby responded in kind, casting Absorb. A blast of life essence poured into the vortex that formed in his hand. His fingers went numb, but that was all the spell could do. He immediately summoned the crone and dumped every bit of power he'd taken into the spell.

Power lit up the hallway as the figure of an elderly woman cackled into existence with arms raised high. A chorus of wails erupted in all directions as a dozen spectral limbs stretched out of the floor and walls, each surging toward Henwick to hold him in place.

"How?" The man's eyes bulged as the ghostly appendages locked around his arms and legs.

"That old witch left me with a new spell." Digby's tone grew somber. "Unlike you, she was satisfied in leaving the fate of the world in the hands of another."

"Of course that witch trusted you. You are her ilk. A Fool." Henwick winced. Digby sensed mana moving as the cleric cast Regeneration to repair his damaged body enough so that he could focus on getting free of the crone's grip.

"I have had it with everyone trying to tell me what or who I am." Digby stomped toward him.

"You are no saint. You are not a hero capable of sacrificing or kneeling to the righteous when the world requires it." Henwick spoke as if pleading. "Why can't you see that? Why can't you accept your shortcomings? Please, give this up, Graves. Allow someone more suited to take the reins!"

"Oh, I have accepted my shortcomings just fine." Digby stopped in front of him. "I am a liar, a thief, and a scoundrel. Hell, most of what I do is motivated by spite. I know all that. But what you fail to understand is that there are people that have placed their faith in me despite all that. And I am not planning on letting them down."

"That's right." Parker stood behind the cleric. "And you're not turning out to be much of a hero either."

"Indeed." Digby leaned down. "At least I am aware of my flaws. You, on the other hand, seem to think you are above us."

"I have made mistakes." Henwick glared up at him. "Yet I have never done so for my own selfishness."

"The reason doesn't matter." Digby rolled his eyes. "We all mean well."

"But the road to hell is paved with good intentions," Parker chimed in.

"That's actually quite wise." Digby gave her an approving nod.

"It's a saying, I didn't come up with it." She shrugged.

He dropped his gaze back to Henwick and sighed. "I am sorry that things have to be this way. If there was a chance I could reconnect your spark with the soulless husk you left behind to destroy the world, then I would. But the Heretic Seed needs to be restored and that requires that the souls trapped inside be wiped clean."

"I understand." Henwick lowered his head, as if giving in. Then, he snapped his vision back up. "But I cannot allow the Seed to corrupt the world."

Motes of light exploded from both of his hands at once, blasting the spectral hands from his body. Digby leapt back but took a single glowing orb to the hand, leaving a gaping hole in his palm. Another mote of light struck Parker in the thigh. It didn't cause as much damage since she was not deceased, but from the pained expression on her face, it hadn't felt good either.

Henwick took the moment for what it was, grabbing his ax and rushing for the nearest entrance to the coliseum's interior. "I am sorry, but I must leave the caretaker to decide your fate."

That was when a loud screech came from behind them. Both Digby and Parker turned and raised their eyes up to the oversized skull of the caretaker standing in one of the openings in the outer wall. The monster had returned to do its work.

"Damn it!" Digby cast Necrotic Regeneration to close the hole in his hand and rushed after Henwick.

"Shit." Parker limped her way up the stairs behind him.

It was already too late as soon as they reached the inside of the coliseum. Henwick was halfway to the platform at the center of the space. There was no way to stop him from reaching the safe area. Fragments of obsidian littered the floor, with only three statues still standing.

Just Digby, Parker, and Henwick.

Still one too many.

They moved forward to get away from the entryway before the caretaker caught up.

"Digby!"

He winced at the sound of his father's voice coming from the hallway behind him.

"Crap." Parker thrust a finger out toward Henwick as he made it to the raised platform at the center of the space. "He's already safe."

"Indeed. That just leaves the caretaker and us. If you have any ideas, I'm open to suggestions." Digby glanced at Parker, open to whatever input she might provide.

"You go after Henwick." Parker gestured toward the center. "He might be safe over there, but that doesn't mean you can't kick his ass back out."

"But if I enter that circle, the caretaker will count me as safe too. It will only target you." He eyed her sideways as she limped on her injured leg. Neither of them had a healing spell to deal with it.

"I'm still fast enough to stay ahead of the caretaker. I'll be fine if I keep moving." She swung her arms back and forth to limber up. "I'll just lead it around in a circle."

Digby's first instinct was to argue and tell her the idea was stupid and risky, but he suppressed the urge. She had proven herself already, and he wouldn't gain anything by doubting her now.

"Alright. If it gets too close or you get in trouble, join me in the center. You won't be any safer, but at least it will start going after the rest of us." With that, he broke into a jog and checked his mana.

MP: 23/298

He cringed. It wasn't a lot, but it would have to do. At least, Henwick had to be running out as well.

The cleric's face fell as soon as Digby got close. "You have abandoned the woman. I was right not to trust you."

"Oh shut it, Henwick." Digby gripped the short sword he'd forged. "And her name is Parker. You best start using it. She is more capable than you realize."

Henwick leapt back and raised his ax to keep him away from the platform. Digby made a note of the fact that he hadn't used another Smite.

Probably saving the last of his mana for a Regeneration.

Still, ax versus short sword was not a good match up.

"You scoundrel." Henwick charged. "You have doomed that woman—" He shook his head before finally using her name. "You have condemned Parker to death!"

"She'll be fine." Digby slammed his sword into the man's ax in a clash of steel and blood. "I believe in her. Besides, you can save her anytime. Just step off the platform." He forced his way onto the safe area.

"The same can be said for you." The cleric bared his teeth and cast a heal spell in his direction, opting to use it as an attack.

The result sent Digby's body into spasms. "Damn it!"

"How can I trust you to protect the world when you can't even protect one woman?" Henwick raised his ax as Digby fought against the life essence surging through his body. The head of the weapon came down with a solid thunk, impacting with the bone plate that protected his chest. "You're going to have to chop harder than that." Digby threw a wild, uncoordinated kick at his shin.

Henwick fell forward momentarily before shifting his weight to stay upright. His agility must have been as high as Digby's. Possibly even higher, considering the cleric hadn't lost any levels upon his death.

No matter.

Digby flailed on the ground, spinning himself around to swipe at the man's ankle with his sword. The strike merely carved a sliver from his boot, though it served as a reminder for the cleric to keep his distance. Digby took the momentary pause to glance in Parker's direction to make sure the soldier was still in the fight.

"Kick his ass, Dig," she shouted as she led the caretaker in a circle twenty feet away. She looked a little winded and was favoring her leg but with the wide-open space of the coliseum at her disposal, she had enough room to evade it. He snapped his vision back to Henwick just as the cleric was getting back into position.

"Gah!" Flopping to the side, the head of the ax hit the stone inches from Digby's head. Sparks flew from the impact as the sound reverberated through his ears. The only saving grace was that the healing spell that Henwick had cast was finally wearing off.

With control over his body fully returned to him, Digby spun his legs around and kicked himself back up on his feet. With one hand raised, he made sure to be ready for another attack. Doing the math in his head, he was pretty sure Henwick still had the mana for something.

Digby glanced at his mana, reminding himself that the twenty-three points he had wasn't enough to get him very far.

Or was it?

Digby crouched down with one hand on the floor and his other holding his sword at the ready. Henwick adjusted his ax to guard from his blade.

That was when Digby cast Decay.

The spell went to work, wearing away the stone beneath his

hand where Henwick couldn't see. Digby smirked as he closed his fingers around the dust that remained.

What was it that Parker said earlier?

Digby nodded.

Oh yes.

"Pocket sand!" Digby lunged forward with a feint before launching the handful of dust he'd created into Henwick's face.

The cleric struggled to readjust his weapon's position, not expecting the secondary attack. Digby took the opening for what it was and slipped his blade through the man's defenses. A spray of arterial blood coated his face, hot against his cold skin.

A sputtering gasp came from Henwick's throat, his hand clutched over a river of crimson that cascaded down his chest. Mana flowed to stem the bleeding, probably the last few points he had.

Digby wasn't about to give him the chance to heal. Instead, he flipped his sword on his hand and pivoted to strike Henwick down, once and for all.

Then, he hesitated.

"Go ahead then." Henwick knelt on the platform, resting his weight on one hand as he applied pressure to his neck with the other. "I'm out of mana."

The damage he'd caused must have been severe. So much that one Regeneration spell had not been enough to heal it completely.

The sword shook in Digby's hands. "I am sorry it turned out this way."

"Don't be. This is what you are. I thought you might have changed when we agreed to work together, but you are still just a thief and a liar." Henwick spat a mouthful of blood.

"I never denied that." Digby jerked his hand down to finish the cleric, only to stop when a scream came from behind him.

No!

All thoughts of killing Henwick vanished from his mind as he spun to find Parker on the ground. A sinewy, black cord extended from the caretaker's oversized claws. Digby followed the tendril back to the pink haired soldier's leg where a barbed spike had impaled her thigh.

"Finish him, Dig!" Parker gritted her teeth, her eyes focused on him and Henwick.

He glanced at his HUD.

MP: 13/298

Not enough for anything significant.

Digby flicked his attention back to the cleric kneeling on the platform.

All he had to do was finish him.

"Blast!" Digby planted a foot on the ground and kicked off to run in the opposite direction, leaving a shocked Henwick behind.

There was no way he could finish the cleric and save Parker.

He had to make a choice, and he wasn't about to let her die. Not after everything they had been through.

"Get away from her!" Digby activated his Limitless mutation, throwing caution to the wind as he lunged for the caretaker's skull. He grabbed on tight, driving a thumb into the hollow of its eye to hold on and thrusting his blood sword deep into its neck.

The caretaker let out a literal earsplitting scream directly in Digby's face, causing the deceased membranes in one ear to rupture. He ignored it and tightened his grip on his sword. Using his other hand as a fulcrum, he kicked off. At the same time, he spent ten points of mana to reforge his weapon, widening the blade within the monster's neck. Bones snapped and popped in Digby's feet as he launched himself in a circular arc around the creature's head. He took his modified blood sword with him, tearing it through the caretaker's flesh.

"Die, damn it!" Digby howled as his weapon nearly severed the beast's head from its shoulders. His face fell when the handle of his blood forged sword snapped the instant the blade carved into the caretaker's spine.

Panic slammed into him as he dangled, still hanging on to the monster's head. The hollow sockets of the caretaker's skull turned toward him slowly.

"Why can't you just die?" Digby whimpered as he let go in the hope that he might fall safely to the ground. Terror gripped him a second later when the creature's free hand snapped around his arm.

Damn.

The world blurred as the caretaker whipped him up and then straight down again. A dozen bones throughout his body splintered when he hit the ground near Parker. Digby forced himself to sit up only to find his right arm missing entirely. He flicked his eyes back to the Caretaker just in time to watch it toss his severed limb over its shoulder. It hit the platform near Henwick with a wet slap.

Digby groaned at the fact the cleric was still within the platform's safe area, clearly waiting for one of them to die. The thought of it nearly drove him mad. "Where is your honor now? You treacherous zealot."

Henwick didn't budge, his face full of what looked like shock.

The caretaker stalked closer.

"I'm sorry." Parker winced as she pulled at her skewered leg, struggling to stay standing. "I screwed up."

That was when Digby remembered he had a willing source of mana right beside him. He rolled to look Parker in the eyes. "You haven't screwed up anything. There's still a chance! Just don't fight me."

"What?" Confusion swept across her face as he reached his remaining arm to hover over her heart and cast Leach with his last three points of mana. She gasped as a trickle of power began to flow from her to him. "Fine, take it."

Digby felt the massive well of mana she carried relax as she let go, allowing him to drain what he needed. He cast the spell again and again to fill himself back up.

"Digby!" the caretaker cried out in his father's voice as it closed the gap.

"Stop using that voice!" Digby pushed himself up on his remaining arm and focused on the ground at the monster's feet. "You are not my father!" He opened his maw and pushed its width until it covered the stone with plenty to spare.

The caretaker fell back, sinking into the shadowy opening of his void.

"Wait, shit!" Parker lurched forward with a shriek of pain as the tendril attached to the barbed spike in her leg pulled her toward the opening.

"Grab my hand." Digby flopped forward to reach her, lamenting the fact that his other hand was laying over by Henwick. She took hold and braced along with him until she stopped sliding forward. The result only gave the caretaker an anchor to work with. Slowly, the beast began to pull itself up and out of Digby's maw.

"No you don't." He summoned the crone, sending a dozen ghostly limbs up out of his maw to hold the monstrosity in place. Then, he focused on the tendril attached to Parker and called his wraith.

The crimson specter flickered into existence and streaked forward. Digby frowned when it rushed straight past the tendril and slashed at the caretaker's side. A shower of black fluid sprayed through the air only for the wound to immediately close. He tried again, only for the echo of Jack the Ripper to repeat the same attack.

"No, you idiot! Attack the tendril, damn it!" Digby felt Parker begin to slip and cast Forge in the hope of severing the sinewy cord with a blade of blood from his maw. He willed the black shape to form a serrated edge, but even with that, the caretaker's tendrils remained firm.

Parker let out a grunt as the spike in her leg yanked them both toward his open maw. Tears streamed down her face, yet she didn't let go of Digby's hand. He stared at the caretaker as it sank. He couldn't close his maw yet, that would only cut the monster in half. It was sure to regenerate in a matter of seconds. He had to wait until the beast's head went under. Hell, he wasn't even sure if swallowing the thing whole would be enough to finish it off for good. He debated casting Flare, but they were too close. Decay was out as well since the creature had the will to resist it.

"Bloody hell." Digby slipped forward.

Between the two of them they had plenty of mana, but no spells with the accuracy to actually help. He was going to have to close his maw prematurely, otherwise, Parker was doomed. Maybe cutting the caretaker in half would at least buy some time.

That was when Parker did the last thing he expected.

Snapping her tear-filled eyes to the center of the area, she rolled the dice on an insane gamble.

"God damn it, Henwick, help us!" She bared her teeth at the cleric who was still standing within the platform's safe area. "You hear me, you douche. Get your bland ass over here and help."

It was ridiculous. That bastard had won. All Henwick had to do was stay right where he was, and the caretaker would kill at least one of them. The Heretic Seed would simply hand a body to him and send him on his way. Then again, it wouldn't be the first time Digby had bet everything on a gamble. After all, Henwick might have been misguided, but the man he had come to know wasn't evil.

Digby snapped his eyes to the cleric and piled on. "We can sort things out between us once the caretaker is gone. So like she said, get your bland ass over here and lend a hand."

"I'm sorry, Graves, you know I can't." Henwick remained where he was. "I can't trust you."

"Is that really the problem? Is believing in me really so hard? Or is it that you can't give up control?" Digby shouted back while returning his attention to the caretaker to stop it from pulling Parker into his maw.

"I…" Henwick started to respond but trailed off.

That was it.

That hesitation.

There was a chance!

Under all of Henwick's faith and morals, there was at least a shred of doubt.

Parker let out a pained whimper as they slipped closer to doom. Digby strained to hold on to her hand, closing his eyes and shouting in desperation the first thing that drifted through his mind.

"Don't stop believing! You hear me, Henwick? I was just a petty thief, caught in the wrong place at the wrong time. But I will take this road 'til the end. I will stop Autem. You don't have to trust me now, but give me the chance to earn it."

"Did you just quote Journey?" Parker let out an inappropriate laugh along with a cry of pain.

"I don't know who that is, damn it." Digby slipped forward. "Just hold on."

Then, with a sudden snap, the caretaker's tendril went slack. The sound of metal hitting stone echoed through the air as he and Parker fell backward. Digby snapped his eyes open to find Henwick standing before them, his ax's head against the ground where the sinewy cord lay severed. The caretaker continued to sink behind him.

Digby froze, unsure how to respond as the cleric hefted up his weapon. For a moment, he looked like he might raise the ax again to attack. Then, he lowered it to his side. "I know you mean well, Graves. I still don't trust you."

Digby's mouth fell open. "But—"

His words were cut off when a barbed spike burst through the cleric's shoulder to yank him backward. In surprise, his ax fell from his hand. The head hit the ground and tipped back to topple into the opening of the void behind him.

Without thinking, Digby sprang up and threw his remaining hand out to Henwick. "Grab hold!"

The cleric reached out and gripped his wrist with one hand while clutching his shoulder with the other. "You could just let me die."

"I know." Digby fought to hold the man away from the edge of his maw as the sinewy cord pulled taut. "But I won't."

Henwick merely closed his eyes, blew out a labored sigh and let go. "I know you won't."

"What are you doing?" Digby stepped closer and grabbed his sleeve.

Henwick slapped his hand away. "It took me longer than I care to admit, but what you said makes sense. You're doing the best you can. Same as I. In that regard, I can't trust myself any more than I can you. Not to mention, you didn't hesitate to grab my hand just now. Nor did you let Miss Parker remain in danger once she had been hurt. You could have finished me off, but you valued her life over winning."

"Don't be ridiculous, you idiot." Digby shook his hand at the man, pleading with him to take it.

"I'm merely being pragmatic." Henwick smiled. "I will never truly trust you, and I will not leave the world in your hands unless I can remain with you to keep you in line. If I can't return to the world outside, then it's better I be consumed. Least that way I become a source of strength to aid you in your quest, as well as a reminder when the power of the Seed tempts you."

Digby shook his head. It was Sybil all over again. "Why does everyone think putting more pressure on me is the best way to get what they want?"

"Because trust cannot be given easily." Henwick stepped backward toward the edge. "That's just how people are."

"Damn it, you fool. I don't want this." Digby reached for him again, but his hand was slapped away.

"That is life, Graves. You don't always get what you want. I have learned that better than most. What was it you said? Sometimes you just have to play the hand you were dealt." He glanced back at the shadowy opening and the caretaker behind him, its skull sinking into the void. "It seems that now I must do the same."

Before Digby could get out another word, the cleric turned and leapt toward the caretaker with fists raised. Bone crunched as he slammed his knuckles into the beast. He raised his hand again and again, to beat the monster into submission, his knuckles red with blood. Then, together, they both vanished into the darkness.

"Why do they keep—" Digby ran out of words as he dropped to his knees.

"It was the only way." Parker limped to his side and placed a hand on his shoulder as he slowly closed his maw.

Caretaker defeated. 12,430 experience awarded.
Remnant Spark, level 31 Cleric defeated. 3,030 experience awarded.
You have reached level 37. 7,884 experience to next level.
You have 2 attribute points to allocate.
ECHO OF AN HONORABLE CLERIC OBTAINED: By

**consuming a powerful spark, you have incorporated a
portion of its power to your mana system.
HONORABLE CLERIC
When summoned, this spark will manifest and heal one ally.**

Digby's attention was torn away from his HUD when Parker fell against him. He caught her with his remaining arm to keep her from toppling onto her back and looked down at the barbed spike in her leg. "We have to get that out of you."

"I'm okay. I just leveled up a ton all at once and it made me dizzy. This is nothing." She contradicted herself by wincing.

That was when the remains of the sinewy cord hanging from her thigh began to shudder.

"Blast, that damn thing is still alive." Digby grabbed for the tendril only to have it slither away from his hand like a snake.

Parker let out a gasp as the barb in her leg changed shape, scales forming along its surface. A pair of tiny crimson eyes opened at the end, followed by a mouth, and forked tongue.

"Shit! Shit! Get it out! Get it out!" The soldier flailed and fell backward on her rear as the caretaker's tendril-turned-snake obliged her request by slithering through her leg wound until it was free. Parker clutched her thigh and sucked in air through her teeth.

Digby focused on the miniature version of the monster's original form.

Caretaker, friendly.

"What?" He crept toward the serpent as it raised its head, its beady little eyes watching him. "It isn't hostile."

"That actually makes sense." Parker took a deep breath still dealing with the pain of having her leg impaled. "With just us in here, the number of souls matches the number of bodies available outside. The caretaker doesn't need to kill us anymore."

Digby glanced at his HUD.

2/2

"That's not exactly comforting." Digby reached toward the snake just before it flicked its head in the other direction and slithered off toward the chamber at the center of the space. He turned his attention back to her. "Can you stand?"

"Maybe with help." She stared at the hole in her thigh before attempting to push herself up.

"Wait." Digby focused on her wound, remembering what the description of Henwick's echo had said. It wasn't an offensive ability like the others.

Parker held still as he cast the spell.

A figure of white light flickered into existence beside her with hands outstretched. Digby watched as motes of light formed in the air, drawn from the surrounding mana.

"Whoa." Parker relaxed as the hole in her thigh closed.

"My god." Digby placed his remaining hand on her leg in astonishment. With his deathly mana balance, he was unable to absorb the life essence required to heal the living. It was one of his biggest weaknesses. The idea that he was unable to do anything if one of his friends were wounded terrified him. Yet now, he didn't need life essence. No, all he had to do was summon the cleric's echo and let him do the rest. It wasn't an economical use of mana, but it worked. "Looks like Henwick is making himself useful already."

"So is the caretaker." Parker stood up and pointed toward the center of the space.

Digby caught the snake slithering up a pillar near the door of the chamber to coil around the top. In response, the entryway opened without so much as a sound. He picked his severed arm up off the stone and shoved it back into place before looking back to Parker.

"Let's go, this isn't over."

CHAPTER THIRTY-SEVEN

"Everyone stay belted in, this might get a little rough." Becca tightened her grip on the controls of the kestrel as she piloted toward the ship that held Bancroft's hypothetical weapon. She glanced to the side at a second aircraft flying beside her. Alex rode in that one, along with half of Bancroft's men. The other half were in the back of hers, along with Mason, Easton, and a handful of their newly minted Heretics.

Mason had returned from his work at the power station just as they were getting ready to leave for Bancroft's mission. Time was short, so there hadn't been a moment to catch up with each other before they had to head out. Fortunately, she had slipped a note under his door an hour ago to tell him how she felt. She was pretty sure everyone would be rushing around so that seemed like the best way to handle things to make sure she couldn't chicken out at the last minute. The note was short and sweet, and in all honesty got a little not safe for work toward the end, but knowing she had written it was enough to take some of the pressure off. On top of that, she made a point of giving him a firm kiss before they left. From the look on his face, he got the point even if she hadn't said anything. Between that and the note, she was feeling pretty good about herself.

As for Bancroft, he had stayed behind. The debate had been significant, but in the end, they needed to leave someone strong back in Vegas in case a threat showed up. Otherwise the city would have been defenseless. That being said, Becca had ordered Deuce, Elenore, and Sax to stay behind. At least that way, there was some leadership there to keep Bancroft in line. Initially, she was concerned that he might make a move to destroy Digby's body while they were gone, but considering Tavern would never allow that, she was able to push that possibility out of her head.

That was the way it had to be.

The cargo ship appeared on the horizon, and without Digby, the mission was going to be a challenge. It may have been daylight, but there was no telling what sort of revenant mutations they might face, and she didn't have room in her head to worry about what Bancroft might do.

"We have incoming!" Malcolm jabbed a finger against the glass as a few winged forms appeared to take flight from the deck of the tanker. Seven in total.

"I see them." Becca's hands danced across the console to activate the craft's weapons. The guns mounted on the front slid out into position. She pushed the limits of her perception to acquire her target's in the distance.

Revenant Lightflyer, Hostile.

"Shit, they've evolved again. The things can fly during the day!" She opened fire.

"At least it's just the small ones. Let's hope the bloodstalkers aboard haven't evolved too." Malcolm held onto his seat. "Those things are going to be a big enough problem even in a weakened state."

The kestrel beside them opened fire as well. Ducky, Bancroft's illusionist, must have been at the sticks. Only someone with a high enough perception value would attempt the shot at that distance. She couldn't help but wonder who was better.

The bullets ripped through the sky to answer the question.

Revenant Lightflyer defeated, 690 experience awarded.
Revenant Lightflyer defeated, 690 experience awarded.
Revenant Lightflyer defeated, 690 experience awarded.

The kestrel beside them took out another three but missed a the last one.

"Mine!" She let loose another torrent of death from the kestrel's guns, taking out the remainder.

Revenant Lightflyer defeated, 690 experience awarded.

"Jeez." Malcolm eyed her sideways. "Hard to believe you sat behind a drone console for years. I can respect a shot like that when I see one."

"You tend to get good at this stuff when your ex-employer tries to kill you for a solid month." She stared down at the controls. It was strange how foreign the act of firing the craft's guns had felt while experiencing the familiarity of combat at the same time. She had gotten used to the fighting, but she had used nothing but magic for a while now. Apparently, firing modern weapons had become something of a novelty for her.

Becca shook off the thought and looked back into the cabin, making eye contact with Mason. "Okay, everyone get prepared to land. I don't know what is going to greet us, but be ready for anything."

"Got it." Mason nodded despite looking awkward with a sword strapped to his back. The power station he'd been guarding had been in the middle of nowhere, so he'd only reached level ten. From the expression on his face, it was clear he hadn't gotten as used to using magic as she had. Easton and the rest of Vegas's heretics nodded as well, looking just as unsure of themselves.

"Just stay behind this jerk." She hooked a thumb to Malcolm who sat beside her. "Let him get the attention of the revs and hide behind him. You'll be fine."

"Thanks," Malcolm grumbled.

"Welcome." Becca gave him a nod in her most fake polite voice.

"All kidding aside." Malcolm gave her a smile. "I know we don't really get along, but I'm glad to have you on the team. I've seen what you can do out there and you have more experience with the Seed. I'd love to say the Guardian Core is the same, but the Heretic Seed certainly has its differences."

"That some kind of apology for being an ass all week?" Becca eyed him sideways as she brought the kestrel to hover over the ship.

"Call it what you want." He groaned and resigned himself to look out the window at the deck.

She set the kestrel down gently and popped her seatbelt. Mason hit the ramp button at the back. Malcolm gave her a nod and took point. Becca exited right behind him just as Alex emerged from the other craft. The deck was filled with shipping containers.

Before everyone had a chance to gather together, a labored groan came from one of the towers of containers. A massive, clawed hand gripped the side as a bloodstalker lumbered into view.

"Here we go, people." Malcolm snapped his sword from the sheath on his back and rushed forward to take a position in the front.

"Fighters, guard the mages." Mason joined him, having some trouble getting his sword out. "Alex, umm, start enchanting."

On his command, the newly minted Heretics from Vegas assembled into a mostly organized set of two squads. Becca headed to the front with Alex and the rest of Bancroft's men to bracket Malcolm on either side.

The bloodstalker pushed off the wall of one of the cargo containers as if it was exhausted. The wings on its back were folded up tight, clearly unable to fly. Becca focused on it.

Dormant Revenant Bloodstalker, rare.

"It's suffering from the sunlight." She cast Reveal just to make sure there was nothing lurking around in plain sight that no one had noticed. When she found the deck empty, she launched an icicle straight for the bloodstalker's head. The dormant beast responded by covering its face with both hands. The frozen projectile thumped into the flesh of its wrist. She sent a second one out, getting the same result as well as a notification from the Heretic Seed.

Icicle has advanced to rank A. The velocity, size, and hardness of a projectile may be increased by taking additional time to form it. This ability will increase mana cost, by 1 for every second that an icicle is charged.

"Pile on!" Malcolm shouted, causing the entire group to throw everything they had at the creature.

Becca ducked on instinct as a dozen spells flew over her head. Ice mixed with fire as everything slammed into the bloodstalker one after another. It staggered and fell to a knee, one of its main claws slamming into the deck to support its weight. Fire licked at its back and icicles tore at its skin. There was even a bolt of electricity in the mix. Despite the damage, the revenant kept one hand up to protect its head.

"Keep going," Malcolm called out. "It can't fight back while the sun is—oh fuck!"

The revenant proved him wrong, using both legs to launch its weight in their direction. It fell in an uncoordinated slide that bowled through their forces. A few people screamed, getting caught by a swinging limb. Malcolm fell back into Mason. One of his men had not been so lucky, with one of his legs bending forward in a way that it was definitely not supposed to bend.

Becca didn't waste time, casting her newly ranked-up Icicle spell and holding it. They didn't look like they had suffered any fatalities, and the other mages could tend to the wounded. She needed to finish the creature off.

Holding out her hand, droplets of water condensed in the air to swirl into a mass, each forming together to build her projectile. The process was slower than usual, but something else was different, like more power was building up behind it. Becca focused on the shape, willing it into a form that she pictured in her head, a trio of angled fins appearing at the end while a twisted spiral climbed from the point in the front.

"The hell is that?" Alex looked at her sideways.

"Don't worry about it." Becca jumped toward the oversized revenant, hopping a flailing leg as it swept it across the deck. The icicle continued to grow and harden as she held it, the tip of the spike moving to aim at whichever point on the revenant that she was focusing on. She skidded to a stop just as it was shoving itself up off the deck.

"Back off." Mason slid in from the side, the edge of his sword glowing like molten steel. He buried it in the creature's wrist with a hard chop that crunched into bone.

The revenant let out a screech and dropped its other hand to the deck for support. Its face was only a few feet away. So close she could practically touch it. Its hot breath caressed her cheek. Becca took the opening, letting the frozen projectile fly like a missile. A swell of mana from her surroundings pulled inward, drawn by the spell only to explode outward in a shockwave that blew her hair back. Frost formed on her hand and poncho as air blasted the heat of the revenant's breath away. The spike took off for home in a perfect spiral. She kept her eyes focused on the monster's head.

The revenant's screech ended in an instant, its skull detonating outward from the back to spray the cargo container behind it. The frozen projectile slammed into the metal storage unit as well, finally shattering, though not without punching a two-foot dent into the side. The revenant dropped to the deck at her feet, its head shattering into dozens of frozen pieces of meat. Another experience message scrolled across her vision.

"Good god." Mason stared up at her. "The hell was that?"

She shook flakes of frost off her hand. "Icicle. Rank A."

Several of the combat volunteers looked down at their hands, clearly realizing the power that they had obtained.

That was when she heard something from the shadows cast by the shipping containers. Becca snapped her eyes to the darkened space, her Reveal spell negating the darkness to show her a human-sized form slipping out from behind one of the containers. It crept closer.

Revenant Lightwalker, hostile.

She flicked her vision to Easton, who was standing right in front of the shadowed space where the creature lurked. He was staring off into space, probably looking at his HUD instead of paying attention to his surroundings. The revenant behind him moved, picking up its pace to go in for the kill.

"Look out!" Becca grabbed Mason as he was standing up and yanked him backward to use him as a counter weight. The momentum got her moving but there was too much ground to cover. The revenant was already too close, its clawed fingers reaching out for Easton. All he did was look back at her with a confused look on his face as the monster grabbed hold of his shoulder.

"No!" She ran with a hand outstretched. They had only been on the ship for a minute, and they were going to lose someone already.

That was when Bancroft's illusionist, Ducky, slammed a fist into the lightwalker's head, sending it toppling to the deck before it got the chance to strike. Easton jumped forward, realizing how close he had just come to death. Malcolm jumped in to help Ducky.

"Nice try, asshole." He plunged his sword down into the revenant's chest and planted a boot on its stomach to keep it down until it expired.

Becca slowed to a stop, her heart still racing as sweat trickled down the side of her face.

"Jeez, Alvarez." Malcolm pulled his sword free of the corpse. "Relax. You aren't the only one here that's capable of kicking some ass. You gotta learn to rely on us."

She nodded but said nothing in return. He was right. She hated that he was right. After an awkward moment, she gave him a simple thumbs up. It was beginning to become clear that the betrayal that her gut kept warning her about was not actually going to happen.

Once the deck that they had landed on was secure, everyone gathered by the ramps of the kestrels. Becca cast Waking Dream as soon as everyone was together, showing the schematic of a cargo vessel. It wasn't an exact match for the ship they were on, but it was the closest thing she could find in the dark corners of the internet that she could still access, which was not much.

From there, they would need to split up. Alex and Mason would lead the majority of the group to secure whatever weapon Autem had stored below deck. She and Malcolm would head down to the bowels of the ship to place explosives to cover their tracks. It wouldn't be long before Henwick was able to send a team out to secure the vessel, and it wouldn't do to leave the ship there empty. That would be like leaving a sign saying, 'We took your shit.'

At least if they sank the tanker, Henwick wouldn't be able to tell exactly what happened to it. The satellites didn't keep watch on the area at all times and according to Bancroft, they wouldn't have the ship back in their view until the following morning. Hopefully they would be long gone by then, leaving Autem wondering where the ship went. They would have to search the area before reaching the conclusion that it had sunk, and it would take even longer to realize that their enemies had something to do with it. By then, the war could even be over. After all, a lot could happen in a few weeks. The last month was proof of that.

Becca swept a hand through the air, wiping her illusion out of existence. Once everyone was ready, they headed for the nearest passage that led below deck. She stopped short halfway there, slowing everyone else as they got close.

"What is it?" Malcolm leaned toward her.

Before she could answer, a massive hand reached out from an open cargo hold in the deck behind them to drag a revenant bloodstalker into view. A second pair of hands gripped the side of the cargo hold next to it.

"At least we don't have to go looking for them." Becca shrugged.

"Fair enough." Malcolm took up a position beside her. "Let's get this done."

CHAPTER THIRTY-EIGHT

Dread rolled through Digby's stomach as he approached the open doors of the stone chamber at the crown of the Heretic Seed's realm. He'd hoped that everything would simply end when he and Parker survived the gauntlet, but no, there was something more.

He passed the obsidian statues of himself and Parker as he walked, the only two still intact. Digby stopped when he reached the raised platform that had previously been the safe area that he'd needed to reach. The doors loomed in front of him. The chamber within was completely shrouded in darkness.

"Do you want me to hold your hand?" Parker reached for him as she stepped onto the platform beside him.

"No, I don't want to hold hands." He swatted at her.

"Okay, okay." She pulled away. "You just looked scared, is all."

"Of course I'm scared." Digby folded his arms. "We have no idea what awaits us in there. It could be the devil himself, for all we know."

"True." She stepped forward and looked back at him. "But we have come this far."

"I suppose there's no going back anyway." He felt the corner of his mouth tug up slightly as he stepped forward to join her, then he stopped again. "Listen, Parker."

"Yeah?" She tilted her head to one side.

"I am glad you're here." He shook a bit of weight off his shoulders and stepped toward the doors. "I know I'm not the easiest to get along with, so thank you for putting up with me."

"No problem." She walked beside him. "I'm not perfect either, so thank you for not eating me or something."

Without another word, they stepped inside.

Darkness closed in on them as the doors began to swing shut behind them.

"It's a trap!" they both shouted in unison as they ran back to reach the opening only to crash into the stone as the chamber sealed itself shut.

Digby pounded his fists against the cold stone, but the doors wouldn't open. "Alright, alright, we just have to relax."

"You first." Parker slapped him on the arm as he continued to panic despite his words.

"Stop that." He slapped her back, finally taking a moment to calm down.

The space was completely black without a torch or lamp anywhere to light their surroundings. Hell, Digby wasn't even sure where the walls were. They could be closing in on him for all he knew.

They needed light.

"I have an idea." Digby opened his maw on the floor and cast Forge to raise a small spike of necrotic blood up from his void. He made sure to construct supports on the sides to keep it from falling over. Once it was ready, he cast Cremation to set it alight.

"That's better." Parker blew out a relieved sigh as the flickering light reflected off the walls all around them.

They were alone.

"Yes. It's not a long-term solution but it will suffice for now." Digby approached the glossy, black wall of the chamber and examined it. "Obsidian?"

The interior seemed to be made of the same substance as the statues outside, as well as the Heretic Seed's obelisk out in the real world. Sweeping his vision around him, the space didn't seem to be manmade. Instead, the wall jutted off at odd angles like a crystal of some kind.

"Odd." Digby spun around. "There's nothing in here."

"I'm not so sure." Parker wandered through the space.

Digby eyed her. "You feeling something? Something to do with your messenger class?"

"Maybe." She closed her eyes and took several deep breaths. "That feeling I had. It's like the world is thinnest here. Or maybe that there is someplace else we can reach. It's like the Seed is trying to connect us to something. And the feeling has gotten stronger after I gained some more levels."

"What are you at now?"

"Level seventeen." She looked back at him.

"That's odd." Digby folded his arms and tapped a finger in his elbow. "You should have gotten a new class at fifteen."

"Maybe messenger doesn't have the same options." She shrugged.

"Maybe." Digby stepped closer to her. "Can you use your Mirror Passage using the wall?"

"I think so, but I need a destination in mind." She opened her eyes. "Plus, I would need a body to inhabit, or the destination would have to be immaterial like this one." She reached out to touch the nearest wall only to pull her fingers away a second later when the whole place came to life with activity.

Circles of white runes expanded out from where she'd touched the wall, like ripples on the surface of a water in the rain. From there, they swept across the walls, creating more ripples until the entire chamber was illuminated by thousands of runes. It was pure chaos.

"What did you do?" Digby moved to the center of the room.

"I don't know. All I did was touch it." She inched closer to him as well.

"Well, you did something." Digby raised his hands prepared for some sort of attack, only to look foolish when none came. "What the…?" He trailed off as the activity settled down.

Then, one by one, images came.

Some he recognized.

On one wall, the castle that he'd died in filled one surface of obsidian. The picture was dim and washed out to a point where it was represented entirely in grayscale. Dozens of other images blanketed the space as well. Digby shifted his view, finding the street where he'd fought Jack, and the ghost town where he'd faced that gunslinger. There were also many images of places he didn't recognize.

"Oh wow." Parker slowly looked over the space. "It's like looking through a history book."

"What do you mean?" Digby furrowed his brow.

"These all look like places that people have built over the centuries." She walked around the chamber, examining the walls.

Digby scratched at his chin. "Maybe it's showing us the memories of where the Seed's fragments have been. Some sort of history of the Heretics?"

"Maybe—" She cocked her head to one side. "Wait, no, that can't be right."

"What?" Digby dropped his hand to his side.

"I mean that." She pointed over his shoulder.

Digby turned to find an image of a gothic castle that filled one of the obsidian facets. His jaw dropped as he took it in. The only way to describe it was… impossible. A landscape of ice surrounded the structure as its spires reached into the sky. Some were so narrow that he couldn't tell how they could stand on their own. Even stranger, the image was brighter than most of the others, with hints of color fading in and out like a dream.

"I take it that isn't a place that has existed in this world?"

"Nope." Parker stared at it. "It looks like something out of a fantasy movie. I'm pretty sure people couldn't build something like that and still obey the laws of physics."

"What is it then?" Digby placed his hand against the image. "A world beyond this realm?"

"I don't know, but it feels closer than some of the other places." She reached forward to touch the image and for an instant, the view changed to focus on a reflective surface of ice that might have served as a mirror. The image vanished a second later as if slapping her hand away. "Okay, I guess that's not our destination."

"Alright, so maybe we just have to figure out which of these places you can access with a Mirror Passage." Digby scanned the rest of the room to see if any of the other images stood out. He stopped at a picture of a tall building bearing a massive banner hanging down one side. "How about this one?"

"I hope not. I don't like the look of that banner. There's something very Third Reich." Parker touched it but it vanished just like the other.

"And this one?" Digby pointed to another image showing a relatively ordinary street with a large school building.

"What the what?" Parker gasped. "That's my old high school. I went there back in the nine—" She winced and slapped a hand over her eyes before she could finish the sentence.

"You alright?" Digby eyed her.

"I'm okay. Just got a sharp pain in my head." She brushed her fingers against the image just as it blinked out of sight.

"I guess that's not the place either?" Digby shrugged.

"I guess that confirms that these images are the memories of the Heretics. That one must have been mine." She shuddered. "Kind of unsettling, though."

"Indeed, I understand that all too well." Digby moved on.

She glanced at the spot where the image of her hometown had been only to look away and rub at her temples. She shook her head and turned away. A second later, she rushed across the place and slapped her hand against another picture.

It didn't disappear.

"This is it." She nodded decisively.

"Are you sure?" Digby stepped to her side to take in the image.

It was brighter than the others and had more color, to the point where it almost looked real. The scene was simple. There were no castles or impressive buildings. Just a bar lined with stools and an array of bottles shelved behind it. A mirror hung on the wall behind the shelves.

Digby furrowed his brow. "I could see Tavern being drawn to such a location, but I can't imagine why we would find anything useful there."

Parker kept her hand pressed against the image. "This one is it.

I'm sure of it. The Seed is practically inviting us in. I can take us there. I can feel it."

"Could it be a trap?" Digby frowned, not liking the idea of being invited anywhere.

"No way to be sure." She shrugged. "But we did come this far. The Seed might not have taken our side with that battle royal bullshit, but now that we're all that's left, it should want to help us."

"Fair enough," Digby shifted his view to the largest surface that might function to open a passage.

"Only one way to find out." She raised her hand to the glossy, black wall as the reflected light of Digby's fire grew brighter. The surface rippled and warped until the passage seemed stable.

"Do you still want to hold hands?" Digby let out a laugh.

Parker smirked and grabbed hold of his hand. "Why not? Don't want you to get lost now."

Then, without hesitation, she pulled him forward.

CHAPTER THIRTY-NINE

"We split up here." Malcolm stopped when they reached a stairway.

Alex skidded to a halt behind him along with everyone else. "Shouldn't we stay together?"

Some of the low-level Heretics ran into each other in the doorway behind them. Alex could hear Mason trying to keep them organized. Clearly, he was having a little trouble since the group had so little training. It was understandable. It wasn't that long ago that being a Heretic was something Alex had needed to get used to, after all.

Fortunately, the revenants up top had gone down easy, leaving little opposition to get below deck.

"We've brought plenty of people." Malcolm shook his head at Alex's suggestion of staying together. "We should be able to handle things." Skyline's former knight grabbed a duffle bag from one of his men while barely paying attention to Alex or the people in the back.

"He's right." Becca nodded to Alex. "We're on borrowed time, to some degree. Autem will make it out here at one point. It could be a half hour from now, or it could be days. We have no way to know."

"We probably shouldn't waste daylight either." Malcolm zipped open the bag and checked its contents before closing it again. "We still have a few hours left, but if we have to move our whole group through the ship to plant explosives, that time is going to run out fast. And we don't want to be here when every rev lurking below deck goes into night mode."

Alex sighed. "I guess that makes sense."

"That means you're with us." Louis gave him a somewhat friendly punch in the arm.

"Yay." Alex suppressed an eye roll as Roland, Nat, Sullivan, and the rest of Vegas's Heretics took up a position behind him. The only one who had stayed up top with the kestrels was Ducky. Alex may have had plenty of conflicts with the mercs, but now, Bancroft's guys seemed committed to being pals. Alex still wasn't sure if he was buying it. Kristen had never had anything nice to say about them. Well, technically, she never had anything nice to say about anyone. He smirked, finding that he actually missed the skull.

I hope Kristen is having a good time back in Vegas. He'd left her on his workbench with a television running.

Becca interrupted his thoughts with a sigh. "Sorry to saddle you with these guys, but hold down the fort while I get the charges placed. And don't let my boyfriend get eaten."

"Okay, sure, I'll keep him safe." Alex laughed and elbowed Mason in the side.

"Hey." The soldier elbowed him back before reaching a hand to Becca. "Don't you get eaten either."

"Let's all try our best not to get eaten, alright." Easton threw up his arms, clearly still stressed from almost becoming a meal back up on the deck of the ship.

"Good plan." Malcolm nodded.

Becca shook her head. "Anyway, I'll keep me and Malcolm concealed so we can avoid any fights. As long as things go smoothly, it shouldn't take long. We'll meet you back on the deck when we're done."

"Okay." Alex took her word for it.

"Just make sure this weapon that Bancroft thinks is here gets dealt with." She gave him a look that said volumes. Alex had known her long enough to know when she was feeling conflicted. She probably didn't fully trust Malcolm or the rest of Bancroft's men either.

"I'm on it." Alex gave her a thumbs up and a look of his own that said the same.

With that, Becca headed down the stairwell with Malcolm.

Mason slipped to the front of the group just before she disappeared to add a final, "Be careful."

She stopped for a moment and gave him a smile. "I will."

A moment later she was gone, the sound of her footsteps growing quieter by the second.

"She knows what she's doing." Alex placed a hand on his shoulder. "And we have a job to do too."

Mason nodded and took charge of his men. "Alright, let's move."

Louis took point and waved the rest of the Skyline guys on. Alex made a point to keep an eye on Roland just in case the rogue had something up his sleeve.

On the upside, the group's training did make it easier to move through the ship. As much as Alex hated to admit it, the ex-mercenaries did know what they were doing. At least, they knew a whole lot more than the rest of Vegas's new Heretics. Even Easton, who had training, seemed to have been thrown off balance by gaining magic.

Alex pushed the concern out of his mind. The new Heretics would learn and gain experience. In time, they would be strong enough to hold their own without depending on Bancroft's guys.

They headed for the cargo hold without any delay. Aside from a few dormant revenants lurking about, the ship was in relatively good condition. The lights didn't work, but the vessel was undamaged. For some reason, Alex had been expecting the corridors to be rusted to hell. That was probably the influence of movies and games. Too much survival horror apparently.

Fortunately, the revenants hiding in the corridors were no match and they gave their people an opportunity to get some experience. Under Mason's orders, Louis and the other mercenaries hung back to let the newer magic users take down the easy prey whenever possible. Alex made sure not to take part so as to not screw up the experience. He still wasn't sure why he and Becca were counted as separate when the Seed awarded points, but he added that to the list of things that he would need to figure out.

It wasn't long before they reached the heavy metal hatch that led to the cargo bay. Mason commanded one squad of his Heretics to secure the hallway while sending the second group to stand guard on the other side. He split the remaining four of Bancroft's men between the groups to keep them out of the way and went for the cargo hatch.

"Small problem." Mason stepped aside. "Do you know how to hack an electronic lock?"

Alex looked to the side of the hatch to find a number pad attached to a heavy locking mechanism. "Umm, hacking is kind of Becca's thing. Besides, there's no power, so that thing isn't opening anytime soon."

"Damn." Mason stepped back. "Too bad Dig isn't here. He could just Decay his way right through the wall."

"Actually." Alex smirked. "Maybe I can do the next best thing."

He may not have had a spell that could rust its way through steel, but everything had a melting point and that was something he could manage. Alex focused on the stainless-steel locking bolts and cast heat object. It wasn't the fastest way in, and it heated up the hallway enough to make everyone within ten feet of the door sweat, but it worked.

In less than ten minutes, the lock was a malformed piece of scrap. A couple crowbars took care of the rest. Once the hatch was open, Alex cracked a handful of glow sticks and tossed them inside to chase the darkness back. Mason slipped in once they were sure that there were no revenants waiting. The creatures might have been dormant, but that didn't mean one wouldn't try to take a bite if they stumbled into them.

"It's safe." Mason flicked on a headlamp.

Alex followed, hesitating the moment he set foot onto a walkway that wrapped around the cargo hold. It was huge with a wide-open space directly below them and several rows of shelves and containers at the far end. There was no way to know what was in them without looking through everything. Then again, it wasn't hard to see what was the most important.

Alex lowered his gaze to the open space below, where a lone crate was strapped to the floor. "I guess that's our weapon."

"That's not all that's down there." Mason gestured to the far end of the space.

Alex swallowed as dozens of eyes the color of dying embers stared up at them from the shadows behind the shelving.

"The ship's crew must have come in here to hide when the revs got on board. One must have been bitten." Mason leaned on the railing of the walkway. "Will they come after us if we go down there?"

Alex thought about it. "They should be too weak to climb the ladders, but there's enough of them down there that they have the advantage. My guess is that they will back off once we get down there but swarm once we get further from the exit."

"That's not great." Mason grunted at the creatures. "I guess we get some of the mages to lob some fireballs at them from here then."

"Nah. Don't want to risk damaging anything that's stored in here, and honestly, we don't know how magic will affect this weapon. Besides, I have just the thing for a situation like this." Alex reached into one of the many pouches on his armor and pulled out a set of warding rods. He tossed them down the nearest ladder a moment later. They hit the floor and bounced back up as if repelled by a magnet, the set separating into four individual rods that floated into position in a ten foot wide square.

"That supposed to be safe?" Mason eyed him suspiciously.

"Yup." Alex started down the ladder. "I've been working in the garage the last few days. Plenty of revenants are still hanging around there and the warding rods haven't failed me yet." He set foot on the floor of the cargo hold as he finished speaking and tossed another set of warding rods out to make a path that the revenants couldn't enter.

"If you say so." Mason slid down the ladder.

Yeah, I'm going to stay up here with everyone else," Easton

commented from above. "You know, to guard the flanks. And, you know, not hang out with a bunch of revenants."

Alex waved a hand in front of one of the creatures, getting no reaction. "They might as well be behind a concrete wall. But that's probably a good idea regardless. We don't want too many people wandering around in here. Now where is this weapon?" Alex ventured into the space, his head lamp cutting through the shadows.

That was when he saw it.

At the center of the cargo hold sat a metal crate the size of a sarcophagus. Autem's weird cross-like emblem was etched onto the top, making it look even more like a coffin. The sides were lined with latches to keep the lid on. Alex couldn't help but let his mind run wild with what might be inside. He had hoped it would be another famous item with a mass enchantment like the ruby slippers he had stashed under his bed back in Vegas, but judging by the size of the crate, his mind went in a different direction.

Alex shuddered at the thought that the casket-sized crate might house a corpse. When thinking about what Autem might consider a weapon, it could be anything.

An ancient monster, older than Digby?

A Heretic from the past.

There was only one way to be sure.

Alex started popping the latches on one side of the lid.

"You sure we should open it?" Mason stepped around the other side.

Alex hesitated. "No, but I would like to know what's inside it before I bring it back to Vegas with us."

"Fair enough." Mason worked on the other side.

Alex swallowed hard as he popped the last of the latches, half expecting something to burst out from under the lid. He relaxed a second later when nothing did. From the lack of color in Mason's face, he had been expecting the same thing.

"Let's hope it's nothing too weird." Alex nodded to himself and lifted the lid to slide it off the crate. His blood ran cold as soon as he saw what was inside.

Mason took a large step backward. "Is that what I think it is?"

Alex stared down at the cone shaped hunk of metal. It was painted green with a radiation symbol on the side. "Obviously, I have not seen one in person, but I think that's a nuclear warhead."

"That's what I thought." Mason let out a heavy sigh.

"I don't know what I was expecting." Alex leaned on the crate to support his weight while his knees trembled. "But it wasn't this."

"I know what you mean." Mason looked down at his hands. "With all this magic stuff, a nuke seems so…"

"Barbaric?" Alex finished his sentence.

"No, I was going to say it seems so normal."

"Oh." Alex shook his head. "Sorry, I guess that makes sense too. I've just been so entrenched in magic and runes for the last week that it's hard to believe we used to fight with missiles and stuff."

"Well, technically, there's still plenty of nukes out there, if you think about the submarines that are floating around. I'm sure the captains of those vessels are still out there. I doubt they have launch capabilities but still, they aren't gone."

"That's terrifying." Alex took a deep breath. "I'm not sure which is worse, the fact that you're right about there being nukes out there, or the fact that we're now in charge of one. I am so not ready for this."

"Same." Mason folded his arms.

That was when a revenant hissed from just outside the ward behind him.

"Yar! Motherfucker!" The soldier leapt back to the crate and spun around to see the creature wandering harmlessly. "God damn it! Jesus Christ."

"You okay?" Alex arched an eyebrow.

Mason leaned against the crate. "No, I'm not okay. Monsters, nukes, magic. I didn't sign on for any of this."

Alex made eye contact with him, realizing just how out of his element the soldier was. "I get that. I was nobody. I never thought I would be stuck in the middle of this stuff. But hey, at least you have some military training, right?"

"Yeah, great." Mason stabilized himself. "I was in the army for less than a year and it sure as hell didn't prepare me for this."

"At least we get cool swords, though." Alex tried to be encouraging.

Mason only glowered back at him.

"Yeah, okay, not helping. I get it." Alex pulled his radio from his belt and thumbed the button. "Hey Becca, we found the weapon."

A moment of silence went by before she responded. "Okay, Malcolm and I have placed half the charges. What is the weapon?"

"It's a nuke," Alex responded in his most deadpan tone in order to convey the absurdity of the answer.

"A what?"

"A nuke." Alex sighed. "You know, like the thing that blew up Seattle."

"Yeah, I know what a nuke is," she snapped back. "But what the hell? Why does Henwick have one?"

That was when Malcolm joined the conversation. "It makes sense. Might as well keep something from the old world. An ace up his sleeve as all of you in Vegas would say."

"Sure." Alex tapped his other hand on the crate. "But do we even want to take this thing?"

"I sure as hell would," Malcolm answered matter-of-factly. "Think about it. All we have to do is bring it close to Autem's settlement on the east coast and, boom, no more Autem. That would just leave us with Henwick to deal with, provided we can lure him off the fucking moon."

"That's awful." Mason grabbed the radio. "Have you forgotten that a large portion of Autem's personnel is made up of people that were not given a choice and children that they have indoctrinated? I don't know what you guys in Skyline were used to, but I don't think we're okay with nuking a bunch of kids."

"That is a fair argument," Becca chimed in. "I know I don't have the best track record on judgment calls, but maybe we should remove nuking the east coast from the list of options."

"Okay." Alex took back his radio. "But if we aren't going to use it? Do we even want to take it with us? We could just sink it with the ship."

"I wouldn't recommend that," Malcolm interjected. "That would slow Autem down, but they would find it eventually. I get what you're saying, but it's better that we have control over as many pieces on the board as possible."

"He's not wrong," Becca added as if agreeing with the man left a bad taste in her mouth.

"Okay, then." Alex nodded. "We'll get the warhead secured and load it into a kestrel."

Taking his thumb off the call button, he dropped his radio to his side and stared down at the coffin-sized crate. Then he looked back to the ladder he'd climbed down to get there.

"Now how the hell are we going to get this thing out of here?"

CHAPTER FORTY

Digby braced for the crash that was sure to announce their arrival. From the image that he'd seen of the stranger tavern at the other end of Parker's Mirror Passage, there were shelves of bottles blocking their exit point. To his surprise, the crash never came. Instead, he simply tumbled forward toward the counter of the bar. He braced again for impact. Yet again, confusion filled his mind when the collision never came.

Flailing wildly, he simply passed through the counter like a ghost until he came to a stop on the floor.

"What." Digby landed flat on his back on a floor of hardwood, though strangely, it didn't feel rigid. No, it almost seemed pliable and capable of flexing against his weight like a mattress.

Then he noticed something firm underneath his legs.

"Get your dead ass feet off of me." Parker kicked at him from where she lay on the floor a few feet away.

"Don't kick me." He swatted at her boots. "It's not my fault I landed on you."

"I don't care." She kicked him one more time before stopping.

"What happened to let's hold hands?" Digby spat back. "Your friendly sentiment seems to have only gone so far."

"Well, that was before—" Her complaint ended the second she

sat up to find a bar stool with one leg passing through the middle of her leg. "Okay, that's weird."

Digby reached for the counter to pull himself up, completely forgetting that he had passed through it a moment earlier. Predictably, the same thing happened, leaving him with nothing to grip. He stumbled back on his ass to sit beside Parker on the strange squishy floor.

"Alright, what is happening here?" Digby furrowed his brow.

"Ghost stool." She pointed to the barstool passing through her leg as if that was an explanation.

"Something tells me the stool is not part of the equation of us manifesting in a spectral form." Digby glowered at her.

Parker scrunched up her nose for a second then readjusted her finger to point at herself. "Oh, we're the ghosts."

"Indeed." Digby looked around, noticing a strange haze in the air that was thicker and darker until it blocked out everything beyond, like they were surrounded by fog. Examining their surroundings, the mirror and bar seemed to be the clearest point in the room. He didn't dare venture too far from there.

"I'm not sure how much I like this." Parker stood up, wobbling a little on the squishy floor.

"Well, don't blame me, you brought us here." Digby did the same.

"Sure, but what even is this?" She waved her hand back and forth through the bar.

Digby peered into the dark edges of the space. "It's like we're in some kind of bubble that only extends so far."

"So does that mean there's nothing beyond what we can see?" Parker took a step toward the darkness that surrounded them. "Or does it mean that we just can't see beyond the edge of our bubble?"

"I don't know." Digby examined the room.

As far as he could tell, it was a normal tavern. The bar was made of polished mahogany and the furniture was beautifully crafted. There was an element of care in every aspect of the place. Even the light fixture hanging from the ceiling carried an element of simple elegance.

Approaching the bar showed him dozens of unique and inter-
estingly shaped bottles, each with an elaborate label. Vodka, bour-
bon, rum, absinthe. It was all spirits. Many of the labels looked
hand drawn, complete with decorative lettering and designs. It was
obvious that he would never find anything like them back in Vegas.

Digby took a breath, inhaling a strange sense of calm. Despite
the fact that they had just magicked their way into a completely
unknown place, surrounded by darkness, he felt safe.

But why?

As intriguing as the place was, he failed to see why the Heretic
Seed would want to send him there. For that matter, he had no
way to know where they were.

"Oh damn." Parker bumped into him as she took a step back,
her mouth hanging open. "I know where we are."

"What?" Digby snapped his focus to here. "Where?"

She merely pointed to a wall barely visible at the edge of their
bubble. Digby squinted to see through the haze that obscured the
view. There was definitely something written. The lettering glinted
in the fog as if written with silver paint, otherwise they would
never have noticed it. Digby read the stylized text, his jaw falling to
match Parkers as he finished.

The Hanging Frederick.

"What the devil?" He took a step back.

"I don't know, but it has the same name as that board game
cafe we stayed in back in California." Parker took a deep breath.

"Yes, that was the building that bore an enchantment." Digby
scratched his chin. "If I remember, it was called a surrogate
enchantment. Something about that place being a copy of another
tavern that bore the same…" He trailed off as the gears in his
head began to turn.

"What if this is the original?" Parker turned to look at him.

"But why would that even matter?" Digby shook his head,
having trouble wrapping his mind around the place. "Why would
the Seed send us here? Where on Earth even is this place?"

"It's not Earth." Parker shook her head.

"How do you know?" Digby shot her a look.

"Messenger, remember." She pointed to her chest with a

thumb. "The fact that I was able to open a passage means that this place is an immaterial realm, just like the one the Seed created for its Heretics to duke it out in. It's like we stepped out of one dream and into another."

"A dream, eh?" Digby took a step toward the edge of the fog. "Fine, then I suggest we push on through the haze and find out who this dream belongs to."

"I wouldn't do that if I were you."

Digby froze as a woman's voice came from just beyond the haze. Parker had the opposite reaction, leaping four feet in the air only to fall on the floor when she landed.

After processing the information that they were not as alone as he thought they were, Digby raised a hand to cast a summon and send his wraith after the threat. "Show yourself!"

A moment of silence passed followed by the sound of footsteps coming closer. Digby kept his hand raised as the figure of a woman emerged from the fog.

"I have no idea how you wandered into this place, but I don't think leaving this cloud of essence that you brought with you would be good for your health." She stopped a few feet away with her arms folded and a confident smile on her face. Her clothing could only be described as appropriate, just a black vest and white dress shirt with a long apron over slacks. A green neck tie hung loosely from her neck.

The woman's seemingly uniformed appearance was disrupted by her hair, as it defied the normal spectrum similarly to Parker's. Except instead of pink, hers was green and tied back neatly.

Digby clenched his teeth, still feeling that something was off. He tried to analyze her, but the Seed apparently was unable to tell him anything, or just didn't feel like it.

Then he spotted it. The telltale detail that explained everything.

Throughout the woman's appearance, the color green seemed to be a theme. Hell, even her fingernails were painted a shade of emerald.

So why, then, were her eyes a familiar crimson?

The caretaker!

Digby didn't hesitate. Instead, he cast wraith without a second thought. The spectral form of Jack the Ripper flickered into view before streaking toward her. She didn't even try to dodge as the spell washed over her harmlessly.

"Seriously?" The woman arched an eyebrow.

"Dig, what the hell?" Parker shot him a look like he had just said something rude. "We should at least ask questions before leaping to murder."

"Yes, I would recommend that as well." The woman nodded.

"I don't need to ask questions." Digby kept his hand raised. "Look at her eyes. It's the caretaker."

"Oh." Parker jumped up and took a combat ready pose that she had probably seen in a movie.

"Relax." The caretaker held up both hands. "The Heretic Seed's magic is not compatible with this plane of existence."

"What do you mean?" Digby held his ground.

The caretaker gestured around the space. "The essence of this place is not the same as where you came from. I don't know how you managed to find your way here, but the only reason you didn't cease to exist the moment you arrived is because a cloud of your home essence flowed in with you."

"Shit." Parker ceased her combat stance and pointed to the side. "The edge of the fog is closer."

"See, she gets it." The caretaker dropped her hands to her sides. "You do not belong here, and this plane is actively trying to purge you from it. Casting that spell just now burned off a portion of the essence that you brought in with you. The more you throw magic around, the faster your existence here will be erased. Get it?"

Digby narrowed his eyes at the caretaker, debating on if he should trust her or not. Everything he knew told him not to. Then again, his gut told him he was safe. "Fine."

"Good." She let out a breath. "Now, why don't you tell me how you got here? Obviously, you're Heretics, but there shouldn't be a way for the mortal world to reach this place."

"Mortal world?" Digby's eyebrows climbed all the way up his forehead.

"Yes, that much should be easy to guess." The caretaker nodded.

Digby flicked his eyes to the pink-haired soldier beside him. "Damn it, Parker. You sent us to the land of the dead."

"Don't blame me." She shook her head furiously. "I never said I knew what I was doing."

"Wait…" Digby looked back to the caretaker. "Is this hell?"

"No."

Digby nodded. "Heaven then?"

"Sorry." The caretaker leaned from side to side. "It's a little more complicated than that."

"Of course it is." He deflated.

"Look, you don't have a lot of time here." The caretaker tapped her foot. "So let's save the earth-shattering revelations about the great beyond for later." She looked at Parker. "What's this about you casting a spell?"

"I'm a messenger class. I cast Mirror Passage to get here," Parker blurted out. "Will I be able to cast it again to get back to where we came from?"

"You should be able to as long as you don't wait too long." The caretaker arched an eyebrow. "But Mirror Passage is not a spell I have heard of. It seems the Heretic Seed can still manage a few surprises even without me."

"What do you mean, without you?" Digby eyed her. "How are you the caretaker?"

"Me?" She gestured to a metal name tag pinned to her vest. "My name is Abby. And yes, I am the caretaker of the Seed." She paused. "Or at least I used to be."

"Alright." Digby glanced to the edge of the fog, noting that the space they occupied had shrunk a little more. He winced and asked the next question he thought of as to avoid wasting valuable time. "What made you lose your place as the caretaker of the Seed?"

"I'm dead." Abby gestured to herself. "Some idiot shattered the Seed's obelisk and left my spark with nowhere to go." She gestured to her surroundings. "Hence the change in my existence."

"Oh." Digby cringed, realizing that he was the idiot she spoke of. He asked another question, hoping to keep that detail to himself. "What is that monster that took your place?"

Abby furrowed her brow. "If you came into contact with a fragment of the Seed, it should attempt to replace me by entangling with your spark. Though, that would only be a temporary fix and the result would not be a true caretaker. Nor could you access the Seed's full capabilities."

"What if I restored the Seed's obelisk?" Digby meant for the question to sound hypothetical, but it ended up sounding like a boast.

"That would be... impressive." The caretaker walked past him to slip behind the bar.

"Indeed." Digby gave her a slight bow as if to say, ta da.

"Yes, well, if the obelisk is whole again, then a caretaker would need to be selected from the sparks that had come in contact with the Seed's fragments." She grabbed a glass from beneath the counter and set it down. "I assume the both of you were among those sparks?"

"Yes, I was." Digby stepped up to the bar.

"But I wasn't," Parker added. "I was yanked in at the last second. We don't know if it was an accident or if the Seed did it on purpose. All I know is that the caretaker turned into a horrible monster and murdered everyone that was trapped in there except us."

Abby eyed her. "Your class has never existed before. I doubt the Heretic Seed did that by accident."

"Oh." Parker sounded disappointed.

"As for the caretaker turning into a monster. It probably shouldn't do that either. Though if the Seed was unable to properly choose a spark to take my place, then something must have gone wrong with whatever process you used to restore the obelisk." Abby grabbed a bottle labeled absinth and poured it into the glass.

"Well, there is still one fragment of the Seed that didn't get restored with the rest. Right, Dig?" Parker reached for the glass on the counter only for her hand to pass through it.

"I poured that for me. You are not capable of drinking anything here, remember?" Abby stared at her for a second before slapping a hand on the counter. "More importantly, why would you try to restore the obelisk without having all of it? Do you have any idea how dangerous that would be? The results could be," she gestured to herself and the room around her, "completely unpredictable."

Digby attempted to slap the counter back, looking foolish when he passed through it. "Now you listen here, we couldn't include every fragment because one of them is lodged in my heart."

She stared at him with a perfect deadpan expression. Then she looked back to Parker. "I'm starting to understand this a little." She pointed at them both. "You two aren't the brightest, are you?"

"Insulting us is not helping." Digby narrowed his eyes.

"Okay, I think I get it." She set a small spoon across her glass and placed a cube of sugar on it. "The Seed tried to pick a new caretaker but has no way to finalize the process. That's the first problem. The second is that it can't stop the process once it starts so, as it is, it can't release you."

"And that's why it sent us here?" Parker leaned to one side. "So that you can fix it."

"Not quite." Abby pulled a small eyedropper from beneath the counter and dropped water on the sugar cube resting on her glass. "I can't actually fix anything. I have no real connection with the Seed other than knowing how it works."

"So you can't help?" Digby threw up his hands as the fog around them closed in to a point where he could only see a few tables nearby. "What is the point of sending us here, then?"

"I didn't say I can't." Her eyes bulged for a second. "But what that Seed has done here is, well, insane. I can't even explain how it did it, and I was its caretaker for a few thousand years."

Parker gasped. "You're how old?"

"That's a bigger question than we have time for." Abby glanced to the end of the bar that was beginning to fade into the haze that surrounded them. She punctuated her statement by dropping the sugar cube into her glass and stirring it with the spoon that had held it. "None of this should be possible, but somehow in the Heretic Seed's broken state, it saw a possibility and threw everything it had behind it." She grabbed her glass and knocked it back. "I can't fix it. Actually, I don't think the Seed meant for you to meet me. I think it just wanted you to open a passage to this plane."

"Why?" Digby furrowed his brow glancing behind him as the haze closed in.

"Because the Seed needs you to fix the problem." Abby tapped her finger on her empty glass. "It needs you to put the last fragment back where it belongs, but you can't do that while trapped inside it. The reason you're here is this." She waved her hand around at the shrinking bubble that they existed in. "The Heretic Seed just needs to interrupt the caretaker selection so it can return you back to your body."

"And traveling here will do that?" Parker stepped closer to the bar to stay away from the edge of the fog.

"It should." Abby nodded. "If that passage spell was able to pull essence with you from the Seed, then it should do the same from here."

"And that will release us from the Seed's clutches." Digby started to understand.

"It would have to." Abby nodded. "You would be introducing a flood of incompatible essence into the Seed. It would have to stop everything it was doing to purge it. With the selection process halted, you would be released. Then you just need to put the last fragment back where it belongs to fully restore the Seed."

"Oh my god, I'm the task manager." Parker slapped a hand to her cheek. "The Seed literally pulled me in here to force quit a task that stopped responding."

"What?" Digby looked at her sideways.

Her eyes widened. "It needs us to turn it off and on again."

"Wait, wait, wait." Digby waved a hand back and forth. "But if I remove my fragment and put it back into the obelisk, what will happen to me?"

"You will become the new caretaker," Abby responded matter-of-factly.

Digby's mind flashed back to the copy of himself that had normally appeared to represent the Seed. If he was understanding things, that entity was an incomplete caretaker, and this soul was shared between it and his body. If he removed the shard, what did that mean for him? He shook his head at the idea. "But what will happen to the me that exists in the world?"

"Your spark would become the new caretaker of the Heretic Seed and your body should continue to exist separately. So nothing significant would change." She shrugged. "I think."

"What do you mean, you think?" He fought the urge to slap the immaterial counter, knowing that doing so would only make him look stupid. "It can't possibly be alright for me to walk around without a soul."

"I haven't been the caretaker for eight hundred years. I'm rusty." She threw up her hands. "And everything about this situation is in uncharted waters. Don't even get me started on this messenger stuff. I don't know what the Seed is leveraging to get that done, but this Mirror Passage spell is not something within its power."

"That's not good." Parker took a step back only to jump forward again when the edge of the fog closed in behind her. "Crap, we have to go."

"Alright, alright." Digby stepped closer to the mirror they had arrived through until he was standing halfway inside the bar's counter top. His mind raced, struggling to think of another question to ask before they had to leave. There was so much he didn't know. So many answers he didn't have. He cursed himself for wasting so much time. It was impossible to pick just one question. In the end he blurted something at random.

"What happened to you when you became the caretaker?"

"I gave up my physical body." Abby stood a little taller as if proud of the sacrifice.

"Dig. I'm opening a passage." Parker raised a hand to the mirror.

He ignored her and locked eyes with the caretaker of the past. "Why give up your life?"

"Someone had to." Her eyes began to well up. "The rebellion would not have survived otherwise."

"It's open." Parker grabbed hold of his shoulder as the room faded all around them.

"I'm sorry." Abby shook her head. "But you have to——"

"Not yet." Digby held his ground, feeling like he had just scratched the surface of something more important than anything else. "What rebellion? Who were you fighting?"

Abby's face drained of color as if she was in shock that he didn't already know. Then she spoke. "The Nine."

The bottom dropped out of Digby's stomach all at once. "The Nine... are real?"

Abby stared at him with crimson eyes as the fog blotted her out of sight. Her voice reached through the gloom. "You think the Nine... a myth?"

"Now, Dig!" Parker yanked him back as the Hanging Frederick Tavern faded out of sight.

The words of the caretaker of the past echoed through his mind as he fell into the passage.

You think the Nine... a myth?

He was a fool indeed.

He hadn't even considered the possibility.

It was just too much.

Everything was about to change.

CHAPTER FORTY-ONE

Becca sprinted down the corridor of the cargo ship that had apparently housed a nuclear warhead before the world ended. Her cloak flapped through the air behind her, giving only glimpses of the bright red lining within.

Alex should have been getting the nuke out of the cargo hold any minute. She glanced back at Malcolm as he kept pace behind her. They were almost done with their half of the job as well, leaving them a couple charges left to set. Once they were finished, the explosives would poke enough holes into the ship's hull to sink it into the depths where it would take Autem months to find it.

"Not long now." Becca slowed to a stop at the next hatch.

"What was that?" Malcolm did the same.

"Nothing. Just counting how many stops we have left." She patted the near empty duffle bag she wore slung over her shoulder.

"Should be just two charges left to set. Then we can send this boat straight to hell." He walked past her and peeked through a small, round window embedded in the hatch. "Shit."

"What?" Becca pushed forward.

"See for yourself." He got out of the way.

There had been little opposition so far as they traveled the corridors, just a few dormant revenants here and there. They didn't even need to kill them. Becca had just kept them concealed and they walked right by. Looking through the darkened window, though, showed her their first real problem.

A few dozen eyes reflected in the dark.

Revenant Lightwalker, uncommon, hostile.

"Shit is right. They're all Lightwalkers." She pulled away from the window as a few revenants' attention found her. "The corridor is about fifty feet long and packed with them."

Malcolm leaned against the wall. "I don't like the odds of fighting our way through or trying to stealth our way past them in such close quarters."

"Same. Probably best to err on the side of caution." Becca tapped a hand on the locking wheel that held the hatch shut. "I'm just glad these things don't know how to open doors. This thing isn't even locked."

"I can agree with that." Malcolm nodded. "Think you can find us a way around?"

Becca cast her Cartography spell to map out the corridors that weren't blocked by a door. The image of a network of corridors stretched out in the air, only visible to her. She debated keeping it secret to make sure that she was the only one who knew the path just in case Malcolm did have something up his sleeve. The thought reminded her of everything that had gone wrong recently. Bancroft's men had plenty of opportunity to make a move already. If she had learned anything, it was that she had to start trusting people eventually.

Becca cast Waking Dream to show the map to Malcolm as well.

"You really do come in handy." He traced his finger through the image finding a passage further down. The detour would let them bypass the corridor of Lightwalkers, though it would also take them out of their way by a wide margin.

"Right here will work." He nodded. "And it's definitely safer."

"Okay, then." She canceled the spell to close the map.

"Lead on." Malcolm gestured for her to go first.

The detour took them up a level and then back down. Fortunately, it also brought them past one of the two remaining sites where they needed to place a charge. Once it was set, they circled back and headed toward their original destination. They crossed paths with a pair of dormant revenants on the way but her newly ranked up Icicle spell handled them easily enough. She frowned at the lack of experience.

For once it didn't matter who killed them. The inactive creatures just weren't worth anything.

Maybe they should have fought their way through that corridor of Lightwalkers after all. At least that would have got her close to another level. She immediately regretted the thought when they reached the other end of the corridor that they had taken the detour to avoid. The hatch was closed at that end as well, trapping the revenants within. Though, unlike the other side which could be opened easily by spinning the locking wheel, this side had a wrench shoved into the mechanism to ensure that it couldn't be opened from within.

"Damn, the ship's crew must have lured the Lightwalkers into the corridor and trapped them inside." Malcolm approached the wrench, making a point not to touch it.

"Yeah." Becca placed her hand on the hatch. "I can only imagine what went on here. It seems like the crew put up a good fight."

"Didn't do them any good in the end. Kind of pisses me off. Most of them were civilians, with just a few guys from Skyline. My guess is Autem didn't even bother prepping them for what might happen." Malcolm blew out a sigh that ended in a growl, then he shook his head and headed down the hall toward the stairwell where they needed to place the last charge. "Come on, let's get this done so we can sink this floating tomb and head back to Vegas."

Becca nodded and followed along.

According to the schematic she'd found, the stairway ran up against the front hull of the ship. There was something unsettling about the fact that they had placed enough C4 throughout the vessel to poke two dozen holes in it. Becca reached in her duffle to retrieve the detonator. It was just a simple stick with an activation toggle and a trigger. She made a point to hang onto the device. Sure, she had been making an effort to be more trusting but there was no way she was going to let Malcolm hold it. Not until she and everyone else were safely outside.

Opening the next hatch, she found that her schematic was slightly different than the actual ship. Instead of a stairwell, the hatch simply led to a maintenance shaft. It traveled down about three levels into a darkened space below. A ladder lined the wall.

Malcolm cracked a glow stick and tossed it in to light the way. "Looks clear." He breathed a relieved sigh. "No need for both of us to climb all the way down there." The knight held out his hand and stepped to the ladder. "Pass me the last charge and I'll get it placed while you keep an eye out up here."

"Sure." She handed him the last block of C4.

"Be right back." Malcolm carefully stepped down onto the ladder and began to climb down. He'd only made it a few rungs before the hairs on Becca's neck stood on end.

"What?" She spun around, unsure what she had even picked up. There hadn't been a sound. It was almost like she'd sensed a change in temperature. Like a warm body was sneaking up on her. It could only be one thing.

A sensebreaker.

Becca cast Reveal, glad for the Cloak of Steel that ensured her safety. Her jaw dropped as her vision flickered into grayscale and highlighted a figure directly in front of her.

It wasn't a sensebreaker.

No, it was so much worse.

Heretic, level 29 illusionist, hostile.

Panic flooded Becca's mind as a Conceal spell unraveled to reveal Ducky, the illusionist that she had been working with for the last week. Before she could react, something yanked on the back of her cloak. Nearly falling, her hand snapped out to catch the railing as she glanced back to see Malcolm pulling on the bottom of the garment with everything he had.

"I fucking knew it!" Her gut screamed, 'I told you so.'

She had been right all along.

The. Whole. Damn. Time.

Ducky planted a boot to her chest and shoved. The combined effort of him and Malcolm launched her over the edge. Time seemed to slow as she fell past the traitorous knight.

The smirk on his face was infuriating.

Becca hit the bottom with a solid thud, her cloak's barrier taking the impact. She immediately fired off an Icicle, trying to hit Malcolm before he could get out of the way. The frozen spike shattered against a barrier of his own, showering the air in glittering fragments. He must have cast it when her back was turned.

"Nice try." He climbed up. "I'm surprised that fall didn't knock you out."

"I'm tougher than I look, you ass!" She shoved herself back up and reached for the ladder, leaving out the fact that her cloak made her almost indestructible.

"We'll see." He vanished over the edge just before throwing something down.

Becca's eyes bulged as she recognized the block of plastic explosive that she had handed him just a moment before. Her mind raced, passing through a moment of panic before she remembered that she had the detonator. She slapped her hand to her belt as the charge tumbled down.

"No!" Her hand came up empty.

Malcolm must have snatched it when he grabbed her. The C4 hit the floor at the base of the ladder. The status light on the top of the block lit up.

"Shit!" Becca leapt with everything she had, grabbing on to the ladder over a dozen feet up.

The sound of the hatch closing above met her ears.

There was no escape.

Then everything went white.

———

Alex fell against the ladder that led to the upper walkway of the cargo hold as explosions rocked the ship. His head hit one of the metal rungs before he toppled backward.

"What the hell happened?" His head spun.

"The charges went off early." Mason struggled to keep the warhead steady as one of the other Heretics from Vegas hoisted the bomb up to the walk way.

Alex started to shout to Louis but failed to get a word out before one of the dormant revenants in the cargo hold reached for his head. He glanced to the side, realizing he'd fallen halfway out of the perimeter of his warding rods. He cast Fireball and lobbed it at the foe without looking. It splashed against the creature's chest, setting the revenant alight. It screamed and shrank away, claiming a lock of blue hair from his head in the process. He cast Purify Water on one of his flasks just in case he or Mason got bit. Then he crab-walked his way back into the safe area.

"What happened?" Alex rushed back to the ladder as everyone on the walkway hoisted the warhead up to the top.

"We need to hurry and get the nuke to the kestrels," Louis shouted as he took over for one of the other Heretics to help carry the warhead.

"Forget about the stupid bomb. We need to find Becca. She could be hurt." Mason climbed up to the walkway as Alex followed close behind.

"Yeah, and we need to take a count of the other Heretics to make sure none of them were caught in the blasts." Alex reached the walkway just as Louis and Nat set down the warhead in the corridor outside. Both of Bancroft's men drew their swords as soon as their hands were free.

"Wait! No!" Alex's mind screeched to a halt as both of them turned their blades on a pair of Vegas's Heretics that were standing on the walkway. Blood sprayed from the unsuspecting men as Louis and Nat cut them down. Their bodies fell over the rail where the revenants below moved in for the meal.

"No!" Mason reached for his sword.

"You bastards." Alex did the same.

That was when something hard pressed up against his forehead.

Alex froze, dead in his tracks as a Conceal spell unraveled, leaving Roland standing directly in front of him. A revolver was held in his hand. The sight of the weapon threw him for a loop. It had been a while since anyone had tried to hurt him with something so mundane as a firearm.

Roland grinned and squeezed the trigger.

Alex willed his magic to cast Barrier as the cylinder began to turn. A gunshot shattered the air.

Then there was nothing.

CHAPTER FORTY-TWO

"Where am I!" Digby sat up in a dark room.

For a moment, he wasn't sure where he was. It was only minutes ago that he was somewhere in the realm of the dead, having a conversation with the original caretaker of the Seed. After running out of time there, Parker had pulled him through a Mirror Passage to return to the realm where he'd been trapped. A few seconds later, the world within the Seed had vanished.

Apparently bringing a cloud of incompatible essence back into the Seed's realm really was enough to release them back to their bodies in the real world.

"Parker?"

The messenger didn't answer.

"They must be keeping her someplace else." Digby felt the familiar texture of a felt poker table beneath him. He really was back in Vegas.

"Finally."

Digby blew out a relieved sigh and rolled to the side.

"Gah!"

He fell to the carpet, having not realized that he had been laying on the edge of the table.

"Glad no one was here to see that." Digby pushed himself up, unsure what time of day it was. With the difference in how time flowed in the Seed, there was no way to know. Hell, he could have been there for years for all he knew.

Stumbling over to the wall, he found a light switch. He flicked it on and found himself in some kind of storage room. Shelves of supplies lined one wall. The poker table he'd been laying on had been shoved against the other side. Rebecca or Alex must have moved him from where he'd passed out. Taking a step, he realized he was still dressed in the clothes that he'd been wearing from before he'd gone on his little trip into the Seed. The expensive slacks, dress shirt, and vest were considerably wrinkled but that was about it. Even better, he was still wearing his coat and had both shoes. He glanced around the room, finding his staff leaning against the wall.

"Could have used you back there in the Seed's realm." He snatched the staff up, then checked his attributes.

STATUS
Name: Digby Graves
Race: Zombie
Heretic Class: Necromancer
Mana: 362 / 362
Mana Composition: Pure
Current Level: 37 (9,578 experience to next level.)

ATTRIBUTES
Constitution: 35
Defense: 41
Strength: 39
Dexterity: 39
Agility: 44
Intelligence: 63
Perception: 48
Will: 49

AILMENTS
Deceased

Satisfied that he had both kept the levels he'd earned within the Seed and regained the extra fifty mana that the Goblin King's pauldron provided, he checked his void contents.

VOID RESOURCES
Sinew: 31
Flesh: 15
Bone: 28
Viscera: 15
Heart: 33
Mind: 27

"Much better." He'd been struggling so much just to find scraps back in the Seed's immaterial realm, so it was a relief to once again have plenty to work with. He double checked his minions as well, finding Tavern right where they should be. Asher was listed along with his coven.

That was when he noticed the status ailments.

Rebecca: MP 384/384, UNCONCIOUS
Alex: MP 325/325, UNCONCIOUS/SILENCED

"What?" He snapped his head toward the door. "What the hell is going on?"

If he didn't know any better, he'd say they were in the middle of a fight. He held still for a moment and listened to his surroundings.

"Hmm, no gunfire or screaming."

Maybe the conflict was elsewhere. The thought sent a wave of dread rolling through his body. What if Autem had found them somewhere out there in the world while they were gathering resources for the fight ahead of them? "I have to get moving."

Rushing toward the door, Digby sent a mental call across his bond with Asher. The deceased raven responded with an excited feeling, clearly overjoyed that he'd woken up.

You've returned.

Digby sent a thought back. *Indeed. Where are Rebecca and Alex?*

Asher responded calmly, *Away.*

Very well. Digby shoved through the door into the hall of one of the guest floors. "Now where the hell is Bancroft?"

That was when the last person he expected answered.

"He was down in the dining area last time I saw him." Hawk simply appeared in the hallway in front of him.

"Gah!" Digby leapt backward and raised his staff, nearly jabbing the boy with the butt of the weapon on instinct. "Where the devil did you manifest from?"

Hawk stood a little taller. "Analyze me."

Digby lowered his staff and did so.

Heretic, level 15 Rogue.

Digby's jaw dropped. "You've grown stronger."

"Damn right I have." The boy slapped a hand to his chest. "Just got back from a patrol. I got plenty of XP with Bancroft's mercs away. Just hit fifteen and got Conceal. So you know, I'm gonna use it."

"Yes, I see that." Digby shook off the subject. "But more importantly—" He ran out of words when Hawk rushed forward and punched him in the side.

"More importantly, where the fuck have you been? I was so freaked out that you wouldn't wake up." Hawk finished his attack with a hug.

"Yes." Digby awkwardly patted the boy on the back, unsure what else to do. "It is a long story that will have to wait. You mentioned that Rebecca and Alex are away. Where are they now?"

"No idea, just that they and most of our Heretics are on some mission." Hawk started walking. "Bancroft knows the rest. You know, because he's not twelve. And people tell him things."

"Good, take me to him." Digby followed. "From what I am seeing on my HUD, they may be in danger."

"What?" Hawk's tone grew serious in an instant.

Digby nodded. "Their mana looks full, but they both have status ailments that concern me. It looks like they have been captured or something."

Parker rushed in the hallway a second later, wearing a set of those green garments that Digby had seen Lana wear. "Dig!"

Digby cringed the moment he saw her. "You look like death."

The pink haired woman did indeed resemble a corpse.

She punched him straight in the stomach. "I know, you ass. Lana has been keeping me alive with fluids and magic, and I've leveled up a ton without eating anything. I am hungry enough to eat you, god damn it. Now, where is everyone? I woke up dressed like this, and haven't seen anyone important on my way down here. I don't even have any underwear."

"That is more information than I require." Digby ignored her attack and kept walking.

"We're going to find Bancroft," Hawk added.

Parker growled to herself, clearly stressed by the situation. She stomped down the hall behind them without any further argument. Digby filled her in with what he saw on his HUD on the way. The only thing she had been able to tell him was that the time was midafternoon since she could see the sun outside the window where she was being kept.

Of course, there was still the question of completing the Seed's restoration, but everyone agreed that Rebecca and Alex came first. It wasn't long before Digby burst onto the casino floor.

He nearly tripped over his own feet the moment he did.

"How long have I been gone?"

Last he'd seen, they had been using a small portion of the casino as a communal space while lighting it with the bare minimum to save on fuel. Now, though, it was barely recognizable. The entire place shined brighter than anything he'd ever seen. Not only that, but they had opened up more of the floor. Hell, they had even turned on the fountains. It was incredible.

Even more shocking was the people.

Sweeping his vision across the space, Digby estimated that there were at least a thousand going about their business. There had only been a couple hundred back when he'd entered the Seed.

Where did they all come from?

"It's been about two weeks." Hawk shrugged. "Becca negotiated things with a group of survivors that were hiding out in the

Hoover Dam. We took in most of their people, and they set us up with electricity."

Digby shook off his shock and kept going. He could process things later. There wasn't time to get caught up. Not when his coven was in danger. He tried his best to ignore the stares he got from nearly everyone around him. Clearly his reputation had preceded him.

The fact that he was an angry-looking man with white hair and a staff was sure to make it clear to the newcomers who he was. From the fearful expressions on many of their faces, they were well aware of his zombified condition. His perception wasn't as powerful as Rebecca's, but even with what he had, he could make out the whispers.

"Oh my god, that's him."

"He's a zombie?"

"How many people has he killed?"

"How many people has he eaten?"

They kept coming, though he did notice a few of the original survivors that had been with him since the beginning in the mix. Their presence had an impact on the narrative as well.

"He saved you from what?"

"He killed how many revenants?"

"He almost looks human."

Digby ignored the onlookers and stomped his way toward the establishment that they had been using as a dining area. Hawk and Parker struggled to keep up. He stopped short when he found the place empty.

"They moved the dining area." Hawk caught up. "We needed someplace bigger."

"'Cause of all the people," Parker assumed as she brought up the rear.

Digby rolled his eyes. "Gee, thank you for telling me sooner."

"You got too far ahead," he defended before shaking his head and marching off in the other direction. "We don't have time to argue. My sister is in trouble."

"Sister?" Digby followed.

"Yeah, Becca." Hawk headed toward one of the larger spaces

in the casino that they hadn't been using. "Apparently, I lived with her parents before the world ended."

"Her parents? The ones that abandoned her?" Parker asked.

Hawk stopped for a second. "No, they were…" He trailed off. "It's a long story. I'll let Becca tell it."

"Alright." Digby let that little revelation fade into the back of his mind as he walked over a bridge that passed over a decorative canal that separated part of the casino. His mind flashed back to his time in the disjointed realm of the Seed. The inclusion of the feature looked out of place within the interior of a building, like whoever had put it there had simply forgotten that rivers were supposed to be outside. Hell, there were even boats in it. Clearly the space was built to resemble an exterior street. Even the ceiling was painted to look like the sky.

Following Hawk, Digby reached an open area filled with tables. Many of the casino's inhabitants populated the space. Some ate sizable meals, while others clearly had less. None of them looked starved but still, Digby arched an eyebrow at the inconsistency.

"Now, where is Bancroft?" He slammed the butt of his staff down hard on the opulent tile floor, causing anyone that wasn't already looking at him to turn in his direction.

"Graves?" Bancroft sat, looking up at the sound along with everyone else, his mouth hanging open. In front of him lay a ledger of some sort and a pile of poker chips. From the look on the man's face, it was clear he wasn't expecting to see him so soon.

"Indeed. I have returned." Digby approached and leaned forward to place his free hand on the edge of the table. "Now where are Rebecca and Alex?"

Bancroft furrowed his brow and closed the ledger that he was writing in. "They are on a mission."

"I know that much." Digby eyed the man. "But why is Becky unconscious and why is Alex unconscious and silenced? Just who are they fighting out there?"

"Yeah, the last time I checked, revenants couldn't silence anyone," Parker chimed in to back him up.

"Yes, that was more your people's kind of thing." Digby

narrowed his eyes at the man. "And I might add that you look a little too comfortable here."

Hawk's face grew serious. "Start talking."

"Yes. Start explaining, Charles." Digby leaned into the boy's attempt at intimidation.

Bancroft hesitated a moment before glancing around the room. Then stood up and began to gather his things, making a point of carefully transferring the poker chips into a bag. "Graves, I realize you are concerned and that is understandable. However, we have a lot of new citizens of this city, and you are causing a scene. We should take this conversation somewhere less public. I know it is hard to sit back while your people are in danger, but that is part of being a leader. Besides, their mission has taken them several hours away and they have both of our kestrels. It would be nightfall by the time you reached them and by then the operation would be over. There is nothing you can do for them right now. Not only that, but the fact that your people are unconscious and not dead would have to mean that my men have intervened in some way to keep them alive despite whatever injury they have suffered. I'm sure if you wait, those ailments will resolve themselves."

"That sounds awfully convenient." Digby glared at him.

"I hope you aren't seriously thinking that I had something to do with your people's status." He let out a very business-like cackle, as if Digby would be a fool for even thinking it.

"Did you?" Digby slapped a handful of poker chips out of his hand to throw him off balance.

Anger flashed across Bancroft's face as a strange shimmer passed over the chips. It was clearly magical in nature. That was when Elenore and Deuce rushed in. Someone must have told them he was back. Sax wandered in behind them. They punched through the crowd that had gathered, but didn't interrupt.

Digby glanced at the people watching then back to the poker chips on the floor as they shimmered. "What the devil is that?"

"That was a few hundred dollars' worth of currency that you just slapped to the floor." Bancroft went to pick them up in a huff.

"Currency?" Digby furrowed his brow as the bizarre statement caught him off guard. "We are in the middle of a war with an organization that wishes to destroy us. What on earth do we need currency for?"

Bancroft glanced from him to the chips on the floor, then to the people staring at their exchange. "We need a foundation on which to build a future. And this is not the time or place to discuss such things."

"Wait, shit, does that mean I need to get a job?" Parker started to panic a little.

"You have a job. You are a soldier." Bancroft finished picking up the poker chips. "And yes, the people here will need to work from here on out."

Digby looked around the room at the survivors in the dining area, connecting the dots of the inconsistency that he'd noticed earlier. A memory of going hungry as a peasant back in his time rose to the surface of his mind.

"Are you insane?" Digby slapped the chips away again. "This is not Skyline. You can't simply return to your way of doing things. A horde needs food."

"Fine, if you want to do this now in front of everyone, I won't stop you." Bancroft pushed back. "You are right the people need food, but the difference here is that these people are not a horde of the dead."

"People, horde, it's all the same." Digby waved a hand back and forth, only realizing how his words might have made him sound after they had spilled from his mouth. The gasps of onlookers confirmed it. Digby cringed.

"Umm, maybe nix calling human beings a horde." Parker gave him the universal sign for stop talking by swiping a hand back and forth in front of her throat.

Digby shook his head at the misunderstanding, noticing that many of the onlookers tensed up. He wasn't sure what Bancroft was trying to do by making him look bad, considering he could just tell Tavern to shut him up, but then again, ordering the man's skeleton around would only make him look worse.

Unless that was Bancroft's plan.

The conniving snake must have been trying to give him enough rope to hang himself with. Without Rebecca and Alex around, then there would be no one to defend him. Depending on how bad he put his foot in his mouth, the rest of the city would burn him at the stake all on their own.

Digby suppressed the urge to shout. He had come too far to fall for that. Not only that, but he understood the people of Vegas better than Skyline's ex-commander. He was sure of it. Besides, now that he understood Bancroft's plan, he could set a trap of his own. With that in mind, he threw out the bait.

"Don't be ridiculous, Charles. There's little difference between a horde and people."

Bancroft jumped on the opportunity. "I don't expect a zombie like you to understand, but——"

"But nothing." Digby raised his staff and slammed it down again, this time raising his voice to make sure that everyone could hear him. "My point is that a leader is only as good as those that support them. This is as true for lords as it is for necromancers. I realize that this may be my undead perspective, but you don't build a future on the backs of the starving, be they live or dead."

At that, the people around them relaxed.

There was little point in pretending to be human. That would only be a lie. No, if he wanted to win over the people, he had to be honest for once.

Digby took the moment to earn some extra points. "There is a difference between asking people to follow you toward a common goal and obligating them through a system of inequality." He kept the sacrifices that Sybil and Henwick had made back in the Seed in his mind. "I don't claim to be worthy to stand at the top of this city, nor do I even want to, but at least I understand that a leader must earn their place here and I dare say that you have not done so."

With that, he actually noticed some people around him nodding. Bancroft must have been taking advantage of his absence a little too much while he was away.

That was when the last person he thought would show up to help appeared in the entrance.

"Mister Graves?"

Clint, the zombified necromancer that Autem created, stood at the entrance to the space with a garbage sack in his hand. At first, Digby barely recognized him. The zombie looked much more stable than he had the last time he had seen him.

Flying in above him was Asher.

"Mister Graves!" Clint broke into a jog, rushing across the casino floor. "Mister Graves!" Several people got out of his way as he ran, which was probably wise considering his habit of snapping at the living.

"Okay, slow down." Parker walked toward him as he approached, making sure to keep her hands to herself.

Clint bowed his head, clearly looking away as to not be tempted to take a bite.

Looks like he has come a long way.

Asher flapped to Digby's shoulder and gave a nod in agreement.

Clint has done well.

Bancroft didn't seem to agree. "What are you doing, Clint? We spoke about this. You need to stay away from the living."

"I know, I know, but—" The zombie lowered his head, avoiding eye contact to resemble his previous demeanor a bit more.

"But nothing, you have to understand that your presence is a health risk." Bancroft tried to take the garbage sack from him, but he pulled it away.

"Hear him out." Digby held up a hand, unsure what the zombie had thought so important. "He is a zombie master, and what he needs is support, not condemnation."

Clint made things more complicated by reaching into the bag and pulling out a skull covered in gold. "I found her in a dumpster a little way down the strip while I was gathering minions. Someone has tampered with the runes that Alex engraved to keep her spell active."

"Yes, I was almost murdered." Kristen's voice came from the skull. "Again."

"Engraved?" Digby looked over the gold covered surface, finding a series of symbols carved into the metal. Some of them had been scratched beyond recognition. "What is the meaning of this?"

"Alex has been experimenting with the runes you guys brought back from Autem." Hawk pulled a bundle of warding rods from his pocket. "He's been making some cool stuff. He was able to do something to the skull to keep the Talking Corpse spell going without recasting."

"And someone sabotaged the engravings?" Parker examined the skull next to Digby.

"Yes." Clint placed the skull down on the table so they could see better without him holding it. He stepped away from anyone living, probably just to be safe. "The Talking Corpse spell had nearly run out when I found her. I refreshed it just in time."

"Who would try to murder an already deceased seer?" Digby glared at Bancroft as accusingly as he could.

"Don't look at me." He placed a hand on his chest. "You can ask Tavern if you don't trust me."

Digby eyed him but refrained from asking his minion in front of everyone. Clearly it was a trap. Besides, Bancroft would never have left a loose end like that open. If he had something to do with what was going on, then he must have found a way to hide things from Tavern.

"Okay, who did, then?" Parker ran a hand over the scratched runes on the skull's surface.

"She wouldn't tell me." Clint shrugged.

"Why the hell not?" Digby picked up the skull and stared into the hollows of Kristen's sockets.

"Because I don't feel like it," the skull responded, sounding a little unsure.

"Well too bad, you have to answer me remember?" Digby shook the skull. "Who did this to you?"

"Alright, fine. You twisted my arm. Oh wait, I don't have those anymore." She sighed. "It was Malcolm."

"Your knight did this?" Digby snapped his attention back to Bancroft.

"I have no idea why he would." The man shrugged, sounding sincere.

"You expect me to believe that?" Digby shook the skull at the man.

"Again, you don't have to trust me, you just have to ask Tavern. I have given no such order." Bancroft shook his head.

Digby let his stare linger on the man for a moment before raising Kristen's skull up to his face. "Alright, why did Malcolm do this, and does this have anything to do with my coven being in danger?"

"I don't know why." She took a curt tone. "And I don't know if this has something to do with Alex."

"Well that isn't helpful." Digby rolled his eyes, ignoring the fact that everyone in the area was now watching the exchange intently. "You must know something."

"I don't. I would have to answer you if I did. Remember?" Kristen fell silent.

Bancroft continued to gather his things. "We will have to speak with Malcolm to find out more. There is always the chance that there is a reasonable explanation. I certainly can't explain him going rogue."

That was when Kristen spoke up without being asked a question. "Wait."

"Yes?" Digby arched an eyebrow at the fact that she hadn't insulted him or complained about something.

"I don't know anything." She hesitated for a long moment. " But if you asked me something else, I might."

"What the devil does that mean?" Digby stared at the skull.

She remained silent.

He shook her and repeated his question. "What the devil does that mean?"

"It means figure it out, you deceased moron!" she shouted back.

"No, you tell me, you deceased irritation!" He shook her again, this time with both hands for added leverage.

"Dude, you're being too direct, just ask what she thinks Malcolm is up to." Parker interrupted the idiotic argument.

"Oh." He settled down. "Why do you think Malcolm tried to kill you?"

"Whoa…" Tavern suddenly interjected, speaking from Bancroft's mouth on their own.

The crowd gasped at the deathly tinge that filled the man's voice.

"My bad, brah. But this dude just clenched his whole ass," Tavern explained as eloquently as they could.

Digby snapped his vision to the dude in question. Other than Tavern's comment, Bancroft looked calm, or at least he did before Kristen started talking again.

"It was Bancroft."

"What? I did no such thing." He swept a hand through the air. "How could I?"

"You wouldn't have to." Kristen began to spill information like a dam had burst. "Might I remind you, I was a seer. I may be dead, but I still see things and know enough to put it all together. Even if it is just a theory. The fact that you had prepared a team of mercenaries just in case you ever found yourself on Henwick's bad side says it all. If you went to such lengths, then you would almost certainly have a way to signal your intent to your men in a way that a moron like Tavern wouldn't notice."

"Hey," Bancroft's possessed skeleton complained.

"Oh please." Kristen let out a ghostly huff. "You are the collective remnants of a fraternity that clearly had less than five brain cells to share between them which has left you unable to focus on anything but drinking. It would not be difficult for Charles to slip something past you."

"Eh, that's fair." Tavern shrugged using Bancroft's shoulders. The gesture made the man look ridiculous, considering the horrified expression on his face.

Kristen continued her accusation. "If we accept that Bancroft could have easily signaled his men to eliminate me, then the motive is easy enough to figure out. If he had an intent to make a play for control of this city and the Heretic Seed, then I'm sure he would be concerned about the amount of time I have been spending with Alex. I may not have cooperated with the artificer, but he has gleaned enough information from our interactions to make some impressive advancements in the runecraft technology that he has been experimenting with. That would be enough for someone like Bancroft to question my loyalty. That would make me a risk. And for as long as I have known him, he has not been one to leave things to chance."

"Those are just your assumptions." Bancroft took a step away from the skull.

"That may be, but it still fits our current situation." She didn't let up. "If you intended to eliminate Graves here, then the first thing you would do is remove anyone that could stand against you. Then all you would have to do is make sure Alex and Rebecca expire while on a mission and have your men dispose of Graves's body afterward. With the necromancer gone from this world, your skeleton would have no one to give them orders. You would be free."

Anger bubbled in Digby's chest at how plausible the deceased seer's theory was. It was immediately replaced by an overwhelming dread. "I have to get to them."

"What?" Parker snapped her head to him.

"If what she says is right, then Rebecca and Alex are really in danger. We have to get to them as soon as possible or they might not survive." He turned abruptly, leaving Bancroft on his own.

It was likely that Kristen knew what she was talking about, meaning that his coven was up against an entire squad of Heretics close to their level. Even if Kristen was wrong, he couldn't take the chance. There simply wasn't time to do anything about Bancroft.

Hawk followed after him, clearly concerned as well. Parker brought up the rear.

"But what about Charles?" Kristen asked as he held her at his side.

Digby stopped for a moment and looked back, finally feeling confident that the people watching would understand his methods. "Tavern, take Bancroft upstairs and don't let him leave his room. Stop him any way you can if he tries to escape or use magic."

"Got it, boss." The infernal spirit spoke from Bancroft's mouth as his body started walking toward the stairs.

Anger flooded the man's face. "But you can't prove I had anything to do—"

Digby stabbed a finger in his direction. "I will deal with you when I return."

Asher let out a caw to back him up.

With that, Digby stormed off. "Now, how do we get to my coven without a kestrel?"

Hawk jogged to catch up. "I have an idea."

"Perfect. Lead on, then." Digby didn't even question the boy as he led him into the parking garage and to what looked like a car covered in a tarp.

Parker cocked her head to one side. "Aren't Alex and Becca on a boat?"

Hawk answered her by yanking off the tarp.

Digby nearly dropped Kristen's skull. Clearly his apprentice had been busy. "Alright, please tell me Alex left some sort of operating manual."

CHAPTER FORTY-THREE

Mason gasped in pain as he pressed his hand over his gut.

Blood trickled through his fingers.

He rolled to the side to look down into the cargo area from where he lay on the walkway above.

Alex lay on the floor near the edge of the area where he'd set up the warding rods. One of his eyes was gone, leaving a gaping hole in its place. Mason gasped, his abdomen protesting with a jolt of pain as he realized that Alex was still breathing. That rogue, Roland, had shot the artificer right in the face before turning his revolver on Mason to fire a round into his stomach. After that, the mercs backed out through the door. The sounds of combat from the hallway outside followed. It was a slaughter. The Heretics that they had brought with them from Vegas didn't stand a chance. For a brief moment, he had heard Easton cry out before Roland closed the door of the cargo hold. After that, all he had heard was muffled violence. Everyone they had brought with them was dead.

His first thought was Becca. She hadn't been in the fight in the hallway, but there was no way to know if she was okay.

His eyes focused on the spot where his mana should have appeared.

It was gone.

"H-how?" He sucked in a breath, unsure what had just happened. It must have been the bullet. He'd been given a crash course in magic just after becoming a Heretic and he'd learned about status ailments. There had to be some enchantment on the bullet that silenced him.

None of that mattered now.

He had to move.

Alex was still alive and he probably wasn't going to stay that way.

God damn it!

Mason reached for the railing of the walkway and yanked himself up. His insides felt like they were full of broken glass but he got to his feet. He pushed off the wall and made his way to the ladder. On his way, he touched the door.

It was hot.

Shit!

They must have welded the lock shut. He pushed the concern away and tried to place his foot on the ladder. He slipped almost immediately, falling a few rungs before catching himself. It hurt like no other pain he'd felt. A moment later, he slipped again, this time falling the rest of the way down. He hit the floor in a crumpled mess, but forced himself to get back to his feet. All he could manage was climbing to his hands and knees.

From there he crawled toward Alex. A trail of blood mixed with sweat from his forehead followed him.

The dormant revenants hiding around the edges of the room were getting brave. Beginning to reach for Alex. Mason couldn't be sure, but one of the artificer's legs might have been poking out of the wards.

"Don't you dare die."

With a labored grunt, he slapped a hand down on the floor to try and get himself up. Pain echoed through his gut like a shotgun blast of nails. He pushed off, getting a foot under him.

The revenants crept closer to Alex.

"Get away from him!" Mason kicked off, feeling like his intestines were being torn to shreds. He snapped his sword from its sheath and slammed it into the shoulder of the closest threat, fumbling the grip in the process. There wasn't enough force in the blow to kill the creature, but the impact knocked it over. "Thank god it's dormant."

The sword clattered to the floor as he fell to his knees beside Alex. Several more revenants closed in, smelling blood in the water. Abandoning his weapon, he grabbed hold of the artificer's arm and dragged him backward. If it wasn't for the enhanced stats from the levels he'd gained, he would never have been able to budge him. As it was, he felt like the guy weighed a ton and a half.

"I am not letting you die." Mason let out a long growl. "Becca would kill me."

He tried not to think about Easton and the other Heretics that they had brought with them. Every time he did, a sharp pang of shame stabbed at his chest. They weren't prepared to fight other magic users and he was supposed to lead them.

A revenant reached out for Alex's leg, but Mason pulled harder. The artificer's boot passed the edge of the warding rod's perimeter just in time.

Mason glared at the creatures as the cargo ship groaned around them. He couldn't be sure, but the floor seemed to be tilting slightly. "Shit, this place is sinking." He placed his hand on Alex's chest to check if he was still breathing.

He was, barely.

"Come on, you've got to wake up." Mason patted the artificer's cheek several times, noticing that there was no exit wound on the back of his head.

That was when Alex responded with a whisper.

"Flask." He accompanied the word with a weak gesture toward one of his pouches.

Mason's eyes widened. Had he cast Purify Water recently? He grabbed the flask from the pouch and took a sip. The cold water splashed down his throat to dull the pain in his gut.

Yes!

They had a chance. The purified liquid wasn't going to do anything about the bullet in his stomach or the fact that he was silenced, but it could stop the bleeding. That could at least buy them some time. He pushed the flask toward Alex's mouth, but he didn't respond.

He slapped him a little harder. "Wake the hell up, damn it!"

"Wha—" The artificer's remaining eye shot open then he cried out in agony.

"I think you've been shot by a bullet that silences you. I took one in the gut too." Mason held up his flask. "I don't know how you're still alive with a bullet in your brain, but we have one enchanted flask here. It might keep you going."

Alex clutched his missing eye with one hand and downed a few mouthfuls from the flask with the other. Mason sat beside him as the wound started to fill in. It didn't have enough power to repair his eye, but it must have done enough because the artificer started to sit up. He sat quietly for a long moment before Mason spoke again.

"Do you know if Becca is alive?" he asked as soon as Alex looked somewhat stable.

"I can't see my HUD, but she's alive, I'm sure of it." He passed the flask back to Mason.

"How can you be sure?" Mason pushed the flask back. His wound was far from healed, but at least it had stopped bleeding.

"I set her up with a new cloak that no one knows about. With that, she should survive anything as long as she doesn't do something crazy. And with us silenced, Becca is more capable than the both of us. If anything, she will be the one rescuing us." He shoved the flask back to Mason. "So don't pull this alpha male shit. I know how much was in this flask and you need more than a sip."

"Fine." Mason grabbed the container and downed the remainder of its contents without pause. His face relaxed as the magic went to work, stitching the wound the rest of the way closed.

Alex took several deep breaths. "Where are Easton and the rest of the Heretics?"

Mason only shook his head.

"Damn it." Alex slammed a fist into the floor.

"I know." Mason lowered his head. "We were supposed to lead them."

"We couldn't have predicted this." Alex sighed. "Bancroft must have been planning this whole operation to get us out of the way. Probably going to have his guys to destroy Dig's body when they get back to Vegas. We have to get out of here."

"They welded the door shut." Mason pushed himself back up to his feet.

"Shit, we're going to need to find another way out before this place sinks." Alex pushed himself up as well, looking unstable.

"How long do we have before we go down with the ship?" Mason tried to sound hopeful.

"Your guess is as good as mine. Maybe a few hours." Alex looked up at the door.

"That sounds right. We didn't bring enough C4 to do any major damage. Those blasts would have just poked a bunch of holes." Mason checked his watch. It was a few hours until nightfall.

The time brought his attention back to the revenants that were gathering just outside the warding rods like they were lining up for a buffet. A dull ache echoed through his gut. Something was wrong inside him, like the bullet was pressing against something sensitive. Hopefully it wasn't anything that would kill him before the day was through.

Alex looked worse, with his eye like that.

Mason reached to the side and tore off one of his sleeves, handing it to Alex. The artificer tied it on at an angle to cover his eye.

Scanning the floor for his sword, Mason found it several feet past the growing group of revenants. Alex's weapon had fallen out of bounds as well when he'd been shot. The artificer hadn't brought another weapon, considering he relied on magic most of the time.

The angle of the floor seemed to be getting steeper and water could be heard pouring into a corridor nearby. The ship's walls creaked to remind him of the ticking clock that hung over their heads.

Either the ship would sink, or the revenants would become active when the sun went down. Both options assumed that they didn't already have internal bleeding or something else that would doom them anyway.

The sand in the hourglass trickled away.

"We might be stuck here for now." Mason pulled a pistol from his belt and checked a spare magazine. He hadn't been ready to rely entirely on magic yet. "I should have enough ammo if the revs go down easy."

Alex nodded, clearly grateful that one of them had been better prepared.

Mason's hands shook as he raised his gun. "I hope you're right about Becca being okay. She might be our only hope of getting out of here."

"I hope so too." Alex sighed.

"It would be better if Dig would wake the hell up." Mason let out an annoyed grunt.

Alex looked back at him. "You never know, he might be rushing straight here even as we speak."

CHAPTER FORTY-FOUR

"Where did you learn to drive?" Digby slammed his face against the passenger side window of a car that Parker had called a Camaro. The beefy vehicle spun out of control for the seventh time since leaving Vegas. Asher flapped her wings to stabilize herself as she slid across the dash.

"I hate everything that is happening right now." Lana clung to the back of the driver's seat as Parker struggled to get the car under control again.

"Everyone just shut up. This thing is way sensitive and doesn't even have a working speedometer." The pink-haired soldier gripped the wheel, her knuckles turning white. "I literally have no idea how fast we are going, and the braking system can't really keep up with this thing's top speed."

"Surprise, surprise, something Alex builds doesn't work as intended." The skull of Kristen the seer rolled across the floor in the tiny back seat.

Lana lost her grip on the driver's seat and fell against the side of the vehicle along with Digby. "I'm so going to hurl."

"Don't you dare," Digby snapped back. "You are far too close to me."

Lana looked to the floor of the back seat as the car spun across the desert at well over a hundred miles per hour.

"Don't throw up down here either," Kristen shouted from the floor.

"Just hang on." Parker pulled on the wheel. "I think I'm getting the hang of this."

The car began to even out.

"It's about time." Digby pushed himself off the window and settled back into his seat as the front of the car spun back in the direction they were traveling. Asher hopped into his lap.

Actually, after what Alex had done to the vehicle, calling it a car might not have been correct for the mere fact that it no longer had any wheels. In their place, a system of welded supports stretched out from the sides of the vehicle to connect to a layered section of metal plating that ran along the sides. It was all riveted together. According to Kristen, Alex had engraved a few hundred runes into the various plates that controlled and manipulated the absorption and flow of mana.

The result was a vehicle that floated three feet off the ground and seemed capable of traveling at a speed that one could only describe as insanity. It was clear that Alex had not intended for it to move that fast, since the steering became a bit unreliable at top speed. Though, considering the distance they had to travel to reach the cargo ship and the danger that his coven was in, Digby was willing to push the vehicle to its limits. At least that way they might reach everyone before nightfall. After that, there was no telling what might happen.

"Everyone okay?" Parker blew out a relieved sigh as she pressed on a pedal that realigned a system of runes beneath the hood to increase the vehicle's speed.

"I think so." Lana flopped back into her seat. She had been able to keep her lunch down, after all.

"I am still dead, but I suppose that's to be expected," Kristen responded from the floor.

"Yes, yes, woe is me." Digby waved a hand through the air.

"Oh right, no one cares," the skull responded back.

"Actually." Digby turned and reached back to grab her off the floor. "Speaking of caring, why did you tell me about Bancroft's plan?"

Kristen scoffed. "You asked, I didn't have a choice."

Digby squinted at the skull. "Yes, but you told me to ask about what you thought."

"I…" Kristen fell silent.

"Let me rephrase that." Digby stared into the hollows of her eyes. "Why did you ask me to ask you a question that would force you to tell me about Bancroft when you could have avoided it?"

"I don't know." She sounded lost.

"That isn't much of an answer." He set her down on the dash next to Asher now that the car had stopped spinning.

"Well that's all the answer I have." She let out a ghostly sigh. "I may have to tell the truth, but that doesn't always mean I know the answer."

"Maybe spending so much time with Alex showed you that we aren't so bad." Parker glanced at the skull before quickly flicking her attention back to the road to avoid losing control of the vehicle again.

"Yes, Alex does have a way of growing on you." She gave a self-satisfied chuckle. "Like a fungus."

"See, maybe you're turning over a new leaf," Lana added from the back seat.

"I'm a haunted skull, I don't think starting over is an option," she snapped back. "I'm merely an abomination like the zombie sitting in the passenger seat."

"That's not very nice." Digby folded his arms as the zombie in question.

Parker laughed. "Maybe the real friends are the monsters we met along the way. Wait, that doesn't sound—"

Her comment was interrupted as a torrent of gunfire tore through the road ahead of them.

"Shit!" The soldier spun the wheel this time, yanking it back again to keep the car under control as it turned to streak across the desert sideways. White hot bullets pelted the hood of the vehicle, just missing the driver's seat.

"The hell was that?" Lana covered her head.

Digby lowered the window and shoved his head out, the wind whipping through his hair as the car flew sideways at around a hundred and fifty miles per hour. A scan of the sky found two kestrels looping back for a second pass.

"Damn, that must be Malcolm and the rest of Bancroft's men on their way back from the ship." Digby pulled his head back in. "I suppose they can't let me live considering I still hold Tavern under my control."

"That confirms my theory at least. Bancroft is behind it all." Kristen rolled off the dash to land on the seat next to Parker. She let out a haunting gasp as soon as she landed. "My word, girl, you're hurt."

Parker winced. "I think something ricocheted off whatever Alex has replaced the engine with."

Digby's eyes bulged as he noticed a wound on her chest. She was right, there was a hole in the dash where the bullet must have come from. "How in the devil are you still driving?" Digby stared at the soldier.

"I told you, I'm getting the hang of this." She coughed a spatter of blood along with the comment.

"It went right through." Lana leaned forward. "There's an exit hole on the back of her seat. Oh shit, I think it just missed me." She shook her head. "But I can heal her."

"Yay." Parker let out a wet sounding chuckle.

Lana started casting. "We should be alright, but we are sitting ducks. Someone needs to do something about those kestrels before they shred us."

"That's probably a job for me." Digby picked up Asher and placed her in the back seat next to Lana before reaching for the window. "Just keep the car moving straight for a bit."

"Oh, sure, anything else?" Parker clung to the wheel as the wound in her chest closed.

Digby ignored the comment and shoved his head out the window.

"What are you gonna do?" Parker winced.

He pulled his head back in. "Well, with what they know about me, they're going to expect a clever ruse or plan to trick them into giving up the advantage."

"And you have a plan?" She shot him a look.

"No, I'm going to climb onto the roof and launch myself straight at them." He let out a wicked cackle. "They won't see that coming."

Parker's mouth fell open. "And you call me irresponsible."

"I know, I am horrible hypocrite." Digby shoved his head out the window again to leave her behind.

Outside, the ground rushed by in a blur. It took every bit of courage he had to climb out. Using the supports that held the engraved plates that kept the vehicle in the air for footing, Digby pushed off to reach the roof. For a moment, he was nearly blown right off by the force of the wind. He snapped his free hand onto the edge of the window and held tight as he got into a stable crouch. His coat flapped behind him as Lana reached out to pass him his staff.

He checked his mana.

MP: 362/362

"Alright, let's make this count."

The only chance he had against two aircraft and six powerful Heretics was to take them fast and by surprise. Without any minions to back him up, they would be sure to end him if he let them get their bearings.

Digby glared up at the kestrels.

Both were coming in low but making sure to stay high enough to keep out of range of his magic. Considering the fact that a Decay spell could potentially take a kestrel out of the air, that wasn't a bad plan. Lucky for him, he'd never given them a complete idea of his abilities. Then again, it wasn't like he could fly either.

Or can I?

Digby threw reason out the window and opened his maw, placing his foot over the shadowy portal.

This is a bad idea.

There was no telling how much damage he might sustain, but that was a problem for future Digby. Waiting for the right moment, he let the aircraft come closer, their guns spinning up for another barrage of death. He had to time things right. Too soon and they wouldn't be in range. Too late, they would rip the car beneath him to shreds. The kestrels opened fire, cutting a swath through the road behind the vehicle, pavement exploding into the air.

Now!

With a thought, Digby held his staff tight and activated his Limitless mutation. Then, he cast Forge. A post of necrotic blood erupted from the shadowy opening of his maw; one end formed to cradle his foot as it launched a payload of angry zombie. Spending the extra mana to reforge the shape, the pillar of blood exploded upward to increase its length and his momentum along with it. He jumped just as the forged post grew too thin and snapped. Every bone in his right leg splintered with a dozen audible cracks as he soared over a hundred feet into the sky. He cast Necrotic Regeneration not only to handle the fractures, but to deal with whatever damage was sure to follow.

Both kestrels attempted to retarget their weapons, but it was too late, he was already casting Decay. Sparks flew from the front propeller of the kestrel on the right, followed by a burst of smoke and flame. It veered off course, heading for the desert below. Digby reached the apex of his leap, feeling gravity begin to pull him back down. The other kestrel slowed in an attempt to get out of range as he started to fall.

"No you don't!" Digby tucked his leg and opened his maw on the bottom of his left boot to forge a small disc of blood beneath him. He closed his maw and reopened it on the new formation, then cast Forge a second time. Again, a post of black blood erupted from the shadowy opening, this time in mid-air to throw him at an angle. The bones in his other leg snapped as he flew straight for the craft's front window.

Digby locked eyes with a terrified Ducky as the illusionist struggled to pull the kestrel away. He still wasn't sure if the man's name was a nickname or not.

Oh well, it won't matter for long.

Digby cast Decay as he hit the craft, the glass of the kestrel's window shattering around him. "Surprise, Ducky!"

Flipping his staff behind him, Digby used it to catch both sides of the opening. He stopped in an instant, dislocating his shoulder in the process. It popped right back into place as his Necrotic Regeneration spell continued to keep him going.

The stunned illusionist let out a horrified gasp, unable to cast anything to save himself before Digby could cast Five Fingers of Death. Broken glass sliced at his cheek as he drove his hand into the man's chest to flood his mana system with the deathly curse. Ducky choked out a final scream as he succumbed. Digby glanced at his HUD.

Heretic, level 29 Illusionist defeated. 2,826 experience awarded.

Digby checked his mana.

MP: 242/362
MINIONS: 1 Zombie

"Gotcha!" He cackled as he reactivated his Temporary Mass mutation and swapped his target from himself to the newly recruited member of his horde.

Roland and Nat stood behind Ducky's reanimated corpse as Digby stared daggers at them from his place crouched like a gargoyle on the console of the kestrel. The afternoon sun lit his back and the wind whipped through the air. They jumped back as slabs of necrotic muscle formed around Ducky's zombified body.

Roland didn't wait for the minion's armor to form before pulling a revolver from a holster and aiming it at Digby.

"I think not." He ducked behind Ducky's growing bulk as a bullet slammed into the monster.

Nat jumped in as well, raising his hand to fire off a spell.

Digby did the same, ripping his hand free of Ducky's chest and casting Absorb to shield his minion. A blast of life energy exploded from Nat's hand, pelting the console around him with motes of light while he and his armored zombie remained unharmed.

Nat fired a second blast into the swirling vortex of Digby's Absorb just as plates of bone slid across Ducky's face to form a horned mask.

"Get to work," Digby commanded the oversized zombie as Ducky stood from the pilot's seat and turned around to squeeze himself through the cockpit door and wrap his clawed hand around Nat's head.

Roland fired at Digby again with his revolver, but the motion of the craft sent the bullet into the controls. Sparks flew from the impact. Without a zombie to shield him, he was forced to abandon his assault. The risk of a bullet hitting his brain was too great.

Glancing back, he found the desert rushing closer and closer. It was time he returned to land anyway. The craft spun in a lazy circle as Digby threw himself off. He cast another Necrotic Regeneration as he landed in a roll. Several cracks were audible from his limbs, and he lost a bit of control, but his magic got him moving again.

The craft went down a hundred feet away, skidding to a stop in the dusty clay that bracketed the road. Digby grabbed his staff and pushed himself back up before sweeping his vision across the scene. The other kestrel had landed rough but somewhat intact on the road. It was a pity to destroy the aircraft, but there wasn't time to be gentle. Digby limped for a few feet before whatever was broken in his leg repaired itself.

"Are you fucking insane, Graves?" Malcolm, Bancroft's knight, appeared from the back of the first kestrel that went down.

"What?" Digby hesitated as Louis and Sullivan appeared behind him. If Digby remembered right, they were an enchanter and pyromancer respectively.

"We are carrying a nuclear warhead, you idiot." Malcolm tapped his head. "Maybe you should think for once before attacking everything, you undead monster."

"And maybe you shouldn't have attacked my friends." Digby glanced behind him, unsure where Parker and the others were. He'd lost track of the car shortly after jumping.

"Orders are orders, but I assume you know that already." Malcolm snapped his sword from his sheath. "I'm sorry that it came to this, but your people are as good as dead. They'll never get out of that ship before it sinks."

"We'll see. I'll just have to deal with you quickly and be on my way then." Digby swallowed the dread in his throat, hoping the man's words were a lie. He stalked forward, holding his staff at his side regardless. If he knew anything, it was that Becca and Alex were resourceful. If they truly were trapped, then they would find a way to survive. He just hoped his new summoning spells would be enough to take Malcolm down.

"We can't let you leave here, Graves. You get that, right?" The knight smirked. "My men are experts at dealing with monsters."

"Yes, yes, you can't have me running back to Vegas and telling Tavern to kill Bancroft. I understand." Digby glanced at his HUD as a message streaked by.

Heretic, level 30 Cleric defeated. 2,926 experience awarded.

He looked over his shoulder as the hulking zombified form of Ducky pushed his way from the wreckage of the other kestrel. Behind him, he dragged the body of that cleric, Nat. At the pace the monster walked, he would never make it to him in time to be of any use. Digby couldn't help but notice the absence of a kill message for the rogue. He didn't see him lurking about either. He filed that away as another detail that future Digby would have to deal with and returned his attention to Malcolm instead.

"Time to put you down for good." A shimmer of blue light washed across the knight's body as he rushed forward. Sullivan and Louis followed close behind him.

Digby wasted no time, summoning a crone and a wraith together.

Malcolm raised his sword to block as the two spells flickered into existence. The crone went for him, sending a dozen spectral limbs of the lingering dead bursting from the road to grab hold of the knight's legs. He swatted at them with his sword, but the mundane weapon merely passed through the spirits.

Digby took the opening and sent his wraith after Sullivan behind him, the crimson form streaking toward him with a blade gleaming in the afternoon sun. The pyromancer didn't know what hit him.

Perfect!

Digby broke into a run as blood exploded from Sullivan's chest and neck. He could almost hear the echo of Jack the Ripper gloating from within his mana system.

Heretic, level 31 Pyromancer defeated. 3,026 experience awarded.

Digby sprinted forward as Malcolm struggled against the crone's spectral limbs. He skidded to a stop a second later when Louis enchanted the knight's sword. The blade lit up like molten steel as Malcolm swung it through the crone's magic to cut it away in an instant.

"Blast!" Digby cursed the man, remembering that the enchant weapon spell was able to destabilize other magical constructs.

"Going to have to try harder than that, asshole." Malcolm started running toward him.

Digby darted to the side as the knight swung for his head. The blade tore through the air so close he could feel the heat of the enchantment against his skin. Rolling to the side off the road, he came to a stop on the dry clay of the desert.

Malcolm gave chase only to stop short just before leaving the pavement. He yelled for Louis to stop as well but the man skidded onto the dusty ground.

"Too late." Digby grinned as he cast Burial. The desert opened beneath Louis's feet in response, dropping him six feet under. His muffled scream was cut off by sand and clay. A moment of silence went by as Digby stared at Malcolm, daring him to take a step off the safety of the road.

Heretic, level 30 Artificer defeated. 2,924 experience awarded.
You Have reached level 38. 9,576 experience to next level.

All attributes have increased by 1.
You have 1 additional attribute point to allocate.

Louis must have run out of air.

"What's the matter, too scared to follow?" Digby dropped his extra point into agility and smirked at Malcolm. Apparently the knight hadn't realized that he was no safer on the road than he was in the sand. He focused on the pavement, ready to open his maw wide enough to swallow the man whole.

"No, I'm not scared." Malcolm relaxed his shoulders. "Just waiting."

That was when Digby heard the bark of a gun as something slammed into his lower back.

"Gah!" Digby opened his maw on the ground behind him and cast Blood Forge, but nothing happened.

A look at his HUD told him why.

It was gone.

A mage killer bullet!

"Damn!" Digby spun away from Malcolm and activated his Limitless mutation. He might not have access to magic, but silencing him would do nothing against most of his zombie abilities. Leaping in the direction the shot had come from, a shocked Roland materialized as the rogue's Conceal spell unraveled. Digby swung his staff with both hands, snapping the shaft in two against the man's nose. "I have fought better rogues than the likes of you."

The loss of the weapon was regrettable, but it could be replaced. His maximum mana ticked back up thirty points as the amount he'd donated to the item was restored.

Roland fell backward, clutching his face. A trickle of crimson streamed from a nearly unrecognizable nose. Digby let out a wild growl. There was more where that came from. He lunged for his throat, teeth first. The rogue threw up a hand to protect himself. Digby chomped down to tear through the man's glove and ripped a meaty chunk from his hand. He slammed his fist into the rogue's face again, hearing every bone in his wrist snap under the strain of the impact.

Dazed, the rogue lay there, unable to stand.

Digby fought every instinct he had to stop himself from tearing into his throat right then and there. Dinner would have to wait. Malcolm was sure to be on him in seconds. Leaping with his three undamaged limbs, he threw himself further from the road. The sound of an enchanted sword tore through the air behind him. A blade bit into his leg just below the knee. Digby landed face down in the dusty ground. His leg plopped down a few feet away.

"Not again." He kicked off with his uninjured foot to evade another slash. Rolling to his back, he found Malcolm standing over him. Digby scooted back to get away, moving as fast as he could with a broken arm and missing a leg. All his Limitless mutation could do was keep him moving.

"Did you really think you were gonna win, you undead piece of shit?" Malcolm stomped after him, plunging his sword into Roland's chest as he passed by.

With Louis dead, there was no saving him from Digby's bite. Sure, the rogue could have held out for a few hours, but the curse would have ended him the moment the sun set, and the only enchanter left was trapped in a sinking cargo ship.

Malcolm pulled his blade from the body of his comrade with hate burning in his eyes. "You are going to pay for that."

"Now, now, hold up a second." Digby continued to scoot away, trying his best to keep a dozen feet between himself and the knight. "Perhaps we can work something out here." He scrambled to buy time, blurting out whatever lie he could think of that might at least slow the man down. The look on his face told him nothing would work.

Digby focused on the ground to open his maw in the path of Malcolm's foot. He might not have been able to spend the mana to enlarge the opening while silenced, but he could at least try to take off his leg.

"Nice try." The knight glanced down as he stopped with his foot hovering over the shadowy opening. "Somehow, I'm not surprised you would try to attack while simultaneously begging for your life. That's just the kind of monster you are. No pride."

"What did pride ever do for anyone?" Digby scoffed.

"It lets them live with themselves when the fight is over."

Malcolm stepped over his waiting maw and kept walking. "Having pride means you can sleep at night."

"Well, I'm dead." Digby inched away from him. "So I don't sleep."

Malcolm let out a sigh. "You realize no one is going to miss you, right? The people back there in Vegas just keep you around and act like they respect you because they think they don't have a choice. I'm willing to bet that they won't even bat an eye when they find out I took you out. They'll just let Bancroft take charge and move on. If anything, they'll be grateful for the normalcy he can give them."

"He just wants to run the world, just like Autem. Charles saw a path to power through the Heretic Seed and went for it. All he wants is to be at the top of the food chain, so don't talk like he's any better than me." Digby pushed himself up on his elbow. "I might be a walking corpse, but I understand humanity more than you think, and I'll tell you the same thing I told him. A leader is only as strong as their horde, be they zombie or human. No one stays in power for long when they look down on the people beneath them."

Malcolm raised his sword and broke into a jog. "We'll see about—"

His words were cut off by Alex's modified Camaro as it blew past at nearly full speed. The knight in its path simply exploded mid-sentence, his body bursting from the impact. Digby's mouth fell open.

All that was left was a boot.

Heretic, level 32 Knight defeated. 3,124 experience awarded.

"I suppose that answers the question of where the car went." Digby dropped back into the sand as the vehicle took a wide circle around him. It was clear Parker was having trouble slowing it down. Around a minute later, the car came to a stop, its pink-haired driver leaping from the driver's seat.

"Shit, Dig! Are you okay? I lost control of the car when you jumped and had trouble slowing down enough to get back to you."

"Better late than never." He sat up. "Now someone find my leg while I get this bullet out of me."

"Oh god." Lana covered her mouth as she swept her eyes across the scene from the back of the car. "I'm not sure I know what part belongs to who."

"Well, figure it out." Digby wobbled his way up and tried to stand. "As much as I would like a break, Rebecca and Alex don't have that kind of time."

Asher cawed as she flapped out to help search for his foot.

"Got it." Parker closed her eyes as she picked up his missing extremity and tossed it in the car. "You can patch yourself up on the way."

"Good thinking." Digby hopped his way toward her as the armored form of Ducky's zombified corpse finally reached him, still dragging a body behind him. Digby let out a groan. "Of course you get here now."

CHAPTER FORTY-FIVE

Becca woke to the sound of the cargo ship groaning as she inhaled seawater through her nose.

"Shuck!"

She coughed repeatedly as her sinuses burned.

That was when she realized she was upside down.

Her foot was wedged between the wall and a bent rung of a ladder. Water sloshed around her head. The level was rising, slow but steady. She must have woken up when it reached her nose.

"What happened?"

She raised her body up to grab onto what remained of the ladder and unwedged her foot to flip herself right-side up. Clinging to the wall, her head ached. Everything was blurry, making it hard to even read her HUD. It felt like her brain was ready to burst out her ears.

Then she remembered the betrayal.

Malcolm and Ducky had pushed her down the shaft and tossed one of the C4 charges in after her. Clearly, they had intended to blow her up.

"So why am I not splattered all over the walls?"

Becca looked her body over, finding herself unharmed. Actually, there wasn't even a scratch. Her Cloak of Steel had done one hell of a job keeping her safe.

"Thank you, Alex."

Then again, she had been knocked unconscious. The barrier the cloak produced around her must not have been able to protect her from the internal trauma of having her head slammed against a wall by a concussive blast. She was lucky the impact hadn't liquefied her brain.

"That explains the headache and blurred vision."

If it wasn't for the fact that her Regeneration spell activated while unconscious, she probably wouldn't have woken up at all.

"Wait, how long have I been out?"

She checked her watch.

"Shit!"

It had been hours.

Not only that, but the sun was due to set in just thirty minutes.

A wave of dread crashed into her. She shook it off. There wasn't time to freak out. She had to find Alex and Mason and the rest of the Heretics. She checked her HUD, finding Alex's name right where it had been, though the addition of a silenced status next to his readout gave her reason to worry. Hopefully Mason was faring better. She tried not to consider any other possibility. Fortunately, she noticed something else before her mind fell down a spiral.

Digby's name was back.

"It's about goddamn time."

She couldn't project herself to him while hanging from the broken ladder, but she was sure he would be heading straight for them. After all, if she could see his name, then that meant that he could see hers. He must have noticed she'd been unconscious as well as Alex's silenced status. If that was the case, then he would be tearing his way to them. Without a kestrel, it would still take him hours to reach them by land, but the thought still gave her a feeling of calm.

Despite the knowledge that help might be on the way, the shaft she occupied was flooding little by little with every passing second. She couldn't just sit and wait for rescue.

Getting into a more stable position on the ladder, she surveyed the space. There was about ten feet from where she was and the floor of the shaft. Most of which was full of water. She glanced up. The door she'd entered through was about twenty feet above her. The water was coming in from somewhere below. Considering that, the hole had to either be small or, more likely, Malcolm had closed the hatch up above. In that case, the air pocket was the only thing keeping the water out.

Becca took a breath. The oxygen was definitely getting thin.

"Good thing I woke up before I ran out of breathable air."

She looked back up. The hatch couldn't have been completely airtight, or the water level wouldn't be rising, but if she opened it, the shaft would probably fill up quickly. That could be a problem. The corridor above had to still have air, but the path back to the ship's deck wasn't guaranteed to be clear.

Becca opened her map of the ship to find the shortest route back to the cargo bay where she'd last seen Mason and Alex. If she had to guess, Malcolm's men must have trapped them there.

"Alright, step one. Get out of here. Step two, project myself to Dig and make sure he knows what happened. Three, check on my boyfriend to make sure he's okay. Four, rescue said boyfriend."

It was a long list.

She hesitated, remembering something else. "Step five, tell him you love him."

With that, Becca dropped into the water, letting out an involuntary gasp. It was colder than she'd expected. After catching her breath, she ducked under. There was always a chance she could squeeze through whatever hole the C4 had made. That would certainly be easier than traveling through the ship. As much as she hated to, she slipped off her cloak so she could swim easier. The garment shimmered as she removed it, its nearly impenetrable barrier releasing.

Free of the garment, she swam to the bottom where a nearly two-foot gash had been torn in the ship's hull. Struggling, all she could do was reach an arm out. There was no way her shoulders were going to make it. Instead, she did her best to peek out. It was hard to make anything out through the water, but it looked like the surface was still close. By her best estimate, the deck of the ship should still be above water.

Becca pushed away from the hole and swam back up to the ladder. "I guess I'm going through the ship, then."

She tucked her cloak under her arm and crouched back on the remains of the ladder to spring up to the next rung. The climb was easy from there. She slipped back into her cloak when she reached the hatch, feeling better when its barrier reactivated. The handle of the door was in the locked position.

Holding her breath, she pulled it down.

It moved.

"Oh, thank god."

She had been worried that Malcolm had placed something into the handle to wedge it closed. Then again, he had tossed a bomb down at her face. He probably assumed that had been enough to take her out. Of course, he could have come back to check when a kill message never appeared on his HUD, but escaping the ship was probably a priority.

The air-pressure changed all at once when she opened the door, her ears popping in protest. She ignored it and pushed into the corridor, closing the hatch behind her to keep the place from flooding. Thankfully the hallway was mostly dry. With a little luck, she might be able to make it back to the cargo bay without a problem.

Before doing anything else, she sat down and projected herself to Digby. A second later she opened her eyes.

"What the hell?" She tensed her entire illusionary body as she found herself in the back seat of a Camaro with the scenery passing by at nearly two hundred miles per hour. Parker sat at the wheel.

"Christ!" Lana jumped against the window as soon as she noticed her.

"Becky?" Digby turned around in the passenger seat.

"Yes, holy shit. You're really back." She shook her head. "Sorry, I don't have time to catch up. I just need to tell you where we are and that Malcolm and his guys betrayed us."

"I know." Digby groaned.

"Who do you think is splattered all over the hood?" Parker glanced back, hooking her thumb at the chunky red substance that coated the front of the car. It covered most of the windshield except for a space in the middle where the wipers had streaked it away.

"Oh, gross." Becca recoiled for a moment.

"Yes, very unpleasant." Digby made eye contact with her. "What about you? Malcolm said you were trapped."

She shook her head. "I think I can get out, but I have a lot of ground to cover and the ship is sinking. I don't know about Mason and Alex. I'm going to check on them now."

"Good." Digby nodded. "We're almost there, so if you can get them out, we'll be there shortly to pick you up. If not, I'll get in there and find you one way or another."

"Thank you." Becca let out a relieved sigh. "I have to go. But… I'm glad you're back. Vegas has been hell without you."

With that, she released her projection and opened her eyes to the ship's corridor again. She wasted no time in casting the spell again, this time sending herself to Alex. Relief swept over her as soon as the cargo hold came into view.

Mason stood by an empty crate and Alex leaned against a ladder. There was no sign of anyone else but they both were alive. A number of dead revenants littered the floor around them.

"Oh thank god." She rushed to Mason.

"You're alright!" He started walking toward her but quickly clutched his stomach and leaned back against the empty crate.

"Yeah, I'm fine thanks to the cloak Alex made." She stopped in front of him, wishing she wasn't a projection so she could throw her arms around him. "Are you?"

"I'll live." He winced. "I have a bullet lodged in my gut though. I think it's silencing me. Alex has one too."

Becca turned to look at the artificer.

"Right in the brain." He pointed to his foot for a second before looking down and readjusting to point at his head. "Not sure how I'm alive, but I'm not asking questions. My guess is that it's lodged somewhere I don't use."

Becca cringed. "That's horrible."

"Yeah, I know." He nodded.

"Okay. At least I know where you are." She turned back to Mason. "I'm coming for you, so hang on."

He nodded.

She released the spell immediately. As much as she wanted to stay with them, she had to reach them for real. Standing up in the hall, she got moving.

From there, Becca sprinted past the hatch that led to the corridor full of revenant Lightwalkers. She blew out a relieved sigh at the fact that they were still trapped as she headed for the path that she had traveled on the way there. The ship listed toward the back, causing every hallway to angle downward as she moved. She made it through two bulkheads before running into a dead end.

Becca's heart sank as she waded into knee deep water leading up to a closed hatch that hadn't been closed before. Looking through the circular window embedded in the door, she saw nothing but water and darkness.

"Shit."

She placed her forehead against the window for a second. It was cold against her skin. There was no telling how much of the path was flooded and there was no way she was going to hold her breath long enough to make it to the surface. Not to mention she might not be able to make it to Mason and Alex. She blew out a sigh to calm her nerves.

"I guess that just leaves the Lightwalkers."

With that, Becca pushed away from the door and turned back toward the corridor full of monsters that she had been avoiding. Every instinct in her body screamed at her to turn back, only to be shut down by her more rational side that reminded her that there was no other choice.

"At least I have you." Becca checked the shoulder straps that held her cloak in place.

There may have been over a dozen revenants waiting to drink her dry, but technically none of them could actually hurt her as long as she was wearing Alex's gift. Provided none of the creatures managed to pull the cloak off her. With that in mind, she approached the hatch that someone had wedged a wrench in to keep closed. She hesitated as soon as she looked inside.

There they were, right where she'd left them.

The horde of monsters filled the corridor, ready and waiting for their next meal to walk in. At first, she debated concealing herself and attempting to slip through the passage undetected. Though, the moment she opened the hatch, every revenant in the hall would turn in her direction. Sure, most would probably be fooled, but it would only take one of the monsters to unravel the spell if they were to get too curious. If that happened, the entire swarm would be on her in seconds. That was a chance she couldn't take.

"Okay, fine, so I have to take out as many as I can, as fast as possible."

A charged icicle would have the destructive power to cut through a few of the creatures at once considering how close they were packed together in there. She thanked the Heretic Seed for finally ranking the spell up. It might actually save her ass. Granted, even if she killed half of the revenants, that still left plenty more to take her down.

Becca checked her mana.

MP: 384/384

She nodded at the read out as a plan began to form. She started by setting up a decoy. Conceal plus Waking Dream left her invisible with a copy of herself standing next to her. That brought her mana down to three hundred and fourteen.

Plenty left.

"I hope."

Becca stepped into position. As much as she wanted to take a minute to psych herself up, there wasn't time to spare.

With that, she cast Icicle and held the growing projectile, letting it float above her hand.

"I hope this works."

She pulled the wrench free of the hatch's locking wheel and pulled the door open. Several revenants snapped their attention to her, or more accurately, the copy of her standing beside her. Becca plastered a surprised expression across her illusion's face for realism, before sending it running in the opposite direction.

Five of the revenants passed right by as they raced after her. She'd hoped more would have fallen for the trick.

"Oh well, here goes nothing." Becca stepped back from the open hatch and aimed the massive icicle floating over her hand at the nearest creature, making sure that there were more targets behind it. Then, she let it fly.

A blast of cold air hit her face as the projectile launched, leaving a layer of frost on her cheeks. The revenant she'd fired at let out a sudden screech. It was cut off in an instant, the Lightwalker's chest practically exploding on impact. The frozen projectile drilled through the corridor, taking off the head of another revenant as well as the arm of third.

"Good enough!"

Becca charged in while the Lightwalkers were stunned. Ducking to the side, she leveraged every attribute point she'd ever gotten to jump and kick off the wall to slip past a threat that hadn't been hit by her attack. Another swiped at her face, just barely missing her cheek as she landed back on the floor. A third caught her wrist, but she hit it in the chin with an icicle that burst up through the back of its skull. She lobbed a pair of fireballs over her shoulders with both hands an instant later, hoping to keep the creatures from following her.

Her mana dropped to two thirds.

"Come on!"

She pushed herself forward, casting an icicle as she plowed into another Lightwalker. The projectile spiraled through its chest to knock it off balance.

Putting her weight into her shoulder, Becca planted her elbow into the collar bone of another threat. She sent another spike of frost into its gut to make sure it fell. It went down, cracking its head against the wall on its way to the floor. It wasn't enough to kill or overpower the creature's healing ability, but it would at least keep it down for a few seconds.

All she had to do was make it to the next hatch.

"Almost ther——"

Her encouraging words were cut off with a gasp as a revenant that she hadn't noticed leapt up from the floor. She'd thought it was dead, that she had killed it with her first attack. She struggled to push it out of the way, but its pale hands snapped around her shoulder. She hit it hard with an icicle, but another set of hands grabbed onto her leg from behind.

Another of the creatures rushed her, practically tackling her against the wall. It bit down on her thigh as more and more of the Lightwalkers skittered their way toward her.

Becca glanced down, feeling a minuscule amount of relief as a blue glow emanated from her leg where one of the creatures was trying to chew its way through her cloak's barrier.

"Ha! I'm the freaking woman of steel."

She reached forward and grabbed hold of a pipe that ran along the wall. Another of the revenants leapt on her back, but she pulled herself forward. Another set of jagged teeth clamped down on the back of her shoulder. It felt strange, like a massage that had gotten a little too aggressive.

Again, she reached out and dragged herself forward, taking another large step toward the hatch at the end of the corridor. Letting go of the pipe for a moment, she thrust her palm into one of the Lightwalker's faces and cast Icicle. The frozen projectile formed directly in its screeching mouth. She flicked a few extra points of mana into the spell and let it fly. The back of the revenant's head burst with a spray of crimson.

"I am not letting you goddamn things eat me!"

She snapped one hand around the pipe on the wall just as the creatures began pulling her back. With her free hand, she pumped another frozen spike into the nearest open mouth. Another set of jaws closed, this time around her leg, as she literally dragged several of the creatures toward the hatch with her.

MP: 131/384

That would buy her... maybe six more icicles. Becca tried to look back to get a count of how many more Lightwalkers were

484

behind her. All she could catch was a bunch of pale blurs. That was when a screech echoed down the corridor from the direction she'd come from. Then another.

"Shit, the revs that chased my decoy must have circled back."

Becca felt the weight of another pair of hands latch onto her. She wasn't even sure how many of the creatures she was dragging with her. She pushed on regardless, even as a pale hand covered her face. She was almost there. The hatch was only a few feet away. Becca launched another two icicles to try to clear the last of the threats in front of her.

Finally, she reached for the locking wheel, despite the dozen or so hands that tried to pull her back. She let out a victorious howl when she saw that the hallway beyond was not flooded. She might actually make it. Becca turned the locking wheel, fighting for every inch as the revenants struggled to rip her hands from the hatch.

The metal door creaked as freedom came closer and closer. Then, the lock released.

"Yes!"

Becca planted a foot and shoved the hatch open. The revenants dragged her backward three feet as she let go.

"Fuck!"

Becca reached out to find the pipe she had used before, catching hold a second before falling into the swarm. The revenants grabbed and bit at her all over, but the cloak's barrier held. Becca took a moment to breathe. Somehow, she needed to get out of the corridor and close the hatch behind her. Otherwise, the Lightwalkers would attack her non-stop the whole way back to the cargo bay, and she simply did not have the time for that.

She checked her mana.

MP: 91/384

That left her with four more attacks.

"Shit."

There were more than three revenants on her. Not only that, but she was pretty sure some of the creatures she had already attacked were getting back up. Her only saving grace was that the swarm was behind her. She held firm to the pipe on the wall, her entire hand white.

All she could do was try to kill enough of the creatures to get herself free for the few seconds she needed to make a run for it and close the hatch. A pale hand curled its fingers through her ponytail, just to make things more difficult.

"Let go of me!" She bared her teeth as she cast Icicle, letting it charge enough to form an edge on the projectile. She reached back to angle the spell at the back of her head before carefully letting it go. The blade of frost shot through the base of her ponytail before slicing through one of the revenant's hands.

"That's one." She lamented wasting the spell. "Three more icicles left."

Becca glanced back to find one of the Lightwalker's heads in her periphery and blasted it the hell off.

"Two left."

A set of teeth clamped down on her waist and she responded with another spike of frozen death.

"One!"

Becca yanked herself forward a step before firing off her last spell. The projectile thumped into a revenant's eye socket.

MP: 5/384

"God damnit!"

Becca nearly fell as at least five more of the creatures tried to drag her back, their pale hands clawing at her cloak. The barrier held, but the garment had also become as much a liability as it had been her protector. The creatures held firm, the cloak's fabric balled up in their hands. In fact, that was all they had a grip on.

"Seriously?" she complained.

It was obvious what she had to do. The cloak had to go. It didn't matter if she was invincible if she couldn't escape. The ship would just sink, and she would never make it to Mason and Alex. Either that, or the barrier protecting her would simply fail and leave her defenseless to be drunk dry.

"Fine!"

Becca reached for the clasp under her right shoulder while holding onto the pipe with the other hand. She popped the clip, feeling the weight of the revenants lessen only for her other shoulder to catch the tension an instant later. She let out a gasp as they tried to jerk her backward.

With a final string of expletives, she reached for the clasp under her other shoulder and squeezed the release. All at once, the revenants fell away from her. She tore her leg free of the last few grabby hands and leapt for the open hatch. The Lightwalkers screamed and screeched behind her, her enhanced senses telling her there were only milliseconds to spare. The sound of hands and feet slapping against the floor filled the corridor, a half dozen revenants lunging for her back.

Becca grabbed hold of the hatch and swung it shut just as a mouth full of jagged teeth slammed into the other side of the door. She planted her feet and pressed all her strength against the door as another of the creatures slammed into it, nearly throwing it open.

"Not today, you ugly ass vampires!"

The hatch thumped and jerked but she pushed harder until, finally, it closed with a thud. Immediately, she spun the locking wheel to trap the creatures inside forever.

She collapsed against the hatch the instant it was closed. Her entire body hurt. Every muscle was on fire. She gasped for air, taking a moment to simply hate everything that had just happened. Then, she reminded herself that there wasn't time to rest.

Becca shoved herself up off the floor.

Her body felt heavy. Like she was still carrying the weight of a half dozen revenants on her back.

"I will rest later."

"Right now, I have people to rescue."

CHAPTER FORTY-SIX

"Oh no, oh no, oh no." Digby tensed every undead muscle in his body as Alex's modified Camaro sped across the sand of a Californian beach, heading straight for the ocean.

"I really hope you know what you're doing." Lana dug her fingers into the headrest of his seat.

"This should work." Parker sounded confident before contradicting herself with an unhelpful, "I think."

Asher hopped down from her perch on the dash to hide down by Digby's feet.

"Don't worry." Kristen's skull let out an uninterested sigh. "If it doesn't work, you'll all die. And really, how bad could that be?"

"You're not helping!" Digby clung to the handle above his door with both hands.

"I know, that's why I said it." Kristen's tone took on an all-new level of smugness.

Digby closed his eyes and braced for impact.

Then, nothing happened.

He cracked one eye open, half expecting to have been splattered all over the surf. Yet, he was still in one piece. As was the modified vehicle around him. He leaned against the window to find the dark blue blur of water passing by at nearly two hundred miles per hour.

Parker let out an awkward chuckle. "See, what did I say?"

"Yes, yes." Digby let go of the handle he'd been clinging to and settled back into his seat. "I never doubted Alex's craftsmanship for a moment."

"I did," Kristen added in a solid deadpan. "Honestly, most of his creations so far have either exploded or ended up becoming mana-fueled vibrators."

"Tell me more about these vibrators?" Parker smirked.

"You would be interested, wouldn't you?" Kristen groaned.

"Everyone shut up. We are driving full speed across nothing but water in a Camaro that Alex cobbled together with things he found in a casino." Lana continued to dig her fingers into the seat cushions. "It is a miracle we aren't dead. I don't have the nerves left right now to listen to a skull talk about magic vibrators."

"Indeed. No one wants to hear about vibrators." Digby grumbled to himself, "Whatever that is."

"Yeah, everybody grow up." Parker refocused on her driving as if she had not been involved in the inane conversation.

"Yes, please do." Kristen did the same.

Parker gestured to the horizon. "Okay, this cargo ship was last spotted only a few miles off the coast, so it will come up on us fast."

"Provided it hasn't sunk yet," Kristen added.

"You're still not helping." Digby narrowed his eyes at the skull.

"I am still not trying to."

"Bah." Digby grabbed the skull and tossed her in the back seat next to Lana and glanced to his HUD. Alex was still silenced, but his name was at least listed, meaning he was alive. Hopefully Becca had found him and escaped already. "I'm sure our people are fine. Now keep a look out for this boat."

"There it is." Lana lunged forward to point out the front window.

Digby followed the line of her finger off to the right. There was definitely something there. Though, he wouldn't call it a ship. At least, not anymore. Only the hint of a hull peeked out from the waves, with two thirds of the vessel completely submerged. A formation protruded from the water, like some sort of building.

"I think that's the bridge." Parker circled the sinking ship while she began the lengthy process of slowing the car down.

The sun hung just above the waterline, filling the sky with an otherworldly, pink and orange glow that filtered through the clouds. It had taken hours to get there, leaving only ten minutes or so before dark. Digby squinted at the vessel only to immediately gasp as the car curved around to the other side where a crowd had gathered on top. At first, he thought it was the Heretics that they had sent on the mission with his coven, that somehow, Malcolm had let them live.

Then, they got closer.

The pale forms of a swarm of revenants crowded onto what was left of the ship's deck. Digby's heart sank when he noticed the massive hands of a revenant bloodstalker hanging onto the side. The creatures must have been in the lower levels of the vessel when it began sinking and escaped to the surface. Strangely, they huddled together on the section of the deck that was already submerged rather than staying where it was still dry. It was like they were trying to hide in what little shade was available without drowning.

His hopes rose again when he didn't see any of the people from Vegas amongst the group. There was a chance that they were trapped inside along with Alex. Then again, Malcolm didn't mention them while he was gloating, so there was also a chance they were dead.

"Hurry up and get us over there." Digby fidgeted with the door handle.

"I still have to slow down." Parker kept the car in its circular path. "I may have gotten the hang of this, but we've still been pushing this thing way faster than anyone should ever be driving it as it is."

"Then get close and I'll jump." Digby opened the door a crack. "There's a swarm of revenants onboard that thing, and they're all going to become active the moment the sun sets."

"Okay, I'll do what I can." Parker jerked the wheel to the side.

"But you're going in alone. We're still going too fast for us humans to jump out and not die."

"Fine. I'll make do." Digby glanced down to Asher by his feet. "When they slow down a bit more, take flight and keep an eye on the sky. Warn me if anything approaches."

With that, he hoisted himself through the window and carefully placed his foot on the supports that held the engraved plates onto the sides. Once Digby found some stable footing, he dove for the ship.

Hitting the water at literal breakneck speeds, he cast a Necrotic Regeneration on impact. A moment went by where he struggled to control his body, but the spell pulled everything back into place in seconds. From there, he splashed to the surface.

Digby's mind flashed back to the moment that he'd entered the Seed's realm where he had been alone in an endless ocean. He shook off the memory and swam forward. As difficult as it was to move with his coat on, losing the extra mana it provided was worse. There was no telling what he would have to do aboard that ship, and it wouldn't do to be left wanting.

Ducking under, he swam for the ship's deck. He stayed under as he reached it, not wanting to alert the revenants waiting there that he was coming. Instead, he followed the incline of the deck up until the water became shallow. From there, he could see the legs of the swarm. There had to be over a dozen.

Not for long.

Digby crawled along the ship's deck until he could peek through the waves at the group. Then, he opened his maw and pushed its width to take in the center of the group. The moment he did, a sudden surge hit him. It was like nothing he had ever felt before. At first, he wasn't sure what it was, and then it dawned on him.

It was the water.

Without thinking, he had placed his maw on the deck of the ship where it was still under the surface. The effect acted as a double-edged sword. On one side, the revenants shrieked in protest as the ocean dragged them into his maw, a whirlpool of death forming above to drink in the sea. He even sucked down a few fish.

At the same time, it felt like the balance of his void's resources felt off, like it couldn't fit the volume that he was pouring into it. The sensation made him dizzy and blurred his vision.

It was like being drunk, or worse, poisoned.

"Gah!" Digby snapped his maw shut, slicing the last of the revenants in half as they struggled to break free of the whirlpool's current.

14 dormant revenants defeated. 0 experience awarded.

They may not have been worth anything, but at least they would serve to become worthwhile resources.

With the swarm gone, Digby thrashed his way out of the water and up onto the portion of the deck that was still above water. His vision swayed and churned as the imbalance in his void weighed on everything he was.

"I have to get rid of this water." Digby stumbled to his knee, his wet hair plastered to the side of his face.

Before he could do anything about it, the bloodstalker hiding at the edge of the ship decided to take advantage of the opening. A lumbering shadow engulfed him as the massive creature climbed out of the water, its bulk backlit by the setting sun.

"Get away." Digby threw out a hand to summon his wraith.

Nothing happened.

Summon Echo canceled due to a disruption in mana equilibrium.

"Blast!" He lunged to the side as the enormous revenant did the same toward him. The beast slammed into the deck like a drunken mess, just barely missing him. Digby fell onto his side and rolled, having just as much trouble moving. It felt like the entire ship was swaying.

Well, it was, but his condition exacerbated the disorientation.

The only thing that saved him was the bloodstalker's inability to access its full power while the sun was up. Though, that advantage was dwindling by the minute.

Digby rolled onto his back and scooted up the incline of the deck to get away from the massive threat. The revenant slid down into the water only to thrash its way back onto its hands and feet. From there, it crawled toward him, its heavy limbs slamming into the metal deck with a hollow bang accompanying each step.

"I said get back." Digby focused on the space in front of the creature and opened his maw. At least that still worked. Then again, he couldn't open it any wider than its default with whatever disruption the water he'd taken was causing. It was like he'd been silenced again. The bloodstalker simply crawled over the tiny opening.

"Damn." Digby pushed himself backward as the beast clawed its way toward him. He swept his vision over his surroundings. "I could really use some support again, Parker."

Unfortunately, the car was still spinning across the water nowhere near the ship. It looked like Parker had lost control of the vehicle for a moment. From above, Asher cawed at the revenant, unable to do anything on account of the fact that she was too small.

That was when Digby's back hit a wall.

"That's not good." He glanced up to find the building-like section of the ship that held the command area. A massive claw slammed down on the deck only inches from his feet. The revenant scraped away the paint of the metal surface with a grinding screech. Digby pulled his legs away. The wall behind him almost seemed to push him toward the bloodstalker. "No, this is not good at all."

In a desperate act to deal with both his problems at once, he focused on the wall behind him and opened his maw again. The six-inch shadow appeared again, but this time, he called forth the water.

The enormous revenant opened its jaws, ready to bite down on Digby's head, only to get a mouth full of ocean as a torrent burst from his maw.

"No fun, is it?" Digby let out a wet cackle as the small opening of his maw blasted the creature in the face. From the sheer volume of liquid, he must have swallowed a few swimming pools' worth.

The bloodstalker threw up a hand to shield its head. It slipped the instant it did, having trouble supporting itself with just one arm. The sunlight was still working against the creature. It fell back a few feet, creating a little room for Digby to work.

He pushed himself up to a standing position, his head just beneath the torrent of water rushing from his maw. A dead fish flopped out of his void along with the severed hand of something he'd eaten. He kept his focus on the water, hoping that he could limit the number of usable resources he lost along with it.

The revenant cried out in protest as it slipped again.

"Try killing me now," Digby gloated just as the flow of water began to slow enough to let the creature get back up. "Oh damn."

The bloodstalker regained its footing and started moving. Digby tensed as the flow of water behind him faded to a weak spurt. He raised his hand and tried to summon his wraith, hoping that he'd gotten rid of enough water. Again nothing happened. The revenant crouched down as if preparing to lunge. Digby's eyes bulged. At that range, the beast would simply crush him with its weight. He flicked his attention to the water that still poured from his maw, then back to his target.

"Come on." He cast wraith again. "Come on."

The revenant kicked off.

"Gah!" Digby leapt to the side, getting out of the way at the last second as the beast slammed into the wall. He skidded to a stop and spun to face the oversized creature. That was when he realized his vision wasn't blurry anymore. He wasn't having trouble moving either.

"Finally." Digby cast wraith, this time sending the flickering crimson form of a murderous echo into action. It streaked forward, blade gleaming. He barely saw the impact, it happened so fast, but the spray of blood that showered the deck confirmed the hit.

The bloodstalker shrieked and turned in his direction. The attack had landed, but it would take more than that to kill the beast. Digby obliged, sending his wraith out again and again.

The echo of Jack the Ripper tore through the revenant bloodstalker like it was performing an autopsy. Crimson light

494

streaked back and forth, each strike releasing a geyser of blood. After three more summons, the beast simply came apart at the seams.

The revenant dropped to the ship's deck, its limbs barely attached to its body. It slid down the angled surface with a wet squeak until it came to a stop.

Digby let out a relieved sigh and spent the majority of his mana to open his maw wide enough to swallow the bulk of the creature. He didn't even wait for it to sink into his void before he turned away and began searching for a way into the ship. He found an entrance right next to where he'd been backed up against the wall. A hatch was embedded into the side of the section of the ship still above water. Granted, at the rate that the vessel was sinking, it wouldn't stay that way for long.

There wasn't time to wait for Parker and the others. Digby looked up to find Asher in the sky as he pulled the hatch open.

Show Parker to this door so she can follow.

Digby cast Leach to draw some of his minion's mana as she cawed in confirmation. Then he headed inside.

The corridor was dry beneath his feet. "At least there's that."

Digby started down the hall for a moment before stopping and going back to close the hatch. If the ship sank up to that point, there would be nothing stopping the entire ocean from flowing in after him. He just hoped he wouldn't be inside the place for that long.

A glimpse of the sun falling toward the horizon reminded him how close they were to nightfall. "I hope there's no more revenants inside."

He shook off the worry and started moving, regardless of the fact that he hadn't a clue about the layout of modern ships.

"If I was Rebecca and Alex, where would I be?"

Before he got too far, the sound of metal hitting metal drew his attention. Digby stopped to listen. It came again and again.

"That has to be them." He rushed off in the direction of the sound, traveling down a few corridors as well as a set of stairs. Dread swelled in his chest as water met him at the last step. Even worse, a body floated face down in the hallway. He rolled it over with his foot, his heart sinking when he recognized one of their people from Vegas.

He hadn't interacted with them much, but he recognized the corpse's face from when he had fought alongside the survivors to save the casino.

Wading further down the corridor, he found several more bodies. He didn't recognize all of them, but most were from Vegas like the first. Malcolm must have killed whoever he couldn't trap. He tried not to think of the good people that had met their end. It was such a meaningless way to die.

He made a point to leave their bodies as they were without dropping them into his void. It was unlikely that he would be able to go back and retrieve them for the burial that they deserved, but it wouldn't be right to eat them either.

Instead, he pressed on, the water growing deeper as he walked. The incline of the vessel seemed to be getting steeper as well. Fortunately, it wasn't long before he found the source of the sound.

"Why won't you fucking open?" Rebecca stood in waist high water next to a hatch in the wall. She clutched a metal pry bar in her hands.

"What the hell are you doing, Becky?" Digby sloshed his way down the corridor toward her.

Rebecca's eyes went wide as soon as she saw him. Tears streaked her cheeks. She looked desperate. Then without a word, she lowered the pry bar and threw her free arm around him.

"Hey now, it's alright. I'm here. We'll get them out." Digby froze, not expecting a show of warmth from her. Normally she just said something snippy and got on with things. She shivered in his arms.

She followed the brief hug by letting go and immediately slapping him in the shoulder, her teeth chattering from the cold. Clearly the situation had taken a toll on her nerves. "What took you so long? They're trapped and I can't get in alone."

"Hey stop." He tried to shield himself as she fell back into her usual attitude.

She slapped him one more time before raising the pry bar.

Digby backed away a little worried she might swing it at him. "Hold on now, we can talk about—"

"I'm not going to hit you. Just help me." She turned toward the hatch and whacked a clump of metal attached to some sort of lock that was holding the door closed. "Malcolm welded it shut. Can you Decay your way through?"

"I should be able to." Digby stepped closer and placed his hand to the hunk of scrap that was holding the hatch shut. "I saw corpses. Did any of our side survive besides you three?"

"No." Rebecca stepped aside. "Malcolm killed them. I haven't found all of the bodies, but I haven't had time to search. I can't even find Easton. Bancroft's guys must have got him too. The only reason I'm alive is because Alex gave me a cloak that let me survive a block of C4 to the face. I had to leave it behind, though."

"That's a pity." Digby cast Decay on the clump of metal melted to the door lock, sending a wave of rust across it that traveled to the wall.

"How did you leave things with Bancroft?" Rebecca caught her breath. Now that he could see her in person, it was obvious she had been through a lot while he was gone.

"I have Tavern keeping him in his room." Digby cast Decay again, causing the rust to reach further up the wall. "You're sure Alex and Mason are in here?"

"I projected in to them after I spoke to you in the car." She tapped her ear. "They're both alive but they were shot by some kind of silencing bullet. They healed the wounds with a flask, but they couldn't take out the rounds. Alex looked okay, but has one in his fucking brain." Her voice wavered. "Mason has one in his stomach."

"A mage killer bullet." Digby groaned, hoping he'd never hear of the things again.

"A what?"

"Never mind. It's not important now." Digby pushed his spell further. "I've brought Lana. She and Parker should be parking the car up top as we speak. If anyone is hurt, she can handle it."

"Parking the car?" She shook her head in disbelief. "I still can't believe you rode in that death trap."

"It got us here, didn't it?" He grinned as he cast another Decay. "Alex's creation leaves a lot to be desired, but it certainly moves fast enough."

"Dig, that thing isn't finished." She looked back to the door. "It barely has brakes."

"I've noticed." He blew out a sigh, feeling relieved. She had been with him since the beginning of his time in this new world. Sure, their situation was a little grim, but it was good to see her again after being trapped in the Seed's realm for so long.

"Great, so we're riding in Alex's nerd experiment all the way back to Vegas." She shivered and rubbed her arms to warm up. "Did you find out how to make more magic users on your trip through the Heretic Seed?"

Digby hesitated as he cast another Decay, still unsure what he was going to do. Increasing their forces was more important than ever now that Malcolm had killed so many of the new Heretics.

Still though, there was a cost, and giving up his soul wasn't a price he was sure he was willing to pay, even if it was the only way to unlock the Seed's potential. His original goal of becoming human again was growing further out of reach.

Digby decided to give her a vague answer to avoid thinking about it.

"Yes, we've found some answers." He cast Decay again, feeling the wall creak under the weight of the water. "But right now, we need to survive the day."

That was when the lump of scrap holding the hatch shut crumbled in his hand.

"That's it." He pulled his fingers away and reached for the handle. "Give me a hand."

Rebecca got into position with him to help pull the hatch open. By the time they were ready, the water had reached Digby's chest, forcing him to activate his Limitless mutation just to get the door open a crack against the weight. Water rushed into the space as he felt a bone in his hand snap.

"Holy shit, Dig. I knew you would come." Alex rushed to the opening on the other side, ready to help push the door open a little more. A scrap of bloody fabric covered one of his eyes.

"Is Mason still okay?" Rebecca let out a grunt of effort as she pulled on the handle.

"I'm upright." The soldier choked out in a labored voice from behind Alex. He looked like he could barely stand.

"Shit, are you okay?" Rebecca's voice climbed higher.

"Yeah, I can make it," the soldier answered back. From his tone, it sounded like a lie.

"As long as we get out of here and get him to Lana, he should be fine." Alex got his body between the door and the wall and pushed. "I can't purify any more water while silenced so he's been going downhill."

"I said I'm fine." The soldier pressed against the other side of the hatch to help.

"No, you aren't, you look like death." Rebecca cast a Regeneration on him as the door began to open the rest of the way.

"Thanks, that should keep me breathing until someone can get this bullet out—"

Mason's words were cut off by a loud creak from the door. Panic flooded Digby's body as the lower hinges snapped. They must have rusted through from the repeated casting of Decay.

Alex let out a yelp as the bottom of the hatch bent toward him. The top hinges gave way a second later, causing the entire door to fall at a diagonal that carried the slab of metal through the opening along with the water.

Digby grabbed Alex's arm as the hatch slammed into his leg and threw him to the side. "Hold on."

The door crashed into the railing behind them and fell down into a lower section of the cargo hold. Mason barely avoided getting hit. Unfortunately, the railing he was leaning on was not as lucky.

"Wait, no!" The soldier fell back, his hands clinging to the metal handrail as it bent backward, leaving him dangling over the pit below.

"I'm coming!" Rebecca stepped forward, gripping the door frame with one hand to hold her ground in the middle of the rushing water as she reached out toward Mason with the other.

Digby pulled Alex into the corridor behind him and helped

him get away from the opening before returning to help Rebecca reach Mason as he hung from the broken railing. The soldier still didn't look well. It was as if the bullet inside him was causing some sort of continuous damage. The healing magic could only do so much.

If that wasn't bad enough, the screech of a revenant came from somewhere inside.

"What?" Digby squinted into the darkness, unable to see anything.

"Shit, there's two revenants crawling out from under the shelves in the back," Rebecca shouted, being the only one with the perception to see them.

"We must have missed them when we swept the place." Mason clung to the broken railing as it bent to take him further from Rebecca's hand.

"The bottom of the ladder is warded so the revenants shouldn't be able to…" Alex started to explain from the hallway, before shaking his head and adding, "Crap! The water."

The screech of a revenant came again from inside.

Rebecca fired an icicle off in its direction. "Shit, I missed." Her voice sounded desperate as Mason hung over the cargo hold, the water pouring down like a waterfall beside him. She switched her focus back to him as she threw her hand out again. "Reach for me!"

He looked down. "The water took out the warding rods. There's nothing holding the revs back but the water!"

Digby threw himself against the side of the cargo hold's entrance, trying to get a full view of the room. It was too dark to see much. He cast a Decay into the space anyway hoping that the creatures might stay back. A pale face emerged from the shadows just as the spell hit in a wave of emerald light that sent the creature back into the dark. "I'll try to hold them off!"

Rebecca nodded and reached for Mason's hand. There were still several feet between her and the soldier. He kicked at the air, trying to gain enough momentum to get his feet back on the walkway. The color of his face and his labored breathing made it obvious that he wasn't going to make it.

Rebecca shot Digby a look. "I'm going to let go of the door frame, so I need you to catch me."

"Are you insane?" Dread surged through Digby's mind. "What if I lose my grip on you?"

"It's the only way. I can't get an angle on the revs to take them out and I'm not going to reach him like this. So get ready." She made it clear she wasn't going to take no for an answer.

"Fine!" Digby adjusted his position and clasped his fingers around her wrist. She let go the moment he had her, holding onto his wrist in turn. He cast a Necrotic Regeneration to keep up with the damage that overworking his body might do. The idea that he was the only thing standing in the way of her and certain death screamed at him not to screw up. If he lost his grip, the revenants below would be on her the moment she fell. The only reason they hadn't climbed up to get her and Mason, was that there was a couple minutes left before sunset.

Rebecca cast a Regeneration on Mason again to repair the continuous damage that the bullet inside him was doing. It wasn't a permanent fix, but it might help him get moving.

"I don't know if I can make it." Mason's legs kicked weakly in the air. The healing spell seemed to be having less of an effect.

"I am not leaving you here, damn it!" Rebecca put all her trust in Digby's grip and pushed out into the flow of water to throw a hand out to Mason. "Now grab on and stop looking like you're going to make some sort of stupid, heroic sacrifice."

Mason's eyes flicked around the room as if she hadn't just called out exactly what he had been thinking. Her words lit a fire under him, pushing him to move a little faster. After a few seconds, he managed to kick his foot high enough for her to catch his pant leg.

"That's right." Rebecca pulled him closer, so that he could get his other leg onto the walkway. "I have you."

The pair of revenants below screeched from somewhere just below. Digby couldn't see them to hit them with another Decay.

Mason took one more look down before shifting his weight to take Rebecca's hand. The railing gave way the instant he did. She jumped to reach him, nearly tearing Digby's arm out of the socket in the process. Her fingers curled around the end of Mason's sleeve just before he went over the edge. Together they fell sideways into the center of the doorway, twisting in the rushing water.

Digby let out a terrified cry as one of the bones in his wrist snapped. The jagged edge burst up through his skin, his arm threatening to give way.

Rebecca clung to Mason. The soldier pulled himself closer as both of their legs dangled over the edge. The pale hands of the revenants below clawed at their boots from the darkness.

"No!" Digby cast another Necrotic Regeneration to hold his failing limb together.

"Hold on!" Alex dove into the doorway, his knuckles white against the other side of the door frame as he threw his other hand around Rebecca's wrist.

The broken bone sticking out of Digby's wrist tucked itself back into his arm as they worked together to pull their shivering friends back into the corridor where it was safe. All four of them huddled against the opposite wall as the water flowed past them. The three humans shivered, while Digby regretted that he could do nothing to warm them.

"Okay." Rebecca threw Mason's arm over her shoulder as she cast another heal on him. "We can't stay here, no matter how tired we are."

"Indeed. We must flee before this vessel reaches the bottom of the sea." Digby pushed off and took Mason's other side. It was clear something was wrong the moment he took the brunt of the soldier's weight. As it was, he could barely stand.

Alex limped his way to the front of the group, finding one of the bodies of one of their Heretics as they moved. With a pained expression, he pulled the sword from their sheath and kept walking. There was nothing they could do for the fallen.

Fortunately, there were no more revenants in their path back to the deck. Even better, the water hadn't reached the floor above, leaving the path back to the hatch that Digby had entered through mostly dry. Only a trickle of water ran into the ship from the hatch as he approached the exit.

He gasped when he saw why.

Water sloshed against the little round window that was set into the hatch's surface at eye-level. Through the sliver that was still above sea level, the sun lit the sky in a dying glow of red and orange as it sunk into the horizon.

"Shit." Rebecca stopped dead in her tracks as soon as she took in the view. "We'll never get the hatch open with that much water against it."

"Wait, we might be alright." Digby pressed his face against the window as a figure swam toward them.

Parker appeared through the waves to stop in front of the hatch. Asher landed on her shoulder. The pink-haired soldier held a rope up to the window. The implication was clear, she was going to use the car to pull the door open.

Digby glanced back to Alex. "Can that vehicle of yours get the hatch open?"

"It should." He leaned against the wall.

"Okay." Rebecca glanced around, looking a little frantic. "Everyone needs to hold on to something because a literal ocean's worth of water is going to rush in at us. If anyone falls, they're going to get swept all the way back down to the cargo hold."

Digby's eyes widened. "That would be bad."

Parker rapped on the window before giving a thumbs up to indicate she'd secured the rope to the door. Digby struggled not to panic. The hatch would open at any second.

"Alright, everyone grab on." He focused on the wall at the waterline and cast forge to send a flow of blood across the metal to form several sturdy handles. Then he made sure he had a solid grip on Mason who looked like he was on death's door. He wasn't going to be much help.

"I got him." Alex stepped in to help hold onto the barely conscious soldier.

Everyone else got into position just as the hatch began to creak in protest. It cracked open a second later, letting in a narrow spray of water that grew into a deluge. Then, all at once, the hatch swung open, hitting the corridor with a wall of roaring water.

"Gah!" Digby fell back against the wall as the wave crashed into him. He nearly lost his grip on Mason in the process but caught ahold of a strap on the man's chest protector. The current was so much stronger than he expected. It was all he could do just to remain where he was without being washed back into the bowels of the ship.

That was when Parker appeared in the door with a rope tied around her waist. "Shit, is Mason alright?"

"He will be." Rebecca clung to a blood forged handle on the other side of the hall. "Just get him to Lana."

"Okay, yeah." Parker tossed a loop of rope around Mason's shoulders and began to pull him free of the rushing water. She stopped as she passed Rebecca. "Grab on."

Rebecca shook her head. "No, take Alex, he's hurt too."

"I'm good for now." He nodded. "I can get out with Dig."

"No!" Anger flashed across Rebecca's face. "You get the fuck out now. Don't act tough. We've lost too much today."

Alex winced at the sudden shift in her tone. "Okay, sorry."

Digby helped him reach Parker where he was able to help keep Mason's head above water as they used the rope to pull themselves out of the sinking ship.

"Alright, we're next." Digby inched his way toward the edge of the door.

Rebecca clung to the other side of the opening as an ocean of water rushed between them. She looked small, huddled against the wall with her head against the metal. That was when Digby noticed how pale she was. She hadn't looked that bad a moment before.

"Becky, come on." He beckoned to her to start making her way to him.

"Dig." She kept her head against the wall, avoiding eye contact. "I need you to tell Hawk I'm sorry."

"What?" Digby's face fell.

"Tell him!" she shouted back. "Mason too."

Digby let out a growl. "No, I don't know what you're on about, but stop it right—"

"I'm not coming." She finally looked up, giving him a look at her face as flecks of orange shined in her eyes.

"No..." Digby glanced at his HUD to see a word hanging there next to her name.

CURSED

He immediately looked to the sky outside as the last rays of sunlight died in the distance to shroud the ocean in darkness.

"It was when I was dangling over the walkway down in the cargo hold." Rebecca winced before letting out a defeated sigh. "One of the revenants tagged my leg."

"We have to get you out of here." He threw a hand toward her.

"You can't. Alex is silenced and we don't have anyone else that can cleanse the curse. I've been bitten before; I know how much time I have. We only have a minute or so before I start trying to kill people."

"We'll find a way, Becky." Digby's voice climbed higher. "We'll figure something out."

"I'm so thirsty, Dig." She let out a whimper that sounded less human than her words. "I'll rip out Parker's throat first. Then Alex. Then Mason. I won't stop. You'll have to kill me."

"I am not leaving you here, damn it!" He slapped a hand into the rushing water between them.

"You have to." She twitched to the side, hitting her head against the wall.

"No!" He forced his way closer, fighting against the water. "You are the first friend I've had, and I am not letting you give up."

"You know..." She let out a weak laugh. "I don't think you've ever called me your friend before. At least, not to my face."

"Well, it's true." Digby held out his hand, praying that she'd take it. "You are the only one that understands me and has the will to fight me when I'm wrong. I need you. I can't do this alone."

"Yes, you can." She locked eyes with him and smiled, showing a set of elongated fangs. "You are a better person than you think."

"Then take my hand," he pleaded with her. "Believe in me one more time."

Rebecca's face softened, but she said nothing as the sound of rushing water filled the silence.

Then, finally, she reached out.

"That's it." Digby's fingers grazed hers.

His heart died all over again when she didn't take his hand.

Instead, an icicle formed in the air above her palm.

"I'm sorry." Without hesitation, Rebecca flicked her wrist, plunging the shard of frost straight into her heart. She let go of the wall and stepped into the center of the rushing water to let the ocean take her away.

She was gone in seconds.

Digby stood in the corridor with his hand outstretched.

He glanced back to his HUD just as her name blinked out of existence.

"No!" Digby shook his head and stepped into the current just as Parker appeared in the doorway to grab him.

"What the hell are you doing?" She held firm to him. "Where's Becca?"

"Dead." The word felt like a knife in his chest, even as he said it. "She was bit."

Parker gasped. "I'm so sorry."

Digby tried to wriggle free of her grip. "Let go, I have to find her body. I'll cast Talking Corpse like I did with that skull."

"No." Parker grabbed him tighter. "That wouldn't be her."

"Then I'll find another way." He elbowed her in the side.

Parker winced but didn't let go. "You can't. We have to go. Lana says Mason is septic. We have to get him back to Vegas and get that bullet out. Alex needs attention too."

"But I can't just—"

"I know." Parker threw her arms around him as he struggled. "I know."

"But..." Digby trailed off.

She held him tight. "There's nothing we can do."

CHAPTER FORTY-SEVEN

The ride back to Sin City was uneventful, other than a few revenants that ended up as splatters on the Camaro's windshield.

Digby didn't say a word the entire way.

It was all too much.

The image of his friend being carried away by the ocean, down into the depths of that ship, was all he could see.

It took near continuous Regeneration spells for Lana to keep Mason alive. He was rushed to the casino's infirmary the moment they arrived. Alex was taken there too. He wasn't in immediate danger, but there wasn't a reason to take chances.

Digby had no reason to argue.

Besides, he had other things to deal with.

Aside from Deuce and his men that stood guard, most of the city was asleep. The rest wouldn't be waking up until dawn. Digby wasn't sure what to tell them about their losses. The fact that so many had died would be devastating.

A nagging voice in his head told him it was his fault. That if he hadn't spent so long within the Seed's realm, maybe things would have gone differently. He shook his head.

No.

For once, something wasn't his fault. Rebecca was more

capable than him at most things. She had done everything right with the information available to her. He would have made the same choices. There was no failure there.

Just a betrayal.

Digby stood outside the door to Bancroft's room as Hawk stood behind him. The boy hadn't gone to bed that night. Instead, he waited for Digby to return. The news was harder on him than anyone, yet he held back all but a few tears. Clearly, he was used to losing people.

Then again, sometimes the pain children hide was far worse than what they showed. Digby thought about his own childhood and the hurt that he held in back then.

"Are you going to kill him?" Hawk's tone held a cold hatred that hadn't been there before.

"No." Digby grimaced as every impulse in his deceased body screamed at him to kick in the door and rip Bancroft's throat out with his teeth. Hell, he should have ordered Tavern to tear themself free from the man's body, piece by piece.

"What do you mean, no?" Hawk's tone grew louder. "Bancroft killed my—"

"I know!" Digby snapped back, his voice dripping with venom. "I know. But there are worse things than death, and I am not about to let Bancroft go so easily."

Hawk didn't argue. "Then what do we do with him?"

Digby dragged his fingernails down the surface of the door. "We can use one of the casino vaults, there are plenty of barred rooms there. That will make a good enough dungeon. He can rot there until I make up my mind. Besides, Charles is the least of our troubles."

"What?" Hawk's face fell.

"We still have a war on our hands and no army to fight it." Digby let his hand fall to his side before turning abruptly and stomping his way down the hall.

"Where are you—"

Digby stopped short and held a hand out to the boy. "Do you have a blade?"

"Yeah." Hawk pulled a pocket knife from a pouch and flicked it open.

Digby took it as he pushed in through the door that led to the high-roller suite. He could feel the pull of the Heretic Seed on the shard in his chest as soon as he entered the room. It was as if Alex's Mend spell was still trying to pull it from his body.

He stopped in front of the obelisk and stared at the indentation where the fragment belonged.

"What did you want the knife for?" Hawk's voice wavered.

Digby answered him by stabbing the blade into his chest at the edge of one of his bone plates. He didn't even bother unbuttoning his shirt. It had been ruined by the night's fighting anyway.

Hawk gagged as Digby pried one of his bone plates to the side and dug the knife in. With a twist, a rib cracked and he tossed the bloody knife to the floor.

Digby jammed his fingers into his chest, the same way he had back in the Seed's realm to remove a bullet. The Heretic Seed demanded a sacrifice. According to the original caretaker, he would continue to exist just as he had, but there was no way to know what giving up his soul would mean.

Nobody ever said power came cheap.

He hadn't been sure he could pay the price, but now, his spark just didn't seem important. Not after all they'd lost. No. Not after all that had been taken from them.

A sickening squelch came from his chest as he pinched his fingers around something small and jagged.

"There you are."

Digby pulled the Seed's fragment from the home it had rested in for eight hundred years and held it up to the light. It was hard to believe that something so small could be so important, or that his very soul could be held within it. He held it for a moment, wondering if he would notice a difference now that he had removed it. Now that his soul had been severed from his body.

Nothing seemed to change.

What good is a soul anyway?

"Is that what I think it is?" Hawk looked out of the corner of his eye, clearly not wanting a full view of the hole in Digby's chest.

"Indeed." He turned the shard in his fingers as black blood dripped down his wrist.

"Are you sure you want to do this?" Hawk took a step away.

"No." He let a horrid chuckle bubble in his throat. "But this apocalypse has already cost us all so much. I think it's time we made the world pay us back. And we're going to need power to do that."

Digby reached forward, holding the fragment closer to the obelisk. He could feel it trying to slip from his grip.

Fine, take it.

He let go.

The fragment snapped back to the obelisk like a magnet to fill in the indentation where it had come from. At the same time, something broke inside him. Something that he hadn't ever realized was there.

Then, just like that, he couldn't even remember what having a spark felt like.

All he knew was that something was gone.

"That's that, then." Digby shook off the feeling of loss that drifted through his chest and placed his hand against the now-flawless surface of the Seed. There wasn't even a seam.

Standing in silence, he waited for some kind of indication that the process had worked. That the full power of the Seed had been reached.

A long moment of nothing passed by.

Then the message came.

Heretic Seed restored.

Digby grinned as the tiny ring at the edge of his vision snapped to the center and multiplied to show several lists of new information on the Seed and its capabilities. He skimmed his eyes past it all to one line at the bottom, a message from the new caretaker.

Get moving, you undead copy. The world won't save itself.

Digby frowned. Apparently the version of him that now lived as a part of the Heretic Seed was just as arrogant as always.

That was when Asher sent a thought across their bond.

It approaches.

Digby swept aside the Seed's new information windows and turned to Hawk.

"The Heretic Seed has been unlocked. I want you to get the word out. All who want magic shall have it. We will need every one we can possibly get. This city is going to war. And I'll take this fight all the way to the Nine if we have to."

The boy nodded.

Digby locked eyes with him. "When you're done, we shall deal with Bancroft."

"Where are you going?" Hawk's face grew hard.

"Out." Digby headed for the door. "It seems one of my minions has found his way home after completing an errand for me."

Without another word, Digby headed straight for the casino's entrance. From there, he marched into the night. The revenants that roamed the strip ignored him. His blood wasn't worth drinking. When he made it to the street, Asher flapped down to his shoulder. A feeling of sadness radiated from the raven.

"I know." He scratched at her wing. "I miss her too."

He stopped as a hulking form entered the street in front of him. The familiar armored zombie that he had created earlier.

"Hello, Ducky. It seems you had a bit of a long walk."

His minion responded by kneeling to remove the load that it carried strapped to its back. A radiation symbol stared up at him from the bomb that Malcolm had tried to steal. Digby ran a hand over it as a chuckle rose in his throat. It grew into a rumbling cackle.

"I'm not losing anyone else." He turned back to the casino, motioning for his minion to pick up the weapon and follow. "It's time we show this miserable world exactly what we can do."

EPILOGUE

Darkness swirled like oil on the surface of a puddle as a spark of light swelled within the void. It grew to a dull glow, the energy of the unknown trickling in to stoke the fire. Slow but steady, the point of light grew as if too much at once could not be contained. Time stretched beyond perception. Was it a second? A minute? Hours? There was no way to be sure.

Becca's eyes snapped open.

She took several deep breaths as the memory of her death played over and over in her mind. The look on Digby's face had been heartbreaking. She didn't even know the zombie was capable of an expression like that. From there, her thoughts fell to Hawk, the brother she'd barely known. The brother she'd left behind. Then there was Mason and the note she'd slipped under his door.

There was so much. She felt tears welling up in her eyes. So much she'd left behind.

Becca rubbed her hand on her chest.

Then she stopped and looked down.

Where was the icicle?

She distinctly remembered impaling her heart with a spike of ice.

Becca yanked on the collar of her shirt so she could see the wound.

It was gone.

The panic she'd felt began to subside. It ramped back up when she looked for her HUD.

It was gone too.

"Where am I?" She snapped her head from side to side, unable to see anything beyond her own body. A strange darkness wrapped her body like a blanket. Its edges were hazy, like she existed alone in a bubble drifting through a void.

That was when she realized she was sitting on something.

She slapped her hand down without a second thought, feeling a weird bouncy sensation. There was something beneath her. She dragged her hand against it. Something soft. The texture of velvet caressed her fingers. Staring at the cushion, she could see slivers of red emerging from the hazy bubble that surrounded her. It was as if the space she existed in was expanding slowly.

After waiting a minute, things started to solidify. Becca pushed her hands across the cushion she sat on to find the edge. It was some sort of bench. Behind her, another upholstered surface supported her weight. As the hazy bubble expanded, she ran her fingers across decorative filigree and brass detailing that framed the bench.

Wherever she was, it was fancy in a strange, vintage sort of way.

Reaching her foot down, she found a floor of hardwood. After testing it with her weight, she stood up. She could feel a steady vibration along with a rhythmic ca-chunk through her feet. By now, the space she existed in had grown enough to reveal another bench seat facing the same direction as the one she had been sitting in. She furrowed her brow. Then she reached her arms out to her sides. One hand found nothing but empty space, the other touched glass.

Becca turned to press both hands against the surface. She couldn't see through it, but it was definitely some kind of window. Her mind filled in the blanks. The benches, the windows, the vibrations.

"I'm on a train."

Becca pushed into the aisle, finding that her cloud of existence came with her. Above, a ceiling of decorative paneling curved overhead along with brass handrails. She reached for one and let herself hang there. She paid attention to the movement off the car, it leaned to one side and tilted up toward the front of the train. She was traveling in a circle but also up, like some sort of spiral.

Finally, she allowed herself to start exploring the possibilities.

"I'm dead."

She blew out a sigh, remembering everything she'd left behind and all that she still had to do.

"I'm surprised I'm not haunting Earth with all of my unfinished business." She groaned.

That thought begged the question, where was she?

Becca stood in the aisle for a long moment, letting the space she existed in expand further. For a moment, she debated walking forward to see if there was another car to the train she was on. The shroud of darkness that closed in around the other end of the compartment made her think twice. Instead, she just stared into the gloom, feeling like it was staring back at her.

It wasn't long before she noticed something glinting in the shadows.

Something crimson.

"Who's there?" She stepped back and raised a hand on instinct.

A pair of red eyes blinked at her just before a hand reached from the gloom. Becca froze as five green fingernails touched down on the back of one of the benches.

"Who are you?" Becca held her ground.

The figure continued to emerge from the darkness, color swirling around as they pushed into the hazy bubble she existed in.

Becca's mouth fell slack.

It was a woman.

She wore a vest and pants, like some sort of classic bartender. Her hair and necktie matched the emerald green of her fingernails. The only break from that pattern were her crimson eyes.

"Hello Rebecca." The woman blew out a sigh and relaxed her shoulders. "We need to talk."

ABOUT D. PETRIE

D. Petrie discovered a love of stories and nerd culture at an early age. From there, life was all about comics, video games, and books. It's not surprising that all that would lead to writing. He currently lives north of Boston with the love of his life and their two adopted cats. He streams on twitch every Thursday night.

Connect with D. Petrie:
TavernToldTales.com
Patreon.com/DavidPetrie
Facebook.com/WordsByDavidPetrie
Facebook.com/groups/TavernToldTales
Twitter.com/TavernToldTales

ABOUT MOUNTAINDALE PRESS

Dakota and Danielle Krout, a husband and wife team, strive to create as well as publish excellent fantasy and science fiction novels. Self-publishing *The Divine Dungeon: Dungeon Born* in 2016 transformed their careers from Dakota's military and programming background and Danielle's Ph.D. in pharmacology to President and CEO, respectively, of a small press. Their goal is to share their success with other authors and provide captivating fiction to readers with the purpose of solidifying Mountaindale Press as the place 'Where Fantasy Transforms Reality.'

Connect with Mountaindale Press:
MountaindalePress.com
Facebook.com/MountaindalePress
Twitter.com/_Mountaindale
Instagram.com/MountaindalePress

MOUNTAINDALE PRESS TITLES

GameLit and LitRPG

The Completionist Chronicles,
Cooking with Disaster,
The Divine Dungeon,
Full Murderhobo, and
Year of the Sword by Dakota Krout

A Touch of Power by Jay Boyce

Red Mage and
Farming Livia by Xander Boyce

Ether Collapse and
Ether Flows by Ryan DeBruyn

Unbound by Nicoli Gonnella

Threads of Fate by Michael Head

Lion's Lineage by Rohan Hublikar and Dakota Krout

Wolfman Warlock by James Hunter and Dakota Krout

Axe Druid,
Mephisto's Magic Online, and
High Table Hijinks by Christopher Johns

Dragon Core Chronicles by Lars Machmüller

Pixel Dust and
Necrotic Apocalypse by D. Petrie

Viceroy's Pride and
Tower of Somnus by Cale Plamann

Henchman by Carl Stubblefield

Artorian's Archives by Dennis Vanderkerken and Dakota Krout

APPENDIX

NOTEWORTY ITEMS

THE HERETIC SEED
An unrestricted pillar of power. Once connected, this system grants access to, and manages the usage of, the mana that exists within the human body and the world around them.

HERETIC RINGS
A ring that synchronizes the wearer with the Heretic Seed to assign a starting class.

THE GUARDIAN CORE
A well-regulated pillar of power. Once connected, this system grants temporary access to, and manages the usage of, the mana that exists within the human body and the world around them.

NOTEWORTY CONCEPTS

AMBIENT MANA
The energy present with a person's surroundings. This energy can

be absorbed and use to alter the world in a way that could be described as magic.

MANA SYSTEM
All creatures possess a mana system. This system consists of layers of energy that protect the core of what that creature is. The outer layers of this system may be used to cast spells and will replenish as more mana is absorbed. Some factors, such as becoming a Heretic will greatly increase the strength of this system to provide much higher quantities of usable mana.

MANA BALANCE (EXTERNAL)
Mana is made up of different types of essence. These are as follows, HEAT, FLUID, SOIL, VAPOR, LIFE, DEATH. Often, one type of essence may be more plentiful than others. A location's mana balance can be altered by various environmental factors and recent events.

MANA BALANCE (INTERNAL)
Through persistence and discipline, a Heretic may cultivate their mana system to contain a unique balance of essence. This requires favoring spells that coincide with the desired balance while neglecting other's that don't. This may affect the potency of spells that coincide with the dominant mana type within a Heretic's system.

MASS ENCHANTMENTS
Due to belief and admiration shared by a large quantity of people and item or place may develop a power of power of its own.

SURROGATE ENCHANTMENTS
An enchantment bestowed upon an object or structure based upon its resemblance (in either appearance or purpose) of another object or structure that already carries a mass enchantment.

WARDING
While sheltering one or more people, a structure will repel hostile

entities that do not possess a high enough will to overpower that location's warding.

RUNECRAFT

By engraving various runes on to a surface through the use of the Artificer's Engraving spell, a object make be empowered with a magical trait. When used in combination, a variety of results can be achieved.

INFERNAL SPIRIT

A spirit formed from the lingering essence of the dead.

HERETIC & GUARDIAN CLASSES

ARTIFICER

The artificer class specializes in the manipulation of materials and mana to create unique and powerful items. With the right tools, an artificer can create almost anything.

DISCOVERD SPELLS:

IMBUE

Allows the caster to implant a portion of either their own mana or the donated mana of a consenting person or persons into an object to create a self-sustaining mana system capable of powering a permanent enchantment.

TRANSFER ENCHANTMENT

Allows the caster to transfer an existing enchantment from one item to another.

MEND

Allows the caster to repair an object made from a single material. Limitations: this spell is unable to mend complex items.

INSPECTION

Description: Similar to a Heretic's Analyze ability, this spell examines an inanimate item with more depth, allowing the caster to see what materials an object is made of as well as enchantments that might be present.

ILLUSIONIST
The illusionist class specializes in shaping mana to create believable lies.

DISCOVERED SPELLS:

CONCEAL
Allows the caster to weave a simple illusion capable of hiding any person or object from view.

VENTRILOQUISM
Allows the caster to project a voice or sound to another location.

REVEAL
By combining the power of the enhanced senses that you have cultivated, this spell will reveal the position of any threat that may be hidden to you and display as much information as available. This spell may also be used to see in low-light situations.

MAGE
Starting class for a heretic or guardian whose highest attribute is intelligence. Excels at magic.

POSSIBLE STARTING SPELLS:

ICICLE
Gather moisture from the air around you to form an icicle. Once formed, icicles will hover in place for 3 seconds, during which they may be claimed as a melee weapons or

launched in the direction of a target. Accuracy is dependent on caster's focus.

TERRA BURST
Call forth a circle of stone shards from the earth to injure any target unfortunate enough to be standing in the vicinity.

FIREBALL
Will a ball of fire to gather in your hand to form a throwable sphere that ruptures on contact.

REGENERATION
Heal wounds for yourself or others. If rendered unconscious, this spell will cast automatically until all damage is repaired or until MP runs out.

VERITAS
Decipher truth from lies.

CARTOGRAPHY
Map the surrounding area. A previously mapped area may be viewed at anytime.

MIRROR LINK
Connect two reflective surfaces to swap their reflections and allow for communication. The caster must have touched both surfaces previously.

DICSCOVERED SPELLS:

NECROTIC REGENERATION
Repair damage to necrotic flesh and bone to restore function and structural integrity.

CARTOGRAPHY

Send a pulse into the ambient mana around you to map your
surroundings. Each use will add to the area that has been
previously mapped. Mapped areas may be viewed at any time.
This spell may interact with other location dependent spells.

CREMATION
Ignite a target's necrotic tissue. Resulting fire will spread to
other flammable substances.

CONTROL ZOMBIE
Temporarily subjugate the dead into your service regardless
of target's will values. Zombies under your control gain +2
intelligence and are unable to refuse any command. May
control up to 5 common zombies at any time.

SPIRIT PROJECTION
Project an immaterial image of yourself visible to both
enemies and allies.

ZOMBIE WHISPERER
Give yourself or others the ability to sooth the nature of
any non-human zombie to gain its trust. Once cast, a non-
human zombie will obey basic commands.

BLOOD FORGE
Description: Forge a simple object or objects of your
choosing out of any available blood source.

MESSENGER
Determining factor to access this class is unknown.

POSSIBLE STARTING SPELLS:

MIRROR LINK
Connect two reflective surfaces to swap their reflections
and allow for communication. The caster must have
touched both surfaces previously.

MIRROR PASSAGE

Create a passage between two reflective surfaces capable of traversing great distances. The caster must have a clear picture of their destination.

ENCHANTER

Starting class for a heretic or guardian whose highest attribute is will. Excels at supporting others.

POSSIBLE STARTING SPELLS:

ENCHANT WEAPON

Infuse a weapon or projectile with mana. An infused weapon will deal increased damage as well as disrupt the mana flow of another caster. Potential damage will increase with rank. Enchanting a single projectile will have a greater effect.

PURIFY WATER

Imbue any liquid with cleansing power. Purified liquids will become safe for human consumption and will remove most ailments. At higher ranks, purified liquids may also gain a mild regenerative effect.

Choose one spell to be extracted.

DISCOVERED SPELLS:

DETECT ENEMY:

Infuse any common iron object with the ability to sense and person of creature that is currently hostile toward you.

HEAT OBJECT

Slowly increase the temperature of an inanimate object. Practical when other means of cooking are unavailable. This spell will continue to heat an object until the caster stops focusing on it or until its maximum temperature is reached.

APPENDIX

FIGHTER
Starting class for a heretic or guardian whose highest attribute is will. Excels at physical combat.

POSSIBLE STARTING SPELLS:

BARRIER
Create a layer of mana around yourself or a target to absorb an incoming attack.

KINETIC IMPACT
Generate a field of mana around your fist to amplify the kinetic energy of an attack.

SPECIALIZED CLASSES

NECROMANCER
A specialized class unlocked buy achieving a high balance of death essence withing a Heretic's mana system as well as discover spells within the mage class that make use of death essence.

STARTING SPELLS:

ANIMATE CORPSE
Raise a zombie from the dead by implanting a portion of your mana into a corpse. Once raised, a minion will remain loyal until destroyed. Mutation path of an animated zombie will be controlled by the caster, allowing them to evolve their follower into a minion that will fit their needs.

DECAY
Accelerate the damage done by the ravages of time on a variety of materials. Metal will rust, glass will crack, flesh will rot, and plants will die. Effect may be enhanced through physical contact. Decay may be focused on a specific object as well as aimed at a general area for a wider effect.

DISCOVERABLE SPELLS:

ABSORB
Absorb the energy of an incoming attack. Absorbed energy may be stored and applied to a future spell to amplify its damage.

BURIAL
Displace an area of earth to dig a grave beneath a target. The resulting grave will fill back in after five seconds.

CONTROL UNCOMMON ZOMBIE
Temporarily subjugate the dead into your service regardless of target's will/resistance. Zombies under your control gain +2 intelligence and are unable to refuse any command. May control up to 1 uncommon zombie at any time.

EMERALD FLARE
Create a point of unstable energy that explodes and irradiates its surroundings. This area will remain harmful to all living creatures for one hour. Anyone caught within its area of effect will gain a poison ailment lasting for one day or until cleansed.

ANIMATE SKELETON
Call forth your infernal spirit to inhabit one partial or complete skeleton. Physical attributes of an animated skeleton will mimic the average values for a typical human.

FROST TOUCH
Freeze anything you touch.

TALKING CORPSE
Temporarily bestow the gift of speech to a corpse to gain access to the information known to them while they were alive. Once active, a talking corpse cannot lie.

FIVE FINGERS OF DEATH

Create a field of mana around the fingers of one hand, capable of boring through the armor and flesh of your enemies. Through prolonged contact with the internal structures of an enemy's body, this spell is capable of bestowing an additional curse effect. Death's Embrace: This curse manifests by creating a state of undeath within a target, capable of reanimating your enemy into a loyal zombie minion. Once animated, a zombie minion will seek to consume the flesh of their species and may pass along their cursed status to another creature.

SUMMON ECHO

Temporarily recall the echo of a consumed spark to take action. The actions of a summoned spark may be unpredictable and will vary depending what type of spark you choose to summon. More control may be possible at higher ranks.

MURDEROUS WRAITH

When summoned, this spark will manifest and attack a target that is currently hostile to you. Due to the skills of the consumed spark, this spell has a high probability of dealing catastrophic damage to a target.

CRONE

When summoned, this spark will call upon the remnants of the lingering dead to grab hold of a target and prevent movement. This spell will last until the target is either able to break free, or until canceled.

HONORABLE CLERIC

When summoned, this spark will manifest and heal one ally.

HOLY KNIGHT (GUARDIAN ONLY)

A class that specializes in physical combat and defense. This class has the ability to draw strength from a Guardian's faith.

TEMPESTARII
A class that specializes in both fluid and vapor spells resulting on a variety of weather-based spells.

AREOMANCER
A class that specializes in vapor spells.

PYROMANCER
A class that specializes in heat spells.

ROGUE
A class that specializes in stealth and movement spells.

CLERIC
A class that specializes in life spells.

PASSIVE HERETIC ABILITIES

ANALYZE
Reveal hidden information about an object or target, such as rarity and hostility toward you.

MANA ABSORPTION
Ambient mana will be absorbed whenever MANA POINTS are below maximum MP values. Rate of absorption may vary depending on ambient mana concentration and essence composition. Absorption may be increased through meditation and rest. WARNING: Mana absorption will be delayed whenever spells are cast.

SKILL LINK
Discover new spells by demonstrating repeated and proficient use of non-heretic skills or talents.

APPENDIX

TIMELESS
Due to the higher than normal concentration of mana within a heretic's body, the natural aging process has been halted, allowing for more time to reach the full potential of your class. It is still possible to expire from external damage.

ZOMBIE RACIAL TRAITS (HUMAN)

BLOOD SENSE
Allows a zombie to sense blood in their surroundings to aid in the tracking of prey. Potency of this trait increases with perception.

GUIDED MUTATION
Due to an unusually high intelligence for an undead creature, you are capable of mutating at will rather than mutating when required resources are consumed. This allows you to choose mutations from multiple paths instead of following just one.

MUTATION
Alter your form or attributes by consuming resources of the living or recently deceased. Required resources are broken down into 6 types: Flesh, Bone, Sinew, Viscera, Mind, and Heart. Mutation path is determined by what resources a zombie consumes.

RAVENOUS
A ravenous zombie will be unable to perform any action other than the direct pursuit of food until satiated. This may result in self-destructive behavior. While active, all physical limitations will be ignored. Ignoring physical limitations for prolonged periods of time may result in catastrophic damage.

RESIST
A remnant from a zombie's human life, this common trait grants +5 points to will. Normally exclusive to conscious beings, this trait allows a zombie to resist basic spells that directly target their body or mind until their will is overpowered.

VOID

A bottomless, weightless, dimensional space that exists within the core of a zombie's mana system. This space can be accessed through its carrier's stomach and will expand to fit whatever contents are consumed.

ZOMBIE MINION TRAITS (AVIAN)

FLIGHT OF THE DEAD

As an avian zombie, the attributes required to maintain the ability to fly have been restored.

BOND OF THE DEAD

As a zombie animated directly by a necromancer, this creature will gain one attribute point for every 2 levels of their master. These points may be allocated at any time. 7 attribute points remaining.

CALL OF THE DEAD

As a zombie animated directly by a necromancer, this minion and its master will be capable of sensing each other's presence through their bond. In addition, the necromancer will be capable of summoning this minion to their location over great distances.

ZOMBIE MINION TRAITS (RODENT)

SPEED OF THE DEAD

As a rodent zombie, the attributes required to maintain the ability to move quickly have been retained. +3 agility, + 2 strength.

BOND OF THE DEAD

As a zombie animated directly by a necromancer, this creature will gain one attribute point for every 2 levels of their master. These points may be allocated at any time. 7 attribute points remaining.

CALL OF THE DEAD

As a zombie animated directly by a necromancer, this minion and its master will be capable of sensing each other's presence through their bond. In addition, the necromancer will be capable of summoning this minion to their location over great distances.

ZOMBIE MINION TRAITS (REVENANT)

BOND OF THE DEAD
As a zombie animated directly by a necromancer, this creature will gain one attribute point for every 2 levels of their master. These points may be allocated at any time. 9 attribute points remaining.

NOCTURNAL
As a zombie created from the corpse of a deceased revenant, this zombie will retain a portion of its attributes associated with physical capabilities. Attributes will revert to that of a normal zombie during daylight hours.
+8 Strength, +8 Defense, +4 Dexterity, +8 Agility, +5 Will

MINOR NECROTIC REGENERATION
As a zombie created from the corpse of a deceased revenant, this zombie will simulate a revenant's regenerative ability. Regeneration will function at half the rate of a living revenant. Minor Necrotic Regeneration requires mana and void resources to function. This trait will cease to function in daylight hours when there are higher concentrations of life essence present in the ambient mana.

MUTATION PATHS AND MUTATIONS

PATH OF THE LURKER
Move in silence and strike with precision.

SILENT MOVEMENT
Description: Removes excess weight and improves balance.
Resource Requirements: 2 sinew, 1 bone
Attribute Effects: +6 agility, +2 dexterity, -1 strength, +1 will

BONE CLAWS
Description: Craft claws from consumed bone on one hand.
Description: .25 sinew, .25 bone
Attribute Effects: +4 dexterity, +1 defense, +1 strength

PATH OF THE BRUTE
Hit hard and stand your ground.

INCREASE MASS
Description: Dramatically increase muscle mass.
Resource Requirements: 15 flesh, 3 bone
Attribute Effects: +30 strength, +20 defense, -10 intelligence, -7 agility, -7 dexterity, +1 will

BONE ARMOR
Description: Craft armor plating from consumed bone.
Resource Requirements: 5 bone
Attribute Effects: +5 defense, +1 will

PATH OF THE GLUTTON
Trap and swallow your prey whole.

MAW
Description: Open a gateway directly to the dimensional space of your void to devour prey faster.
Resource Requirements: 10 viscera, 1 bone
Attribute Effects: +2 perception, +1 will

JAWBONE
Description: Craft a trap from consumed bone within the opening of your maw that can bite and pull prey in.
Resource Requirements: 2 bone, 1 sinew
Attribute Effects: +2 perception, +1 will

PATH OF THE LEADER
Control the horde and conquer the living.

COMPEL ZOMBIE
Description: Temporally coerce one or more common zombies to obey your intent. Limited by target's intelligence.
Resource Requirements: 5 mind, 5 heart
Attribute Effects: +2 intelligence, +2 perception, +1 will

RECALL MEMORY
Description: Access a portion of your living memories.
Resource Requirements: 30 mind, 40 heart
Attribute Effects: +5 intelligence, +5 perception, +1 will
Units of requirement values are equal to the quantity of resources contained by the average human body.

PATH OF THE RAVAGER
Leave nothing alive.

SHEEP'S CLOTHING
Description: Mimic a human appearance to lull your prey into a false sense of security.
Resource Requirements: 10 flesh.

TEMPORARY MASS
Description: Consume void resources to weave a structure of muscle and bone around your body to enhance strength and defense until it is either released or its structural integrity has been compromised enough to disrupt functionality.
Resource Requirements: 25 flesh, 10 bone.
Attribute Effects: +11 strength, +9 defense.
Limitations: All effects are temporary. Once claimed, each use requires 2 flesh and 1 bone.

HELL'S MAW
Description: Increase the maximum size of your void gateway at will.
Resource Requirements: 30 viscera.

Attribute Effects: +3 perception, +6 will.
Limitations: Once claimed, each use requires the expenditure of 1 MP for every 5 inches of diameter beyond your maw's default width.

DISSECTION
Description: When consuming prey, you may gain a deeper understanding of how bodies are formed. This will allow you to spot and exploit a target's weaknesses instinctively.
Resource Requirements: 10 mind, 5 heart.
Attribute Effects: +3 intelligence, +6 perception.

PATH OF THE EMISSARY
Demonstrate the power of the dead.

APEX PREDATOR
Description: You may consume the corpses of life forms other than humans without harmful side effects. Consumed materials will be converted into usable resources.
Resource Requirements: 50 viscera

BODY CRAFT
Description: By consuming the corpses of life forms other than humans, you may gain a better understanding of biology and body structures. Once understood, you may use your gained knowledge to alter your physical body to adapt to any given situation. All alterations require the consumption of void resources. Your body will remain in whatever form you craft until you decide to alter it again.
Resource Requirements: 200 mind
Limitations: Once claimed, each use requires the consumption of void resources appropriate to the size and complexity of the alteration.

LIMITLESS
Description: Similar to the Ravenous trait, this mutation will remove all physical limitations, allowing for a sudden

burst of strength. All effects are temporary. This mutation may cause damage to your body that will require mending.

Attribute Effects: strength + 100%

Duration: 5 seconds

Resource Requirements: 35 flesh, 50 bone, 35 sinew

MEND UNDEAD

Description: You may mend damage incurred by a member of your horde as well as yourself, including limbs that have been lost or severely damaged.

Resource Requirements: 50 mind, 100 heart.

Limitations: Once claimed, each use requires a variable consumption of void resources and mana appropriate to repair the amount of damage to the target.